Moving On

Moving On

A NOVEL BY
Kathleen Haun

Aventine Press

Published by Aventine Press
750 State St. #319
San Diego CA, 92101
www.aventinepress.com

ISBN: 1-59330-718-7

Printed in the United States of America

Dedicated to those

who have had to move on,

one way or another.

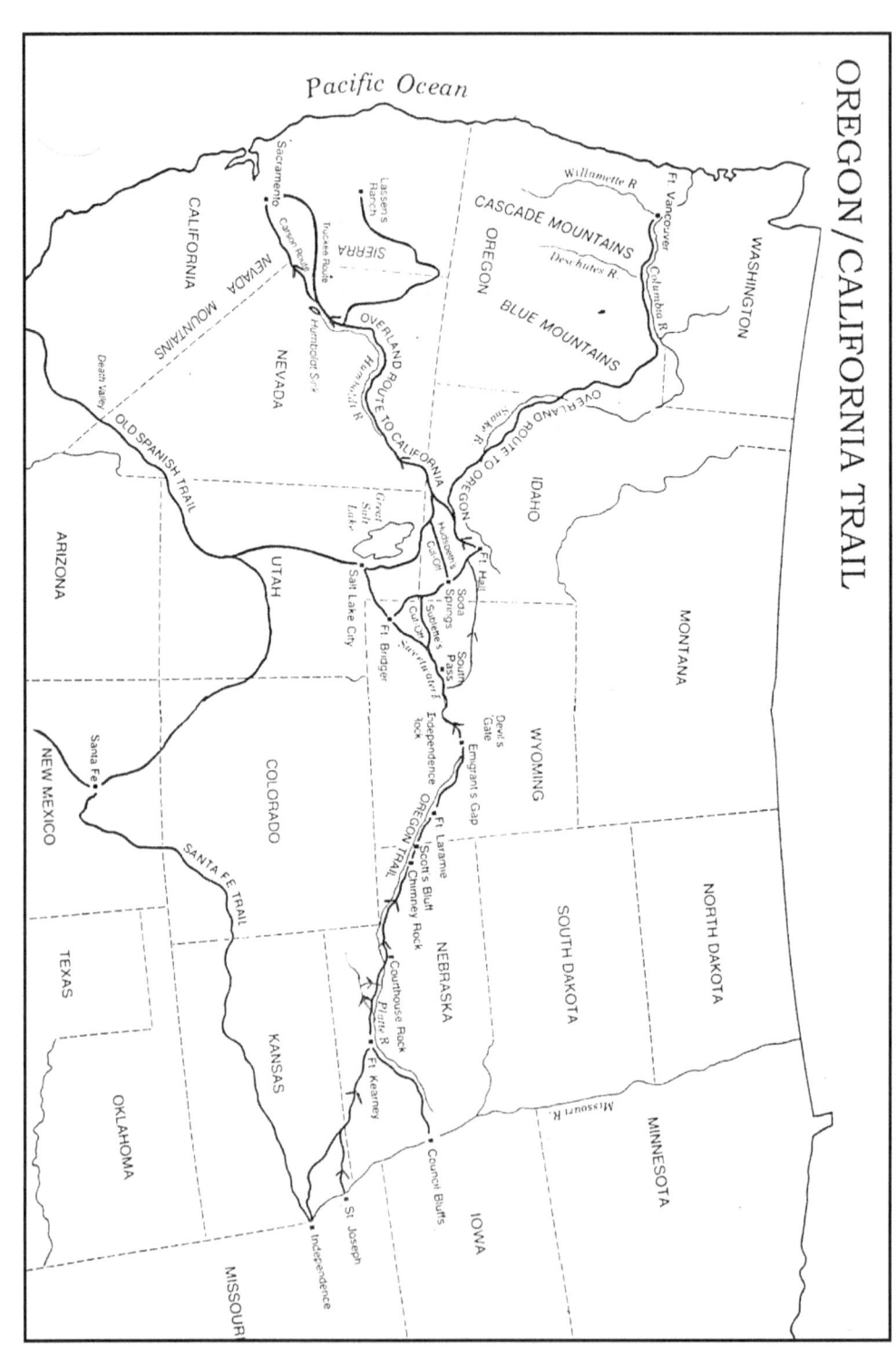

OREGON / CALIFORNIA TRAIL

Pacific Ocean

WASHINGTON

Ft. Vancouver
Columbia R.
Willamette R.
CASCADE MOUNTAINS
OREGON
Deschutes R.
BLUE MOUNTAINS

Sacramento
Lassen's Ranch
SIERRA
CALIFORNIA
NEVADA MOUNTAINS
Carson Route
Truckee Route
OVERLAND ROUTE TO CALIFORNIA
OVERLAND ROUTE TO OREGON
Snake R.
IDAHO
Humboldt Sink
Humboldt R.
NEVADA
Ft. Hall

Death Valley
OLD SPANISH TRAIL
Great Salt Lake
Humboldt R.
Cut Off
Soda Springs
Sublettes
Cut Off
South Pass
MONTANA

ARIZONA
UTAH
Salt Lake City
Ft. Bridger
Sweetwater R.
Independence Rock
Devil's Gate
Emigrant's Gap
WYOMING

NEW MEXICO
Santa Fe
COLORADO
Ft. Laramie
Scott's Bluff
OREGON TRAIL
Chimney Rock
SOUTH DAKOTA
NORTH DAKOTA

SANTA FE TRAIL
NEBRASKA
Courthouse Rock
Platte R.
Ft. Kearney

TEXAS
KANSAS
Council Bluffs
IOWA
Missouri R.
MINNESOTA

OKLAHOMA
St. Joseph
Independence
MISSOURI

PROLOGUE

My connection to the families of the Eastern Sierra of California, and those of Lone Pine in particular, did not end after publishing the letters of Emily Eastman and the memoir of her daughter Whitney. (*Dear Carrie, Letters From the Eastern Sierra 1878 to 1899*, published 2006, and *Passing Storms*, published 2007).

In 2008, Emily's great great granddaughter sent me the manuscript of the book that follows. Her cover letter reads:

"Dear Ms. Haun,

"Last week I found a note from my Great Great Grandmother Emily Eastman among the effects of my mother, Rose. The note was dated 1946 when Emily was 86. In it, Emily asked my mother to pass the manuscript on to me. Gran Emily is a legend in our family. Those of us composing the generations that have followed her, were told about her adventures in the Eastern Sierra of California in riveting detail.

"Gran felt the life story of her friends Abe and Nancy Carrington to be intensely private, but that was because those involved were so close to her heart. But she also felt that when enough time had passed, the story could be of interest and even value. I know that I react differently to life's difficulties since reading the full story of the Carringtons' 1863 journey west by wagon train. Finding out how they ended up in Lone Pine, California in 1870 has solved a mystery for me that Gran would never discuss with anyone.

"I'm a senior citizen now, with no children to whom I can give this manuscript, so I feel it should be given to you, to be published when you think it proper."

Rosalee

After Lewis and Clark traveled west to the Pacific Ocean in 1805, restless men longing for adventure or a better life began wondering if it could be found in the Far West. Most decided to stay home. Then, in the 1840's, rumors of gold in the Western Territories and California reached those in the East. This offered the perfect justification for men to prove that the Far West could be home to more than trappers, mountain men, and missionaries.

By 1860, it was a common event for wagons from the East to head west every spring on a migration that carried them across the plains, the Rockies, and through what was referred to as "the Great American Desert". By 1863 over 300,000 people had traveled the famous California, Oregon and Mormon Trails.

The emigrants from the east quickly learned that their lives, whether in cities or on farms, had ill prepared them for what they were encountering on the trail. By the time they reached the Far West, they had also learned that an individual's personality and character could impact their immediate survival, as well as their future happiness.

Some of the words, phrases, descriptions and attitudes in the context of the following story may offend some readers. However, to edit what was then common regarding both terminology and attitude, would give less of an impact to the reader's experience of this unique period in America's history. Part of our appreciation comes from realizing how much things have changed in the last 150 years, and how little.

Kathleen Haun, 2010

CHAPTER ONE
LONE PINE, CALIFORNIA
1946

Fifty years ago I was given the burdensome responsibility of a secret. Now, before it's too late, I have decided I must release it to the judgment of future generations.

My name is Emily Eastman and I have lived my life in a small pioneer town in the Owens Valley that runs along the eastern flank of California's Sierra Nevada Mountains. I was born just before the Civil War, before railroads crossed the country, before the telephone and radio, and before automobiles and airplanes. For transport I knew only horses, wagons and stagecoaches, and towns with three-story brick buildings were a community's pride.

Lately I've been thinking about how precious life is, and how fleeting a time we are given to enjoy it. I've lived long enough to have seen the world change dramatically, although I think of myself as simply a wiser version of the young woman that stepped off a stagecoach in the dirt plaza of Lone Pine in 1878.

Lone Pine has changed too. The plaza and the stables are gone, and stagecoaches no longer raise dust as they pass through. The creek has been diverted so it no longer flows across Main toward the river, and the dirt of unpaved roads has been replaced with asphalt.

The genesis of the secret I referred to earlier began in 1863 when the United States was a country not as united as it is now. It was embroiled in what some referred to as *civil strife*, but which was actually a shameful war that should not have been, yet needed to be. Across the rest of the country there were also battles among the many tribal nations, and confrontations between tribes and settlers. Yes, the 1860's were very difficult years, especially for those who desired to cross from one side of the country to the other as part of a wagon train.

Most of the movement West occurred only 66 years ago, but the current generation of young people seem to know remarkably little about it. The courage and sacrifice of those composing history's greatest mass migration of people should not be forgotten. Consequently, I have decided to tell Abe and Nancy Carrington's story.

They described much of their life to me throughout the years I knew them, but after Nancy gave me her diary in 1895, I discovered just how much they had kept to themselves. What Nancy never knew was that Abe had also given me his journal with the direction not to tell Nancy.

On the last page of her trail diary Nancy wrote:

"Looking objectively at the whole of our time on the trail, it could be assumed that everyone on our wagon train experienced the same thing. But that isn't true. Yes, each day was a shared routine, but the experience of it was different for each of us. Within our long undulating canvas city that crossed rivers and streams, and that moved over the flat prairies, rolling hill country, dry deserts and steep mountains, we each had daily achievements and losses that belonged only to ourselves. I could only record what was happening to Abe and myself, and some of what I observed around me.

"I now realize that what we endured belongs to history. I have therefore made no changes to the diary, leaving alone even the more bold portions that I never dreamed would be read by others, but that were written to help myself cope with it all. I have been shown several of the diaries kept by other women on the various trains and they were very bare-bones. They were intended to be read either by later generations or relatives back East to whom they were to be sent. There was no one Abe and I had left behind other than beloved friends.

"I have in Lone Pine a good friend of 17 years whom I can trust. Even though she is considerably younger than Abe and me, she has an unusual wisdom gained through a life of challenge and daring. So, to posterity and Emily Eastman, I leave this diary."

Nancy Carrington,
November, 1895

☆ ☆ ☆ ☆

WESTERN MISSOURI
MARCH, 1863

The calendar said it was still winter, but it was an unusually warm day and a light shawl was all Nancy Carrington required. She sat on the top step of the porch fronting a small log house where she could easily hear Alice inside sleeping soundly in her cradle. Two large cur dogs, one black and the other brown but both with long fluffy tails, dozed at her feet. Even when she looked up, her hands never stopped as she shelled peas into a wooden bowl on her lap. Trying to keep clean the long white apron that covered her homespun brown wool dress, Nancy brushed an errant pea pod onto the ground. The black dog snapped it up and crunched it between his teeth. So the other dog wouldn't feel left out, she tossed him one as well.

Nancy cast her eyes fondly over the neat rows of the vegetable garden to the south of the house, then took in the sturdy red barn to the north and the smoke house beyond it, the two storage sheds, the three-sided shed where the anvil and forge awaited a mule to be shod, and the cold house over the creek that ran through their small apple orchard. Nancy reminded herself to retrieve some butter and eggs that were kept cool there in lidded stoneware crocks.

Her eyes wandered to the acres of plowed black furrows, and a deep sense of pleasure rose up and forced from her a sigh of the utmost satisfaction. It had taken ten years of hard work--hot summers sweated and icy miserable winters endured--to get the farm looking this good. However, where in the past they had produced enough to sustain their family as well as trading or selling their excess harvest, that was no longer the case. Abe said the land was wearing out.

They had thought in the past that it might be possible to someday send Harold away to college. Now they weren't so sure. Almost nine, he was the younger of the two boys, and was not at all interested in the farm. Instead, he loved to learn new things about the world around him and had accumulated an impressive library of books. Todd, his fourteen year old brother, loved the farm and never had to be asked to do his chores, often even doing those assigned to Harold. In return Harold occasionally did Todd's homework for him, but just poorly enough that the schoolmaster was fooled.

Todd was well-suited to the hard work of farm life. He was tall and strong, and acted more like a responsible sixteen year old. When his father explained how to do something, Todd paid attention and seldom needed a second lesson.

Baby Alice was only six months old, and both parents considered her an unexpected blessing. Abe called her God's reward of a girl for Nancy for putting up with an all-male household for so long.

The only dark shadow in their lives was the fearful War of Secession. The fighting was spreading toward them, and Missouri was a border state that could go either way. Although most likely Abe would join the Union Army, he saw points for both sides. Of more urgent importance to him was what would happen to his family if he left them.

Nancy quickly returned her attention to the bowl on her lap. Abe was heading to the chicken coop, carrying two full pails of feed, and she didn't want him to see her watching him. Tall, lean, and strong without being overly muscular, his long confident strides propelled him across the yard. He removed his hat to wipe his brow and his light brown hair caught the afternoon sun, turning it a brassy gold that complimented his brown eyes. Even as dusty, damp and tousled as he was, the strength of character and humor in his face showed plainly, and she thought to herself that she was a fortunate woman. She had thought so since the day she met him fifteen years before.

Feeding the chickens was normally Nancy's job, but Abe had offered to do it for her today, probably because he knew that she was fixing a big Sunday dinner and that Harold needed to be kept quiet while getting over a cold. Many of her friends' husbands expected their wives to do their regular chores no matter how busy they were, or even if ill.

Nancy had known from the beginning of their courtship that Abe had a gentle soul. He loved to hunt and was a crack shot, and their table regularly had fresh meat on it. At the same time, killing a domestic animal that he knew well because of injury or old age was difficult for him. But Abe was a very practical person, and he always did what was required. Little did she know right then that his willingness to make bold and expedient choices could lead to tragedy.

When Abe finished with the feeding, he put the pails away in the barn and walked toward the house. How pretty Nancy looked, he thought, settled as she was on the porch steps with her long skirts and white apron bunched around her legs. He smiled at the thought of those shapely legs, knowing that only he had ever seen them or felt their softness beneath his hands. Others might admire her face, but only he had knowledge of her body, and it made him eager for that night.

Before sitting down on the step next to her, Abe reached for a few of the bright green pods and popped them open, slowly chewing the raw nuggets. Nancy smiled as she recalled the many times she had watched him do this, and felt once more the closeness that she and Abe too often took for granted.

Abe leaned his back against one of the supporting posts of the sagging porch roof, stretched his long legs out before him and sighed deeply. Removing his hat, he ran his fingers through hair that was still fluffy from its weekly scrubbing the night before. The small tub had been filled with creek water heated on the stove, then visited by Nancy, followed by Abe, and lastly the two boys.

Catching Abe looking at her with that funny crooked smile she so loved, Nancy tried not to blush as she thought about the night to follow. They would send the boys to bed early, shortly after the baby was sound asleep, and then they too would go early to bed. She marveled that after all these years he could still make her feel loved and wanted, and thrilled at his touch.

Abe looked away but didn't stop smiling. He knew by the color in her cheeks and the way she looked up at him through her long lashes that Nancy was thinking about their time alone later that night. He was glad she was not one of those prim women who thought private relations a chore, or worse yet, a duty. He knew too that her preparing a big Sunday dinner was her way of expressing her love for him. That was why he had decided to wait until the next day to tell her about the decision he had made that would so dramatically change their lives.

Before following Abe inside the house that he had built for them ten years before, Nancy looked out over the farm again.

She never tired of the feeling of proud ownership mixed with a little awe at the fact that it actually belonged to them. With three healthy children and having just turned thirty, she knew her life was good.

Marrying when she was fifteen and Abe sixteen was not that unusual in 1848. Some girls married older men at even earlier ages to get away from abusive situations, or because they were orphans, or because they were the oldest of families too large to be able to feed everyone. Abe was of the second and Nancy of the last, and although younger than her brothers, she had been the first to marry.

It had been expected that Abe would inevitably lose touch with those at the orphanage, but Nancy had been cut off from her four brothers soon after she had moved from Council Bluffs at the time of her marriage. Her parents had died a month later, and letters from brothers never fond of her became gradually less frequent until her letters to them went unanswered.

The next morning Nancy emerged from the house a little earlier than usual, and as she always did, walked to the barn for the chicken feed. While the hens clucked contentedly and scratched around in the dirt while eating, she carefully gathered their eggs. When finished, she set the basket gently on the ground outside the pen and carefully fastened the gate. To assert his dominance, the big red rooster jumped up on a tree stump in the corner of the pen and crowed. The way he proudly surveyed his hens reminded her of the day before when she had surveyed the happy circumstance of their life.

Holding onto the gate post, she leaned against it and let tears run freely down her cheeks. The night before Abe had informed her that a man had made him a good offer for the farm, and he had accepted. They would be leaving on a wagon train for Oregon in three weeks.

She and Abe had seen the dust in the distance as wagons headed to St. Joseph, the nearest jumping off point for wagon trains heading west. Maybe she had been naïve in refusing to realize how the war would affect them, but she had never thought they would be one of those families. More men were needed to replace those soldiers who had died or deserted, and Abe was torn as to his proper role. Abe had made the decision that protected his family.

Knowing all of this, Nancy grudgingly admitted that she saw the wisdom of their leaving immediately. So she wiped her face on the skirt of her apron, smoothed it back down over her simple homespun gray dress, and forced herself to face the reality of their situation. Then she prepared herself to tell the boys.

Sitting across the table from their parents later that morning, the breakfast plates pushed aside, Harold and Todd were silent as they absorbed what they had just been told. Todd was a study in brown--dark hair, eyes and olive skin, and now his mood darkened too as he contemplated leaving the farm. He had planned on working it with his father before someday inheriting it, and his sense of loss was great.

Harold, by contrast, was a lighter child altogether. His unruly sandy hair often straggled across the fair skin of his forehead almost into his golden brown eyes. His curiosity and eagerness for new ideas and adventures had always amazed Nancy. Harold never saw himself staying on the farm anyway, so the news did not upset him. But Harold knew this move would be bad news for his brother, and immediately sought a way to find a positive aspect to it by asking, "They have a college in Oregon, don't they?" While Nancy smiled at her intelligent son, Abe frowned.

Realizing this must be a crushing turn of events for his father, Todd decided not to show his disappointment and said, "The land in Oregon is said to be very fertile, especially in the Willamette Valley."

"Yes, son, it is. And that's where we're going."

Abe pulled out *The Prairie Traveler*. Since 1859 it had been one of the main reference sources for those heading west. "Mr. Marcy's pamphlet is much more accurate than the Hastings '45 guide, and I think we'll be well prepared for what lies ahead of us. There are more forts, short cuts, and toll bridges over the rivers now. And even some trading posts along the way."

Harold frowned as he thought of leaving his beloved schoolmaster and said, "Can't we wait a few more years? There's bound to be locomotives heading that way sometime in the future."

Abe laughed. "That may not happen until the next decade, and we have to leave now."

"Why?" Harold asked.

Todd turned to him. "The fighting is getting closer. We'd best be out of here soon or we could be in the thick of it."

"We're too young to be called up," Harold protested.

Todd laid a hand on his brother's shoulder. "Dad isn't."

"Oh." Howard looked at Abe and for the first time saw him as someone other than just his father.

"Whenever the fighting does get here," Abe told them as he stood up, "we at least will be gone." The boys nodded solemnly and reached for the guide book.

Abe explained to them what he understood about their journey. "Our wagon train is supposed to have about 50 wagons in it. It's been organized by an experienced leader who has taken a large group across, as well as a small train returning east. We'll be leaving in April before the grass has grown very much, so we'll carry grain for the animals. By the time it's gone, we'll have reached good grazing.

"Each one of us men will sign a contract of obligation. In it we agree to be bound by the Colonel's decisions and to aid him any way we can."

Nancy, who had spoken little while watching her children's reactions, added, "The agreement emphasizes that the individual interest of each person is also that of common concern to the whole company."

"That's right," Abe agreed. "So you boys will have to be on your best behavior for the four months we're on the road."

"Four months!" they exclaimed together.

Abe chuckled. "How long did you think it would take?"

"Two months," Todd mumbled. Not wanting to look ignorant, Harold said nothing.

Nancy said, "Some in the past have taken even longer." She chose not to worry the boys with common reports of illness, injury, lack of grazing and starving animals, and Indian troubles in some of the years of crossing.

"Well, don't worry," Abe encouraged his family. "All the men share the guarding and herding chores of the loose stock. I expect you two to help your mother, even if she asks you to look after Alice."

Neither boy looked particularly enthusiastic, but both nodded their heads obediently.

"What about our dogs?" Todd asked.

Abe took a deep breath. "Our train doesn't allow them. Some wagon trains use them for guarding and hunting, but there's been problems with dogs pestering the stock or barking all night at unfamiliar sounds."

Harold had trouble controlling the quiver in his chin. It would take the boys, not to mention Nancy, several days to come to terms with the necessity of leaving their dogs behind.

"Will we have to leave all our animals?" Todd asked."No," Abe told him. "Mr. and Mrs. Ivey will take our hens, although we'll start out with fresh eggs packed in sacks of corn meal to protect them. We'll slaughter the hogs tomorrow, so we'll have that pork. And we'll take the milk cow, four steers, and the two big mules to pull the spring wagon to St. Joseph. And of course Flame."

They all smiled at this last pronouncement. Abe had raised his sorrel quarter horse Flame from a foal, and they knew he would never sell him or leave him behind.

Nancy told the boys, "The larder is pretty full right now, but we'll have to buy more appropriate supplies in St. Joseph.""Will we eat buffalo along the way?" Todd asked, ever the practical planner.

"We can't count on that," Abe said. "We'll get antelope, rabbits and anything else for fresh meat when we can, but we mustn't count on anything other than what we have in the wagon."

"We'll be seeing deserts?" Harold asked. He had read books about the Far West and had seen a map marked with the Great American Desert just the other side of the Rockies.

"Oh yes, we'll see the desert," Nancy reassured him, unsure exactly what that meant other than hot and dry.

"Anything we can't take, the new owners will keep." Abe spoke in a voice more subdued than the boys had ever heard before. He had tried unsuccessfully to convince himself that the $10,000 he had gotten for his acres and buildings compensated for the shattering of his family's future expectations. Nancy laid a hand on his forearm and squeezed it reassuringly.

"What about our wagon?" Harold asked.

"We're getting a new one in St. Joe," Abe told him. "It'll have a ten foot box and will carry all our things. With the number of supply depots along the trail, that should be all we need. It's got a hickory box, tongues and hounds, and osage orange for the hubs, ash for the felloes and framework, and oak spokes on the wheels. Of course, they're reinforced with iron, but as little as necessary. We'll be carrying about 2,000 pounds. All the wood will be well-seasoned so it shouldn't shrink too much in the deserts."

"Wow," Todd breathed. "Will we get more mules to pull it?"

"No, son. We'll buy three yoke of oxen. They're much cheaper than mules and they eat scrub more willingly." After a slight hesitation and a quick sideways glance at Nancy, Abe added, "If they die, we can use them for meat."

Nancy tried to divert the boys from such a harsh reality. "It also means we'll be traveling slowly so the cow can keep up. We'll put the morning's milking in a pail at the back of the wagon so the constant movement can churn it into buttermilk by dinner. Harold, this will be one of your chores."

Harold rolled his eyes but nodded before asking, "Why not get a grand Conestoga wagon?"

"They're too large and heavy and require more animals to pull it," Abe explained. "They're okay on flat and straight trails like the Santa Fe, but we'll be going over the Rockies and fording a lot of streams and rivers."

Harold smiled and asked, "I guess we'll be seeing the elephant, huh?"

Abe smiled at his son's use of the old gold rush phrase that meant experiencing unexpected adventures and challenges. He nodded his head and watched Harold smile. Todd remembered their dogs waiting for them on the front porch and thought that they were already seeing the unpleasant side of the elephant.

After they had talked a little longer, the boys went outside to help their father while Nancy reviewed her list of supplies. Several sources of information were available to her, including the *Marcy Guide* published at the request of the government.

It described the clothing for men, including undershirts and overshirts, boots for horsemen and stout shoes for men on foot, a gutta-percha poncho, a broad-brimmed hat of soft felt, a coat and over-coat. It even suggested such items as green or blue glasses enclosed in a network of wire as protection from the intense glare of the sun, but at least charcoal to be wet and smeared under the eyes. However, there was no mention made of clothing for women or children, or any item they might need.

The list that made her uneasy was the one suggesting the arms they should bring, which included guns and knives. Abe had a cap and ball Colt and a new Henry repeating rifle, but her unease was because this inventory of weapons reminded her of why they might be needed. So many horror stories had reached those in the East, not only about the many different tribes across the country, but also about rogue white men who masqueraded as Indians while massacring and plundering wagon trains and homesteads. Local tribes took the blame, and so these white men were branded "white Indians". With a shudder, she pushed her mind away from such things and returned her thoughts to more practical considerations.

After reviewing the rest of the lists for camp equipage and food, Nancy sat and wondered how they would pack it all into the wagon. Then she thought of those precious personal items she felt could not be left behind. Abe assured her they could buy furniture when they got there, or he could make it, but she insisted that the small chest left her by her mother could not be replaced. And how could she leave behind the good china Abe had bought her with the money made from their first harvest? Or Harold's much loved books?

How especially could she leave behind Mr. and Mrs. Ivey who lived on the farm a quarter mile down the road? These dear friends had built their house on the east edge of their property so they could be close to Abe and Nancy who had built on the western edge of theirs. So much had been shared: construction projects, meals on most Sundays, holiday celebrations, hunting trips, and afternoons spent canning their combined garden harvests. But the best that had been shared had been the laughter and comfort of agreeable companionship.

A bright red cardinal called from a tree outside and she remembered someone saying that they had no such fiery feathered beauties in the West. In that moment, the bird became a symbol of all that would be left behind and all that would be different. The next chortling call prompted fresh tears that poured over Nancy's cheeks like sheets of rain. Hearing the chatter of the boys as they neared the house, she heaved a deep chuttering breath and wiped her face on her apron. When the boys came in shoving and laughing, she was at the stove with her back to them and they noticed nothing wrong.

Abe entered right behind the boys just as Nancy told them, "You need to spend some time with your school books. Get up in the loft until supper and work on your penmanship."

They offered the universal children's response of "Ahhh...", but still they climbed the steep ladder. Abe came up behind Nancy and put his arms around her waist while kissing the side of her neck. He had heard the crack in her voice.

"It'll be all right, Nan. It'll be hard leaving here, but in a couple of years you'll be glad we made the move. The land is perfect for farming in Oregon and you'll make new friends. And we'll have something better to leave Todd."

She nodded her head. "You didn't mention Harold in that."

Abe chuckled. "Well, I'm trying to make peace with the fact that our Harold will probably be a doctor or lawyer or something fancy like that. Definitely not a farmer."

"Abe, remember when I was carrying Harold and we told Todd that he was going to have a brother or sister? Remember what he said?"

After a moment of thought, Abe laughed. "Oh, yeah. He called it a *golden moment* in his life."

"We never knew where he got that phrase, but we've made good use of it over the years."

"Like when I foaled Flame."

"Yes," Nancy acknowledged with a smile, "and when Harold won the spelling contest at school."

"There were ten and eleven year olds in that contest." Abe couldn't hide his pride.

"That's why Todd called it Harold's golden moment."

"What's your point?"

"Well, maybe this is our golden moment. Gold is usually hidden before it's revealed, right? Well, that's how I've chosen to think of this move."

"Nan, you're a prize." He grinned and stroked her hair.

Nancy turned to him and put her arms around his neck. "You're a good man, my love. And goodness should be rewarded."

Nancy saw Abe flush as she kissed him and held her body against his, knowing that he could use such a moment of intimate reassurance. From that moment on Nancy made sure to hide more carefully any grief she might have about their leaving.

The following weeks went by swiftly, each day filled with regular chores as well as packing items in their spring wagon. Since the guidebook only told in detail what a man should pack, Nancy had to use her imagination based on common sense for the rest of them. The boys could be considered small men, but Alice had her own special needs. For herself, two wool dresses and two of calico, an extra shawl, a heavy coat, two cotton aprons, and stout boots over the ankles would suffice. For dressier occasions she packed two scarves and a lace collar.

The guidebooks explained the basic structure of each group traveling west. The wagon master would serve as the ultimate authority not unlike a ship's captain, with scouts to assist him along with a trail cook to prepare meals for this group alone. Wranglers would care for the loose stock with the help of the men from the train. Each evening when they stopped for the night, the wagons would form a circle around the cattle, milk cows, and ground-tied horses. They would leave the next day in a new order, with the front wagons that had breathed clean air the day before now moving to the rear. However, those who broke the rules in some way, such as not being ready to leave in the morning on time, would be forced to catch up and travel at the very end of the line.

When the wagon train stopped at night the women would be expected to set up camp, start the cooking fire, prepare the evening meal, and assign chores to the children. Meanwhile, the men would make sure their animals were fed and watered and doctored if necessary, and repairs made to overloaded and stressed wagons. Most important, water barrels were to be filled whenever the precious liquid was available.

Small tents would be set up if the wind allowed. If there was no room in the wagon, or if it was very hot, then bedrolls would be laid out beneath the wagon. Most people brought thin pallets with feather or horsehair stuffing for this purpose.

The men were expected to gather together most evenings to discuss the next day's route, as well as any situations that might need resolution. Consequently, these councils could take the form of a hearing if a traveler needed chastising for an act that had endangered the others.

The women were instructed to take that time to mend clothes or prepare fixings for the next day's breakfast or noon meal, which would likely be a cold one. This brief nooning would be a time for the animals and people to have a bit of rest in the heat of the day, as well as an opportunity to nurse the sick and care for children, who would lead more independent lives than ever they had at home.

Everyone would be expected to be in bed as early as possible, because the wagons had to be ready to roll at sun-up, which meant rising at four if they wanted a hot breakfast. Daylight was the only time the wagons could move safely, and the light was too precious to waste.

By the time the Carringtons were ready to leave home, Nancy's eagerness still did not match that of Abe. She had heard stories about the early gold rush camps with dozens of saloons and honky-tonk palaces surrounded by clusters of old tents and ramshackle cabins, some set up by the prostitutes that followed the miners from camp to camp. Although she had been told that considerable refinement had occurred in the towns of the West since then, she was not convinced and fretted that there was too much unknown that confronted them.

There had been many good reasons for people to go west over the past dozen years, beyond the reports of gold and silver. There had been from the beginning the need for goods and services for the prospectors, and the benefit of leaving behind the diseases of crowded Eastern cities. People also looked forward to the 160 acres of free land being offered if worked for a minimum of five years by the claimant. Fleeing a decimating war that dragged on with no end in sight was the most recent reason. But only those who could afford the $1,000 for the trip could realistically consider leaving.

After reviewing the information available to them, Abe and Nancy decided to be brutally pragmatic. Therefore, they decided to leave behind that which was too heavy or bulky, and not absolutely essential. Neighbors within close proximity and the new owner of the ranch were the beneficiaries of their prudent decisions.

All of these cherished friends were present and waving as the heavily laden spring wagon pulled out at dawn. Nancy took so long in saying goodbye that Abe had to call to her twice while trying to ignore the weeping of the women. With a final hug of her dear friend Elsie, Nancy wiped the tears from her face and climbed up next to her husband.

Abe wasted no time moving them forward while Nancy waved again to those dear to her and they waved back while standing in the middle of a narrow dirt road under the overhang of trees that the Carrington boys had so often climbed. She sat forward, swallowed twice and determined not to shed more tears. Abe had been very patient with her so far, and she didn't want to press the point.

CHAPTER TWO
ST. JOSEPH, MISSOURI TO
THE COAST OF NEBRASKA
APRIL-MAY, 1863

"I start this new journal on the eve of a great change to our lives. May God keep us in mind, and safe."

Nancy

"Bought this journal in St. Joe. Most men keep one so I guess I will too. Our wagon is sound, our supplies sufficient, and the family as prepared for what comes next as I can make them. We pull out at dawn tomorrow."

Abe

It pricked Abe's conscience that he wasn't eager to rush into battle. He understood the states rights issue, the economic pressures that lay at the heart of certain states wanting to secede from the Union, and why others didn't want slavery in their state. While Abe fundamentally abhorred the idea of slavery, he also understood the cost to the farms and plantations if they suddenly lost their workers or had to pay them the same wages as free men. That is, if that was what *free slaves* meant. Like most people he knew, he wasn't sure. But more than anything else, he didn't think it wise that the country should be weakened by the secession of any state from the Union.

He remembered the violence over the last several years created by the Missouri Bushwhackers, the Kansas Jayhawkers and John Brown's rebellion. So in his heart, he knew which side he would join if given the chance to choose, but he would be leaving his family to their fate while surrounded by the violence of war. This was not something he was willing to do, especially with an alternative so readily available to him.

When a man too old to fight had shown interest in his farm, Abe had reduced the value by $2,000 and after offering to include the furniture, equipment and much of the stock, had begged the man to buy it. He felt bad that he hadn't told Nancy about that, but he promised himself that he would when they were happily settled in Oregon.

Beyond his desire to be away from the spread of war, Abe had been fascinated by the stories of Jedediah Smith, John Fremont, Kit Carson, Joseph Walker and the other great frontiersmen. When he had read of their adventures and accomplishments it had always left him feeling that there must be more to life than walking behind a plow, and climbing into bed each night with nothing to look forward to except more of the same.

While Nancy had proudly maintained their small home, Abe had worried and dreamed. Although never really expecting to go West, he had still enjoyed thinking about how they could do it. It made him feel a little less a prisoner of his failing farm. Then, after years of listening to stories about free land in Oregon, Abe had started thinking that maybe they *should* go there. So in the privacy of the barn he had read the guide books written by men who claimed to have first-hand knowledge of the routes.

Unfortunately, many a misled emigrant learned too late that some of the authors of the guides had not actually traveled the whole of the various routes they wrote about with such authority. Abe also had no awareness that the attitude of even the most benign Indian tribe during the 1840's and '50's had by the early 1860's evolved into acrimonious resentment.

Sitting behind the two mules pulling their farm wagon toward St. Joseph, Abe looked next to him at his pretty wife holding their baby before glancing over his shoulder at his boys. Abe thought of those men who had made the journey over the last dozen years that had written letters to family left behind in the States. Abe had heard some of these read out.

They had described the abundance of their harvests after the fertile prairies had been plowed and planted. Others described the Oregon forests where they had cut timber to build their houses, corrals and barns. Some had bragged about the abundance of game that had ended up on their dining table, not to mention the huge fish caught in the rivers. They had expressed surprise at the lack of intimidation by local tribes, and had all written of helpful new friends ever ready to lend a hand.

But most of what had been written to relatives and friends had been an effort to reassure those left behind. Not that their glossy accounts were not true, but they avoided much of the daily drudgery, loss of life, violent storms, lack of good water and the resulting dysentery, and the constant fear of insufficient feed for the animals. The letter writers especially did not relate to their families their constant underlying fear of Indians, whether justified or not.

After the Carringtons arrived in St. Joseph, Abe picked up their new wagon. The boys stayed with their father to help him finish the interior and then transfer their supplies into it. Nancy meanwhile visited the town and was impressed with so many people and wagons now crowding its edges. Nancy tried to picture how it had been in the past when there had been present double or even triple the number of wagons waiting to leave. Some of the wagons were new and some not long ago were hauling hay on a farm, but all were now being loaded and made ready to go forth into an unknown future.

Over the next few days Abe and Nancy's wagon train gathered together under the watchful gaze of Colonel Langley Luster. He had led another wagon train West in 1858, and then returned in '61. Although the title of Colonel was probably complimentary, no one really cared, and his bearing was certainly military.

On the other hand, he had a gentle and almost whimsical smile, a laugh that caused even the most dour person to smile, and an appreciation of the ironical that often caused his dark eyes to twinkle. But those same eyes could in an instant turn as hard and black as obsidian, leading men to wonder who the real Colonel Luster was.

The women didn't care. They thought him courteous and handsome. They noted, without being observed doing so, his shoulder-length black hair streaked with gray, the thick brows over sensuous eyes, the long straight nose, the full lips and his simple neat mustache. As one woman coyly stated, "Why should he wear a beard? He has nothing to hide."

More than one person had commented that even when the Colonel was focused on what you were saying, you knew he was also aware of everything else happening nearby. He wore his side arm low as though it was an extension of his body, and this caused some to surmise that he might have once earned his living with it, although no one said this out loud.

Abe and the boys transferred their things to the new wagon and then parked it outside of town near the others of their train, after which they corralled the new oxen. When Abe was told that Colonel Luster wanted to talk to all the men, he obediently joined the others in the shade of a large tree.

The Colonel began by welcoming them and introducing the scouts. He told them of the supplies they must have in their wagons, and those heavy things they should leave behind if they had been foolish enough to pack them in the first place.

The men listened carefully to the list of items they would need and prepared to purchase what they lacked. However, most of them ignored what the Colonel said about leaving behind their heavy plows, bags of seed, sheet iron stoves, crates of china, and boxes of books. Or even the extra 20 pounds of bacon. They should have known better, having heard of the rare few who had been able to carry such heavy items all the way through. True to human nature, however, each thought they could be that exception.

Their hankies were barely dry of tears shed while parting from family and friends, but the women of the Luster train were discovering between themselves common bonds. Not least of this was their shared inexperience and consequent trepidation of what was to happen to them out on the plains. Nevertheless, Nancy was amazed to meet so many women with boundless confidence in their ability to persevere through anything.

The second day after the Carringtons reached St. Joseph, Abe left Nancy at their camp. Todd and Harold, a litany of instructions and warnings ringing in their ears, had joined a small group of other boys who were determined to explore the town.

Abe wanted to purchase a few supplies, but he also thought it might be a good idea to gather what information he could. He moved among throngs of men of different backgrounds, professions, economic solvency, and nationality. They wore brown or grey wool trousers held up by the grip of tight waist bands or suspenders, and some had their pant legs tucked into stout high-top boots. Shirts were either red or blue, solid or striped, and wool or cotton. Any individuality was achieved by the addition of vests, jackets, and neckerchiefs. Their hat, whether straw or felt, was broad-brimmed and usually well worn.

The young boys among them wore much the same clothes, except that their pant legs were seldom tucked into their boots.

But regardless of their differences, Abe walked among men who were bound by a common experience so momentous that it overshadowed everything else in their lives. The men were not unaware of this, and it allowed them to more easily introduce themselves and join conversations.

They discussed what they planned to do in the West, but whatever else they described, most concluded by saying they wanted a better life for their families. Abe flinched when he realized that their explanations were much the same as his own, and often sounded more like a justification for leaving than a reason for being in the West.

Some of the men said they were holding to the hope that there was still gold and silver in the mines so they could amass a fortune. Others said they hoped the mines were still active so they could sell their products or services to the miners. Still others talked of the fertile farming land in Oregon. Then there were those few men who said nothing of their reason for going so far. This caused suspicious glances in their direction, but wisely no comment. There was, however, no mention by any of them of the war they were leaving behind.

Meanwhile, Nancy stood next to a wagon so new she could still smell the tang of the sawn lumber that had not long before been several varieties of tree. With Alice napping soundly in her basket at the rear of the wagon, Nancy turned her attention to her list of supplies.

The Carrington wagon was loaded with everything necessary for survival and, Nancy smiled to herself, the small chest that had belonged to her mother. It was filled with extra clothes for the children and the medicines they were told to bring such as quinine, castor oil, whiskey and hartshorn for rattlesnake bites. Nancy had been taught that hartshorn, the scrapings of the antler of a stag, was a good absorbent in the system, and she had occasionally made it into a jelly as a stimulant after illness. But her reason doubted that it could absorb the venom of a snake bite, and she fervently hoped she would not have to find out for sure.

Most of the room in the wagon was taken up with food. She fretted that the 600 pounds of flour and 100 pounds of bacon might not be enough until they could re-supply. There was a bag of hard crackers, 10 pounds of rice, 10 pounds of green coffee beans, 25 pounds of loaf sugar wrapped in blue paper, 20 pounds of salt, three bushels of dried beans, compressed blocks of dried peaches, plums and apples, corn meal with fresh eggs buried in it, two buckets of lard, a keg of vinegar, a jug of molasses, a firkin of butter, half a wheel of hard cheese, and various spices. Because both boys would have a birthday while on the trail, Nancy had hidden a fruit cake among the boxes as a treat. She had been told they would have many opportunities to restock their provisions while still east of the Rockies, so she tried to rest easy about what they had packed.

A strong breeze rippled the white canvas that covered the bent ribs of thin hickory arching over the wagon and Nancy glanced up at it with pride. It had been carefully waterproofed with linseed oil, although she had been told that as soon as it got wet the canvas would expand and become water tight. As suggested, she had sewn onto the underside surface of the canvas half a dozen muslin pockets where small items could be tucked away. For privacy, and to protect the interior from the effects of wind, the opening at the front and back could be closed to a small hole by simply pulling on a puckering string.

There was no painted slogan on their canvas top, although many of those nearby had them. Some declared determination to reach their destination, *Oregon or Bust*, *California Calling*, while others remembered their beginnings, *Goodbye New England*. One family proclaimed *Happy Times*, which showed an optimism that for them was not destined to last.

Nancy ran her hand over the smoothly sanded wood of the wagon bed. It had been carefully built to make it as impervious to water as possible. The side boards slanted four inches outward with a parallel board inside a few inches from it. Between these was set the ends of the bent bows that held up the canvas top, as well as Mackinaw blanketing that would help to waterproof the bed. Abe had spent the day before building boxes along the inside edge to hold supplies. They were lidded and just wide enough for a person to sleep on at night if they needed to be out of the rain. Most clever of all, Nancy thought, was the wagon's false floor that created a little over a foot high space for tools, extra kingbolts, linchpins, chains, and other items impervious to water.

Abe had packed the wagon with burlap bags of grain for the stock to eat until they reached good grazing, after which the bags would be used to hold buffalo and cattle *chips* to burn in place of wood on the plains. Nancy made a few fussy changes in the arrangement of sacks, barrels and kegs so she could more easily reach the roasted coffee beans, tins of tea, a jug of maple syrup, and a crock of pickles.

She had already made sure she could reach the few cooking utensils she had been allowed: Dutch oven with reflector, tin-ware kettle and coffee pot, cast iron skillet, small coffee grinder, china teapot, round wooden hoop sifter, two butcher knives and a whetstone, a long-handled ladle, two gourd dippers, a spice box with individual small boxes inside, and tin plates and cutlery. Once again she made sure that her cherished matches were still wrapped in their heavy waxed paper, and close to hand. There was, however, a flint packed away just in case.

The boys would sleep in a small tent if the weather allowed, so the ropes and stakes were settled at the back of the wagon for easy access at night and so the tent could act as a tarp during the day. Among other items packed inside was a sewing basket, palm and pricker for sewing the canvas top, a spade, a small butter churn, bars of soap, bundles of candles for the lantern, a washboard and small tin tub, a small folding table, four camp stools, and a chamber pot with a well-fitted lid. Nancy was divided between relief and fastidious concern when she realized that she would be unable to press her washed clothes, but smoothing irons were heavy, and it would take too much wood or too many chips to keep the fire hot long enough to sufficiently heat them.

The wagon was a storage room of a remarkable practicality; a ton of goods packed in such a way that the wagon could also serve as a bedroom if necessary. Nancy thought the whole thing very clever, and was proud of their home on wheels. She was also relieved that it was only temporary.

After again checking on the sleeping Alice, Nancy lowered her sore muscles onto a camp stool and leaned against one of the large wagon wheels. She closed her eyes and let the soft breeze dry the sweat on her forehead while her thoughts wandered back to their journey to St. Joseph. Abe had enjoyed a little hunting with the boys so there had been less need to use up so many of their supplies. Nancy had taught Todd how to diaper his baby sister in case the need arose, and his first efforts had occasioned much laughter, including that of baby Alice. The boys also learned how to make coffee and biscuits. When they responded to their accomplishments with pride, Nancy wondered why she had not thought of doing this before.

But there had been disturbing moments too. Several farms along the way had only recently been abandoned, but weeds were already growing up around the buildings. It reminded Nancy of their old home, and the fact that for now they had no home at all.

They had passed several large and well-cultivated properties where slaves had been toiling in the fields. It was the first time Nancy, and many of those coming in from the northern states, had seen slaves. Some of the men wore shackles, and one man's back showed the oozing cuts of a recent whipping. It had been a disturbing experience, and a stab to the conscience of many as they were once again reminded that they were leaving behind those willing to die for a cause. But still, not one man turned his wagon around.

There was a new sound in St. Joseph. In the late 1850's the steam trains of the Hannibal and St. Joseph Railroad had arrived, and its presence was one of the reasons the stores were so well stocked. Nancy stood up and turned in the direction of the arrival platform, wishing that the steam belching monster continued all the way to the West Coast. But like most people, and regardless of those who talked of it as a reality within the decade, she had little faith that such a thing would ever be possible. After all, there was the challenge of the mountainous terrain of the Rockies, not to mention the Great American Desert, and then the final barrier of the Sierra Nevada.

Nancy's attention was diverted to a man in the distance on horseback. He was talking to a group of men standing around him and she recognized who it was more by the respectful attitude of the men than her ability to clearly see his features. Everyone on this wagon train had put their faith in the experienced person of Colonel Langley Luster. For a fee of $125 he had promised to guide them across, although as Abe told Nancy, the road was so deeply rutted now that a blind man could find his way. The Colonel not only knew the route, but also the best river crossings, which Indian tribes could be trusted, and how to survive the long distances between water sources.

Colonel Luster was known to be a very cautious man. So much so was this true that some men had scoffed at him behind his back. He was aware of this, but didn't care. They didn't have the lives of over a hundred men, women and children to account for on a daily basis. Consequently, upon the arrival of each family who had committed themselves to his care, the Colonel made sure they knew what they were doing.

Each wagon owner, or hand hired on to drive in exchange for food and transport west, was made to unhitch his team. They then had to hitch it up again, and were asked to drive it in a large figure eight. They were timed in the process and watched carefully. Those that had been fumbling their way through the process for days on the trail while getting to St. Joseph were properly trained. Those who had been doing it for years when not under a time constraint were shown short cuts. If by chance they did a speedy and good job of handling their teams, they might be asked to help the greenhorns having difficulty.

Because of the Colonel's stubborn insistence that every man perform for him or the scouts, he often had to later win over some man's resentment. Until, that is, the resentful man witnessed damage caused by someone who didn't know how to control his fractious team. No man was taken at his word that he knew what he was doing about anything. The Colonel had believed a man on the first train he had taken across, and had discovered his mistakes only after someone died.

Abe was more used to mules, and getting his new oxen to move right and left to his commands of "gee" and "haw" was a challenge. Bob Cook, the scout that had been assigned to work with Abe, explained to him the mastery of such activity. Bob found Abe a quick and able student with a great deal of self-deprecating humor, and took an instant liking to this tall Missourian. He added Abe to his mental list of those men he *might* be able to count on in a difficult situation.

Bob's perpetual squint made others think he was always suspicious, but it was just his sensitivity to the sun's glare. This opinion of his personality was heightened by the way he wore his hat low over his eyes and the short mustache that shadowed his mouth. In fact, their assumption did fit him well, as he trusted no one until they were tried in the fire of experience.

The Colonel also made sure the women knew how to produce a meal from a kettle nestled in hot coals. The women enjoyed what they called their classes because it allowed them to meet one another. They talked of home, where they were headed, caring for children on the trail, and ideas of meals that could be cooked on a campfire.

So closely parked were the wagons that Nancy only had to step away a few feet to introduce herself to a woman with a gentle face and large brown eyes. Similar to Nancy and the other women, her hair was tucked under a short-brimmed cotton bonnet that was tied securely under her chin so the frequent gusts of wind could not unseat it. These were not the bonnets so often associated with pioneer women, with deep coal scuttle brims. Those were saved for the times when they would be walking in the hot sun.

Nancy picked up a fussing Alice from her basket and stepped forward. "Hello, my name is Nancy Carrington."

"Nice to meet you. I'm Effie Howard." Her smile was bright and friendly. "Your baby is adorable."

"Thank you." Curious about everything related to their situation, Nancy asked, "Have you met Colonel Luster and his scouts?"

"No, but my husband has. He says the Colonel is tough but fair." Effie wiped her hands on her apron. "Still, I can't help feeling a little anxious."

"I know what you mean." Nancy's emotions at the moment were a stomach-gnawing dread mixed with an eagerness for unknown adventure that she had not known before was in her. But she merely told Effie, "So much can happen on the trail from what I hear."

"Oh, I don't mean that." Effie waved her hand, chasing away such a mundane matter. "It's just that I'm used to cooking big meals at home. That won't be possible for the next few months. I'm concerned about keeping my husband and son fed properly." Looking around her, she added her judgment on all other women. "No hog and hominy dinners for my men!"

Somewhat taken aback at the woman's priorities, Nancy thought to herself, "I hope that's the worst concern she has on this trip."

"Do you hear someone crying?" Effie suddenly asked Nancy.

They listened for a moment and then slowly approached a wagon a short distance away. Inside was a young woman of about nineteen whose tears had saturated her handkerchief.

"Excuse me," Effie interjected softly. "Can we help you?"

The woman looked up and sniffed. "Oh, lord. Did you hear me crying?"

"I'm afraid so," Nancy told her with a gentle smile. "Are you ill?"

"No." The young woman jumped out of the wagon and smoothed the skirt of her dress. "I'm Mrs. Ashe. We're from Virginia. The only thing wrong with me is that I'm so homesick I just can't stand it."

Both Effie and Nancy nodded, then introduced themselves. "Are you going to California or Oregon?"

"Oregon. We're going to buy a farm there."

"Well," Nancy told her, "from what I hear, the winters there are a lot milder than those in Virginia. It's a small blessing that maybe you can look forward to."

"Yes, that's something, I suppose." Mrs. Ashe took a deep breath and smiled. "You know, I feel much better. Maybe it's because I have two new friends."

Effie added for both herself and Nancy, "And you can call upon either of us any time you want."

"Do you have children?" Nancy asked her.

"Not yet. We've only been married a year."

The women's attention was directed to the sound of Harold and Todd laughing as they tossed sticks with several others boys a couple of wagons over.

"Any of those yours?" Nancy asked Effie.

"Yes. My Charley's the one with the gray floppy hat."

Nancy smiled as she recalled seeing Effie's kind assistance to some of the other women, and was glad to have made her acquaintance. The day before all females over thirteen years of age had been gathered together by scouts Bob and Chris, and instructed on how to start a fire with a flint in case they ran out of their precious matches.

Some of the women were better at it than others, but all had accomplished the task at least once before they were allowed to return to their wagon. The session had produced a few frustrated tears, as well as some surprisingly colorful curses learned from a husband or father. Effie had thought this scandalous until she saw Nancy fighting a smile, at which point she returned Nancy's wink.

Now, as they returned to their wagons, Nancy asked, "Are you going to California or Oregon?"

"Oh, Oregon." Effie colored slightly and looked grim. "We don't want to mingle with the element in California."

Nancy stopped herself from laughing since she was familiar with the popular opinion of Californians as rough, coarse, and opportunistic. She merely commented, "We just want to live on good land near a river."

"The Willamette in Oregon?" Effie asked eagerly.

"Yes."

"Us too." Effie smiled. "Oh, wouldn't it be nice if we were neighbors? We'll be getting to know each other so well on the trip. I miss my wonderful neighbors back home."

It was not the first time Nancy had heard someone refer to the home so recently abandoned as though they had last seen it years before. To her, nothing could have been a greater indicator of the women's commitment to a new life.

Abe walked along the noisy town's muddy streets crowded with full freight wagons being driven by loudly swearing freighters. He passed the crowded saloons and gambling parlors, and made his way around a small group of men in front of the harness and saddle maker's shop where he inhaled the rich scent of tanned and raw leather wafting from inside. Next door to it he bought Nan a small milk pitcher at the tinner's shop, thinking that its riveted construction might survive the coming months of heavy use.

Flour dust filled the air around a mill as he hurried past on his way to the rope maker's shop, after which he loitered in front of a livery stable along with men watching the farrier shoe a large horse. He ignored the clothing and hardware establishments, but listened to trail rumors from a gunsmith while he purchased more powder and caps.

He joined half a dozen men gathered on the worn wooden walkway outside the gunsmith's and listened to them talking about some people that had arrived by river boat. He was curious about how much time they had saved in getting to St. Joseph by traveling this way. One man, having spent five weeks on the road just getting to St. Joseph, asked, "It'll take 'em some time to get their wagon built and supplied. And what wagon train will they join? The Luster train, and another just forming, will be gone in a day or so."

Another man was better informed about these particular individuals and said, "I don't think they care. There's ten families in the group and they're going to travel together, just them."

The men were suddenly subdued and looked at each other while shaking their heads, all aware of the lack of wisdom in traveling with so few wagons through areas where the Indians were hostile to even large well-armed wagon trains.

"They're using teams of six mules," the first man said, "so they'll at least be traveling fast."

Everyone shook their heads again, showing their doubt that these people, so independent and so much in a hurry, would survive. They were doomed if they made even the slightest mistake in their preparations, such as carrying too much weight or too few supplies, or if they came across bandits wanting their mules, or a tribe seeking retribution, or if illness beset them. It was too depressing to consider further and the men suddenly changed the subject.

Making his way back to their campsite, Abe passed a corral where one of the wranglers from the Colonel's staff was working with a man who had never before driven oxen. The difficulty of this was increased by the fact that none of the animals in the team had pulled together before and were not easily adjusting to their new work mates. The dust filling the air was rife with shouts of "gee" and "haw" and "ho" mixed with colorful and varied invective the women in the area pretended not to hear. It would seem that all of the oxen were named *son-of-a-bitch*. Half a dozen mostly naked men from the local Sac tribe sat on the ground near the corral watching the Anglos struggling with their oxen. They could often be heard laughing.

Abe had been taught by his old friend and neighbor Bryan Ivey how to drive an ox team and during the long boring hours on the way to St. Joseph, Abe had practiced in his mind. But this mental exercise had helped little when it came time to actually work with the animals, so he had been glad of Bob Cook's help. Several of the men who had finished earlier working in the corral were now resting in the shade of a tree. After Abe introduced himself to them, he asked, "Did any of you hear the particulars about the man killed on the edge of town last night? There's a rumor about it in town."

"It's no rumor," the one called Buran told him. "He was camping alone and off aways from everyone else. He was hit over the head with something, then robbed of his valuables. No one saw or heard anything except a horse riding out fast sometime during the night."

Abe said, "I heard that his rig and supplies are being sold at auction in town tonight."

"Yeah, that's right," Buran said. "His supplies are being divided up among the poorer families on the train."

After Abe returned to the wagon, he called to the boys who were talking to Charlie Howard, and they spent the next hour practicing how to unload and reload the regularly used items in the wagon. Food, water and cooking utensils had to come off quickly and easily twice a day. If they needed to make room for one of them when ill or injured, they had to know how to rearrange the wagon to accommodate that too.

Abe sent the boys off to get water at the town's well, and then told Nancy what he had seen and heard. He joked about some of the men learning to work with their teams, and explained that because they were using oxen he would carry a long stick and drive the animals from the ground.

Those with mules or horses would drive their teams with long reins from within the wagon while sitting on a barrel or box at the inside front. This was different from what most were used to doing when driving a buckboard or spring wagon with a seat up front. But with the flat front of the wagon between themselves and the animals, the driver was protected from the weather, clods of earth or rocks kicked up by the teams, or even arrows or bullets if the wagons were under attack.

Abe checked his pocket watch and told Nancy, "The Colonel has asked us men to bring our guns to a meeting with the scouts while dinner is being prepared. I'll see you in awhile." Before leaving, Abe kissed Nancy on the cheek and called out to the boys to mind their mother, an unnecessary directive.

Unlike many of their friends, Todd and Harold were not regularly disciplined by way of the belt or hair brush liberally applied to their backsides, although each had made one trek to the woodshed. Years later Abe would discover that this common disciplinary practice, and many much harsher, had been observed by the tribes watching the many trains passing through their lands. It had created an irate reaction from some tribes, as they considered such treatment the abuse of a child, and they resented even more that they were the ones referred to as heathens.

Abe was soon settled on the ground with the train's other 80 travelers sitting three-deep in a large circle. Each man had his side arm, rifle or old musket in front of him, and many were grumbling their displeasure.

Bob Cook, the head scout, stood in the middle of the circle. "It's important that we're comfortable with each of you being able to handle your weapons. I can't begin to tell you the number of emigrants that over the years have accidentally killed themselves and other people, including family members. And all because they weren't as practiced in handling their weapons as they thought they were. So I want you to dismantle your weapons, clean them, reassemble them and load them."

Complaints were still heard from some of those fully capable of handling their guns efficiently and safely. Abe, instead of complaining, helped those men on either side of him. Some present were from cities and had never even touched a gun, and these definitely benefited from guidance during this meeting. When Bob was convinced that everyone knew enough that they just might not kill themselves or each other, he prepared to dismiss them. Then the Colonel walked up to the group.

"I just want to remind you to lighten your wagons." When many of the men claimed they had already done that odious task, the Colonel nodded his head and flung up his hands. "You only think you have. But I know some of you have given in to your women and are keeping things you know should be left behind. Think it over well and be sure you don't have on board any useless trumpery. Dump the furniture, plows, and china now. Your teams and wagons will last a lot longer." He waited for neither agreement nor argument, but simply turned on his heel and walked away.

Abe returned to their wagon in the company of Buran. He was a muscular dark haired man in his early thirties with a long drooping mustache, a quick smile, and an outgoing manner. Until recently he had been a shopkeeper in an Iowa border town. When they reached the Carrington wagon, it was revealed that Buran was the breadwinner for Effie and Charlie.

Over a shared dinner the men told of their training sessions that day and answered the boys' many questions. When mentioning some of his purchases, Abe commented, "Good thing we don't need too much more. We'd be using up our travel money."

"Prices that bad?" Nancy asked.

"Well, not really." He smiled at his exaggeration and Nancy smiled back. They understood each other well, and Abe's expansive descriptions were a never-failing delight to her.

Buran told them, "In the last two decades the St. Joe merchants have made a fortune off us overlanders. Now that there are fewer wagon trains, the merchants are trying to make up for it by charging us higher prices."

Abe asked, "You really think the locals pay less?"

Buran looked at this naïve farmer with pity. "Of course they do."

Effie spoke up. "As long as I can cook good meals for my men, I'll be happy."

Buran smiled at her in a tolerant if somewhat condescending manner. "Effie prides herself on setting a good table."

"Well, she certainly does that!" Nancy exclaimed. She took another bite of Effie's apple cobbler, knowing it was the last of the fresh fruit the Burans had brought with them. Nancy told Effie, "There's a German couple on our train, and the smells from their cooking fire were very different than I've smelled before."

"Spices," Effie declared. "I'll have to make their acquaintance in case they have something I can swap for."

"You'll want to meet the several Irish families then," Nancy told her. "I hear they're traveling with fresh lamb."

Effie sniffed loudly. "Irish! I don't think so. They're probably going to California."

Nancy was for a moment taken aback. She then remembered how poorly treated the Irish were in some quarters.

Effie continued, "At least I don't think there's any Chinese on the train. I suppose we'll have to deal with them in the West though."

Buran spoke up. "Two families have darky servants with them. One has a Nigra girl and the other has a young buck."

Effie shrugged. "Oh, well, servants." That seemed to cover that.

Somehow Abe and Nancy had thought that with so many different people thrown together and needing each other for their daily wants, it would cause such intolerance to be set aside.

They quickly realized that for some this would be too much to ask, at least this early in the trip.

Later that night, in the privacy of their bed beneath the wagon, Nancy whispered to Abe, "Effie may be a bit of a worry wart, and locked into some common attitudes, but she means well. But even if they're right about the prices here, we can afford to pay them and I bet they can too."

"We should be able to restock several times," Abe murmured. "It's not like we're traveling in the '40's when there were only a few trading posts, no stage stations and only a couple of forts along the route."

Nancy got up and checked the basket at the back of the wagon holding the sleeping Alice. Abe joined her, catching Nancy's shawl before it fell from her shoulders. He wrapped it around her again along with his arms, and she leaned into him to bask in the brief moment of intimacy.

Abe shook his head in wonder as he looked down at the unexpected gift of his daughter, thinking to himself how beautiful she was. Aloud, he only said, "I sure wish I could sleep as sound as she does."

Nancy smiled, knowing from the sound of his snoring every night that he did. "Only last month I was wishing she was walking." Looking around at all the large wagon wheels and dirt, she added, "Now I'm glad she's not." They went back to bed and slept the heavy sleep of the exhausted.

The next afternoon the Colonel watched a wagon pull into camp and recognized the two old mountain men he had signed on when he had been in South Dakota the previous winter. They had said they were headed to California, but wondering if they would actually show up, the Colonel had started to question whether or not he should get under way without them. He now turned his thoughts to the challenges of the next few days.

The Colonel was eager to leave behind the busy crush of the city and get back out on the trail. There he was in charge, and everyone had to follow his orders. Bob Cook was unaware that the Colonel had once heard Bob refer to him as "the best kind of dictator". Remembering now those words, it made the Colonel smile.

The Colonel was a little taller than most of those around him and thick across the shoulders. He knew his deep voice was made for commanding others, and had learned how to use it to his advantage so that troublesome people wouldn't try to see how far he could be pushed. Whether or not he did it on purpose, he dressed to affect an image of power. He wore a knee-length coat of supple brown leather over a blue flannel shirt, and his dark blue pant legs were tucked neatly into tall brown leather boots. An old wide-brimmed black hat crowned his head. There was not one thing about him that suggested weakness or indecision.

Nancy watched the Colonel ride past. When he tipped his hat to her, she smiled at him and only just resisted the urge to curtsey. When she noticed Abe giving her a strange look, she quickly asked, "Where are the boys? They were supposed to come right back after visiting with Charley Howard."

"Two wagons just showed up. One the Colonel expected, but not the other one. The boys wanted to watch the owners get checked out by the scouts."

The two laughing boys soon joined their parents, overflowing with energy and excitement, and a trail of dust billowing behind them as they skidded to a stop. Todd began an animated description of what they had witnessed, and Harold listened with his typical attentiveness whenever his brother spoke.

Finally Harold said, "Mom, there were six huge oxen in this guy's team. Some were dun colored like ours, but two are black and white like a cow. They're hauling a big plow and bags of seed and..."

Todd turned to his father and cut in. "They're carrying little sticks wrapped in burlap. The man says they're grape vines and he's going to make wine from the fruit. That's something we should think about if we get enough land."

Harold continued his description of items they had seen in other wagons, many of them heavy and bulky, and doomed to be dumped along the trail. When Harold finished with wagon contents, he started telling his mother about some of the rough men he had seen among their fellow travelers. "But I wasn't afraid of them. I was with Todd."

Todd acted as though he cared little about his brother's near worshipful attitude, but it secretly made him feel proud and grown up.

As Nancy listened to what Harold was saying, she was secretly pleased. He usually reported his observations and adventures to her first, unlike Todd who always turned to Abe. Nancy knew Todd not only wanted to please his father, but was also eager to be a man. Thankfully Harold was content to be a boy for a little longer.

When Todd saw his father begin to load a barrel into the wagon, he rushed forward to help. Nancy started to tell him it was too heavy, but changed her mind at the last moment, as Abe had warned her about being overly solicitous of the boys on this trip. It was not hard to follow his suggestion, since there was so much to do.

The wagon in front of them was suddenly sent rocking by two rearing and squealing mules just hitched on. The two wheelers were old mules used to pulling together, but the front two were new to the team and were uneasy with the strange smells of the two animals behind them whose noses were not far from their tails. In fact, all around the Carringtons were mules, horses, and oxen unused to one another and that were creating havoc. They screamed in protest, reared and snorted, and all the while kicked up dust into air already thick with it.

Pete Hastings, owner of the team in front of them, yelled and swore at his rowdy mules. His wife stood back and wrung her hands when her husband hit the animals with the business end of a whip. Seeing Nancy watching, she moved closer and introduced herself as Mrs. Pete Hastings.

They only had time to exchange a few sentences, but the woman ended with, "I will come by later so we may converse, if there is enough time for it. You may call me Lona."

That's the way she talked. Not *"If there's enough time, I'll come by so we can talk."* Nancy wondered if they were of a certain culture, although her husband's speech was not stilted. However, like most women of her class, it would never have occurred to Nancy to inquire outright and possibly be considered impolite.

The Colonel approached, barking sharply at the Hastings's unruly mules as he passed them, "Whoa!" The animals slewed their bulging eyes around at this human who spoke with such commanding authority and miraculously settled down. The men standing around watching this knew they had been shown a valuable lesson. They just weren't sure what it was.

Bob later told Abe, "Pete ought to speak to his mules like he does his poor wife. She's learned to mind him without argument." Abe wisely chose not to repeat this comment to Nancy and described it in his diary instead.

That evening the Colonel gathered together wagon owners in groups of twenty and talked to them about what they could expect over the next few days. As he answered their questions, he learned valuable information about each one of his charges. It was important for him to know which of those on this trip were experienced in handling firearms, herding stock, or leading men. Even more important to him, he needed to know which men were apt to complain and be disagreeable, or create fear in the others.

From among those in the Carrington's group he chose one man to join others that would be the first to stand guard duty the night after they crossed the river. Abe was glad he was not one of them, although he knew it would eventually be his turn.

The Colonel rode past some of the women working on starting a fire with a flint. He listened to their good-natured laughter, and watched as those more adept helped those who were not. This pleased him, for he knew how valuable this cooperative spirit would be to them out on the trail. He noted their clean new aprons, the freshness of their skirts and their tidy braids of hair, and he smiled. He knew how brief a time this cleanliness would last.

Not long after the Colonel left them, Bob Cook rode through the crush of wagons and examined each rig. On the near side of thirty, some of the men surmised Bob might have a mix of foreign blood. He was not very tall, but he was wiry and strong, and his good humor showed on his dark-skinned face, at least until he was challenged or severely irritated. Bob had freighted on the old Santa Fe Trail, and had a reputation for being capable and fair. He was happy answering people's questions, but anyone who argued with his instructions quickly learned that he expected to be obeyed.

Bob stopped next to a few wagons and told the owners that immediately after they crossed the river they were to rivet the ends of the bolts that secured the running gear. "If the wheels have to be taken off again, the ends of the bolts can be easily filed away," he explained. "Much of the trail is going to be rougher than anything you've ever seen before."

A few of the older men were unconvinced, thinking of themselves as perfectly fit for any situation that might arise. They glared at Bob with an expression that said clearly, "How dare this youngster tell me what to do!" Bob only smiled to himself, knowing better than these greenhorns what challenges lay ahead.

Sitting atop his calm, well-trained horse, Bob stopped in front of the Carrington wagon and called for the attention of those families nearby. "Okay folks," he addressed them, gesturing to encompass eight wagons, "you'll be the last group to leave tomorrow morning. Get ready to roll out at dawn. Sixty-one wagons in all have shown up."

As Bob rode away, Abe stood next to Nancy with an arm around her shoulders. "Want to turn back?"

She looked up at him in surprise. "No. Do you?"

"No, but I thought I should bring it up now. Once we're on the trail, there can't be any such thought."

"I know." She looked up at him and hoped her smile was steady.

Both knew that over the years some people had turned back soon after starting on the trail when confronted by its harsh realities. These people had then been on their own without the protection of a large train, and for some it had been the end of them. They had become lost or had been set upon by Indians or bandits. Abe and Nancy had agreed before starting that there was only one direction they would be traveling, and that they would stay with the train "no matter what".

In the chill of early morning and not long after first light, Nancy loaded the children into the wagon. Abe managed to pull their rig in line third from the end. This meant that for several days they would be eating dust until they rotated closer to the front. Abe thought about apologizing to Nancy for not assuring their start nearer the front of the train, but knowing that it was something she would have to get used to eventually, he kept silent.

A wagon passed them headed in the opposite direction. As it passed, Nancy could see a woman weeping inside just behind the front wall of the wagon. Her husband sat next to her, a dejected picture of quiet shame. He was driving two large mules instead of the recommended four to six, and the overworked animals strained to pull the wagon.

Abe explained that when he had been in town the night before he had noticed some of the men from their train drinking and gambling in the saloons. The man passing them with the weeping wife had been one of these, and had lost his family's travel money. This meant they had to return to the war-torn States, and would probably never again be able to start West. Nancy felt so grateful for Abe's good common sense that in a spontaneous burst of appreciation she leaned toward him and kissed him on the cheek. Abe did not pretend to misunderstand the gesture and smiled back at her.

As they stood by their wagon waiting their turn to start forward, Nancy watched with curiosity the small groups of Sac, Pottawatomie and Winnebago Indians that hovered on the edge of town. The people of St. Joseph seemed used to them and they were mostly ignored. But for those from the East, the Indians tending their chickens, dogs and elders, afforded something of interest. The women of the train, however, watched somewhat furtively, as many of the men wore only a few strips of hide haphazardly placed where it most pleased the Anglos.

A few of the braves lounging near the Carringtons were watching with studied disinterest as the wagons began to roll forward. Nancy wondered what they thought of these strange vehicles and the people in them. Were the emigrants simply a source of occasional handouts and therefore grudgingly accepted into their lives?

One near group of Indians were rubbing the smoked entrails of small fat animals over their naked limbs. The smell was almost as repugnant as the sight of the slime on their dark skin, and Nancy looked away in disgust. At the same time, she reminded herself that to these indigenous people many of her own customs might be curious.

Since the buildings of St. Joseph were clustered near the Missouri River, its swiftly flowing waters had to be crossed first thing in order to head west. As the first wagons to cross neared the water, those behind them came to a stop. Nancy fretted that it might take too long to get everyone across that day, especially those like themselves stuck at the end. But there were several ferries working and not long before dusk the Carrington wagon came to the river.

A scout they had not previously met came by on his large bay horse and introduced himself. Chris Payne was a tall clean-shaven man somewhere in his thirties, but when he removed his hat to wipe his face with his forearm, Nancy noticed a rapidly retreating hair line of thin black hair. The skin around his large hazel eyes showed deep wrinkles and he squinted at people as though trying to figure out their peculiarities. Chris was quick to make sure that everyone realized he was to be respected every bit as much as head scout Bob Cook.

Abe asked him why it had taken all day for them to get to the river. Chris explained that while the wagons could be ferried across, the stock had to swim and that could only be done when the sun was not glaring on the water.

"What happens if it is?" Nancy asked.

"If the stock can't see the opposite shore, they swim in circles until exhausted. Sometimes they can't make their way back to the near shore, so they drown."

Realizing how woefully ignorant he was of the ways of the trail and how poorly prepared he was for what lay ahead, Abe had to forcibly shake off the wave of doubt that brought tightness to his chest. As though reading Abe's mind, Chris smiled and said, "Don't worry. You'll learn quickly. And you always have me to help you." As an after thought, he added, "And of course Bob too."

When at last they were only two wagons away from their turn to ferry across, Abe and Nancy watched men tie a young strong steer to the back of a boat and row across with it swimming behind. The last of the cattle, which included those the Carringtons had brought along for food, readily swam after this leader and were soon gathered on the opposite shore.

After unhitching their team and rolling their wagon onto the ferry, the wheels were detached and set beside the wagon bed. Abe made sure Flame was securely tied to the raft before climbing on with the boys, while Nancy held Alice in her arms where she sat next to the wagon. Three of the Indians from the town helped push their ferry out into the river. Abe, like many of the other men, tossed the Indians a coin in appreciation, after which they returned to the side of the road to await the approach of the next wagon.

The ferry was merely a platform made from hewn timbers large enough to hold one wagon disconnected from its team, which swam along side. It was guided by two huge sweeps or oars at the back, each of which took a well muscled man to keep the whole assemblage from being swept downstream by the current. Abe sat near where Flame was tied and never took his eyes off him.

The Luster train was fortunate to cross the Missouri on a calm day, with the wind that so often kept the ferries on shore now mercifully absent. Once on the opposite shore, they attached the wheels to the wagon, retrieved their oxen, hitched them up, and got out of the way of the next ferry set to arrive behind them. As Abe commanded the left lead oxen to "Giddup", Nancy prodded it with a stick, and it slowly started forward.

A small tan mutt belonging to one of the Indians that had helped pull the ferry to shore ran past barking at a squirrel. Just as Nancy smiled at this playful action, two arrows whizzed through the air. At Nancy's feet the dog lay on its side with one of the arrows all the way through it, and nearby the squirrel was pinned to the ground with the other. Both animals gave a last twitch as the nearly naked Indian nonchalantly approached, tossed the dog into the water and dropped the squirrel into a deer skin pouch slung over his shoulder. He walked down the road away from the congested town without a backward glance.

Nancy fought an urge to be sick and turned her head away from the river, glad that the boys in the back of the wagon had not seen this display of casual violence. She pulled her shawl more securely about her shoulders, held Alice a little tighter, and looked to the other side of their wagon. There she saw Harry Jones, the third scout. It was his regular assignment to ride ahead to look for water and grass, and assess their next camping place.

Harry was old enough to have gray at his temples and in his short beard, and the deep lines of his dark leathery face gave evidence to his years of living under the sun's influence. Next to him rode a trapper, a man somewhere in the direction of fifty whose wagon was two back of the Carrington's rig.

Having seen Nancy's reaction to the Indian, Harry gave her his most comforting smile and tipped his hat. "All the Indians we'll encounter aren't like that, ma'am."

The mountain man, known simply as Croat, gave a short bark of laughter. He wore wool pants but his shirt and coat consisted of several layers of hides, and his hat had at one time been an animal with gray fur. Beneath it his hair was long and dark gray, although it had probably seen a razor more recently than his scraggly beard. This last showed a patch of reddish brown below his lower lip. Some of the men assumed this was his original hair color and others thought it due to the juicy wad of tobacco usually tucked into his cheek. The women simply refused to think about it. But the only truly ominous thing about Croat was the large knife always sheathed at his side, and the rifle in its sling on his back.

Croat's lips parted in a yellow grin and he explained his retort of laughter in response to Harry's reassurance. "Yeah, some Indians are better, but some'll do that to a man." He rode away with a nasty chuckle hanging in the air.

"Don't pay him any attention," Harry said. "He's just shootin' his mouth off to get a rise out of you."

Nancy watched both men ride away and tried her best not to feel intimidated. It occurred to her that her future was now to be filled with men of harder natures and humors than any she had known before, and that she had best accept that fact and adapt. To do otherwise could lead to a permanent state of shock.

After the wagons crossed to the west bank of the swiftly flowing Missouri, they continued up the old creek road to Mosquito Creek. Here the wagons stopped while the Colonel and his scouts rode along the line of wagons to make sure the wagons had weathered the first water crossing. It was a good thing they checked. Several men had forgotten to rivet the wheels of their wagons after attaching them, and three families had to be shown better methods of packing their shifted goods.

At Wolf Creek they settled down to eat their first supper on the trail, and Nancy quickly realized that even without high winds it was going to be difficult keeping the food free of grit. The boys exchanged a look after their first bite of the beans and transferred it to their father who gently shook his head at them. Abe told his exhausted wife, "Boy, Nan, this sure tastes good."

Harold nodded and Todd made a noise that sounded close enough to agreement that Abe was satisfied. Nancy choked on her gratitude as well as the hard crunch in the beans, and after that remembered to remove the pot lids with her back to the wind so her long skirts could shield the food.

The next morning when Harold looked down at his pancakes, he said, "Why is there pepper in these?"

Todd sank an elbow gently in his brother's side and whispered, "They're skeeters."

Harold hesitated only a moment before asking, "May I have more syrup, please?"

Nancy smiled and passed the jug to him. Abe chuckled before also reaching for the jug.

At seven in the morning the air was filled with the sounds of long black whips cracking over the backs of oxen, and men shouting at both their animals and their families. Wagons creaked as they rolled forward while men herding the loose stock whistled and yelled to hasten the animals forward.

At the next water crossing each wagon owner paid their 50 cent toll to a Sac at the log bridge and then passed over. This routine had been established since the late '40's, and people then as in '63 complained bitterly.

Except for the first few days of awkward adjustment to the teams, the uneven road, and the unfamiliar routine, the first leg of the journey passed without incident. During this time the wagon train settled into a surprisingly comfortable routine, and covered a little over 100 miles to a camp just past Marysville, Kansas.

While supplying themselves at Marysville, they enjoyed their time in a town again. It was only a small community of board shacks, but there was a supply depot, a blacksmith, a barber, and two drinking houses. The town was located there as the result of a route established in 1849 for travel from Ft. Leavenworth, Kansas to Salt Lake City. The best part of it for the travelers was the convenience of a bridge over the Big Blue River, where Sac and Fox Indians collected a twenty-five cent toll.

As the travelers waited in line to use the bridge, they reviewed with pride their week of contending with strong winds that had ripped some of the poorer made canvas tops, the crossing of more muddy gullies than they could now count, the difficulty of cooking some nights with little more than pea grass for fuel, and the surprising number of rattlesnakes killed at each stop. While crossing the Nemaha River after sliding down its steep bank, they had shuddered with horror at the thought of those crossing when the river was higher. There was much gratitude among the travelers at this reflective juncture in their journey. It almost made the homesickness less pronounced.

Only a few of the wagons had so far broken down. Men had learned quickly how to make all kinds of repairs, helping with the work on their own wagon and watching the work done on those belonging to others. This last was, of course, accompanied by advice and opinion, but it was accepted in the spirit given. The Colonel and the scouts, noting the poor workmanship of a few wagons, wondered how long they would last, and how much of a delay it would cost the entire train while they were repaired.

The animals, however, were now accustomed to pulling together. Men once unused to guiding oxen from the ground had learned how best to keep them going, and harder yet, how to stop them. Women had quickly learned how to organize the brief nooning, as well as how to set up the night camp and get everyone fed with a minimum of sand in the food.

People now knew how long each daily task would take, and who in the family was most capable in doing it. Those assigned to dig the latrine trench knew to dig it half on one side of a boulder or bush, and half on the other. The standard of women to the left and men to the right was a strict one, and no one ever thought to break from it. Out on the flat prairie it would be dug in an arch so people could keep their backs to one another. This was the main reason for women steadfastly choosing to wear dresses instead of men's pants, as the long skirts gave them at least some modicum of privacy.

The latrine trenches were to be filled in before the wagon train left the area. This had not always been done in the early years of the migration, and many felt this to have contributed to at least some of the cholera that had been so common then.

Each morning the Colonel's old cook sounded a bugle to rouse the sleepy people to another day closer to their goal. In the still air of dawn before the wind began to blow, the murmur of voices could be heard giving instructions and making demands. Responses were mixed with the sound and aroma of breakfast being made, children laughing as they carried water from the stream in coffee pots, tents being struck and stored, cows mooing until milked, oxen being yoked and horses or mules hitched to wagons.

All children who were old enough to walk had a job to do, the task appropriate to their age. They commonly looked out for younger siblings, so that sometimes eight year olds cared for their four year old brothers and sisters. Older children gathered wood and even helped prepare the evening meal. But after dinner, when the men lit their pipes and visited or played cards, and the women were mending or preparing meals for the day to follow, it was time for the youngsters to play their games. Sometimes those in their teens danced or sang.

The noise of teams being hitched acted as a prompt for people to brace themselves for another arduous day, and when a second blast of the bugle sounded, everyone knew they had better be ready to move out. If they were not, they would have to move out of line and watch everyone pass until they could get into position at the end of the line. They had been told that if they were so tardy that they were left behind, they would have to travel alone. The fear of such peril, explained in gory detail by the Colonel, kept everyone on the Luster train determined to never experience such a circumstance.

By seven in the morning the wagons disappeared from the comfort of the camp site. The dust raised by their departure settled again to the earth, and once again the local animals, snakes, lizards, beetles, and mosquitoes were left alone to get on with their peaceful existence. That is, until the next wagon train arrived and decided to make that area their camping place.

The empty rolling prairie that stretched out beyond the length of their view, destitute of tree or large bush, was the landscape through which their journey proceeded. The farmers admired the rich earth that grew the grasses thick and long, and the women inhaled the fragrance arising from the wildflowers that brought color to the drabness of their monotonous days. But they didn't linger, because the Colonel said they were moving through the home of the horse Indians, and the train was an unwelcome guest.

Every couple of hours Nancy allowed herself a few moments to rest by riding in the wagon while feeding or just holding Alice. She could then watch the loose animals being herded as a group not far from the train, as well as over a hundred people walking beside their slow moving rigs in an effort to spare the teams the burden of their added weight. Few people rode inside their wagon unless old or ill, but when the children grew tired they were put inside, and sometimes the women used this as an excuse to do the same when the road was smooth. But the men either walked or rode a horse. To do otherwise would be to lose status and risk ridicule.

The men had quickly learned how to circle the wagons at night, the tongue of each wagon snugged against the rear of the one in front of it, leaving the perfect distance for chains or ropes to reach from one to the other. In this way, no animal could escape the corral formed by the circle of wagons. From the time the wagons stopped, it only took ten minutes for the teams to be removed and the barricade formed. The teams were then driven to pasture before being returned to the safety of the enclosure for the night. It was an efficient choreography of movement, and had quickly become second nature to everyone.

Because the heat of the day was now steady, Nancy changed into a lighter weight gingham dress with a blue apron that covered only her skirt. It felt good to be wearing clean clothes again, but she knew she needed to wash the other one as soon as possible. There was no telling what might soon happen to this one, what with popping grease, thorns ripping at the hem, a baby that occasionally threw up, and the mud of rain storms.

The first time that Indians showed up shouting "How do" and "tobac" while pointing at any visible food, there was nervous commotion among the families. But the Colonel had prepared them for this and they knew to give them the food. It occurred often enough that most families kept aside bread that had turned stale in the dry prairie air or meat that had turned rancid.

If the Indians pressed for ammunition or liquor they were steadfastly refused it, and instead were given small trinkets. Although they took the bent pin or frayed ribbon, it was often received with a comment couched in shockingly imaginative profanity. They had picked up these words from their years of exposure to mountain men and traders, and used the words with a casualness that was sometimes too funny to be offensive. This resulted in the Indian's occasional greeting of "Hello goddams."

Those from the East, not realizing that the Indians had little understanding of the exact meaning of the florid words they uttered, often became incensed. But they learned to keep their mouths shut, for if the exchange went badly, that night the Indians would probably steal at least one animal from the loose stock. The man who had provoked this would then have to stand extra guard duty.

Just east of Hanover, Kansas, they saw their first view of the Little Blue River and reached the point where the St. Joe Road ended. It was here they were to be joined by twenty wagons coming up from Independence and Nebraska City.

As they waited for the Independence train to join them, Nancy and Effie watched their husbands and sons fish the Little Blue and soon baskets were filled with the shining catch. After awhile, Nancy commented to Effie, "Odd, but the river smells a little like a bed of strawberries to me."

"Oh, thank goodness," Effie laughed. "I thought I was imaging it."

Soon they were a train of 80 strong that stayed on a gentle road where nearby was plentiful wood, water and grass. For one week they camped each night on the Little Blue's pleasantly shady banks, so the youngest of those on the train had plenty of energy and often danced or sang. Some even managed a little harmless romancing.

In the main, Abe and Nancy were fortunate in their neighbors and enjoyed their company--Buran and Effie Howard, Pete and Lona Hastings, and Herman and Edna Crotts. Even the mountain man Croat and his taciturn traveling partner Hickly were often helpful in assisting with teams or loading wagons.

Behind these men was a wagon driven by a single man named Gabe who had arrived with those from Independence. These single men were often irksome, but Nancy chose to think of them generously as simple, strong and capable outdoorsmen. She would soon discover how quickly opinions could change.

CHAPTER THREE
NEBRASKA
MAY, 1863

"Tonight the prairie spreads out for miles around us and hosts our tired cattle numbering about 200, all grazing hungrily upon the green grass. White tents and wagon tops shine beneath a bright full moon with a cooking fire blazing near each homestead on wheels. People are talking, playing games, and some even singing hymns, and all are of light heart. We have arranged ourselves into an efficient village, the only difference being that by the time the sun is well up in the sky tomorrow morning, this village will have disappeared."

Nancy

"Sunday layover yesterday. A man was chosen to act as minister. He stood in the middle of the circle of wagons and read from the Bible. He was chosen because he has such a loud voice. Too bad he is heard more often when complaining."

Abe

Just north of Hanover, Kansas, the train crossed the "coast of Nebraska". This often used phrase originated with the French fur traders and the phrase *la cote de la Nebraska;* Nebraska meaning *Platte* and *cote* indicating a line of bluffs along a stream.

Late in the evening, near the Little Blue River, they arrived at Rock Creek Station. They were now 130 miles from the great Platte River and their next major challenge. The station was the typical coaching stop of corrals surrounding a ramshackle building of clay and logs for the family who served the stages. The teams were changed and the passengers were fed, but little else was supplied.

At this station in 1861 James Butler Hickok, also known as Wild Bill, had shot it out with David McCanles, the owner of the station. Horace Wellman and his wife were the station keepers then and eagerly told Abe and Nancy about that day.

"The stage line had hired James as stock tender. McCanles showed up drunk and began harassing me about overdue rent payments. James tried to intervene. Unfortunately, two McCanles men also joined in. It ended in a brief shoot-out that left McCanles and his men dead. Fast draw, that Hickok."

Mrs. Wellman was quick to add, "James was acquitted of murder and since then he's spent his life helping various offices of the Federal Government to maintain order." It would take a number of years for history to register the full measure of Wild Bill.

The train was in a broad valley and the hills were covered in a mat of vivid green short grass occasionally scattered by blankets of white prairie flowers. In this valley they passed Liberty Farm, a stage station on the north bank of the river, about 190 miles west of the Missouri River.

The station was kept by a Mormon gentleman, Jim Lemmon, who was fortunate to have his family with him. The children on the train ran to meet the Lemmon children, and their raucous play and laughter moved to the back of the station. The men checked their stock with the help of Mr. Lemmon and grazed the animals, while the women obtained a few supplies from the society-starved Mrs. Lemmon with whom they shared news of the latest fashions in the east.

One of the stages of the overland road that followed the river for almost 100 miles was stopped at the station for a change of teams. Without preamble, the stage pulled out to the sound of the driver's shouts and the team's jangling harnesses. As it disappeared in a cloud of dust, those on the Luster train stood beside their cumbersome wagons and watched the speed of the coach with envy.

Fifteen miles of travel over rolling prairie brought them to Lone Tree Station, located on Nine Mile Ridge. The monotony of the gently rolling prairie was broken by a single tree atop a far hill silhouetted against a clear blue sky. It only served to emphasize the isolation of the station.

Ten miles to the northwest they came to one of the larger home stations for the stages. It was a long low log building known as Thirty-two Mile Creek Station. The creek itself was a main tributary of the Little Blue and was so twisting that the wagons had to cross its waters three times in order to continue on a straight line. The Colonel had them fill their water barrels, since the next portion would be a waterless section of the trail leading to the Valley of the Platte. Some of the people purchased fresh eggs at the station and had them boiled for their lunch. They traveled the next day quite content at having had such a nice change to what was quickly becoming a monotonous routine.

The Carringtons had enjoyed the arid beauty of this peaceful Valley through which they had just traveled. They had met many industrious, friendly and helpful people, and had been provided important support at a point when it was very much needed.

It was good they remembered their time there as so pleasant, because the following year much of it would be burned out by Indians whose tolerance had ended. In one spectacular raid intended to end the habitation of their land, they would burn the farms, businesses and stations of those the Carringtons remembered so fondly. The ground would be soaked with the blood of the men, women and children they had so enjoyed meeting.

The promise of Fort Kearny ahead made the next day and a half of hard travel more bearable. They were on the divide between the Little Blue and the Platte, and heading due west at 2,000 feet elevation. They had in their barrels just enough water for themselves and their animals, but this did little to give them a sense of refreshment. The dry sand hills gave way to deep ravines and gullies cut by the run-off of the region's heavy rains, and the strain on the wagons was severe. The men were tense with the fear of something breaking on their rigs. The women with babies carried them in their arms and were quickly exhausted, and small children whimpered as they were tossed about inside the wagons.

At last they saw the much anticipated Platte River. Whatever they might have pictured in their minds, what they found was a river that for a hundred miles cut a path that threaded around dozens of islands studded with trees and furred with grass. The edges of these islands were a mess of branches and the flotsam of wagons wrecked while crossing the river.

About nine miles before the fort, they turned west to Valley City, more often referred to as Dogtown. Named after the cute prairie dogs that sat by their tunnels watching the wagons pass, the town itself was far from cute. It was a dilapidated collection of unpainted shacks surrounded by muddy streets and trash heaps. A store, a grog shop and a residence for Mr. Hook, the station keeper, were fronted by small porches now crowded with a rabble of loud men. But the town did have postal service and there were a few outlying ranches nearby.

Mrs. West, a tall angular woman who was often heard whining to her husband when unhappy, waved to the Colonel as he rode by the West's wagon. She asked the Colonel to stop the train so she could mail letters, but he told her she would have to wait until reaching the fort. When she tried to argue with him, he simply turned his horse and rode away, leaving her to complain to her beleaguered husband about such rudeness. The wagon train passed Dogtown without so much as hesitating, and no man was drawn closer by even the promise of the grog shop.

As they descended into the Valley of the Platte they could see spread before them the incredibly wide but shallow river on its way east to the Missouri. Along the banks were willow and young cottonwood trees with short grass growing beneath, while on the many islands breaking the surface of the Platte there were considerably more trees and bushes. This puzzled the travelers until the Colonel explained that local Indians regularly burned the land along the Platte to facilitate their rabbit drives.

That night, only a few miles from Fort Kearny, Nancy lay awake and listened to the sounds of the night. Horses tied on the line within the circle of wagons stomped and munched any grass close by, cattle let loose with an occasional bellow, a wolf in the distance howled his plaintive call, crickets chirped, and what seemed like millions of frogs croaked their wooing of mates. These sounds had finally become comfortingly familiar.

Nancy's mind drifted through the sights and smells and events of the day, and stopped at the memory of a young woman who was part of the group from Independence. Two men had called Nancy's attention to her. "Well, hell and damnation!" Mr. Black had exclaimed. "Look at that."

Mr. Furman had responded with a simple, "Damn!"

Nancy had turned in the direction they were staring. What had made the young woman stand out beyond her pretty blonde looks was the fact that she wore pleated bloomers under a full skirt that ended just below her knees. Her legs had been wrapped in thick black stockings and her leather boots were laced tightly over trim ankles.

"You can see her lower limbs!" Mr. Black had declared, using the socially acceptable term for legs.

Impatient with their affronted tone, Nancy had said, "All women have them, you know."

Mrs. Ashe had joined them, and having heard Nancy's comment, said, "Yes, but our limbs are not visible."

Some of the other nearby men approached and they too gawked at the woman. Most had heard of this bloomer outfit worn by the more progressive of women, but no one present had actually seen a woman so bold as to wear it. Mrs. Ashe turned to Nancy and allowed that the girl could "get away with it" only because she was not yet twenty. Being the same age, she quickly added, "She's not married, of course. No husband would tolerate such clothing on his wife."

Several days later, after watching the young woman climb so easily in and out of her wagon, Nancy began to envy the girl's courage to wear such daring attire. But she would never consider saying so to anyone, not even Abe.

The wagons made good time along the Great Platte River Road, their white covers flapping in the breeze like sails on ships. This was especially true for those wagons with diapers pinned to the canvas so the sun could bleach them clean until the next opportunity to wash clothes.

The wagons strained up to the crest of a low hill and followed it with a steep descent down the other side, repeating this motion for hours as they crossed miles of rolling swales in the grass lands of the prairie. Seen from a distance they looked somewhat like ships tossed on a stormy sea, and consequently over time the wagons had gained the name of *prairie schooners.*

For those riding in these wagons on this part of the trail, it was so miserably uncomfortable that most people preferred to walk even if the effort was difficult. Over a century later this portion of the trail over which hundreds of thousands of wagons had traveled, would still be discernable even when the area became ranches and farms. As though nature desired to pay homage to all this traffic, wheat growing in the wagon tracks would be of a different color and density than that surrounding it.

The Platte to their right was at some points a mile or more wide. The people looked at it with a mixture of gratitude for its presence and complaint that it was not more to their liking. It was not beautiful by any means. It lent them no cooling shade and its taste was foul, and consequently was mostly used for the animals. Nancy was grateful that there were so many creeks leading into the river, and like everyone else the Carringtons stored that water in their barrels.

The women refused to wash clothes in the Platte, much less themselves. In many places its surface was so opaque that if a calf or child fell in, it would be almost impossible to launch a rescue even though the victim might be only inches beneath the surface of the shallow flow. In the cholera years, the disease had been at its worst along the Platte, and the evidence of this was recorded on dozens of rocks used as grave markers that were carved with names and dates. The worst part was that everyone knew there were many more bodies buried in unmarked graves beneath the road they traveled. No, the Platte was not much to their liking at all.

To their left were the low green bluffs that enclosed the Platte bottoms, but which Nancy was surprised to find gave no sense of relief. They had been told this was a good area for hunting and the Colonel said that here they might find deer, and if lucky, buffalo. Even one deer could feed a family through a good number of meals.

Of all those on the Colonel's train, the man most people wanted to avoid after an initial introduction was Croat. Someone said this was his last name, although others thought it his first. No one seemed to have the courage or interest to ask. He was certainly nothing enjoyable to look at, or smell for that matter. His stature was average, and he might have had a fair physique, but it was hidden under a thick bulk of hides that covered his body and hung long over dark wool pants tucked into tall black boots.

His manner of dress, even his peculiar musky scent, might have been forgiven him. But his deplorable manners when eating, his nasty quick temper, and his foul vocabulary kept all but a few from trying. He traveled with another man of similar description, except that Hickly was shorter, his hat a darker fur, and he very seldom spoke.

Jebb, of similar but somewhat cleaner habits and dress, had arrived with those from Independence. He had pulled his wagon in line back of the one belonging to Croat and Hickly, and in front of the friendly Gabe.

Gabe was a stocky man of about fifty, with a long brown beard and short hair under a floppy black hat. He declared himself a miner heading to California, but although he too had been part of the Independence group, he didn't seem eager to spend time with Jebb.

No one regretted that these men preferred their own company. Jebb was especially onerous, being quick to loudly and fulsomely express his sour opinions of practically everything from the weather to trail conditions. But he particularly resented the existence of Indians.

While carrying on about them, he peppered his comments with words and phrases so vulgar that even the most worldly of the men listening flinched. He never gave a hint as to the reason for his hatred. There were no allusions to personal loss or harm, just frequent and colorful tirades at the slightest provocation about Indian customs, dress, diet, conduct, or any other characteristic that might come to his mind. The tribe might change, but the last sentence of every diatribe was always the same. He swore he would kill the first Indian that came within range of his gun or knife.

Although the Colonel hoped he was wrong about the man, he had the uneasy suspicion that Jebb was serious. He knew that the whole train would be in severe jeopardy if Jebb shot at an Indian, so the Colonel had felt it necessary to threaten Jebb with colorful and imaginative retributions if he followed through.

For the last year the trail had been shadowed by a line of telegraph poles along much of the route. This reminder of civilization encouraged people to press on so they could start their new lives, but it also brought to mind those left behind who were enjoying comfortable chairs and savory meals cooked in large stoves.

The Luster train in 1863 had the advantage of crossing most creeks and rivers on at least rudimentary bridges. These were manned by Mormons or Indians who charged a toll and who were supposed to see to the bridge's upkeep. Nevertheless, the tolls were resented by many of the cash-strapped emigrants. Many of the waterways that didn't have a bridge, at least had ferries for hire. Nevertheless, there were still dozens of small creeks and even some stretches of river, that had to be crossed with the teams pulling and swimming as best they could to get their load across.

The other water encountered usually arrived at the worst moments. The first time Abe and Nancy experienced one of the infamous Platte thunderstorms, it first loomed over them for hours in the form of steel gray clouds. At the nooning, Nancy hurriedly buttered the left over morning biscuits and sprinkled them with sugar while trying unsuccessfully to ignore the ominous clouds that were forming overhead. Those who had been lifelong farmers, and were used to judging weather events, declared the clouds to be harmless. But they were unfamiliar with the strange perversity of the weather along the Platte. With a sudden whoosh of wind, the storm dumped its load upon them.

As the rain fell in sheets, men slogged and skidded through the mud while trying to calm their teams. Some hobbled their animals to keep them from bolting beneath the lightening strikes and rumbling thunder. Young children were tossed into the wagons to protect them from the deluge, and the women quickly followed. It took only minutes for many of the treated canvas tops to leak and allow rain into the wagons, and only canvas that was folded into a double thickness held up well.

People who at first thought they could get away from the beating strength of the rain by crawling under their wagon soon were contending with slick black mud that flowed everywhere. Jagged snapping bolts of lightening cut through the sky, illuminating the landscape in vivid detail and showing stringers of muddy water rushing wherever the land was low. Each blinding flash from above was accompanied by a pounding crash of thunder, and children screamed almost as loud as the mules and horses.

Abe stayed by the team with a slicker draped over his head and shoulders while the boys clung to Nancy in the back of their damp wagon. She held a crying Alice tightly in her arms, and although Todd and Harold never would have said so, they were happy their mother insisted they stay with her. Later, in case one of the other boys on the train had seen, they told them, "Our mother needed lots of comforting during the storm." The others claimed the same was true of their mothers.

The storm stopped as suddenly as it had begun and in an hour it was over. The air was crisp and clean, and at least for a few hours there was no dust with which to contend. After bolting down two cold biscuits, the Carringtons spent the rest of the day drying their wagon and its contents. Women spread wet clothes on wheels, wagon tongues and bushes to dry in the bright sun that followed the storm, while the men gathered the loose stock that had scattered.

True to her commitment to cook good meals for her family, Effie Howard had built a small fire to heat stew just before the storm hit. Few women went to so much trouble at the brief nooning. For the entire duration of the storm Effie had protected the fire by holding an umbrella over the fire ring. Her bonnet and dress were soaked, but her fire had blazed on and her family had eaten a hot meal the minute the storm passed. Nancy would never forget the sight of the indomitable woman and her umbrella, and the memory would often serve as a reminder of unyielding perseverance in the face of adversity.

But other than the misery of that bad thunderstorm, the first month of travel had not been too difficult for the Luster train. Lying in their bed under or in the wagon, depending on the weather, at the end of each day Abe and Nancy enjoyed a few precious moments of whispered conversation before plummeting into exhausted sleep. Some of their discussions were about the future of their children, for although the boys got along well with one another, it was also true that Todd and Harold had very different interests. Mostly, however, they talked about trail gossip and their fears of what lay ahead.

Each evening for half an hour after dinner Nancy made the boys attend class with her, refusing to neglect their education. She might have them work at memorizing the multiplication table, spell words she chose at random, or practice their penmanship. Sometimes there was background music that accompanied their studying, offered by a young man with a harmonica in a wagon not far away. This night he was playing *Old Kentucky Home*, and it brought Nancy a wave of homesickness for her old *Missouri* home.

She turned her attention to the boys. They discussed first West Virginia, the thirty-fifth and newest state to join the Union. After that Harold wanted to talk about President Lincoln's reasons for passing the Emancipation Proclamation three months before. Finally, Nancy told the boys they could read by themselves until the light of the fire was too dim.

"Truth to tell," Nancy admitted to herself, "I'm just too tired to focus." She retrieved her pile of mending, pulled her camp stool where she could use a wagon wheel as a back rest, and stared

into the last of the glowing ashes. Just as Nancy felt her heavy
eyes begin to close, Harold looked up from his history book.
    "Mom?"
    "Yes, dear?" Nancy jerked to an upright position and looked
at him across the dim embers of the fire.
    "Have you ever read the Declaration of Independence?"
    "Not recently." She put a hand over her mouth to stifle a
yawn.
    "It's just a long list of justifications for separating from Great
Britain," Harold lamented.
    "Are they good reasons?"
    He took a moment, wrinkling his brow as he considered the
question. "Yeah. I mean, why should someone so far away, who
never even saw our country, tell us what to do and tax us too?"
    Nancy smiled at her intelligent son, feeling pride swell with-
in her. She noticed Todd looking at his brother with a frown
between his eyes, and wondered if he had reached the same
conclusion. Most likely he didn't even understand what Harold
was talking about. On the other hand, Harold had no idea how
to gentle a young animal or plant a straight row of corn, even
after watching Todd and Abe several times. As she returned to
the mending of Abe's socks, she wondered if Harold might not
someday become a lawyer.
    Before Harold could ask further questions, their conversa-
tion was interrupted by Bob Cook as he walked by on his nightly
check of the wagons. He enjoyed watching the people settled
and enjoying their evenings, and had recently begun to make it
part of his routine to accept a cup of coffee from the Carrington
family. He enjoyed visiting with them, but if they sensed his
need for quiet, they went on about their evening routine and let
him sip his coffee by the fire alone. When Abe returned from
checking on their loose stock, he was happy to divide the last of
the pot with Bob.
    After a few minutes of casual conversation, Bob mentioned
that Mr. and Mrs. Shayne were both very ill. Abe had met Mr.
Shayne at the first evening council meeting, and Nancy had only
talked to Mrs. Shayne before the train left St. Joseph. In fact,
few people had seen the young couple after the first few days
on the trail. They had always retired for the night immediately
upon stopping. The families in the wagons forward and behind

them had been feeding their two little boys as well as bringing broth to the couple. It went mostly untouched.

"At least the boys aren't far away from their parents," Bob summarized.

"Mrs. Shayne said she wasn't feeling well before we even started," Nancy told him. "But she didn't tell her husband because she didn't want to be a burden."

Abe grunted. "He wasn't feeling well either, but didn't want to worry his wife."

Bob looked at them and sighed. "They should have stayed home. They might have lived."

Startled, Abe reminded him, "You said they were just ill."

"For now." Bob thanked Nancy for the coffee and walked off.

Late that night there was noisy activity across the circle from the Carrington wagon. The boys became aware of it first and awakened their parents. Nancy and Abe were afraid it meant the worst, and Abe went to investigate. Upon his return he told Nancy that both of the Shaynes had died.

"Oh, those poor children," Nancy exclaimed. "They're not much past five years old."

"Now, Nan, we don't have provision or room for them."

"I know, but..."

"And besides, they're being sent back to St. Joe where they have an uncle."

"How? Is there a wagon falling out of the trip?"

"The Colonel didn't give more particulars."

While the Colonel said prayers and read from the Bible, a small crew of men from the train buried the young couple in one unmarked grave in the middle of the road. Those gathered by the grave sang "Nearer, My God to Thee" and then returned to their wagons to continue their routine.

As the long line of wagons pulled out of camp, they each in turn rolled over the grave. The wheels left their imprint in the soft earth until it was tamped down to match the rest of the hard packed earth of the trail. In this way they hoped the local Indians would not find and dig up the couple's grave.

Later in the day, Bob told Abe that the Shayne children would be escorted back to St. Joseph by two Pottawatomie Indians that had been hanging around the Colonel's wagon since they had left the Missouri River. As shocking a solution as this seemed to everyone, no one could think of a more practical alternative, considering that the children did have relatives. When informed by their husbands of this decision, many of the women were especially disturbed.

Effie Howard told a number of people that she thought it a clever way to get the pesky Indians out of camp without angering them. Although Buran thought her clever for thinking of that, some of those to whom she said this were troubled at hearing the thought put so boldly into words. Not that they disagreed, but they felt it was dangerous to show ones loathing for an Indian so openly. As one man put it, "The savages seem to resent it."

The next morning, just as dawn was beginning to show a glow of warm light in the east, Nancy looked out from the back of the wagon. There passed not far from the train the silhouette of two skinny horses each carrying an Indian brave with his arms wrapped around a child snuggled in front of him. The wagons had traveled almost 200 miles from St. Joseph, but no doubt the Indians knew a much shorter route for those on horseback. These braves were now the only protection the children would have against a life that had suddenly taken their parents, and Nancy felt her throat tighten as she tried to imagine what the children were feeling.

At that night's council meeting, Colonel Luster assured the men that the Indians had a very high regard for children and would see that they got home. He did *not* tell them that being boys, if their tribe was small, they might be tempted to keep the children. But the Colonel refused to deal with a group of angry women hounding him about something he couldn't change, so he kept silent about it even to the men. A cunning Jebb, who had spent a lot of time on the plains, gave the Colonel a smirk as he walked away.

"God, I dislike that man!" the Colonel mumbled to himself.

Of all those who had arrived on the Independence train, the boys seemed to like Gabe the best. He was one of only half a dozen single men on the train, but he had a small farm wagon drawn by four large mules and a riding mule tied behind the wagon. This tagged him as a man of some wealth, even if his worn trousers, stained flannel shirt, worn felt hat and long beard offered a different impression. Gabe liked to tell everyone how good they had it by traveling in '63, and in the comfort of well-made wagons on improved roads.

At an evening meeting, the men discussed the next place they could buy supplies. This launched Gabe into one of his un-invited reminiscences. "I started across in '46 with no wagon. I only had my riding mule and a string of four. I also had two bits in my pocket and never had no reason to spend it. Two other fellas with me had the same setup. We got our food by trading, sharing, digging it from the land or shooting it on the run. There weren't no trading posts and only a couple of forts. What ferries we used was run by Indians. That was as far as the Rockies. We turned back then."

Chris Payne, just starting to scout for wagon trains back then, spoke up. "There were also lots of stock and people drowned, and much of the time they were hungry and thirsty. Most now are happy to be well supplied and pay tolls at bridges. It gets them all the way to the West." He walked away without giving Gabe a chance to respond.

"City feller!" the old man snorted at Chris's back.

Abe shrugged. "I'm a farmer, and I think I agree with Chris." Then he quickly added, "But I won't end up with the same pride of accomplishment as you did." Gabe looked somewhat molli-fied as he walked away.

Abe turned around in preparation of returning to his wagon only to find the Colonel standing close behind him. He nodded to him as he walked past and the Colonel returned his greeting. Not for the first time, the Colonel noted that this tall farmer had a knack for tactfully handling situations.

Two wagons up from the Carringtons were Herman and Edna Crotts. When the short muscular Herman barked orders at Edna, which seemed to be his primary means of communica-tion, there was never a sign that it bothered her. She merely stretched her five feet a little taller and did as she was told, her tight expression suggesting that she already had just that in mind. Edna was in her fifties and childless, and wore her dignity like an armor that nothing could penetrate. But she was always pleasant to others and Nancy liked her.

While the men were dealing with each other at council, Nancy, Effie and Edna sat near the Carrington's fire nibbling on Effie's biscuits and jam. Nancy was roasting green coffee beans and she needed to carefully tend the fire, since one burned bean would adversely flavor the whole pan.

"By the way," Effie told her new friends, "I have extra sassafras root if you need it to thicken a soup. It's already ground up too."

They thanked her for her generosity, after which their conversation ranged from complaining about the limited diversity of meals to the difficulty of washing clothes. They laughed when each admitted that they longed to soak in a tub for at least an hour.

Edna chuckled to herself and shook her head as she brushed ash from her long skirt.

"What brought that on?" Nancy asked her.

"I was thinking about my dear deceased mother," Edna told her. "She would have been horrified at the way I'm living right now."

"Really?"

"Oh, yes. Although Herman is a shopkeeper, I was brought up in Virginia to be a delicate, cultured lady."

"Ah, yes," Effie responded, "the guardian of hearth and home and all things domestic."

Nancy smiled and nodded her head, adding, "And expected to be passive and accepting of whatever men deem right."

Both women looked at her, but it was Edna that said, "Well, I must admit it has never occurred to me to voice any opinion other than that of my husband."

Nancy recalled the many times she had heard Herman Crotts yelling at Edna and looked at her askance, "Not about anything?"

Edna shrugged and said, "Not about anything that really matters." For her, this was a statement of profound independent spirit.

"I must admit I seldom disagree with Buran," Effie said. "But, then, he usually listens to my ideas."

"Does he usually agree with them?" Nancy asked.

Effie grimaced. "Well, no."

Nancy sighed at the not unexpected response. "I have the feeling that after we're on the trail for awhile it may be more difficult for us to show such easy acquiescence."

"Easy what?"

"I mean, being so ready to give in to what the men think without voicing our opinions."

"Do you really think so?" Edna asked.

"We're certainly proving that we're not helpless. And we have no hearth to guard and no home in which to display our homemaking skills." With a teasing smile, Nancy added, "Nor cultured society to judge our moral piety." When she noticed that neither woman realized she was being playfully sarcastic, she quickly summarized, "No, we're frontier women now."

"Meaning?" Edna whispered.

Nancy was losing patience with Edna's naivety and lack of humor. "Meaning we cook in the dirt, wash clothes on rocks, and must accept other people as they are because their help may be necessary to our survival. And the only culture we need care about is that of whatever Indian nation we're passing through."

Both of her new friends looked at her with something akin to awe, but it was Effie that put into words what they were both thinking. "You've grasped the facts of our current situation so quickly."

Edna said, "I think I've been fooling myself into thinking this trip would not change us very much."

"I started thinking about the differences the day after I realized the fact of our going," Nancy temporized. "Maybe I had more time for reflection. I'm sure you would have come to the same realization soon."

"Maybe," Edna admitted, "but I think it best to realize it as soon as possible." She rose up and told Nancy, "Thank you." She walked forward to her wagon deep in thought and looking more disturbed than grateful.

Mention of Indians reminded Nancy of their encounter with Pawnees when they had been at the headwaters of the Little Blue. The men of the train had been told to wear their arms clearly showing while the Pawnee rode alongside the train about twenty yards away on either side. For several miles the Indians had made a great show of their gleaming painted bodies while astride ponies of remarkable sturdiness. Although the quivers tied to their backs were full of arrows, the braves also looked relaxed and disinterested. Scouts Bob, Chris and Harry had ridden along the length of the train telling everyone to keep their arms visible and at the ready, but show no alarm and take no obvious notice of the braves.

"Easier said than done," Abe had mumbled to Nancy.

After an afternoon of this tension, everyone's nerves had been strung tight and many of the women had been sick with terror. No child or woman was seen walking, and the men who had to lead ox teams from the ground had been at the ready to dive under their wagon if arrows flew. That evening at dusk the Indians had disappeared, but their absence had done little to relieve anyone's anxiety.

Nancy brought her thoughts back to the present and told Effie what she had been thinking. "Remember how the next morning we found some of the stock missing? Abe presumed they'd been stolen by the Pawnee."

Effie said, "Yes, but just as we were ready to move out, five braves arrived in camp with the cattle."

"Abe felt bad that he had jumped to the wrong conclusion about the Indians. Then the braves made it clear they expected a large reward for bringing the stock back. Bob explained that sometimes the Indians steal the stock just so they can play this game with the passing trains. Did you know that some of the men were going to refuse to pay?"

Effie shook her head and said, "I know it really angered Buran."

The Colonel had not been misled by the Indians bringing back the horses, but he still had made the owners of the animals pay them a reward. He had even given the braves several plugs of tobacco that he had packed away for just such events.

That night it finally fell to Abe to take his turn at night guard duty. He stood just outside the circle of wagons and quickly realized that when one was tense and straining to hear something out of the ordinary, that was indeed what one heard. It didn't matter that it was just the breeze rustling leaves, the chirps of crickets, the croaking of frogs, or the howls of coyotes. What Abe heard was creeping feet, stealthy breathing, and whispered intentions.

Not long before he was to be relieved at two in the morning, Abe became certain the coyote howls were really Indians passing information about when to attack. Why he would think this, when there had been no problem with the local tribes, he later could not explain. But in the dark of that night, and exhausted beyond any point in his life, he was aware only of a magnified sense of responsibility that ignored the fact that there were several other men also on guard duty. Abe felt the entire train's safety on his feeble shoulders, and the fatigue of the day bunched in the tight sore muscles of his body. Eventually it became a certainty in his mind that danger was near.

A branch cracked about thirty feet from where he stood at the same time that a gust of wind goosed the horses in the corral behind him, several of them jumping sideways. When no one called out the standard "friend of the guard" greeting, Abe reacted by shooting in the direction of the tree from which he was sure had come the sound of a stealthy foot treading on a branch. Immediately men came running to his side, with Chris Payne in the lead.

"What's the matter?" he asked, his gun drawn and his breathing heavy.

"I heard someone over there," Abe whispered, ignoring the fact that the loud report of his gun negated the need to hide his presence. "I'm sure it was someone skulking closer. Maybe an Indian trying to steal stock."

"Let's hope you didn't hit him," Chris told him, "or all hell will break loose."

Upon investigation, however, it was found to be a small pack mule that had wandered in from the loose stock. It lay with a hole in its chest, and would never again carry a pack. Abe felt terrible. Over and over he apologized to its distraught owner, Mr. Frank.

Chris clapped a reassuring hand on Abe's shoulder. "It's not the first time something like this has happened, and it won't be the last. Just be glad it was a mule instead of a man." Abe came very close to being sick.

Mr. Frank was reasonable and forgiving, maybe remembering how close he too had come to shooting at shadows his first night on guard duty. However, he did say, "I expect to be compensated for the loss, you know."

"Of course. What do you think fair?"

The man thought a moment. "How about a couple pans of your good woman's biscuits. My wife's biscuits could substitute for door stops."

Abe swallowed his laughter along with his relief. "I can do that."

The two men shook on it, the deed was put behind them, and the next night Mr. Frank feasted not only on Nancy's biscuits, but also a jug of her buttermilk. Abe delivered it to him along with the recipe, which included exact instructions for his wife.

Not withstanding Mr. Frank's generous attitude, it was days before Abe could rid himself of the memory of the dead mule, or feel that others were not ridiculing him behind his back. However, not once did anyone say a word about it.

After the train was well into Nebraska, the Pawnee in the area were no longer a problem. However, Jebb and Croat could not resist at various times intruding into conversations with stories of the Pawnee's past depredations on wagon trains. Having themselves now experienced the theft of animals, not always returned for a price but sometimes kept for consumption, the emigrants nursed resentment mixed with fear of what more the Indians might do to them. They could still remember the sight of the "brazen savages" riding past, their painted bodies glistening in the sun, their hair cut short except for a small bunch on top, and all hosting an air of distain. Thankfully, this display had not been repeated.

Bob came to Abe at the nooning. "Saddle your horse and come with me."

They rode to a tall rocky cliff about a mile from the stream where they were camped. After dismounting, Bob pointed to a space on the cliff that was covered in names and dates.

"I'll be damned!" Abe burst out. Before him, carved into the rock, were the words *John Fremont and Kit Carson, 1842.* Abe declared, "The boys would love this!"

"Really?" Bob asked.

"Well, Harold would anyway. Todd seems more interested in spending time with that idiot Croat."

"Bothers you, does it?"

"More than it should. But Todd doesn't skip his chores, so I can't really say anything."

"Maybe after awhile Croat will get tired of having a kid hanging around. After Todd gets yelled at, the attraction should disappear."

Abe liked that idea, and only hoped it would happen soon.

Arrival at Ft. Kearny was a time of relief and joy. It had been established in 1848 as protection for the emigrants, as well as protection for the peaceable tribes from the hostiles. It was the teepees of these peaceable tribes that were scattered amid the scrub surrounding the fort.

The Luster train had the opportunity to again refresh their supplies, repair wagons, doctor the teams, and leave mail for eventual transport to the east. A ten mile tract of land had been reserved for the fort, with a portion slightly elevated above the surrounding landscape so the soldiers could observe the countryside east, south and west. The north view was cut off by the timber along the Platte.

There were no tall wooden balustrades encircling it to present an impenetrable wall of protection. There was no need. The land had been purchased from the Pawnee for $2,000 worth of trade goods, so the Indians in the area had always been respectful and had never given much trouble. They preferred to fight one another.

For the last two years the fort had been the first telegraph station west of St. Joseph and Independence, with wire now all the way to the Pacific. But the Carringtons only saw a few soldiers manning the fort, most having been ordered east to fight in the war. Civilians had taken their place, and the fort showed it by its lack of cleanliness and order.

One of the first things a dozen of the women did was to bring their letters to the fort's post office. They handed over their precious missives to Clerk Henry Sheldon, who also manned the telegraph. He was rightfully proud of his job, and explained to the women that the wire had first reached the fort in November of '60 although the actual work of the transcontinental line began in the summer of '61. Only four and a half months later, messages were being sent from coast to coast.

The women listened patiently, but at the first opportunity they asked the young man for reassurance that their letters would reach their destination. Henry knew he could not honestly give such reassurance, but he was nevertheless deeply affected when he looked into the pleading eyes of these women. They were so innocent of the many things that could happen to their letters.

The mail bags might be stolen or lost during a water crossing, or even thrown out to lighten the load if the stage had to sprint away from an attack. At some stations the bags might be left behind if passengers paid enough to take their place. But instead of telling the ladies all of this, he remembered his dear mother in New York and boldly told them, "Don't you worry, ladies. They'll get through." The women returned to their wagons a little happier.

During the nooning Abe and Nancy walked around the fort grounds after Effie said the boys could stay and eat with Charlie. They passed a large building that served as a barracks, office and mess hall not far from several warehouses. Of course there was also the typical blacksmith, stables, corrals and out buildings. The square dirt parade ground, surrounded on three sides by buildings, was empty except for a tall flag pole in the middle and a row of cannons down either side that were shaded by lines of trees. Not far away they could see a small isolated jail near a scattering of Government issue tents.

The stage station was just west of the military post buildings, and it was here that the Western Stage Company's line from Omaha and Nebraska City terminated. Passengers then transferred to Ben Holladay's Overland line. This was why Abe and Nancy saw waiting passengers from the Western line pacing impatiently outside the station. Overland passengers already on board from Atchison had precedence.

Abe and Nancy sat on the edge of a porch and ate their lunch in the shade of the surprisingly mature trees lining the parade ground. Several of the regular mounted cavalrymen rode past on beautifully groomed horses and Nancy noted that several of the younger single women of the train were nearby also enjoying the shade of the trees. The girls followed the men with their eyes while whispering among themselves and Nancy smiled to herself, trying to remember the last time she had giggled.

Just before pulling out the next morning, the Colonel agreed to take on a new traveler. A week earlier the soldiers had rescued a white woman from a Sioux village on the outskirts of their tribal lands. She had been with the tribe for about five years, and had been tattooed on the face to identify her as the wife of one of the braves. She had spoken very little so far, but they had discerned that she had two children by this brave and did not consider herself rescued as much as the victim of a kidnapping by the soldiers. The Commander at the fort assumed this was due to shock and all that she must have endured "while under the influence of savages".

She said her name was White Dove, and refused to reveal her birth name. There was about her an aura of quiet self-contained dignity that never changed, and the long dark hair that was neatly coiled around her head gave accent to her fine features and petite body. Her dress was made from deer skins, but rather than being eager to shed these clothes that proclaimed her captive status, she refused to put on a gingham dress left her by a kind but large woman on a passing stages.

"What she needs," the Commander told the Colonel, "is being once again with women of her own kind. I need someone who can take her away from here in their wagon."

Since the Hastings had no children, Pete agreed she could ride with them. Lona fawned over the young woman and generously helped her to one of her dresses that was more her size. Although White Dove this time accepted the dress, and even ate what was put in front of her, she was sullen and obviously unhappy. For the two nights after they left the fort, she could be heard crying as she fell asleep.

Two miles west of Fort Kearny they came to one of the most dreadful of what could dubiously be called a town. Although named Kearney City, it was more often derogatorily called Dobytown because the buildings were built mostly of adobe and sod. About six such dwellings were occupied by the lowest and most degenerate class of whiskey peddlers, thieves, gamblers and harlots. Near the river in a thicket of cottonwoods was a small house called Dirty Woman's Ranch, which Nancy considered an apt name from the look of the building. Gabe said that only the most depraved of men ever stayed the night there, and beyond that he would say no more, even when the men were alone. The Colonel kept everyone moving past while the gamblers and partially dressed prostitutes standing on the porches waved, whistled and hooted to the travelers. They were pointedly ignored.

On the third night out from the fort there was no weeping from White Dove, and at last she slept soundly. Lona had made the woman walk next to her all day in the hopes it would tire her enough that she would be eager for sleep that night. The Carringtons and the Crotts, their wagons on either side of the Hastings' wagon, were all happy that the woman had finally resigned herself to returning to her white world, and all slept soundly that night.

When they awoke the next morning they discovered their error. White Dove was gone, along with one of the horses. There was talk of going after her, but it was quickly agreed that she had made her choice and they did not want to take time out from their schedule.

Pete Hastings was very put out. Standing by the Carrington wagon with Lona, he declared, "She's no better than a squaw."

"But she has children. Maybe..."

"Don't be stupid, Lona! I say good riddance to the ungrateful bitch." He grabbed his wife's upper arm and dragged her toward their wagon while a tight-lipped Lona had to lift her skirts higher than proper to keep up.

Abe turned to Nancy, who as a woman he assumed should understand. "Why did she return to the Indians?"

Nancy shrugged. "Whatever else she is, or what has happened to her, Lona is correct. She's a mother. And maybe she's in love with her husband. We shouldn't assume that he's treated her poorly, or that her life is unbearable."

That was an idea Abe had not considered, and it gave him pause. Later he shared the idea with Buran, who promptly scoffed at it. "Don't be ridiculous! Indians have no concept of tenderness or romance like women need."

"Why not? A lot of men are good to their wives."

Buran was obviously impatient with the conversation. "Yes, but Indians aren't men like us."

Abe was not convinced, but he knew better than to continue the debate. When he related it to Nancy later, she frowned at him and asked, "Do you agree with him?"

"No. I think men are pretty much men no matter what their origins. Some are good, some are bad, but all have pride, love, hate, and need in common." He turned to her. "What do you think?"

Grateful that he cared what she thought, she answered him honestly. "I agree. But the same is true of women, you know, no matter their nationality."

"Yeah, well, I don't think I'll tell that to Buran." Together they laughed, and with his arm around her waist, they walked toward the back of the wagon to prepare their bed for the night.

Leaving the protection of the soldiers had been for some on the train an emotional wrench. Moving out onto the trail on the south side of the Platte, they found the river even shallower and more uninviting than previously. In all directions there was nothing but a flat scrub-filled plain and the only change was an occasional hillock or slight dip in the land. But as to trees, there was not one.

Never before in the life of these Easterners had they been out of sight of trees plentiful enough for firewood and construction. Out on the plains the sky was a solid glare of blue broken only by the horizon drawing a straight line through the far view. The openness of their position caused many of them to feel exposed and vulnerable, and the occasional funnel of dust whirling around them only exacerbated this. When they added to this their uneasiness from stories they had heard about Indians and the memory of their own recent experiences, many a man and woman spent a sleepless night filled with worry and dread.

Gabe, whenever he could, regaled the men with stories of battles that had taken place in the area between the Pawnee and Sioux back in the early '50's. Most of the time the Pawnee came out the loser. His description of one such battle in May of 1852 was especially grisly and left nothing to the imagination of his listeners. Few of the men related these stories to their wives, and prayed to God that they might soon be rid of the images Gabe had described so graphically.

The long dry grasses of the broad endless plain glowed like spun gold under the morning sun. But like the stubble on the cheeks of an unshaved man, there was new green grass bristling through. There were also large fields of white, yellow, red and purple wildflowers. When the sun warmed the air and the wind was calm, the sweet fragrance hung on the air and became an event unto itself that was talked about for days.

Harold came into camp with one hand gripping his bag full of buffalo chips and the other holding a small bunch of wildflowers. He held out both to his mother.

Nancy was overwhelmed with emotion at the sweetness of his gesture. "Why, thank you, Harold. I can't think of anything I would like better right now." She placed the wild blooms in a metal cup on the little folding table where they would eat their dinner and bent over to kiss his cheek. He quickly looked around to see if anyone had seen this public display, but he was also smiling proudly.

After several days of travel through this primitive and rough terrain, Nancy began to feel a new and puzzling sensation. For the first time in her life, she felt in touch with herself as an individual woman with ideas and opinions all her own. It occurred to her that maybe she was someone more than wife and mother, someone with endless chores and the need to help everyone around her. Maybe she really could have her own thoughts and feelings that need not be shared or approved by anyone else.

She kept this new revelation, and the tiny emerging sense of joy it generated, to herself. Others would surely scoff at her for such independent concepts. But the realization that there was freedom in imagining, and exhilaration in appreciating the beauty of a wild landscape, had stirred within her a new perspective of the world around her and her place within it. She felt powerful, and just a little naughty. What she did not recognize then was that much of this new attitude was due to the way Abe treated her, with a respect of her opinions and trust of her ability.

But the reality of her situation could not be ignored, and she could not escape the fact that she did have people who relied on her--a husband and three children needing almost constant attention, and so many daily chores that there were few moments for such self-revelatory contemplation. So she put aside these new insights and feelings, and resumed the role which life had assigned her.

The approach to Plum Creek over the grassy dunes of the area had been anticipated for some time by the men. Here buffalo might be expected, and indeed many of their wallows were carved into the dirt along the trail. The wagons lurched across the deeply cut ancestral migration paths that thousands of the thirsty beasts had worn into the land on their way from the sand hills to the river. But no animals were seen.

Two stagecoaches passed them and arrived just ahead of the train at the Plum Creek Station. As soon as the wagons came to a stop, Lona decided she would send a telegram to her mother in New York to reassure her of their safe passage. She soon returned looking crestfallen.

"What's the matter?" Nancy asked her. "Is the line down?"

"No. Pete discovered it would cost $5.00 for me to reassure Mother that we're safe and he refused to allow me the sending of the message."

Pete walked past and Lona followed him to the wagon, speaking to his back. "It would mean so much to Mother. She's not well you know."

Pete turned on her and shouted, "Damn it! Hobble your lip woman. Get dinner started." Lona did as she was told.

Moving through an area with Pawnee to the north and Cheyenne to the south caused some tension among the travelers, although the Colonel assured them that the Indians in that area were peaceable. He then encouraged the young people to dance to the tunes played on fiddles and harmonicas. Laughter and song and music filled the night air, and the general mood was soon uplifted. The Colonel stood in the shadow of his wagon and smiled as he watched his people enjoy themselves.

A little over a year later it would be reported in the newspapers that the Plum Creek Station was the only one *not* destroyed by Cheyenne, Sioux, Kiowa and Arapahoe between Ft. Kearney and Julesburg on the South Platte. Although the station building would survive, the settlers in the area would not. All of them would be brutally murdered and scalped, and the whole country would be talking about the Plum Creek Massacre. For weeks all stage lines within 500 miles would be abandoned, and only slowly would traffic through the area resume.

Having been able to resupply at the station, the Colonel's train moved on. That night they camped near a slough of rich grass and good water, and the Carrington clan looked forward to an early night in bed. But just as dinner was over, Gabe stopped and sat down by the fire without an invitation, something he did more frequently as the days passed. He liked this young couple and their two boys, and marveled at the baby that somehow always looked so clean. Besides, Nancy usually welcomed him with a cup of her good coffee.

He told Abe, "Sorry we couldn't find any herds along here."

"Maybe we'll see some further along the way."

"Maybe, but the herds won't be like the ones I saw back in the early '50's." Abe thought to himself that those in the 1850's probably heard the same about the herds of the 1840's. People seemed to glory in describing how the present just missed what was better in the recent past.

Todd and Harold stopped their chores and approached the fire in a state of eager anticipation whenever this mysterious man spoke of the West of old. Gabe played up to their rapt attention. He took a swallow of coffee and savored it, knowing the boys would chafe even more. Then, taking pity on their impatience, he said, "One time I saw thousands of the huge beasts crossing the Platte during a low stage of its flow. It took them hours to cross, and the huge number of them dammed the river. The water rushed up to the animals, and then overflowed the banks."

"Wow!" Todd exhaled.

Gabe saw Abe and Nancy exchange a look accompanied by a poorly hidden smile. "I know you think I'm exaggerating. God knows I'm prone to that. But this time I'm not. There were that many of 'em bunched together half a mile wide and for as long as an hour in their crossing."

Duly chastised for their non-belief, Abe poured Gabe the last of the coffee. Gabe grunted and continued. "Back in the '40's buffalo were thick along the Platte. Sometimes they covered the plains clear to the horizon, especially where Fort Kearny is now. It was early summer when we got there and the bulls were grazing apart from the cows and young ones. If it had been the August mating season, the old bulls would have been defiant and protective of the cows. But right then we could get a clear shot at 'em before they took much notice of us. When the shooting began, and the smell of blood from their dead comrades filled the air, the huge herd panicked and charged toward the river. That's when we saw them damming its flow."

The temperature suddenly dropped and Nancy made the boys get into the wagon and prepare for bed. Gabe left reluctantly, and Abe prepared his and Nancy's bed under the wagon with an extra quilt over them.

The beautiful stage station at Cottonwood Spring, Nebraska, was to be their next stop and an opportunity to refresh their supplies. On the way there they passed several freight wagons pulled by long lines of as many as ten ox pairs, the wagon beds filled with heavy loads of cottonwood trees to be used in building somewhere in the area.

Near a large forest of cedar, they arrived at the McGlachlin settlement, run by a man the Colonel called Mac. When invited to top off their water barrels from Mac's well, they wasted no time. Meanwhile, the Colonel sat on a bench by the door of

Mac's cabin and shared a bottle of whiskey with the old man. The Colonel had brought it along just for Mac. In appreciation for his hospitality, some of the women brought him biscuits or slices of pie. Later that night a fiddle played while the young people danced, and the older ones clapped in time to the music or rested while watching the gaiety.

The following day the train pulled out onto the wide flat plains again. The women marveled at the array of vivid wildflowers dotting the Platte Valley, some forming mounds of color that extended on either side of the road almost as far as the eye could see. Nooning in the midst of this colorful display was a great delight and it raised the morale of everyone.

The men, however, were more enthusiastic about the patches of wild onion. They pulled the plants from the ground and gave them to their wives to add flavor to the limited diversity of meals.

After dinner, Effie stood together in a small group with Nancy, Abe, and Gabe. She called their attention to some prairie dogs several yards from the wagons. "Oh look, two of them are carrying home the body of their wounded comrade. How sweet."

They were not aware of Jebb's presence until they heard his sharp laughter behind them. "They're taking him home for dinner all right. Their own."

Effie squealed in protest, thinking like most people that the animals ate only roots and plants. "Out here you eat what's available," Jebb told them, "and that's true of man or beast."

Nancy glared at his retreating back. "The old ghoul!" She had almost called him a more colorful name, but had caught herself just in time. Maybe, she thought, I've been spending too much time around coarse and uncivilized men.

At the Forks of the Platte the water was crowded with a large number of islands and sand bars. The North Platte continued west, but the South Platte bent southwest away from the North Platte, so the wagons would have to travel along its swift current until they could arrive at one of the main crossings. Before that, however, they camped for the night where the two rivers joined together for a short distance as one turbulent white water tempest.

The rapids were beautiful and powerful, and Nancy thought the force of it a bit frightening. As she always did when needing reassurance or comforting, she cradled baby Alice in her arms and softly crooned an old lullaby. Alice closed her eyes and was soon wrapped in a peaceful sleep that Nancy envied. She smiled as she looked down at her daughter, and laughed at herself for thinking her child more beautiful than any other.

CHAPTER FOUR
NEBRASKA
JUNE, 1863

"I so enjoy visiting with the other women as we walk beside our wagons. The time passes more quickly and I feel the soreness of my feet much less."

Nancy

"The monotony of walking next to the oxen all day is now broken for me. I let Todd relieve me in the morning and mid afternoon. Harold, like the other boys, gathers buffalo chips as we walk and also at night when we stop. The boys make a game of it.

Abe

Nancy dreamt that night about the fort they had passed eight miles before the confluence of the North and South Platte. It was in process of being built in response to local Indian restlessness and was being called Cantonment McKean, named for Major Thomas McKean, 38th Pennsylvania Militia and commanding officer for the territory. There were almost thirty graves near it, laid out in even rows with each having an identical marker. After several name changes, in January of 1866 it would become *Ft. McPherson* in honor of Brigadier General James B. McPherson, killed near Atlanta during the Civil War. The burial grounds at the fort would be declared a National Cemetery in 1873, and would remain such in perpetuity.

As the wagons turned left and away from the North Fork, they headed over O'Fallon's Bluff, the start of sculpted sandstone bluffs overlooking the South Fork of the Platte. The travelers went up and over the hard flat top of the bluff, straining their teams and themselves in the climb, then descended down into a narrow valley covered in bright yellow blooms. Here they found a sign someone had fashioned:

You have traveled 400 miles from St. Joe
120 miles from Ft. Kearny
It is 68 miles to the Upper Crossing
and 40 miles to the Lower Crossing

Around the sign was scattered large ant hills, some as large as six feet across, but only a foot tall. Upon close inspection, Nancy and Effie found that they were decorated with tiny Indian beads that the insects had carried from local tribal encampments, either Pawnee or Sioux.

These tribes were usually warring with one another during the summer months, often so the young braves could bring home enough ponies and other captured goods to qualify themselves worthy to start their own families. But at least while they were focused on one another, they tended to leave the wagon trains alone.

When the Luster train stopped for the day's nooning, Effie and Nancy exchanged leftovers. With a gasp, Effie pointed toward the area of ant hills they had earlier explored. "Oh, dear. Isn't that...?"

Nancy turned to follow the direction of Effie's wide-eyed stare in the direction of the Croat and Hickly wagon. Instead of their normal attire, the two men were wrapped in horse blankets, and nothing else. White legs covered in black wiry hair showed from the knees down, and bright white feet stood gingerly on the rocky dirt. Beyond them, Nancy could see the men's longjohns, boots and hide clothing lying in the sun between the ant hills.

Chris and Abe joined the women. While Abe gawked, Chris rocked back on his heels and laughed loudly. He wiped his eyes and explained, "They're doing that so the ants will carry away the gray-backs that infest their clothes. They're common insects on those who don't bathe much and wear the type of clothing popular with stock tenders and mountain men."

As he walked away, Chris continued to chuckle. Abe and Nancy smiled as they prepared their wagon for the move out, but Effie huffed with indignation all the way to her wagon.

The travelers passed along the South Fork of the Platte as they contemplated the deep water crossing that confronted them. Here was the heart of the West they had recently been hearing about, and even longer had dreamed of seeing. It was a land more arid than most of them had ever seen. What hills there were rose up more as high hummocks of drying and rap-idly fading green grass. With the river to their right and these dry hills to their left, they traveled on a wide easy trail.

The women and children had been collecting buffalo chips for their fires for several miles, and with no wood available, they needed them badly. Although at first the women had found this a repulsive task, they had soon resigned themselves to it once they realized there was often little else they could burn. Those families with children were fortunate in that they could assign this task to them.

Signs of the locally wandering buffalo herds were everywhere, and the oxen knew it. They were able to smell the pungent bison even more acutely than the people, and the teams were more restless than anyone had yet seen them. No longer placid bo-vines doing their job of pulling wagons, the oxen now picked up speed and the men found it difficult to hold them back. Wagons bounced and shook, and anyone riding inside was thrown about and badly bruised.

The Colonel and the scouts rode quickly along the length of the train, shouting for everyone to stop immediately and tie or hobble their oxen. When some of the men hesitated at this strange order, they received a barked command to do as they were told. There was no time for patient explanation.

It was a lesson that had been learned by thousands who had traveled over the years. Oxen could turn a little primitive in the presence of buffalo, and would sometimes attempt to race after their furry cousins even if it meant dragging a wagon after them. Stories of rigs destroyed, and sometimes people injured or killed, were often related. It was better to lose a few hours of travel than to let the oxen too close to the fresh tracks of the buffalo herds. Let the wind clear the air, and the blowing sand cover their tracks.

The small quantity of fresh meat with which Abe and Nancy had started this leg of the journey had quickly been exhausted, and for over a week they had eaten only salted meat. It was the same for everyone else. Walking for miles each day beside their teams, and the hard physical labor required to survive each day's travel, had taken its toll. The idea of fresh meat was very appealing to everyone, so the opportunity for a hunt had been upper-most in the minds of the men for days. Guns, horses and appetites were ready for the first kill.

Col. Luster prepared the train for a one day layover for hunting, agreed upon by the council after the reports from the scouts of good weather ahead. It was not a very large herd they spotted, but they were able to bring down five cows and one young bull. This meant good meat. Taking the prime hump meat, tenderloin, tongue and legs for bone marrow, the rest was left for the local Indians who would eat even the offal.

The carcass would later be picked clean by wolves. When the bones were eventually bleached by the sun, old men who when younger had been hide hunters, would bring their freight wagons to the area and gather the bones. These would then be shipped to the East where they would be crushed and used as fertilizer. Nothing would be wasted in this land of slight offerings.

Nancy and the boys watched in amazement as Chris showed the men how to take the tongue from the mouth of a dead animal. With great effort, the men twisted the animal's head so that its horns were buried in the dirt. With the head thus braced and the nose pointing up, a large cut was made under the jaw, making the tongue easily reached by a long knife.

Chris stood up with a shout of excitement, holding above his head a black tongue dripping blood down his hand and onto the sleeve of his shirt. "Here Colonel, this is for you."

Eager to express their appreciation for the Colonel having gotten everyone this far with so few problems, the other men gave a cheer of approval. The Colonel took it gratefully and later that night had his cook prepare it with prairie onions for the Colonel and the scouts.

Abe was given part of the tenderloin from a cow and some of the leg bones. He brought them to Nancy almost apologetically. She, however, remembered her dear friend Elsie describing what she had once done with them. After carefully burying the bones in coals of brush and buffalo chips for an hour, she removed them and allowed the now blackened bones to cool. They were then cracked and the marrow scraped out, mixed with salt and pepper, and the rich concoction spread on toasted bread. They were surprised to find it delicious and a wonderful change. Too often they ate beans or rice, biscuits and bacon simply because when tired at the end of the day, it was the easiest to prepare.

Croat stopped by after dinner to remind Abe that they were to share guard duty at midnight, but Abe was elsewhere. Todd was brushing Flame where he stood tied to the back of the wagon and Nancy was cleaning up after dinner. Harold was in the wagon where he was reading a story to Alice. Since Edna Crotts had stopped by to visit and was drinking the last of the Carrington's coffee, Croat looked longingly at the pot while scowling at Edna.

"Sorry," Nancy told him shortly. "There isn't any more."

Breaking off a chaw from his tobacco plug and tonguing it to his cheek, Croat sighed with acceptance. "Did you enjoy your portion of the buffalo?"

"Yes, very much." She told him how she had fixed the bones and he nodded with approval. Edna was a picture of dubious consideration as she listened to Nancy.

Croat scratched his stomach and declared, "Hickly and me had the mountain oysters. There were only two, but they were big and we got to 'em quick." He grinned and a trickle of brown tobacco juice bubbled at the corner of his mouth.

Nancy frowned, wondering if the man was purposely trying to be crude. Willing to be generous, she thought that maybe his years of basic and rowdy living had made him unaware of proper topics of conversation with *good* women. But Todd was chuckling, and Nancy glared at him.

Edna frowned with confusion and moved forward. Realizing that Edna was intending to ask Croat for clarification, Nancy took her arm and led her to the back of the wagon, whispering, "Mountain oysters are that part of a steer or buffalo that makes it a bull."

When refined, city-raised Edna frowned even more, Nancy lost patience and snapped, "His balls, dear."

That Edna understood. Her startled response was followed by the choked question, "And people eat them?"

"Yes," Nancy answered more gently. "Braised until tender, or sliced and dredged in flour and corn meal, then fried in lard, they're very tasty." Nancy smiled tolerantly when Edna showed how obviously appalled she was. "They're not for everyone, of course, but many people think them quite a delicacy."

Edna managed a weak smile. "I think I've lived a more sheltered life than I ever realized. Moving West will no doubt be very eye-opening, wouldn't you agree?"

Nancy patted her arm. "Yes, and probably in ways we can't yet imagine. But what a splendid adventure we've set out on."

Making another less than successful effort to smile, Edna slowly walked back to her wagon. She made a wide detour around the retreating Croat.

Jebb passed by with the garrulous Gabe just as Abe returned from checking on their stock. Nancy was surprised to see Jebb, since he seemed to prefer his own company. All three men warmed themselves at the waning fire as the chill of the evening began to settle in. Nancy was determined not to add any of her precious buffalo chips to the fire. It would only encourage Jebb and Gabe to linger and she was ready to see the back of them.

"I'm sorry I have no coffee left," Nancy told them.

"No matter." Jebb pulled out a small bottle from under one of the layers of clothing he wore. Turning to Gabe without offering him the bottle, he nodded in the direction of the Carringtons and asked, "You tell 'em about the Gratton mess what happened up near Ft. Laramie?"

"No." Gabe glanced at Harold who had emerged from the wagon. The suddenly reticent Gabe glared at Jebb and added, "No, I thought better of it."

"Maybe it could wait for another time then," Abe spoke up, realizing that it must be a pretty violent story if Gabe was unwilling to discuss it.

But Jebb continued to speak in his characteristic chopped manner. "It were bad. Sioux were angry."

"Dakotas," Gabe corrected him.

"Well, yeah, they're called Sioux too even if they hate the name. Was a slur used by the French trappers. Anyway, back in the summer of '54 the damn Dakotas were angry." He glared at Gabe, then stared down into the glowing coals. "They'd signed a treaty. They were supposed to get payment in goods for letting wagons cross their land unharmed. But most of the Indian agents kept the goods for themselves. Or at least a lot of them did."

Gabe cut in. "Handsome people they are. The women are good-lookers and the men have great dignity and courage. They pride themselves on that. You'll see for yourself."

But Abe did not want to see for himself. He hoped fervently never to see a Sioux the whole of the trip.

"Yeah," Jebb sneered. "But if they can't get revenge on the person that wrongs 'em, they feel it's okay to get it from anyone related. Maybe a whole other tribe, or the next wagon train that comes along."

Gabe nodded. "Most tribes like the goods that are sent to them by the Government and don't want to do anything that will jeopardize the shipments."

"But some don't care," Jebb said.

Nancy turned to the boys. "You two go to bed now. We'll be leaving early and I want you to get plenty of rest."

"Ah..." Harold began.

Todd cut him off. "Come on. She's right." Todd took his brother by the hand and pulled him off to their tent.

Abe shot Nancy a look and she shrugged. Both knew the boys could probably hear inside the tent not far from the rear of the wagon, but there was nothing they could do about it except hope the story didn't give the boys nightmares.

Jebb said, "Stupid thing to have happened."

"What was that?" Abe asked before he thought to stop himself.

Jebb sighed deeply. "Brule, Wazzazi and Ogallala bands of Sioux. A train of Mormons lost a cow, and some visiting Indian staying with one of the tribes caught and killed it. The Mormon reported its loss at Ft. Laramie to Lieutenant Grattan."

"Young and green," Gabe mumbled.

"Yeah," Jebb agreed. "Grattan took twenty-nine men and a cannon out to arrest the Indian what took the cow." Jebb was into his story and his words came quicker. "It was petty theft at best. Shouldn't have been got after like that. The local chief asked the visiting brave to give himself up. He refused. Young Grattan had to save face, of course. But he overdid it when he fired on the lodge of the thieving Indian. Wounded one of the Indians not involved."

"The young twerp should have been satisfied with that show of force and left," Gabe mumbled.

"But he weren't," Jebb cut in. "When the thief still didn't come forward, Grattan fired the cannon and muskets at the brave's lodge. In the confusion that followed, the Bear Chief of the Wazzazies was wounded and soon died. He'd been there to help the soldiers. Of course the Indians couldn't let that pass. They turned on the soldiers and killed every one of 'em. We passed their graves back at the fort being built."

As Nancy tried to calm the chills pricking her skin, Gabe added, "There's still a lot of tension brewing with the local tribes, even after all these years."

Nancy was glad to finally see the men leave, not wanting to admit how much their stories upset her. Abe was quiet as he helped her ready their camp for sleep. He realized more than Nancy that all around them lay dangerous territory. He had heard many other stories, but he had kept them to himself so as not to frighten Nancy and the boys. He knew that the Grattan story would assail the imaginations of his sons, and Todd and Harold might entertain dreams that would wake them several times. His anger at Jebb took the form of an urge to punch him in the face. It was, of course, something he would never be so foolish as to do.

Abe would never admit to anyone (he could barely admit it to himself), but the story had awakened in him an irrational fear that bordered on carefully controlled panic. He had been impressed with how quickly the Indians had changed from friends to killers. Maybe he had heard too many stories about Indian attacks and massacres, and should put forth more effort to avoid such recitations.

Just east of Brule they came within sight of where they would cross the South Fork of the Platte. It was near the Beauvais Trading Post, which had been a station for the Jones-Russell Pikes Peak stage line since 1859. In 1860 it had also been used as a Pony Express station. The buildings were not far from the river, and the train had plenty of room to circle near them.

Mr. Beauvais came to talk to the Colonel. He was a middle aged man of about forty, large and fine featured. Abe observed that his manner was somewhat subdued and resentful around the travelers, some of whom were put off by his having three Indian wives who had obviously given him a large number of children. Nancy watched Harold join the man's handsome dark-eyed and brown-skinned children as they ran around the trading post, and smiled when they were soon laughing as they tossed rocks at a can on top of a post.

Mr. Beauvais saw this too, and when Nancy brought his wives the last of her stewed peaches made from a block of dried fruit, he thawed considerably. His youngest and prettiest wife gave Nancy a St. Louis newspaper, which over the next week made its way around to all the wagons.

Todd couldn't take his eyes from Mr. Beauvais's young Indian wife. Although fascinated by her dark smoky beauty and knowing that she wasn't legally married to the trader, he also knew that he was not allowed to talk to her. But no one could stop him from fantasizing about her and he smiled to himself. Watching him, Abe was shocked to realize that his son was growing up quickly.

Abe and Nancy visited the hewn log trading post and admired the large number of buffalo robes, elk and antelope skins, and other furs on display. They purchased several plugs of tobacco and a small bag of beads for trade to the Indians during future encounters, and a loaf of sugar for their own use.

The Colonel had decided to take the wagons across in the morning, and thankfully the day dawned with only a slight breeze on the water. Soon the Colonel had the wagons aligned in several long lines and awaiting the crossing.

Nancy joined Abe next to their oxen where they looked across the half mile stretch of river. Not wanting the boys to hear the fear in her voice, she mumbled, "How on earth are we to cross this?"

"It's too shallow for ferries. I'm sure the Colonel will know the best place for us to drive the teams across. Hopefully, it'll be where there isn't quicksand, and the stock can get good footing. That concerns me most." He lifted his hand to his forehead to block the sun as he surveyed the far shore. It was indeed a long way across. Abe took hold of Nancy's hand and they tried not to let fear engulf them.

The slide down to the water's edge was after all not as steep as they had feared when viewing it from the top. But once in the water they were challenged by small islands thick with trees and narrow sand bars that reached out into the water like long beckoning fingers. From the evidence of bones and branches strewn on the shores of the islands, it was clear that they often grasped hold of what floated in their direction. The scouts took their time finding routes across.

The amount of debris in the murky water floating by on the swift current was frightening, but it was into this that they were to launch their wagons like boats upon the sea. Some of the men argued for crossing at the *Upper* California Crossing near Julesburg, but it was over 20 miles further upstream and the Colonel wanted to start as soon as possible. The air smelled strongly of rain. Not surprisingly, the Colonel got his way and they crossed at the *Lower* California Crossing near Brule.

It was important to cross before the rain started to fall on the rapidly melting snow in the near mountains. The Colonel knew that this melt could wash down and overflow the river's banks more quickly than these Easterners could imagine. If not affecting the first of those going across, those doing so last might have to wait until it lowered. In the meantime, they would be cut off from the protection of the others.

So the Colonel chained the wagons together in a span of ten and a wagon length apart so if a wagon bogged down, those behind would have room to go around. Rumors of quicksand were recalled with nervous dread, and each driver was determined not to allow their team to stop, no matter what they had to do to keep them moving.

At first relieved to discover that the water was only two feet deep, everyone was amazed to find the flow such a swift force. It was a constant struggle for the oxen to remain on their feet. Those few men who thought they could easily walk across were saved from being knocked off their feet only by holding onto their wagon bed.

Nancy watched in horror as Ron McQuery, the brother of one of the women she had met, lost his footing. He flailed his way down stream, then disappeared beneath the water before Chris's horse could splash through the water to where he had sunk below the surface. Just as they were about to give up, they saw Ron caught up among debris gathered at the base of a large rock. Several men helped him out of the water and back into his wagon just as he fully regained his senses.

To compensate for the fast current, they were told to follow the scout at the head of their line of wagons, and exactly in his path. The oxen were content to follow the rig in front of them, and the result was that the line of wagons made a wide swing *against* the current and then another to travel *with* the current. This allowed them to work with the current's flow instead of it hitting the wagons broadside. Somewhat amazed, the Carringtons reached the shore almost directly across from where they had entered the water.

Their next goal was to reach the plateau where they would travel toward the North Fork so they could return to its south shore. To do this they were immediately faced with a steep ascent up California Hill. Whips cracked, men whistled and pushed, women and children trudged along on foot to lighten the load, and miraculously the teams dragged their burdens up the hill. At the top, everyone turned to look back and down to the river, amazed at what they had just accomplished. Exhausted they might have been, but they were proud too.

After they checked the stock, they ate a simple dinner and prepared for the next morning's breakfast. No one sang or danced that night, and the Carringtons and their neighbors collapsed into their beds immediately after dinner.

They arose to a sun-filled morning that brought them renewed energy and fresh determination. Only the persistent mosquitoes marred the gentleness of the day, but they were getting used to those.

The land between the forks of the Platte was a strange place. Those of the Luster train were well-conditioned to the rise and fall of steep hills, but here they wound their way between deep canyons carved by hundreds of years of rain run-off. The trail continued over treeless stretches scattered with sandy hummocks that heaved up between the deep gullies. The area had the appearance of a faded and rumpled blanket that had been tossed on the trash heap. Axles were stressed and several cracked, and two wagon tongues were broken. Young Harold was one of only a few who found the region fascinating.

Looking down into the deep crevasses was an unnerving experience and the men concentrated on keeping their teams calm. An out of control rig here would mean certain destruction of the wagon, and most likely the people inside as well, although most of those who were fit enough chose to walk during this part of the trip. Those tending the loose stock kept their animals moving steadily but not crowded.

None of the terrain over which the Luster train had traveled up to then had been as difficult to cross, and the men worried constantly about their wagons, not to mention their exhausted teams. The consequent slow progress grated on the tempers of the impatient, and several quarrels broke out among the men over normally trivial matters. Nancy was not the only woman to find herself snapping at her children. Some women even snapped at their husbands, who responded in turn with even sharper words of their own. Few people escaped from this portion of the trip without hurt feelings and lingering resentments.

Finally they reached the descent to Ash Hollow. The families viewed this next challenge from the edge of a high hill, where they were confronted by a steep slide down to a wide dry ravine dotted with stubby trees. But at least they would then be pointed toward their return to the trail along the North Fork of the Platte.

With the boys on either side of her, and Alice in her arms, Nancy stood at the top and looked down the steep and deeply rutted path to the bottom. The trail was so worn here that it was cut two feet deep into the hard-packed earth, which meant the wagons moved straight as they descended. They had traveled about 640 miles in a little over 40 days on the trail, and this was the first time any of them doubted their ability to accomplish the task at hand.

"How are we to get down this?" Effie asked over Nancy's shoulder. "The steepness is going to propel the wagon faster than the teams can move."

Nancy gave no answer, and instead chose to look beyond the challenge of the descent and gaze over the far hills that rolled away from them. They were covered in the bright green of new short grass that was light and fresh at the top of the bluffs and dark green in the shadow of the bottoms. She tried to picture them camped in the cool shade with everyone safe. Finally she returned her attention to the present and when Abe walked up to her, asked, "Why do they call this Windlass Hill?"

"You'll see."

The Colonel was preparing the windlass as they spoke. He had the back end of one of the largest and strongest wagons facing the edge of the steep drop-off. It was raised and staked firmly to the ground in such a way that the back wheels were left to turn freely with just enough room for a wagon to pull into place behind it and face the downward slope. One wagon at a time was tied to the rope coiled around the back axle, and while a dozen men held onto the rope as well as the spokes of the windlass wheels, they slowly played out the rope until the wagon reached the bottom.

It took three days to get most of them down. With no untoward excitement so far, and with only four wagons to go, the men began the fourth day eagerly. They stretched their stiff and sore muscles and got to work.

Nearby was a small stone hut, and Lona and Effie were writing letters to leave inside. Nancy watched her friends attach a note to their letters that pleaded for anyone heading east to take their precious notes and post them when they could. Each woman laid a coin for postage on top, and prayed it would successfully reach its destination. The Colonel told them they would stand a better chance at the Fort Laramie post office, and the women said they would do that too. It brought a tear to Nancy's eyes to see her friends so desperate to feel they still had some connection to loved ones left behind.

The next time Nancy saw Lona, she was returning to the little stone hut. She almost immediately came back out and returned to Pete who stood by their wagon where she handed him something. The Carrington wagon was the next to be lowered, but Nancy was puzzled by Lona's odd behavior, so she slowly approached the far side of the Hastings wagon. Pete was yelling at Lona, "You're not to waste money in such a foolish manner again, do ya hear?"

"But people have left money with their notes for years."

"Do you have any proof it works?" Lona murmured in the negative. "Then say no more about it! Fetch me some water."

Nancy hurried away before she was seen, angrily wishing she could push Pete down the hill. And once again she counted her blessings.

Late in the afternoon, after the Carrington and Hastings wagons safely reached the bottom, the Hurly wagon was half way down the hill when the rope snapped. The wagon plunged forward, pitched onto its side and the two mules hitched on to hold the wagon tongue up during the descent were knocked off their feet with a sickening thud. Their screams chilled the hearts of even the most hardened.

As the ponderous rig came to rest at the bottom of the hill, men already at the bottom rushed forward. Buran grabbed the mule that was getting to its feet, and Mr. Hurly quickly shot the other one that was screaming as it thrashed in pain. Its legs had been broken in several places.

The Hurly family of father, mother, and two boys carefully inspected the righted wagon and were surprised to find only minor damage. Having two other mules in the loose stock, Mr. Hurly and his oldest boy retrieved them and hitched them to the wagon. Nancy had never been particularly fond of the brusque

Mr. Hurly, but when she saw him turn the surviving mule out to graze and recover with the loose stock, her estimation of the man improved greatly.

Mrs. Hurly, with the help of several nearby women, gathered their scattered belongings and repacked the wagon. Meanwhile, a new stout rope was coiled around the axle of the wagon at the top of the hill, and the last wagon was let down without incident but with much nervous anxiety. With everyone safely at the bottom of the hill, the Colonel once again formed his wagons into a long line of billowing wind-blown canvas, straining animals and footsore people.

As the last of the wagons disappeared into the distance, wolves waiting in the nearby rocks emerged beneath the gliding shadows of vultures flying over the remains of the dead mule. Nature wastes less time than even the most efficient of people.

The wagon train proceeded down two more easy descents and arrived in the cool wooded oasis of Ash Hollow. Camp was set up surrounded by good grass, a flowing stream and wood from the groves of ash trees. Buran came by and said that he had seen an old grave stone when approaching the area, so he and Abe announced that they were going to walk out to it. Effie and Nancy declared they would not be left behind.

Before leaving, Nancy made sure Alice was asleep in her basket and instructed Harold to look in on her in a few minutes. Todd and Charley were assigned the task of collecting buffalo chips and what fire wood they could find.

The two couples hiked to the bluff at the edge of the hollow, and just left of the trail found the marker. It read:

1849 *(the number 4 carved backward)*

R A C H E L   E.

P A T T I S O N.

A G E D 18 J U N E 19TH 49

The men quickly lost interest and moved away while talking about the possibility of hunting. The women lingered by the grave.

"So young," Effie murmured. "Her whole life ahead of her. Wonder what she died of."

Nancy looked beyond their current oasis of shading trees and focused on the wide desolate prairie that spread to the horizon. "Maybe she died of loneliness."

"But she was probably married if she was 18," Effie responded.

Realizing that Effie had missed the meaning of her words, Nancy didn't bother to correct her. She simply turned and walked toward the retreating men. Effie shrugged and followed. Not far from their path could be seen another carved stone that perched a little ways up a steep hill. Effie returned to camp while Nancy climbed the hill with some effort. Breathing hard, she looked down on the rock and saw carved upon it UNKNOWN EMIGRANT'S GRAVE.

Nancy shook her head, took a deep breath and began her way back down the hill. The vegetation snagged at her skirts, and she anticipated later pulling more burrs from the hem, an activity now part of her daily routine. She pulled up several long blades of grass, braided them into a neat circle and returned to the unknown grave where she laid the plait against the base of the stone.

This act of respect only momentarily helped to assuage her sudden dark mood. The sight of the lonely graves disturbed her more profoundly than she could understand and that night they even entered her restless dreams. She awoke feeling almost as tired as when she had gone to bed.

After an early breakfast, and while the boys helped Abe with chores, Nancy wrapped Alice in her extra shawl and went for a walk along the wagons. Although still not familiar with everyone by name, by now she at least recognized them and had spoken to most of the women.

As she passed the cooking fire of the tall gray-haired Mrs. West, that lady darted forward. Nancy had only talked briefly to her twice, but for some reason she couldn't warm to the woman who ranged between cloyingly familiar and stridently demanding.

"Let me see the baby," Mrs. West demanded as she reached for Alice.

Before the woman could touch her, Nancy pulled back the edge of the fabric to reveal her smiling child. "What a bundle of joy she must be for you."

"Yes," Nancy smiled politely, "she's all of that."

Suddenly Mrs. West clapped her veined and arthritic hands. "I'm so glad you came by. I had cut a piece of vinegar pie for you and was going to bring it to your wagon." While the woman turned back to her wagon, Nancy puzzled at this statement. Why, with all there was to do every day, would this woman she barely knew and who traveled ten wagons away, think to cut *her* a piece of pie? Watching Mrs. West, she saw that actually there was only one piece left. Mrs. West rushed back to Nancy with the pie wrapped in a cloth napkin.

"You can return the napkin later," she smiled. Then, her hand gripping Nancy's arm with surprisingly painful force, she whispered, "I want you to promise you'll eat it yourself and not give it to your husband. You deserve a treat."

"Yes. Thank you." Nancy felt like asking how she knew what she deserved, but instead walked slowly back to the Carrington wagon. She could only conclude that the woman had lied. Wondering about anyone who had such a pathetic need to be liked, she split the pie between the boys.

The Colonel decided to let his people spend an extra day in Ash Hollow. Grateful for the presence of abundant clean water, the women took advantage of the opportunity to wash clothes. The young girls on the train stayed near them and, after stripping down to their chemise, went in to bathe.

Nancy watched them with envy, aware of the dust caking her hair and irritating more private areas. Once her wash had been rinsed and piled on the shore, she removed her stockings and petticoats and stated with feeling, "Oh, why not?" She quickly waded to the deepest part of the stream and lay down in the water, letting the cold current wash over her tired body.

As she surfaced, she found that three other women had also decided to be as bold and were splashing one another like young girls. When they all returned to the shore soaking wet, their laughter at one another was something even those women still on shore could not resist. The women and girls retreated to their wagons to change and the boys were allowed to go for a swim.

Because there was firewood available, several of the women decided to prepare in advance some dishes requiring more than an hour over a quick-burning fire of buffalo chips. Some took the opportunity to roast coffee beans and the air was soon pungent with delicious aromas.

The men cleaned their guns, checked their teams carefully and repaired wagons. The most common repair was to the wheels that had shrunk in the dry air, causing the iron rims to become loose. The rims were removed and the dry wood soaked over night until it expanded. In the morning the iron rim was heated in a fire until it expanded enough to allow for slipping over the wooden wheel. When the wheel was then dipped in the cold creek, the iron hissed and cooled, and once again adhered to the wheel.

Nancy sat in front of her fire and sipped coffee. She watched the cattle, horses, mules and oxen that were lying up to their ears in the long grass after eating their fill of it. The boys played cards, Alice played with a spoon and cup, and Nancy felt her sore muscles relax. There would be days ahead when she would look back to Ash Hollow as time spent in Eden.

They sat down to eat their second night in the Hollow just as a party of Sioux men and women arrived out of seemingly nowhere. Abe and Nancy at first were tense and fearful, but the boys were thrilled to be near them. The Indians spread out among the emigrants and chose various fires as a place to rest themselves. The travelers had been warned this might happen, and nervously but politely traded for the moccasins and herbs offered for sale.

With them was a young girl of about sixteen who wore a white man's blue shirt with the sleeves missing. She approached Nancy's fire and looked longingly at the loaf of freshly baked bread sitting on the small folding table where the Carringtons had been about to eat their meal.

Nancy cut off a slice and held the bread out to the girl. After a moment's hesitation, she smiled shyly and accepted it. Nancy held up her hand to indicate that she wanted the girl to stay where she was, and after digging around in her sewing box, hurried back and held out to the girl some bent pins. The puzzled girl looked at the pins lying on the white woman's open hand, but smiled proudly when Nancy attached them to her shirt. When Nancy stepped back to look into the girl's pretty face and realized she was close to starting her adult life, she felt an unexpected fondness for this simple young woman. She only wished that she could explain to her that all whites did not wish her people harm.

The Sioux left as abruptly as they had arrived. At council that night the Colonel explained to the men, "I hope you realize how fortunate we are that the Indians showed us such a peaceable disposition today. In the '40's the tribes were laid low with cholera in this area. It was a time when most every wagon train was full of it. The Indians have the habit of digging up graves to get the clothes and blankets of the dead. But back then it caused them to end up with the same disease as killed the one buried." The Colonel shook his head and looked into the nearby fire, but he gave no voice to his further thoughts.

Gabe, however, had no such restraint, especially since no women were present. "In folk's effort to out-distance the disease, the sickest were sometimes left by the trail in their last hours. Their grave might even be dug while they were breathing their last right next to it. The instant they died they were just rolled into the hole and it was filled in." Gabe stopped and glanced at the Colonel who glared at him and shook his head in warning.

Ignoring the Colonel, Gabe looked down into the fire and continued. "Well, most had stopped breathing first. People knew no one recovered at that stage of the disease, you see, even if it had come on 'em only a few hours earlier. Well, rarely anyway." When some of the men looked outraged at what Gabe was suggesting, he nodded with understanding and added, "They weren't hard-hearted men, really, just scared. And as you know, it's important to stay the course and move on, especially if you're not sure but what you might be the next one to get sick if you stay put."

It was difficult for Abe to imagine having to deal with such rampant disease, considering how difficult it was to get through each of their days while healthy. He therefore decided not to pass judgment on those who might be seen as callous in their actions. He also decided not to tell Nancy or the boys about this aspect of life on the trail.

That night two horses went missing, and the men assumed they had been taken by the same Indians who had visited them during the day. The horses had been valuable riding horses tied to a wagon, just as Abe always tied Flame. Nancy smiled when she noticed Abe spending an unusually long time brushing his beloved horse.

Nancy thought of the sweet young woman to whom she had given the pins and felt conflicted in her feelings, as though by the braves taking the horses her act of friendship had been diminished. She knew she was being silly, and that the young girl might know nothing about the stealing of the stock, but her sense of betrayal lingered.

The next day Lona Hastings asked Nancy to take a turn sitting with Cathy Porter in a wagon a dozen forward. She had been in labor all the day before, and several of the women had taken turns looking in on her. But each woman had a family to look after, and had no idea what more to do for Cathy anyway.

The Colonel allowed the train to stop for the remainder of the day after the nooning, hoping it would speed up the delivery and give the poor woman some comfort. It seemed to help, and after an especially difficult delivery wherein her screams were heard by everyone on the train and probably the Indians not far away, a baby girl was born just before dark. She lived for only an hour. Cathy Porter was so weak that her husband had to carry her to the baby's burial site.

The men had dug a grave among a patch of wild roses, their small pink blooms filling the warm evening air with sweet perfume. Lit only by the brightness of the moon and several lanterns, the Colonel lowered the tiny bundle into the small hole and read a passage from the Bible. As the hole was filled in, Frank Porter carried his weeping wife back to their wagon.

Lona Hastings walked with them and tried to reassure herself as much as the Porters by saying, "At least she's buried in a lovely setting." But at the end of the journey, Cathy Porter would tell Nancy that she would never be able to enjoy the fragrance of a rose without their scent bringing to mind the horrors of that time on the trail.

They continued to travel westward on the south side of the main flow of the Platte. The trail on the north side of the river was referred to as the Mormon Trail, although that sect was certainly not the only one to choose it for travel. However, the Colonel did not want his wagons to cross the Platte more often than necessary, and they needed to be on the south side when they reached Fort Laramie 180 miles away.

Harold noticed his mother writing a letter while Alice, clutching a rag doll, smiled up at her brother from her basket.

After tickling his sister, Harold turned to his mother. "Who're you writing to?"

"Mrs. Ivey back in Missouri."

"You miss her, don't you?"

"Yes, I do." She reached out and pushed strands of hair from his forehead and reminded herself to give him a hair cut soon.

"Where're you going to mail your letter?"

"They have a mail bag at Fort Laramie."

After watching her a few more minutes, he asked, "When we get to Oregon, it'll take her a long time to get a letter to us, won't it?"

"Yes. Many months probably."

"Croat and Hickly are going to California. They said that since Texas seceded from the Union in '61, the stages from St. Joseph have had to change their route. Now they go through Salt Lake City to get to California."

"You and Todd spend a lot of time with those men, don't you?"

Harold wrinkled his nose. "Well, not a lot, but some. Gabe does what Croat calls a lot of jawbonin' about the past, but he's interesting. Todd likes Croat and Hickly's stories. I think they're a little scary."

"The stories or the men?"

Harold looked at her to see if she was serious. Unable to tell for sure, he decided to just tell the truth. "Both."

"I'd prefer that you didn't spend time with them without Todd."

Harold's eyes got big. "I wouldn't dare!"

Along this stretch of the trail, the sharp cold of the night was surprising and unpleasant. It was a cold that set every nerve aflame and every person longing for the relief of warmth. They were gaining in altitude, even if it had been so gradual many had not yet noticed.

Nancy and Abe were relieved that they had survived well the trip so far. That it had been in part due to the Colonel's wise guidance did not escape them, since they had heard many horror stories of wagon trains poorly managed and the fatal consequences of it. But they were also proud of their own developing skills, and consequently felt a sense of overall security.

Each night the wagons now circled quickly and efficiently. Only a few of the wagons had needed simple repairs. The loose stock was exhausted at the end of each day, so they seldom gave any trouble unless spooked by a storm. The train had lost only three steers, three horses, and two mules to accident or theft.

The men on guard duty at night were no longer over-reacting to sounds in the nearby underbrush, having learned to differentiate between a branch breaking under the hoof of a deer or a branch falling from a tree, and a rabbit rustling leaves no longer sent them into a panic of uncertainty. They had yet to see a feared Indian in the night who might not want to harm anyone but might indeed want to steal an animal. The tribes had easily managed their thefts without being detected.

The grass was turning brown in the summer heat, but it was still nutritious and the animals had lost little weight. Dinners were prepared with considerable skill now, and by nine o'clock everyone was usually asleep.

Alice, seldom a fussy baby, seemed to enjoy the rocking of the wagon or being carried during the day, and she slept well at night. When water was too scarce to allow for the washing of diapers, Nancy pinned them to the sides of the wagon's canvas top. Not only did the cloth bleach in the hot sun throughout the day, the flapping in the breeze softened them and few babies suffered with diaper rash.

Nancy lay on their thin mattress beneath the wagon under a sky covered so densely with stars that it looked ablaze with the sparks from a campfire. Her mind drifted to Cathy Porter and how well the young woman was looking, knowing that if Cathy had delivered her baby in an Eastern hospital, she would have been made to stay in bed for two weeks after the birth. Yet here she was, restored to health and already walking more than riding in the wagon. It made one wonder at the wisdom of modern medicine.

Harold and Todd always slept well, even if occasionally awakened by a bad dream after hearing a violent tale from one of the mountain men. Throughout the day the boys walked beside the wagon and collected chips, and after the evening's stop they fetched water and wood if available. Todd was allowed to curry Flame and lead him to grass, but not yet was he allowed the pleasure of riding him. After supper Harold's raucous play with the other boys used up the rest of his energy, while Todd usually found his way to the fire of Croat and Hickly.

Feeling the warmth of his wife sleeping next to him, Abe pulled the blanket up higher around his chin and reviewed the trip so far. As he felt himself dropping off to sleep, his last thought was, "This hasn't been that difficult after all."

Before Chris and Bob allowed themselves to bed down for the night, they made sure all the cooking fires were out, the horses tied properly, the stock settled and the guards posted. Only when they were satisfied would they prepare their bedrolls under the cook wagon next to Cookie, whose real name was Ephrim.

The Colonel was always the last to retire at night. It took him a long time to relax, although he never doubted that Chris and Bob had checked everything thoroughly. He would sit up against a wheel of the cook wagon while making notes in a small journal, roll the two cigarettes he smoked each night, and then think for awhile.

He was pleased that his people were enjoying their present state of sanguine contentment, but he couldn't share it. He was too well aware not only of what *was* ahead of them, but also what *might* be ahead.

CHAPTER FIVE
NEBRASKA
JUNE, 1863

"Maternal love, what a divine state of joy. Maternal loss, what a hell full of pain."

Nancy

"How nice it was to take a short break from the road. We're rested and the boys are looking forward to seeing Court House and Chimney Rocks on the way to Fort Laramie."

Abe

The train was subjected to one of the area's infamous thunderstorms, jagged fingers of lightening flashing across the black sky and illuminating the darkness in short bursts. Thunder rolled over the wagon train like exploding cannons over an army on the march while hail the size of apricots pelted the wagons, followed by rain that quickly melted any evidence of them. After half an hour of this chaos, there was calm again and everyone took great gulps of the rare dust free air.

By now familiar with these erratic storms, the women of the train soon had fresh fires going and the men rounded up the scattered stock. Nancy enjoyed once again reading the slogans on the clean canvas tops, but dinner had to be prepared, so she returned her attention to that task. Life went on as everyone now accepted it to be.

Except that Pete Hastings could not be found. While the men searched around the wagons and out onto the prairie, Lona stood by their wagon wringing her hands. Finally the men found him, lying on his back in a rocky gully with the back of his head bloody and badly smashed. After recovering from their shock, the men brought Pete back to camp.

Lona refused to look at her husband's body. She told Abe, "If you and some of the men would please bury him, I will come after and pay my respects." She walked to her wagon and climbed inside.

The men were stunned. They had anticipated some version of a prostrate wife clutching at her husband's lifeless body while bewailing her loss. Lona's cool response was beyond their comprehension. The women explained that she was overcome with shock, so the men performed the rites of passing for their friend Pete. They dug the grave deep and spread debris over the top so that it would blend into the surrounding prairie. With solemn decorum, the Colonel read the Bible over him.

After the small ceremony, when everyone else had left the grave, Lona approached it slowly. After a few minutes, she knelt down and mumbled a silent and brief prayer. Immediately after returning to the circle of wagons, Lona approached Abe and asked if she could talk to him.

"I know how to drive the team and unhitch them at night. But I'm unsure as to the most efficient method of hitching them to the wagon. If you could show me how to do that, I would be very grateful."

"Of course," he assured her, "I'll come by in the morning and do it for you."

"I'll watch carefully and ask questions if I may. After that, I'm sure I can manage on my own quite well." Abe looked doubtful and the corner of her mouth turned up. "I'm stronger than I look."

As he walked back to Nancy, he kept thinking of Lona's last words and the wisp of a smile that had accompanied it. There had been something there he could not identify. Pride? Satisfaction? Relief? It had been too enigmatic for him to tell.

At dinner that evening, when Nancy remarked on how badly Pete had treated Lona, Abe nodded and said, "I know. He once said a woman worked better when feeling occasionally the back of a man's hand."

Nancy looked at him in dismay. "I never dreamed he was physically abusive with her."

"If I treated you like that I'd be looking for glass in my morning oats." He started to chuckle, but then stopped suddenly, remembering his uneasiness at Lona's last words. Nancy looked at him curiously and he related the conversation with Lona.

"Oh, Abe, you don't think she...?"

"No, of course not."

After a moment, Nancy said, "Of course, the Bible says the meek shall inherit the earth." She shot him a wicked look and added, "It doesn't say how."

Abe and the other men who offered Lona assistance were surprised at how little help she really needed. This was due mostly to the fact that her wagon was pulled by six strong mules, each of which seemed to appreciate the gentleness of this woman. They had after all lately endured treatment by a man who had often hit them when they were already doing their best.

Back in St. Joseph some of the men on the train had thought six mules excessive pulling power for the Hastings light wagon. Now they were glad of it because it made the going easier for Lona, especially considering that she had no difficulty working the lines. In an odd way they were proud of her, like a stray pet they had agreed to care for that turned out to be uncommonly easy to train.

The next day was a long one, punctuated by hours of sweaty, muscle-wrenching effort of walking next to wagons on a deep sandy road. People coughed on the dust, several over-stressed wagon wheels had to be repaired, and the sun beat down relentlessly. Everyone appreciated the early evening stop. Most of the men ate only a light dinner that night before falling into bed and immediately to sleep. The women kept the children quiet and put them to bed early, then used the time for quiet pursuits. Nancy mended clothes for half an hour, but then could keep her eyes open no longer. Lona retired early, the same as the men.

The next morning after stretching out the kinks in their stiff cold bodies, the men checked the stock and readied the wagons. They found that Lona had already brought her mules to the wagon and had hitched on four of them. The women prepared breakfast while the children finished their chores.

Nancy went to Lona and told her to plan on joining them for breakfast each morning because she needed a good meal and might not have time to prepare one for herself. Lona gratefully accepted, at least for that morning. Everyone pulled out in high spirits that day and were eagerly anticipating their next adventure. They had been told this would be Court House Rock.

At that evening's stop, just as Nancy was beginning their meal, loud swearing could be heard from a forward wagon. Todd and Harold raced in that direction before they could be stopped, but they were soon back and both were laughing.

Harold told his mother, "Some woman opened a big pack of bacon she got at the last trading post..."

"And it was green!" Todd finished.

Abe shook his head at the waste. "Cheap meat. It wasn't salted properly."

Todd looked down at the small folding table and a bowl of leafy greens there, and said, "Speaking of green..."

"They're dandelion greens," Nancy told him. "And you'll eat some. I'm going to wilt them with vinegar and bacon drippings. They're good for you."

"Because of scurvy?" Harold asked.

"Yes. The greens and the vinegar will prevent it. So you eat it. You don't want your body to rot."

"Okay, okay," the boys echoed each other.

Later that evening, just as Abe was leading his team to graze, the train was approached by a man riding a large mule and leading a pack train of six smaller ones. His clothing, hat and face were covered in fine dust that he slapped off after dismounting, revealing a young man with a short black beard and bright friendly eyes. He introduced himself to the Colonel as Rod Kingsley and requested permission to stay with the train that night. The Colonel told him to pull up next to Gabe, who generously invited Rod man to share his grub.

While the boys played card games with Charley Howard, Effie brought some sweet biscuits to Gabe and Rod, and Nancy brought a small pot of heavy cream. Buran arrived with their coffee pot, and they all settled down to visit. They were soon joined by Croat and Hickly, who eagerly eyed the biscuits until offered one.

Almost immediately they were joined by a man none of them had spoken with more than a couple of times. Abe had shared guard duty with Bill Rhodes, but had found the burly man surly and unwilling to converse. The few times Bill had attended a council meeting, he had brought with him a long list of petty complaints against others on the train and the scouts who he felt picked on him.

"So Rod," Bill began immediately, "why are you out here alone?"

"I'm going home to my family in Kansas. I traveled with a small train out of Salt Lake City until South Pass. They were too slow so I struck out on my own from there."

"Where you coming from?" Bill asked before anyone else could say anything.

"California."

"Where in California?" Bill persisted.

Rod looked at him with a steady gaze. "Is it important?"

Bill backed down and made a poor attempt at looking as though he didn't after all care. "No, no. No matter."

After a half hour of general conversation, Rod declared he was going to turn in for the night and moved off to his string of mules that had been relieved of their packs. He spread out his bedroll near them.

Bill stood up and yawned loudly, throwing out his arms in a dramatic stretch, and announcing that he too was going to bed. When he was gone, everyone exchanged a puzzled look. All, that is, except Gabe.

He chuckled as he said, "Ole Bill there thinks Kingsley has gold in his packs."

"How do you know?" Buran asked him.

"Stands to reason. The man is coming from California, he's traveling with six mules heavily loaded, and he's in a hurry to keep moving."

Abe shrugged. "I don't know. That's not much to draw a conclusion like that from."

"I didn't say it's true." Gabe scratched the bridge of his nose. "I just think it's what Bill thinks."

They all put such musings to rest and went to bed. In the early morning hours, the Carringtons were awakened by the screaming of a woman followed quickly by shouts of several men. Nancy held the boys back while Abe raced to the scene of the commotion near Gabe's rig. He was just in time to see Bob and Chris wrestling a long bloody knife from Bill's hand. At their feet was a very dead Rod Kingsley.

"He tried to kill me," Bill screamed.

The long and short of it was that after burying Rod, a jury was chosen from those who knew neither Bill nor the deceased. The Colonel acted as judge. Abe and Buran told of the conversation the previous night after dinner. The woman who had screamed testified that she had seen Bill pull the knife out of the dead man's neck.

Bill countered that someone had stolen his knife in the night and that when he had seen it in the dead man, he knew he would be accused so he retrieved it. His explanation of why he had been near Rod Kingsley's camp was vague and different from the first time he had offered an explanation. Because there was no witness that saw him actually stab Kingsley, the jury was divided as to his guilt. They brought in a decision of murder with extenuating circumstances, and the Colonel passed down judgment. Bill was to be banished from the train and turned out on his own.

"You can't do that to me, you son of a bitch," he yelped. "This is Sioux territory."

"Rod Kingsley was willing to go through the area alone. So you can take his place. May God have mercy on your soul." And the Colonel would hear no further argument from Bill Rhodes. Kingsley's mules were turned out with the loose stock, and his few supplies were added to those of the Colonel and the scouts. There was no gold in any of his packs.

The train pulled out with the sun casting warm light over the drying grasses of the flat plain. Bill sat in his wagon off to the side of the trail, but everyone on the train avoided looking at him as they passed his wagon. A train following, that should have seen something of him, later reported that they had spotted no wagon. Nothing was ever heard of Bill again.

The Luster train passed several small Sioux villages peopled by the warrior horsemen and their families, but there was no evidence of tension from the few Indians they encountered. Even so, the Colonel had everyone set their wagons more carefully into a tight circle that night and posted extra guards on the stock.

At dinner, Harold and Todd laughed about the antics of the prairie dogs and Harold mimicked their barking as the wagons passed through their tiny villages. Even though Abe had to finally tell the boys to settle down, the tone of the meal was a happy one.

While they ate, an eastbound Abbot-Downing stagecoach thundered toward them, the driver cracking his whip for more speed. Still, many of the women ran out from the train to flag down the driver in order to hand him letters they had kept at the ready. The driver came to a stop barely long enough to grab the packets, and started out again with the women calling out their thanks and blessings for a safe trip.

It was a calm and pleasant evening, and Nancy took advantage of the early evening stop to give the boys a bit of schooling.

"Okay Todd, here's a question for you. The Kansas Territory covered what part of the country before Kansas was admitted as a state two years ago?"

"Uh..."

"Oh, I know," Harold cut in.

"Okay," Nancy acknowledged him. "What is it?"

"It covered Missouri to the Rocky Mountains." Unbidden, he added, "And the Utah Territory is from the Rocky Mountains to California."

Nancy smiled. "That's right."

Todd asked, "What territory was California in before it became a state?"

Seeing the eager look on Harold's face, Nancy asked, "I suppose you know?"

"Yup," he grinned. "It never was part of a territory."

Todd looked at his brother. "Don't you do anything but read books?"

Nancy left the boys to themselves. Harold took out *Uncle Tom's Cabin* and started to read. Todd brought out a piece of paper upon which he had sketched his idea of how the new farm in Oregon should look. Soon the boys became restless and their high energy brought them outside to seek others of their age.

Some of the young people formed square dance sets while one of the men with a fiddle played for them. Their laughter was in itself a form of music to Nancy. Shrieking young boys ran foot races, while the older ones laughed as they practiced roping an old tree stump.

The joyousness of all this welcome diversion was cut short by the explosion of a shotgun ripping into the night. Immediately all sound stopped as everyone jumped to the conclusion that Indians were attacking, although they quickly realized it was too quiet for that. Confused, everyone returned immediately to their wagon as they had been trained to do. Soon the rumor of "accident" traveled around the circle and everyone relaxed.

An hour later, more to purge what he had seen than a need to socialize, Bob approached the Carrington's waning fire. After checking to see where the boys were and noting that they were at the Howard's wagon, he sat down on a camp stool with a heavy sigh and ran his hands over his face.

Abe asked him, "What happened?"

"Old Burns got a halo gratis." Bob rubbed his eyes with the heels of his hands. "He climbed up into his wagon to retrieve his shotgun and grabbed it muzzle first. The trigger must have caught on something. His chest was directly in front of the barrels."

Nancy swallowed twice and retired inside the wagon until Bob left an hour later.

Because they were in the heart of Sioux territory, the next morning before first light they buried Mr. Burns in the middle of the area where the loose stock had been turned out. They flattened the top of his grave so the animals could walk over it as they left the area, and hoped the Indians would find no evidence of it. Whether or not they had buried him deep enough so the wolves would not dig him out, no one would ever know.

The wagons moved out on schedule, another instance of there being no time for shock. But there was always time for sadness, even for those that one only knew casually.

That night Abe sat down for his dinner with a groan of fatigue. It had been a long day, he hadn't slept well the night before, and he was also depressed after helping bury the careless old man. Mr. Burns had been traveling alone and Abe had helped the scouts distribute the man's things among those with the fewest supplies. A large family with only one wagon had been given the man's wagon.

Hunger gnawed at Abe and for hours he had been looking forward to his first swallow of hot coffee, but when the first sip wet his tongue, his forehead puckered. "What the hell is this?"

"I'm sorry, Abe. We've run out of coffee. I parched some barley. One of the men said it's what the miners used to do."

"I'm not a miner, damn it. If we were low on coffee beans, why didn't you get more at the last supply stop?"

"I miscalculated. I thought I had another bag of beans, but I didn't." She hated to grovel, but nonetheless heard herself say, "I'm very sorry, dear. It won't happen again. I'll get more at Fort Laramie."

He took another sip and realized it wasn't that bad, especially with a little sugar. But he was tired and disgruntled over the bad day, and he was in no mood to acquiesce even a little. Nancy read his silence as continued anger and was more than a little hurt that her efforts were not appreciated.

After dinner they all pitched in to clean up. Exhausted, Abe decided to retire to bed a little earlier than usual. Harold was glad, as he wanted to talk to his mother. Having with Todd heard some stories from Croat that gave him a sense of unease, he was sure his mother could comfort him.

But Nancy was still feeling the sting of Abe's rebuke and thought that if she could get to bed, the usual closeness between them might return. She knew he was tired, but so was she, and the added rest would be good for them both.

Consequently, Nancy told Harold, "Go to bed, dear. You can practice your multiplication tables with Todd if you're not sleepy yet. We'll talk in the morning."

Harold understood how tired his parents were, being as they were so old, so he did as he was told. But he was bored and the mountain man's stories had stirred in him a longing for adventure, at least when he was not shocked at some of the details. He lay awake for a long time that night.

The following morning, after helping Todd fold their tent and put it in the wagon, Harold stuffed his sling shot in a back pocket. He retrieved his carefully saved collection of small round pebbles from the wagon and put them in the other pocket.

Watching him, Todd said, "You really shouldn't do that now. We've got to get ready to pull out."

"I'm not going far." He continued to fill his pockets with pebbles. "I'll be back in a few minutes. A rabbit just darted among the brush over there." He pointed just outside the circle of wagons. "Dad'll be real proud of me when I give it to him for dinner tonight."

Todd thought of going with his brother, but he had been looking forward to helping the men with the loose stock because he had been given permission to ride Flame. So Todd told his brother, "Don't go far," and hurried to join the men. Harold walked away into the brush, intent on finding a fat rabbit for dinner.

A half hour later, Nancy stopped Todd as he returned to the wagon leading Flame. "Where's your brother? We're getting ready to leave."

"He was here a little while ago. He was going to kill a rabbit he saw by the wagon and had his slingshot with him."

Not waiting to analyze the sudden rush of anxiety that threatened to overcome her, Nancy shouted, "Abe!" Instinctively feeling there was something amiss, she added, "Hurry!"

Having just finished hitching the team to the wagon, Abe rushed to her side. "What is it?"

"I think Harold has wandered away into the brush." She repeated what Todd had told her. Without a word of response, Abe grabbed his rifle and called out to Buran. Together they walked into the brush and the network of gullies that ran through the area. They could be heard calling Harold's name.

After fifteen minutes searching on foot without success, they returned to get their horses. Before riding out, they went in search of Bob and Chris. As soon as the Colonel found out what had happened, he gathered two dozen mounted men and they all set out in the general direction indicated by Todd. They then fanned out from there. Against the protests of Effie and the other women, when Nancy could stand the waiting no longer, she herself strode out into the brush.

Abe was on his way back, his throat choked with panic, when he saw Nancy. She was standing on a hillock near one of the many narrow ravines, her long skirts fluttering in the rising breeze while holding a hand to her brow to shield the sun from her eyes. Abe noticed that her other hand clutched at her long apron and he knew that she was wishing that she could grab hold of her son's shirt instead.

Abe rode up to her and looked down into her pale hopeful face. Holding out his hand to her, he slowly shook his head. What little color there was in her face faded away as she reached up to grasp his outstretched hand. Aligned together, they returned to the wagon.

As the minutes dragged by, they waited for word that someone had found Harold in their wagon. They then clung to the hope that one of the men still searching had the good news for which they so fervently prayed. One by one the returning men rode past, each shaking their head while trying not to meet the eyes of the obviously terrified parents.

Todd came to stand by their side, out of breath after running the circle of wagons. "No one on the train has seen him this morning," he reported. But he knew that was not exactly true, because he had seen his brother, and had not gone with him.

Soon after the last man reported to them, the Colonel rode up and dismounted. "I'm sorry. I know this is a terrible moment for you, but we've held up our departure by several hours." He took a deep breath. "Since we rested last Sunday, we just can't wait any longer to leave."

"No!" Nancy shouted. "We need to go out again. We'll find him. I know we will."

"You can stay here if you want, but there's Indians in the area that aren't always as friendly as those we've encountered so far. It wouldn't be a good idea to leave the protection of the train. You have two other children to think about."

By now both Nancy and Abe were white with the strain of so long enduring this horror of a morning. Abe swallowed, cleared his throat with difficulty, and told the Colonel, "But we can't just leave him out there."

"Look, there's another train behind us by a few days. Maybe closer than that if they didn't rest last Sunday. They might find him. When we get to the fort, you can leave word there and if he's found, they'll telegraph ahead to one of the stage stations." As they started to speak, he held up his hands and said, "I hate this, but we have to leave now."

The Colonel clenched his jaw, climbed back on his horse and rode toward the front of the line of wagons. He looked away as he passed Effie and the other women who wept as word spread of the Carrington's tragedy.

Nancy turned to Abe, but he walked away to slump against the front wheel of the wagon. He fought valiantly not to be sick, and tried to calm his racing heart while searching his mind for another option. When he saw the wagon train beginning to move past their position, he took a deep breath and stood up.

With his face set, he slowly walked back to Nancy. Barely able to speak for the painful constriction in his throat, he told her, "Be sure the baby is loaded carefully in the wagon. Todd, go up by the team and wait for me."

"No!" Nancy screamed, grabbing his arm.

"Nan, we have no choice." He cleared his throat and took a deep breath. "If we don't get underway, other wagon trains will get ahead of us and graze the grasses. And everyone's supplies are being used whether we're moving or not. A delay will put the whole train at risk."

"I don't care," she sobbed. "We can't leave. We'll have to pull out of line."

His voice firm, he told her, "No! We're going." Noticing Todd still standing nearby, he told him, "Do as you're told, son." Swallowing his tears and a good portion of guilt, Todd did as he was told.

Abe checked Alice's basket at the rear of the wagon before turning to his wife. When Nancy backed away, Abe dragged her forward while ignoring her pleas. Finally he picked her up and placed her in the rear of the wagon next to the now fussing Alice, then reached for the puckering string and pulled in the canvas.

He walked forward to join Todd by the team and immediately called out, "Giddup". The wagon jolted forward with their rig now at the end of the long string of wagons trailing ahead of them. A screen of dust quickly drifted back and threatened to block even a last scan of the area.

Nancy picked up Alice and held her close. She tried desperately to take in what had happened, even while longing to push it away before it led her into madness. When the baby fussed, she unbuttoned her dress and encouraged Alice to nurse while she continued to stare out through the opening that hid her from view, still hoping to catch a glimpse of movement in the brush. But she saw nothing of Harold, and her mother's instinct told her she never would. Alice settled down to nurse, and Nancy forced herself to weep more quietly.

CHAPTER SIX
NEBRASKA INTO WYOMING
JULY, 1863

"Today I baked bread, mended clothes, and washed diapers. I spread them on the brush and the wagon wheels to dry just before a hail storm hit us hard. Those diapers that were not shredded, froze stiff. The storm passed quickly and when the diapers thawed, they were softer than ever before. I focus on anything good, and I make it through another day."

Nancy

"Yesterday a dozen Indians approached the train about 50 yards off. Mostly young bucks out to prove themselves. They rode slowly along with us, occasionally breaking suddenly into a gallop, and riding back and forth as though looking us over. Their dress was more colorful than usual, as was the paint on their bodies. The Colonel kept us going, but every man was decorated with all their guns and knives. After awhile they rode away, wanting only to frighten us and show us they can create fear if they choose. They succeeded well.

"Our train had its first bad accident today while crossing a rain swollen creek. We paid the toll and one at a time we went over the bridge. One man refused to pay and decided to drive his team across in the water. Thinking the family could not afford the toll, some of us offered to pay for him. The man was affronted and refused. His wife fell from the wagon and drowned. The man appears saddened, but is receiving little comfort from anyone."

Abe

Once again the men on guard duty were nervous at night, with sounds both innocent and suspicious rattling their already taut nerves. Their days had been challenged by the countryside through which they moved. When traveling on a smooth road, everyone would settle comfortably into the rocking sway of their wagon. But then suddenly the road would change to ruts and drop-downs. Sometimes it was steep, sometimes rolling, sometimes rocky, and blessedly eventually it would return to smooth and level. With the stability of the wagons constantly tested, every creak of a wheel induced fear of breakage. Some did fail, and the wagon had to pull out of line while repairs were made. They then had to catch up to the train and travel at the end.

Because of what had happened to the Carringtons, every parent watched their children with a nervous alertness. Boys that before had romped along by themselves were now required to stay with their families. It was not difficult for them to follow orders to stay close to the wagons because the children were aware of the reason for these orders, and several had experienced nightmares of themselves being left behind.

Abe had guard duty again, only this time he was assigned to share his spot with Jebb. To break the boredom after an hour of no conversation, Abe asked, "You married, Jebb?"

"Nope." He spat onto the ground. "Was."

"Oh." Abe decided Jebb preferred another topic. He was wrong.

"Tried plural marriage once."

Abe was glad it was dark so his surprise was hidden. "Oh?"

"Yep. Two years of it. Couldn't stand the crying babies or the women's complaints and demands. All of 'em were expecting at the same time. Looked like they all 'et some bad watermelon and their bellies were swelled with the next crop. So I got out."

Abe blurted out, "You left your wives when expecting and your young children needing a father?"

Hearing the incredulity and anger in Abe's tone, a clearly puzzled Jebb explained, "I only had three women."

Abe was so angry that he had to walk away to keep from connecting his fist with the man's face. Worried for Harold as he was, he was furious that a man could so easily let his family fend for themselves. After that night Abe did all he could to avoid Jebb.

Everyone admired Courthouse Rock and the smaller tower next to it that some referred to as *the jail*. Nancy thought it only a giant lump of rock jutting up from miles of otherwise barren flat land. It was backed by the glare of a cloudless blue sky, and altogether it seemed to her a stark and desolate view. She was in no mood for flights of fancy, and was angry that everyone acted so enthused to see it.

The train finally reached Chimney Rock twelve miles later. They had seen it in the distance for over a day, and Nancy watched everyone's excitement when it was reached. The more they enjoyed themselves, the more her anger grew. Then she began to feel ashamed of herself, realizing that not only had everyone heard about these natural wonders from friends and guidebooks, but they had traveled many drab and boring miles with no scenic change of any kind.

Courthouse Rock had been too far from the trail for the Luster people to visit it and keep to their schedule, but after following the trail while it was only slightly higher than the surrounding marshy meadow, Nancy forced herself to look at what everyone called Chimney Rock. It put her in mind of the funnel that she used to bottle her homemade hair wash after she sat it on the counter mouth down and long spout up. There it was out in the middle of a vast plain showing no other interesting rocky outcropping along the low ridge of bluffs that extended out from the chimney. Nancy had to admit to its uniqueness. That night they saw the Chimney enhanced by an orange sunset sky, and the next morning lit by the rising sun.

After this short and pleasant respite, they continued on through Mitchell Pass, one of several parallel canyons through the line of hills. They traveled through the narrow pass single file with a row of telegraph poles to their left while to their right rose the flat-fronted end of the famous Scotts Bluff looming 800 feet above their rocky trail.

Surrounded by steep clay cliffs of weathered shapes in shades of ochre and rose, only the bravest of the men climbed to the top of the bluff. In the far distance they could see the Black Hills, later called the Laramie Mountains.

That night at council Gabe held everyone's attention when he asked, "Does everyone know the story back of the name of Scott's Bluff?" Not waiting for an answer, he continued quickly. "Scott was a fur trader traveling with a group of men. He got sick and although most of the group went ahead to catch up with another party of trappers, two men stayed with him. They all agreed to meet up by this here rock. But the two men deserted Scott, thinking he'd die soon anyway. When they met up at this rock they told the others that Scott had died and they had buried him. But Scott struggled on and got here by himself, only to find that he had been left behind again. Whether the disease got him, or he starved, no one knows. But the next summer his bones and personal items were found and the real story came out."

No one commented and Gabe came near to pouting. After a long discussion about hunting, the meeting broke up. The morning bugle would sound only too soon.

After emerging from Mitchell Pass, they crossed over several gentle meandering creeks flowing to the Platte. The river was banked with an explosion of wild bush sunflowers and lavender asters, and the people found the velvet gray sage with its sharp pungent odor invigorating. For a few miles they picked up speed.

Faced with the long pull toward Fort Laramie in Wyoming, Bob Cook told Abe that it would take them a little over a week. The roads were mostly of heavy sand that raised choking clouds of dust as they walked under the scorching sun. Abe and Nancy were almost done in. Nancy's lips burned and the salve she had made was not helping. Many people resorted to axle grease, which worked well after one got beyond the taste.

To avoid focusing on her discomfort, Nancy tried to picture the fort from what she had heard of it. Although they never discussed it between them, Abe and Nancy both secretly hoped there might be news of Harold at the fort, and this kept them both pushing forward without complaint.

The train spent an extra day where there was good grass for the animals. Lona picked a large bunch of the black-eyed Susans growing in the area and brought them to Nancy.

"Just a little thank you for all your kindness, and to brighten your table," Lona murmured.

Todd took the flowers and put them in the small tin pitcher while Nancy hugged Lona. Before either was forced to say more, Lona returned to her wagon.

Two wagons needed repairs of their axle-trees, which was common after such jarring down-drops as they had so often experienced. One man had problems with a wheel that was shrinking from the iron rim, but a few wedges hammered in soon corrected that. The large wheels were so well made that they seldom presented more problems than this. Their main drawback was that their large size (four and a half feet in diameter at the back of the wagon and three and a half feet at the front) prevented the wagons from turning left or right at an angle of more than thirty degrees.

After a morning hunt, the Carringtons looked forward to feasting on venison at supper that night. Abe and several other proud marksmen had enjoyed a successful hunt of black-tailed bucks and rabbits. Croat had killed two deer, but Gabe had returned empty-handed. When Nancy found out that Croat had given Gabe a hind quarter, she remembered her mother telling her when a child that no one was all bad.

The sprawl of Fort Laramie, situated on a point of land where the Laramie River branched southwest from the Platte, was a surprise to most of the travelers. It had been a trading post in its infancy, then a walled adobe fort until 1849, and now it was a small city of whitewashed wood buildings, two story barracks, long barns, warehouses and blocks of tents. It was surrounded by a network of roads carved into the earth by the heavy traffic of horses, wagons and walking feet. There was also a scattering of teepees around the fort, with Indians sitting outside the dwellings or wandering between them.

Abe expressed surprise at this to Gabe. "Some of these are the families of the local traders. For years they've taken themselves squaws."

"So some of these children running around...?"

"Cute, huh? But half-breed kids don't fare well in this world."

Abe thought to himself that he hoped Nancy did not find out about this. She had enough to fret over.

Most of the fort buildings were still new enough that the whitewashed wood gleamed in the sun, especially the large two-story building of officers' quarters they called Bedlam. The old original fort of the '40's, with its log buildings and surrounding walls and watch towers of adobe, had mostly weathered into bits of crumbling ruin. Although most of the adobe buildings had been knocked down to make room for the new, some simply had dissolved under the pelting winter rains. In the 1840's, two other forts had existed in the area, Ft. Bernard and Fort Platte, but only Fort Laramie had persisted under the direction of the American Fur Company and its wise trading with the local Indians.

Since 1849 the fort had belonged to the government and was now garrisoned for the purpose of assisting westward travelers with the purchasing of supplies. People could also get advice about the road ahead and protection from the local Utes if it was necessary. There was even a monthly mail service, and several women were eager to find out if their families had gotten letters through to the fort. More likely it would be the mail sent from the fort to the East that would, after months in transit, find its way to loved ones.

Here, as at Fort Kearny, the soldiers were few. Their jobs had been assigned to civilians when the soldiers had been sent east to the war. It was the same at all forts across the country.

One of the few soldiers left in charge told them that the fort had started keeping records of the wagon trains during the early 1850's. He told them it was not unusual back then to have a year that saw upwards of 38,000 men, 800 women and 1,100 children pass through. With them there had been 7,500 mules, 30,000 oxen, 23,000 horses, 9,000 wagons and 5,700 cows. Abe and Nancy were relieved to find that this traffic was much reduced, allowing their wagon train to receive ample attention.

However, the evidence of these travelers through the area was everywhere evident. Those portions of their abandoned wagons that had not been cannibalized by the soldiers lay rotting in the sagebrush. Rusting iron tools were partially buried in the sand, barrel hoops were scattered like fallen leaves, and broken shards of once cherished dishes stuck up through the sand. Hundreds of abandoned books had been gathered by the soldiers and were stacked in a small shed to form a type of library.

Immediately after the wagons of the Luster train circled up outside the fort, Abe and Nancy told Todd to stay with the wagon and keep an eye on Alice. While Todd began setting up camp, they walked the half mile to the fort, where they told the Commander what had happened to Harold.

After commiserating with their situation, he told them, "The next train that arrives here may have him or have heard of him. If not, I'll listen for any word of a white boy with the Indians. But I really don't think either situation to be likely. I'm sorry." Privately, he knew that if the Indians had captured the boy they would either raise him as their own or more likely trade him as a slave to another tribe out of the area. Better the parents think him dead, he thought, so they can get on with their mourning and not hold on to false hope.

Nancy was not aware of it, but Croat had already given Abe his opinion. "Sorry, pard, but your kid probably fell into one of them ravines by where we were camped. The fall would've broke his neck."

Abe had never before wanted to stomp anyone into a lifeless puddle of ooze before, but in that moment the image of Croat in that condition gave him great satisfaction. Buran, accurately reading Abe's face and himself wanting to strike the old man, had quickly grabbed his friend by the arm and led him away.

"Easy Abe," Buran had told him. "After all his years of hard living, he's lost whatever sensitivity he ever had. He probably didn't mean to be disrespectful."

"Part of me knows that," Abe had admitted. "The other part wants to hurt him bad."

"Well, after some of the things he's said to people, I think you'll need to get at the back of a long line." Both men had smiled at the thought.

After their talk with the Commander, Abe went to the trading post for a drink and Nancy walked back to the wagon, where she forced herself to accept what she already sensed. She would never see her younger son again. After blowing her nose, she slipped her long apron over her head and tied it at the back before busying herself preparing dinner. No matter how deep her sadness, her family had to eat.

When Abe returned, he joined Todd where he was milking the cow, took the pail from his son, and placed a hand on his shoulder. "I'm sorry son, but I think we have to accept that Harold is gone." Todd nodded solemnly while fighting the quivering in his chin. He picked up a burlap sack at his feet and moved off to fill it with scraps of wood for that night's fire.

Abe walked slowly back to the wagon, almost smothered by the misery of his loss. But he had no choice other than to simply keep moving and take care of his remaining family. Abe passed Mrs. Porter, glad that she had regained her health after the death of her baby, but he wasn't in the mood to visit.

Mrs. Porter noted Abe's dejected shuffle and correctly read its meaning. She stopped him by putting out a hand and laying it on his arm. "I was just wondering," she whispered, "which is worse. Losing a child you were robbed of knowing at all, or never watching a child fulfill his potential?"

Abe looked into her sad questioning eyes and said, "One is mine to endure, and the other is yours. It's not fair to try and compare one person's suffering to another's."

She nodded slowly and walked away, pulling her shawl tighter around her shoulders even though the sun was warm.

The Carringtons and their neighbors took advantage of the day's layover to repack the shifted contents of their wagons. When the Colonel rode by and saw what heavy items many were still hauling, he told the men to leave them behind. When they simply stared at him, he told them they would regret it when one of their animals dropped from the exertion of pulling such unnecessary stuff. Only one man promised to reassess his contents.

Nancy, however, paid attention, remembering the trunk with Harold's books and clothes still in the wagon. She set aside one book and a shirt, then began dragging the trunk and its contents to the side of the road. Todd ran forward as he entered camp and together they carried the trunk clear of the trail. They turned away from it without either of them having said a word.

With the heavy work of repacking completed, Buran built up Effie's cooking fire and sat down to relax near its warmth. He watched Charlie and Todd move off across the circle of wagons as Croat, Hickly, and Gabe joined him. His rest interrupted, Buran invited Todd and Abe to join them so he didn't have to absorb the full force of these men's personalities alone.

Effie looked around at all the men gathering and headed straight for the Carrington's wagon with her basket of mending. She found Nancy sitting by the fire knitting new socks for Abe and Todd. Bidding Nancy good evening, Effie sat down on a camp stool and picked up a shirt with a tear on the sleeve. Their conversation was relaxed and desultory, and covered a wide range of topics from recipes to preparing their new garden in Oregon, but nothing related to children.

Croat looked beyond the wagons to the fort buildings and said, "Back in '49 some of the soldiers talked people out of their wagons, telling 'em the road ahead was too primitive for 'em. Many an emigrant switched to pack mules, or at least lightened their wagons of hundreds of pounds of excess bacon, as well as the usual heavy items needing to be dumped. The land around here was littered with food, tools, pigs of iron, and farm equipment. Even more than there is now. Some of it the soldiers used, and some of it they sold."

"Why'd the people listen to the soldiers?" Todd asked Croat.

"Because they weren't familiar with the terrain ahead, and they figured the soldiers were. So it was easy to convince 'em that fully loaded wagons couldn't make it all the way."

Hickly spoke a rare few words. "The next year it were the opposite."

"Yeah," Croat agreed.

"What does that mean?" Todd asked them.

Croat had just bitten off a fresh chew of tobacco, so Gabe picked up the thread of the story. "People in the east heard about the trains dumping so much and jumped to the conclusion that they needed a lot less food than they were told to bring. Many starved, or near so, and they all had a hell of a time crossing."

Abe murmured, "Thank God we're traveling now." While everyone around the fire nodded in agreement, Croat stood up and pulled his large hunting knife from its sheath on his bulky thigh. He palmed it expertly, raised his arm and let fly the knife past Abe's left ear. It was all done so swiftly and effortlessly that the stupefied group had no time to react. Then they heard the thrashing in the dirt. A large rattlesnake was fighting against the knife that had it pinned to the earth at its mid section.

Hickly walked up to it and stomped its neck with his heavy boot while pulling out his own knife. He sliced off the rattles and deftly separated the head from the body while casually commenting, "He'll stop kicking in a minute." He tossed the rattles to Croat, who put them in a pocket hidden in one of the layers of hides he wore. "That makes ten this stop, don't it?"

"Yeah." Croat walked over to the snake. He pulled his knife from the now still body and wiped it on the ground before returning it to its leather sleeve. "Anyone want the meat?" When no one answered, he flung the limp body over his shoulder and returned to his wagon. Hickly followed on his heels.

Abe and Todd returned to their wagon, and Effie immediately hurried to join Buran. Todd told his mother what had happened in full if not gory detail. Before going to bed they looked around their wagon with great care, but found no snakes. Still, they all decided to sleep in the wagon and no one complained about how crowded it was.

Over breakfast, Abe told Nancy, "Some of the soldiers were wondering what the Emancipation Proclamation having been passed might mean for the end of the war. I guess it remains to be seen."

"What does it mean for the slaves in the south?" Nancy asked.

"It means that those slaves in the Confederate states are now free."

"What about the slaves in the states that haven't seceded"

Abe looked down and shook his head. "The soldiers said it doesn't apply to those slave states that are loyal to the Union."

"That doesn't seem fair."

"It's probably the only way Lincoln could get it passed."

"Still..."

"Nan, it's a place to start. When the war is over, a lot of things may change for a lot of people."

She nodded her head and poured Abe more coffee. Todd said nothing, but he was thinking seriously about the concept of freedom.

Beyond Laramie the road became rutted and rocky, and everyone found themselves quickly exhausted as they walked up and down a series of steep hills. Along the way, they passed several make-shift signs made by past travelers warning of bad water and bad cutoffs.

The trail passed through a scattering of scrubby pine and cedar that studded the limestone of the Black Hills, bringing views that changed little mile after monotonous mile. Those who initially thought this trip was going to be a jolly adventure were by now thoroughly sobered by the number of tragedies the train had experienced, the challenge of the uneven road, and now the awareness of the possibility of making ruinous decisions. People with exhausted and over-worked teams relented and dumped more of their heavy items, especially the extra ox chains they now realized weren't needed.

After an early stop, with dinner and chores done and with light still available, Abe and Nancy went for a walk around the inner circle of wagons. They passed a boy sitting dejectedly by a wagon with a slab of bacon tied to his neck to treat his sore throat, and hurried on when he scowled up at them.

A man with a violin was playing a gentle tune by his wagon, and a number of people stopped to listen. The young people begged him to fiddle them a tune and soon the foot-stompers and square dancers were enjoying his livelier playing. After a few minutes, Mr. and Mrs. Denton came to stand next to Abe and Nancy.

The Dentons traveled in two mule-drawn wagons with Mrs. Denton's twenty-five year old spinster sister Olivia. They were also the people who had with them a petite and attractive young woman of about seventeen who the family referred to as their negress, and whose name was Sally. She smiled readily and was obviously treated well by the family, having quality shoes, two dresses, a heavy shawl, and a new sun bonnet. Her duties were to cook for the family and do their laundry, as well as look after one ten year old boy who seemed to prefer Sally to his mother. She also drove the second wagon.

As they watched the dancing, Nancy overheard Mr. Denton ask his wife, "Where's Sally?"

"I don't know. Probably somewhere with our Hank. He's been helping her improve her penmanship."

"What the hell does she need to improve herself for?" he demanded. "She's just a darky servant."

"Yes," Mrs. Denton responded, "but in the process, Hank improves his own penmanship."

Mr. Denton grunted what sounded like acquiescence and they walked slowly away.

Abe offered Nancy his arm and they continued their walk. After a few minutes she asked him, "There's only the one other Negro servant on the train, isn't there?"

"Yes, the man with the Reeves family, Tyler Daoud. You saw him by the Porter grave. I talked to him once. Seemed like a decent sort, but unlike Sally, I don't think he's free."

In the dusk of evening Abe missed seeing Nancy blush. She indeed remembered Tyler Daoud. In fact, she found the tall and well-muscled young man rather good looking, and she was still haunted by the incident by the Porter grave to which Abe had referred. Thinking about it now made her wince.

Tyler had gone to the Porter child's grave after he thought everyone had left and laid upon it a small wild flower. When he had noticed Nancy nearby, she smiled and thanked him for his thoughtfulness. He had looked into her face for only a brief moment before remembering to drop his eyes to the ground as he had been taught was appropriate when addressed by a white person, and especially a white woman. He had then turned to walk away.

Mr. Reeves seeing their interaction from a distance, had charged forward while yelling at Tyler, "How dare you talk to a white woman! Get your black ass back to the wagon."

Nancy had snapped at Mr. Reeves, "He didn't talk to me. *I* talked to *him*. He said nothing in return and was about to walk away when you came running up." Changing from anger to sarcasm, she had added, "You've trained him well."

When Abe had joined them, Mr. Reeves turned to him rather than respond to Nancy. "Carrington, you need to teach your woman how to act around darkies."

Abe had been about to tell him where he could put his advice, but Mr. Reeves had roughly herded Tyler back to their wagon. Nancy would never forget that exchange, so surprised at her outspokenness had she been. But she also felt bad that she had put Tyler in a situation that had compromised not only his safety but also his dignity.

One very vocal Secsh on the train was Dave Heath. He was outspokenly and proudly a Confederate sympathizer, and was heading to Virginia City in Nevada to join a friend who had what he called a "paying piece of Sun Mountain." Dave had much to say on the subject of slavery and the importance of slavery to the financial stability of the country. This was something any man could understand, but Dave also did not hesitate to declare, "Slaves are after all bred for hard work and need an occasional good strapping."

The topics of humanity, economics, and secession of states, was one most men had debated over the past few years. However, after hearing Dave's rants and witnessing several times the humiliating treatment of Tyler by the Reeves family, those same men now tried to avoid the topic. They also avoided Dave. This was not entirely because of the unpleasantness of his offensive opinions, but also out of spite for his having awakening in them a portion of their conscience they preferred to keep suppressed.

When Abe told Buran about the exchange between Reeves and Tyler, Buran had said, "Yeah, I've seen the young buck a few times. Works damn hard, I'll say that for him. Must be somewhere in his twenties. No one knows for sure. Reeves told

me Tyler had been taken from his parents when barely walking and sold to a plantation where he was raised by the other
slaves. One of the darky women could read and write, and in
secret taught him. Reeves said when Tyler was about sixteen,
his owner realized he was literate. Tyler and the woman who
had taught him were given six lashes and sold off to separate
owners. Tyler ended up with the Reeves family. But instead of
being against his education, Reeves added to it and used him to
help run his house and barns. That's why they're taking him to
California, so he can help them start their new business. If he
does a good job, Reeves said he could have his freedom in five
years."

"But slavery isn't legal in California, so he'd be free there
wouldn't he?"

"I'm sure Reeves hasn't told him that."

Whatever his intended role in California was to be, Tyler
now herded the family's loose stock, hitched and unhitched the
mules each day, led them to grazing each evening after unload-
ing a small cook stove for Mrs. Reeves (heavy enough to make
the Colonel grind his teeth whenever he saw it), set up a large
sleeping tent for Mr. & Mrs. Reeves, gathered wood and chips,
and variously attended to any work that was of a physical nature. Mrs. Reeves spoke to Tyler in curt tones, and always in
the form of a brusque order. He slept under the wagon on a thin
pallet with only two blankets, and no one ever saw Tyler smile.

Two days after this exchange between Buran and Abe, amid
the normal sounds of the camp awakening, both the Denton
and Reeves families were heard calling for Sally and Tyler.
Abe, with Todd following close behind, walked up to Croat and
Hickly. They were usually the first to know what was happening
in camp. Croat smiled and spat on the ground before saying,
"Looks like the darkies have gone missing."

"Run away, likely," Hickly added with a knowing nod.

After an intensive search, it was confirmed that both servants were gone, along with two horses from the loose stock
belonging to Mr. Reeves. No one had noticed Sally and Tyler
spending much time in one another's company, but they had
obviously gone off together during the night.

There was debate between the two families as to whether or
not they should go after the couple, but the Colonel strongly
argued against it and the families finally decided to continue

on with the train.   It was generally acknowledged that Sally and Tyler would head for the Kansas community of freed slaves where they could hide until certain they were not being hunted.

This new turn of events meant that Mr. Reeves had to learn quickly how to work with the team of mules, grease the wheels and herd the loose stock, and do any heavy lifting. The cook stove was soon left by the side of the road, much to the Colonel's delight, and Mrs. Reeves had to learn how to cook over an open fire. When she first attempted to organize the wagon, she was brought to tears, so Effie and Lona showed her the best arrangement, and Nancy gave her cooking lessons.

Abe and several of the other men, although they thought him a bit of an ass, showed Mr. Reeves how to hitch up his mules. When they received fervent thanks from him, Abe at least regretted his stinging earlier appraisal. The next day Mr. Reeves showed Abe and Buran his blisters on hands that had always been soft and white, shocked that anything so mundane as physical labor could do this to him. Although they couldn't help but laugh, Abe kindly told Mr. Reeves to wear gloves in the future.

Now that Mrs. Denton and sister Olivia had to do the cooking, they were not at all happy about their change of status. When young Hank complained loudly upon being told to help with more of the chores, Mr. Denton boxed his ears and made him drive the second wagon along with his aunt Olivia. After several days, Hank actually began to enjoy it. For the first time in his young life he was not being "tended to" and he was able to experience the special joy of self-sufficiency.

As the people walked beside their wagon, they hoped for anything that might alleviate the numbing boredom of the day and the constant reminder of their sore feet. They were therefore alert as they passed the lonely grave of a woman called Lucinda Rollins who had died back in 1849.

As always when she saw these lonely graves by the side of the road, Nancy wondered what had happened to the deceased. She surmised that Lucinda had probably died of disease, since it was so prevalent in that area back in the 1840's. That someone had stayed to care for her in the midst of fearful disease, and then had lingered after her passing long enough to carve a stone to commemorate her life, was such a sign of love that it almost triggered in Nancy another fit of weeping. But she had chores to do, so she brought her thoughts back to the needs of the moment and soon forgot about Lucinda.

The wagons followed the river along its sweep to the north and continued northwest across the bend at Register Cliff. For over twenty years travelers had painted, carved and drawn onto the rock face their names and place of origin. Many on the Luster train took the time to do the same thing in the few remaining spaces. Abe and Todd took a sharp rock and lightly scratched their names next to one reading "A. H. Unthank 1850".

This brief diversion behind them, the train came to Warm Springs Creek that flowed through a narrow canyon fifteen miles west of the junction of the Laramie River and the North Fork of the Platte. A few people drank the warm water, thinking it to have medicinal properties, and any elixir that offered more energy was welcomed. They rested beneath strange gray cliffs that were home to swallows that swooped through the air while gobbling up mosquitoes and moths. The younger children spent much of their time leaping into the air trying to catch them.

The women begged the Colonel to let them have a day at the Springs so they could launder clothes, and were grateful for his understanding consent. The men took advantage of the stop to graze their exhausted stock and see what there was to hunt.

Lona, meanwhile, was heard to hum as she prepared her meals, fed and watered her team, rearranged her wagon, and washed her clothes. Opinion was divided between those who thought her behavior unseemly and those who were glad she had recovered so well from the loss of her husband.

Leaving Warm Springs Canyon, the wagons followed in the deep limestone ruts between a steep brush-covered hill to their left and the wide shallow river to their right. Many arduous miles of travel lay ahead for the train as they pulled up the steep trail, but the unexpected pleasantness of green trees within their view distracted them enough that it later was remembered as a not unpleasant time.

Having only a light and therefore quickly prepared meal at the nooning, Todd was soon free of chores and wandered off to look at a stone with carving on it. As he approached, he saw the deep cuts of a burial marker. He gasped as he read it.

A. H. Unthank.
Wayne Co. Ind.
Died Jul. 4. 1850

It was the same name as the one at Register Cliff where they had engraved their names. Todd walked back to the wagon with a lump in his throat, suddenly overwhelmed at the stark reality of life's fragility. How different things would be now, he thought, if only I had kept Harold from leaving the shelter of the wagon train. Dreading a return to the family wagon, and his parents' oppressive grief, he chose instead to check on the loose stock. Maybe after that he could find one of the mountain men and get him to share a story with him.

Todd had barely disappeared from the area when Nancy and Effie approached the grave. Suddenly Effie began to cry.

"Effie, what's the matter?"

"Oh, Nancy, there's been so much death along this trail." She pulled her hanky from beneath a sleeve and wiped her eyes. "How do you stand it with what's happened to you?"

Nancy put her arm around Effie's shoulders and led her away. "I stand it because I must. My family needs me. Then, in the quiet of night, I think back to all the times Harold and I spent together. I see all the progressive stages of his life, and somehow it comforts me. It makes me feel that he's still somewhere going on with his life. Just not here with us."

"You mean found by other people? But wouldn't they...?"

"No. I know he's dead." Nancy looked off into the far distance and frowned. "I mean, well, in another stage of living. It's a sense I have, but it's very difficult to put into words."

"Do you mean heaven?"

Nancy shook her head and smiled softly as she walked back to the wagon train. Effie did not follow and stared at her friend's retreating back, thinking her a little strange. But she forgave her because of all she had recently endured.

At Bitter Cottonwood Creek they found shade beneath huge cottonwood trees, along with water and grass, and an easy crossing. Further along the trail Horseshoe Creek flowed into the river. Horseshoe Station stage stop, and the luxuriant meadow grass around it, was a respite of a few hours only but the pure water and fresh mountain air was uplifting. It was a gift of recuperation at the half way point of hard travel through the Black Hills.

At the noon stop, after the food had been eaten and the men were packing the wagons, the women went in pursuit of mountain cherries. Todd went with his mother to help glean the bushes and make sure they had a large share of what was available. While they picked over the bushes like hungry bears, the women admired tangles of wild roses in sheltered spots, blue flax on slopes, and clusters of larkspur that splashed the area in painterly brush strokes of color.

Nancy looked up to see Abe and some of the other men by the tall pines and cedars on the edge of a bluff where they were tapping the trees for resin tar. The wagon wheels needed lubricating often so the hubs would not wear out, and some people had exhausted their supply of axle grease. If a wolf could be shot, the Colonel said they would boil the fat out of it and divide it among those that needed it most. If all else failed, they would have to use bacon grease.

A light rain brought out sweet herb and sage scents. The travelers watched small groups of antelope feeding on the wet foliage, black-tailed deer springing away into the distance, and even a puma in the rocks slinking into the undergrowth. Laramie Peak, the first major landmark west of the fort and shaped almost like a pyramid, was visible from the road as the wagons crested a ridge not far from where they crossed half a dozen mountain streams. Everyone agreed that it had been a day of interesting occupation.

Definitely not enjoyable was the vicious and abrasive rocks that wore the animal's hoofs to the quick, cutting and laming many of them. After several miles of the wheels turning slowly in the deep sand and rock, they found the last six miles of road before La Bonte Station packed hard and smooth. Finally the worst of the pulls through the Black Hills was over.

On they rolled, following the same familiar daily routine. Only now the landscape changed often and at the Wagon Hound Creek crossing there was soft red soil that created a road deep in brick dust. It billowed into the air and set everyone to coughing. Grindstone Butte jutted up near the road, and some of the women gathered rock for use as whetstones with which they could sharpen their knives. Here too, many of the animals pulled up lame. They crossed La Prelle Creek over a natural rock bridge, and finally arrived at Little Box Elder Creek where they camped early.

The early stop allowed the men an opportunity to shoe some of the oxen. To accomplish this laborious task as efficiently as possible, Bob told them to dig a trench about two feet deep and wide, twice as long as the length of an ox and with sloped ends. He then had them lead the animal to the trench and get it to lie down next it. When they rolled the animal onto its back, it slid down into the trench and became wedged. With its feet now stuck up in the air, the men could quickly take care of the hooves and afterwards several men could pull it out quite easily with ropes.

Surrounded by the now familiar fragrant sagebrush, they had circled the wagons close together at the insistence of the Colonel, who could not hide his uneasiness. Ogallala Sioux under old Chief Ottowa were rumored to be *restless,* a word that could mean anything from hungry to out for revenge. While the men had been busy within the circle of wagons with the shoeing of the oxen and other chores, the scouts had patrolled the area with rifles at the ready.

But other than a line of Indians silhouetted on a bluff watching the camp and causing the travelers many terrifying moments, they had no trouble from the Indians. Once again they missed tragedy by a year. In 1864 the Ogallala would wipe out a train there, and take the women and children as captives.

After crossing over the bridge at Deer Creek, they followed the ugly torpid flow of the Platte. Reaching the log buildings of the Platte Bridge Station, they found it manned by the troops of the 6th U.S. Volunteers. It was an open and unfortified outpost that had in 1847 been called Mormon Ferry and had established a trading post for the local Indians, the many passing freighters, and an increasing number of wagon trains in need of supplies.

The trading post was well-designed and not unlike many of its kind, no matter how large the building and the warehouse space in back. The "bull pen" at the front of the store was about eight by ten feet, and this was where the customers stood to look over the shelves of goods and place their orders. The counter that separated this area from the traders was high, almost to a man's chest. This made it more difficult to jump over. A chicken wire screen stretched from the front edge of the counter to the ceiling, with only a small opening through which money and goods could be passed.

There was one door for everyone to enter, and the windows on either side of it were inset with bars of iron. In this way, there could be no more people inside than the clerk could keep an eye on, or that could overcome him before he reached his gun. Those waiting their turn outside often entertained themselves with gambling or even trading among themselves.

Bob told Abe, "We'll find the most securely built of these stores in areas where the tribes have been badly abused and cheated by Indian Agents or the traders themselves."

After filling their casks with fresh water, they crossed the long thousand foot bridge over the Platte that had been built by the soldiers. Here the river turned away from its westward course and curved sharply to the south, and the travelers said good-bye to the Platte. The next river they would see would be the Sweetwater, but it was fifty dreary miles away.

The Colonel informed them that these fifty miles would be their most trying challenge so far. After the wagons came off the bridge, they were headed toward the aptly named Poison Spider Creek where heavy alkali deposits began. The wheels of the wagons cut deep into the white alkali crust covering the barren soil, causing it to billow into the air. This fog of dust followed them for miles and was occasioned by strangled coughing from even those who had before not been afflicted.

Having left behind the protection of the fort, they were nervously aware that they were traveling under the watchful eyes of the Cheyenne. But it would not be until July of 1865 that the tribe's tolerance would run out. Then, 400 braves would attack 25 mounted soldiers.

These troops would immediately return to the fort, and while holding the reins in their teeth, they would fire back at the Cheyenne. Seventeen soldiers would survive, only to reach the Fort and find it under siege by 500 Sioux. The Sioux, however, would quickly retreat when hit by wild bullets from the Cheyenne that were still chasing the soldiers. A wagon train almost to the Fort would also be attacked, and nineteen emigrants would be killed and mutilated before reinforcements could arrive from Deer Creek Station. The Red Buttes Massacre of 1865 would go down in history as one of the worst encounters along the Platte.

Just before crossing Poison Spider Creek and heading south-west, the Colonel's train joined with the Mormon Trail that had so far kept to the north side of the Platte. The road gradually gained altitude while the teams strained through deep sand. Poison Spider Creek had earned its name. It was a slowly moving liquid of foaming dirty white scum. They had experienced this white stuff before in ponds, but there had always been the decent water of the Platte nearby for the stock. The women caring for small children found it especially difficult, as there was no extra water with which to bathe them.

But while the people could wipe the dust from their face throughout the day, the animals' eye lids, ears and nostrils became coated with it and the sun baked this residue into a hard crust. Anything that looked like water caused the teams and loose stock to rush toward it, and the people had a terrible time holding them back.

The bleached bones of long-dead animals were scattered near the poisonous streams and were a reminder of what a lack of vigilance could reap. The Colonel had expected this, and had made sure that everyone watered their stock well before reaching this spot. Therefore, at least for awhile, it was not too difficult to keep the animals away from the bad water. Each night Nancy would wipe the faces of their oxen and the milk cow with a wet cloth, and was rewarded by the fancy that they looked at her with gratitude. Abe took great care to do the same for Flame.

It was a shock to the Carringtons and their friends when they realized that, except for a few places where the water was barely decent enough for the stock, this fifty mile stretch would be a two-day forced march with little good water. It was made more difficult by the necessity of going through what the emigrants of past years had named Rock Avenue. This was an ugly stretch of rock strata that rose in jagged protrusions from the dry wounded earth with only a narrow road for the wagons.

As the people walked next to their rigs in order to lighten the load, the rocks raked the legs of the men, women and children. Then the wind began blowing in gusts that whistled through the rocks and kicked up small pebbles that stung bare skin. The women's skirts were blown about by the wind and caught on the rough stones, the fabric tearing as they jerked it loose.

Nancy looked at Abe's wool pants tucked into high leather boots and felt a momentary burst of envy and resentment.

How easy so many things seemed to be for men: their physical strength, their knowledge of weapons, their ability to step into a bush or turn their backs when *nature called*, never having to give birth, no sore backs from bending over a cook fire for hours, and not having to tend children no matter what else demanded their time.

Then she shook her head and took a deep breath as she realized all they did that she did not: wading or riding in the river while leading the wagons across, standing guard duty in the dark and cold of night, tending the teams and loose stock in all weather, hunting for game, winching wagons down steep descents, doctoring and shoeing animals, fighting hostiles if it became necessary, and just worrying about everyone's safety and welfare as they made decisions that would affect both. Whether man or woman, she concluded, life on the trail was a misery.

After navigating the rock-strewn sandy roads, they emerged into a six mile slog of alkaline pools. The slippery puddles and swampy pits of gelatinous ooze smelled like a slaughter house on a hot day. A few mineral springs broke the horror of this, but there was no refreshment in them, filled as they were with salt, soda, and sulphur. Nancy more than once fought the urge to wretch, even while walking with a hanky over her mouth.

Because the canyon forced the trail away from the river, it was the first time everyone faced such a long length of time without decent water. Many found this more frightening than the possibility of attacking Indians. Thirsty and tired themselves, the men still had to be constantly vigilant of the bad water tempting their loose stock. With the pools so heavily laden with alkali, the animals would die if allowed to drink and several times men were forced to beat the cattle with sticks to keep them away from the tempting water.

These alkali flats, although dangerous to the animals, were still fascinating to the travelers. But it was a short-lived interest, as they were soon exhausted by spending so much time struggling to keep the stock away from the dangerous pools.

Some of the women scraped up a little of the white alkali soda and used it like saleratus for baking. Gabe helped the women with the dusty task, then took some for himself before brushing himself off. "Boy," he declared, "this here's as dry as a long-winded Sunday sermon." The next day the women all agreed they would not be using much of the soda, as it gave an unappetizing green tinge to their biscuits.

The Carrington's oxen had taken their fill of water at the last good spring and were not fighting Abe overmuch, but Mr. Reeves was having a devil of a time with his animals. After Tyler Daoud had left, Mr. Reeves had tried to learn the ways of his mules, but it did not come easy for him. Then one of his mules got away from him and drank before it could be stopped.

Sure to die in agony without efficient intervention, Chris and Bob were summoned. After pulling the mule away from the water, they got it back to the Reeves wagon where Mrs. Reeves was shrieking abusive blame at a panicked Mr. Reeves.

Bob called out, "Get me a chunk of your fattest bacon, quick."

When Mrs. Reeves didn't move and instead continued to scream at her husband, Chris turned on her. "Shut up, damn it. You're just making things worse."

While Mr. Reeves stood by wringing his hands and cursing the mule, an affronted Mrs. Reeves ran to retrieve a large slab of bacon. While she did this, Chris backed the mule up so its butt was pressed against the side of the wagon so it couldn't move away from him. Bob cut off chunks of bacon fat and with the aid of a long stick the scouts rammed the pork down the throat of the struggling mule. Chris then asked for the family's jug of vinegar. They forced the liquid down the mule's throat until he was quiet and drooping from his struggles and all he had ingested.

"He'll be weak in the morning, but he should survive," Chris told the Reeves. "If he had taken in more of the water, this wouldn't work." Turning to the men from other wagons who had been watching in amazement, he told them, "Now you know what to do. But try harder not to let it happen in the first place. Alkaline poisoning is a serious thing and you can't afford to lose any of your stock if you're going to make it all the way through."

The Colonel walked the circle of wagons that night and again tried to convince some of the families to dump their heaviest items. With the Rockies ahead and the gradual but long pull to the top, he told them it would be difficult enough for the teams without carrying unnecessary weight. Some of the men listened to him, but a few still refused to dump their iron tools, mining equipment, and crocks of liquor.

The Colonel made it clear that if their wagon broke down and caused the wagon train too much delay, they would be left behind to fend for themselves. This was motivation enough for several men to change their minds and dump a trunk or a chair or a collection of china, often to the tune of their wife's loud complaining. But even this threat to their safety did not sway some of the wagon owners. The Colonel resisted the urge to yell at them, and instead walked away disgusted.

Alice coughed a lot that night and fussed when she was not coughing. Many of the people on the train were doing the same after days of breathing in the alkali dust constantly floating in the air. But for most, sips of water helped it pass. Nancy wiped Alice down with a little cool water and let her suck on soaked cloths to sooth her throat, but in the morning she was not much better.

Nancy wanted to ride in the wagon with her, but Abe wanted to avoid the added weight for the tired oxen while in such difficult terrain. Consequently, Nancy carried Alice in her arms so she could keep a blanket loosely over her head to filter out the alkali dust.

Already having a difficult enough time of it, they entered an area where large fat crickets blanketed the ground. The hard-bodied insects moved over the trail in an almost solid wash of scurrying and leaping black bodies. The hooves of the teams crunched them, the wagon wheels crunched them, and people walking beside the wagons crunched them. Nancy gritted her teeth and stoically continued walking as she looked into the far distance and tried to picture their arrival there. Occasionally brief feminine shrieks could be heard, and each time it gave Nancy a chill because she was so close to doing the same. Each such outburst was inevitably followed by a stern rebuke from a man who was barely rising above his own repugnance. It was a revolting ordeal that lasted several hours.

Even when the crickets were left behind, they still had to contend with the heat, the alkali and the fatigue. Everyone on the train was bound by the single thought, "Will these fifty miles to the Sweetwater never end?"

Several times someone shouted, "Water on the horizon! We must be to the Sweetwater!" But it was always just a mirage. The only thing beyond that was another far horizon, and when that was reached, it gave a view of yet another.

CHAPTER SEVEN
WYOMING
JULY-AUGUST, 1863

"At one stop we find plenty of all things required and we leave with the animals refreshed. At the next stop the water is bad and there is no grass, and the animals bellow in their misery. It is such a sound that I feel guilty for the food I have, even if rationed."

Nancy

"We had much to eat today, and it was all alkali dust. The oxen are exhausted, their eyes rimmed with burning caked alkali and their noses too. Yet on they go, pulling their burden with only an occasional protest. People are not so stoic."

Abe

Nancy's feet burned, her legs ached from ankle to hip, her lower back was a band of pulsing pain, and as noon approached she shifted baby Alice more often from hip to hip to front. It seemed to comfort Alice, who coughed less when held.

When they finally blessedly stopped or the nooning, Abe told her, "Nan, why don't you leave Alice in her basket in the wagon? You need some relief."

She was easily convinced, and after all, Gabe said they had left the worst of the dust. At Willow Springs there was clean water, a small grove of willows for shade, and nutritious grass for the stock. Tempers cooled, attitudes became positive again, and people talked to one another in more cordial tones. Children were washed even if clothes were not, and Alice's cough was all but gone.

After the all too brief nooning, they were happy to shortly find themselves cresting Prospect Hill after a long pull up its uneven and rocky slope. In the distance lay the Sweetwater

Mountains, signaling that soon they would be approaching the Rockies. The Sweetwater would give them many days of travel in shade with plenty of water and much less dust, and some people were almost jubilant in their anticipation of this leg of the journey. It was easy to not think about the new challenges that would follow, especially since they were still twenty miles from the Sweetwater. Most people had taught themselves to think only about what would come next, and not what came after that.

Crossing the rapid flow of Greasewood Creek, the animals stuck their faces in the water and drank their fill as they made their way across. It was a good thing they did, as the ten miles beyond it were a patchwork of alkali lakes long dry. They crossed them on the edges, and the strong corrosive mineral ate through the soles of shoes and boots already worn thin. Meanwhile, the dust again burned in the nostrils of man and beast, and the people encouraged their teams to pick up speed in their eagerness to get beyond it.

Worst of all for Nancy and Abe was that Alice began coughing again, and worse than before. Nancy and Effie, and any of the other women with a home remedy tried and failed to ease her breathing. Nancy could only keep her comfortable, and hope they would soon be out of the dust.

There was game at hand if one had enough energy to hunt it, but few did. Some of the men at noon killed a few rabbits and a couple of sage hens, but no one wanted to kill an antelope because of the work and time it would take to dress it out. If they had been low on food, as those in the 1840's and early '50's had been, they would have been surprised at how much energy they could muster when motivated by the prospect of starving. As it was, when an old ox collapsed and died, the Colonel demanded the owners cut out part of the meat. He then showed them how to hang strips of it from the bows inside their wagon where it would slowly become jerked beef, if maybe a little dusty.

And then there it was--Independence Rock and the deep blue of the Sweetwater River with its lush banks of green grasses and trees bending around the end of it. Hope reclaimed everyone's expectations, and Nancy now understood why people had talked so enthusiastically about this area. The rock's presence on the flat plane was strange, a huge swayback saddle of granite about 70 feet high and a mile long rising out of nothing. Of course, people had for decades carved their names on it, and those of the early fur trappers were mixed with travelers of the past few decades.

Todd thought the big gray mass of rock looked like a whale he had seen in a book. He fancied it tossed up from some ancient sea onto this dry, treeless valley and just missing the river water. He could only imagine, although he tried not to, that Harold would have loved it.

But it was the swift flow of the Sweetwater sweeping around the huge monolith as it flowed east to the Platte that brought a cheer of jubilation bursting forth from the Luster train. The sweet clear water reflected the brilliance of the blue sky while the low sun scattered glittering diamonds of light across the surface. The story told by Gabe was that fur trappers had years before lost a bag of sugar in the flow, and thus had named it the Sweetwater. Nancy thought to herself that the taste could not be any sweeter than that first sighting.

They nooned near the east flank of the famous monument, and most of the men rode to the rock, the more adventurous of them determined to climb to the top. Even though a strong wind from the west would make the climb difficult, Abe and Todd decided to go with them.

Meanwhile, the women washed their children and then the family's clothes. With the men gone from camp, many of the bolder women, and all of the young girls, quickly stripped down to their chemise and enjoyed a generous dunking. There was much laughter amid the splashing, and Nancy allowed herself to also feel the pleasure of the cool water.

The sun and wind quickly dried their hair and their cotton underclothes while they finished the laundry. Soon the dry gray sage, the rocks and trees along the shore, and the wagon wheels too, were covered with drying clothes flapping in the strong breeze. The women quickly learned to grab the clothes before they were dry enough to catch the wind and blow onto the dirt.

Nancy had just put on a clean dress and apron when Abe and Todd returned. They were still breathing hard from their climb, but Nancy could tell they were energized as Todd described the difficulty of their climb.

"One of the men explained that it's been known as Independence Rock since the '30's when trappers of the American Fur Company spent July 4 camped here." Eager to see his mother once again enthused about something, Todd added, "Croat says that last year a meeting of twenty Masons heading to Oregon found a secluded recess in the rock. It was the Mason's first meeting in the West."

Nancy smiled at him, but said nothing, too worried about Alice to feel enthusiasm for anything as mundane as a rock.

But Todd continued his effort. "It's referred to more often as The Great Register of the Desert, and from the time of the first fur traders it's been a place where they could come together to trade. They left their names on the rock. There's even crosses and other religious symbols on it."

Finally interested in spite of herself, she asked, "Are they all carved into the rock?"

"No. Some are carved, some painted with chalk or axle grease, and some look like ancient hieroglyphics. But I bet the local tribes know what they mean."

Todd then eagerly described what they had seen from above: the miles of alkali flats through which they had just passed, the narrow Sweetwater cutting a meandering path south through a broad rolling plain with the sun glinting off its slow moving water, and their attention drawn to little yellow spots that moved along it.

"We finally realized they were antelope, and that maybe the black mounds further in the distance might be grazing buffalo."

Listening to his son, Abe's thought returned to the sight of the sharp and high mountains to the west that had caught his attention. Gabe called them the Rattlesnake Mountains but the Colonel said they were now called the Granite Mountains. Abe only focused on the mountains themselves, hinting to him as they did that harder travel lay ahead as they approached the Rockies. This, however, he kept to himself.

Todd told his mother, "One of the men said that a huge chunk of the rock was lost back on July 4, 1847. Some men from a passing train exploded old wagon hubs packed with black powder in some crevasses of the rock and blew off several tons of the granite."

"Why?" Nancy asked Abe.

Abe shrugged, but Todd said, "Must have been a hell of an explosion." He grinned at the thought.

Nancy smiled at him, chose to ignore his mild swearing, and said nothing. She thought such destruction wasteful and another example of the underlying violence beneath the thin civilized veneer of men willing to head West without any true understanding of what lay before them. Of course, she reasoned, maybe such actions shared the same source as the men's courage, resourcefulness and perseverance. It was something to ponder later, when the desire became strong to not think about the fatigue of the march forward, or the fact that her daughter was ill.

Todd walked away, crestfallen that he had been unable to convey the excitement of the morning to his mother to boost her spirits. He could not shake the feeling that she blamed him, even if just a little, for Harold wandering away.

He knew he should have tried harder to talk Harold out of looking for that damn rabbit, or even gone with him. But if he had, maybe he too would be missing and probably dead. Again the guilt and shame engulfed him along with the doubt of his ever being a worthy man. The torment of it caught in his throat like caustic bile and almost choked him. Should he talk to his father about his feelings? No, his father already carried too large a burden. Besides, his father would probably tell his mother, and he didn't want that. Better to say nothing and be a man about it, whatever that meant.

The train continued west along the Sweetwater, leaving Independence Rock and its register of names behind them, and to history. With water casks full, wagons repaired, clothes washed and bodies likewise, the people felt fit and ready to continue.Unknown to most of them, the Colonel had allowed such a long rest only because the next leg of the journey was to be a difficult climb over sharp rocks and steep swales in the land. Their progress would be noted by the watchful gaze of the Crow, whose tribal lands extended onto the eastern slope of the Rockies and included the abundant valleys of the Powder, Wind and Yellowstone rivers.

Even though it was summer, Nancy noted snow on the Wind River Mountains to the north and was surprised that Alice still coughed now that the air was clean. She was nursing very little, and even getting her to drink water now was difficult. But as they set up camp in the Granite Mountains, Alice's color was better and she finally breathed easier. Her face was a little flushed and her breathing a bit labored, but she went to sleep without fussing for the first time in several nights.

Just after midnight the second night in these mountains, Nancy got up to check on Alice for the third time. Abe was awakened by her screams. So was Lona, the Howards, and Gabe, who all came running to see what was the trouble. Nancy stood at the back of the wagon, holding the limp body of little Alice in her arms. The baby's blue face was composed in a calm repose from which she would never wake.

Lona and Effie began to cry, and only with great effort were they able to pull themselves together. Their friend needed them. Abe took the child's body from Nancy, although not without a struggle, and Lona immediately wrapped her arms around Nancy and held her close, letting her weep anguished tears upon her shoulder.

Abe closed his eyes and held the baby to his chest for a last embrace, but there was no warmth to be felt and no little hand reached out to grab at his chin. He could not hold back a sob of grief. Buran stepped forward with a small piece of canvas so that Abe could wrap the tiny body within its protection.

The women released Nancy from their arms into those of Abe while Gabe and Buran walked beyond the circle of wagons and up a slope to a small level area of ground. Mr. Reeves met them with a shovel and within minutes the little grave was ready among the bushes heavy with white blooms that glowed in the moonlight. With Abe and Nancy standing nearby, the small group of friends lay Alice in the tiny hole lined with brush, filled it with dirt and small rocks, then tamped it down and covered it with more rock and brush. Soon there was no evidence of a grave at all and everyone hoped it would remain undisturbed, with the brush obscuring it from the Crows who would probably leave it alone anyway if they realized it was a child's grave.

After the Colonel had read a brief passage from the Bible and everyone had returned to their wagons, Abe and Todd led Nancy back to their camp. Abe waited for Nancy to begin weeping again, but she instead stood by the back of the wagon looking silently into the dark while fingering the blankets in Alice's empty basket.

Gathering them to her, she held them to her breast as she would have if Alice had been in them and began crooning the lullaby that Alice had loved. When she buried her face in the bed clothes and inhaled her baby's special scent, the ache and longing she had thought too deep for tears broke to the surface.

Someone later asked what animal it had been that had cried out in the night in such a wrench of agony.

Abe spent the rest of the night in the wagon holding Nancy in his arms, and the next day as they walked next to the oxen, he held her hand. He didn't know what else to do. That night Abe again held Nancy in his arms until she fell asleep, while unshed tears ached in his throat as he dealt with the hollow angry frustration of a man who had found one more thing he could not fix or make right for his family.

During the day Todd had walked behind them, alone in his misery. At night he crouched under the wagon and hugged his knees to his chest while rocking back and forth. What should he say? What could he do to help? He had unhitched the oxen for his father, led them to grass and water, and checked on the loose stock. He had also started the evening fire, heated the left over beans for a dinner only he and his father ate, cleaned up the pots and plates, and milked the cow. But was that enough?

An awkward helplessness engulfed Todd and swallowed up his guilt, squeezing out of his eyes as tears that ran slowly down his cheeks. He was haunted by his belief that his presence was an intrusion into his parent's private grief, and a burden they didn't need. He was convinced that he was a painful reminder to them of the fact that he could have stopped Harold, but had instead selfishly enjoyed himself. Now, with the death of his little sister, his parents would have the added weight to their souls of *two* children dead. So overwhelmed was he by the depth of his own misery and confusion, and too immature to understand a parent's needs, that he failed to realize that he was the child that remained to give his parents solace simply by his presence.

The next day the train reached halfway up the hill that began the Sweetwater Range of mountains. Nancy stood to the side of the road and looked down at the valley they were leaving, knowing that she would never forget that view. The meandering path of the river reflected the puffs of white clouds crowding the blue of the sky and then framed this with its green edges.

However, it was the great bulk of Independence Rock and the wide vista of low hills that held her attention. They now protected the grave of one more child lost on the trek to a better life. But how much better could it be, she thought, when one had lost two children within weeks of each other? How did one recover from such a thing?

Unaware that Bob had approached her, she felt the gentle touch of his hand on her left shoulder from behind. Without turning around, she smelled his not unpleasant musky scent and heard his deep low voice. "You did all you could. Some can handle this trail and some can't. You're allowed to grieve, but you're not allowed to stop living. Just put one foot in front of the other and move on, and trust that it'll all somehow come right."

She reached up to her shoulder and patted his hand and immediately heard him walk away. Turning away from the road that led only to the past, she followed the plodding teams and creaking wagons until the hill was crested, and looking back would have been pointless.

Commented upon in almost every diary kept on the trail, most people had noticed Devils Gate in the distance for the last fourteen miles. Abe and Nancy were not yet ready to see beyond the self-absorbed misery of their grief. Todd, on the other hand, had been looking forward to it and he gave it some notice, although he knew better than to make comment to his parents.

He saw a narrow 400 foot tall slice cut out of the mountain about 300 feet wide at the top but only thirty feet at the bottom. Through this the river filled the gap so that no wagon could follow along the water's edge, which forced them to travel through the hills a half mile to the south. Todd pondered for miles how many thousands of years it might have taken the power of the water to cut this gap to its present depth, and not for the first time he marveled at the awesome strength and resiliency of nature.

This made him think of Harold again, and how he would have loved studying such a phenomenon. When he realized that he had just been enjoying himself, a sudden kick of contrition hit him in the gut. Any further pleasant introspection ceased immediately.

The one good thing about the alkali through which the animals had walked over the past weeks was that those that had earlier developed hoof infections were now healed of it. As the teams strained up the gradual but steady slope of the Rockies, the last two holdout families finally relented and dumped a good portion of their heavy goods. The Colonel was so glad that he resisted the temptation to tell them that it was about time.

The next morning Nancy observed Mrs. George, a woman her own age that had started out from Independence. She had only talked to the woman a few times, and had admired her long blonde hair. Now the woman stood by an old trunk lying by the side of the road while Mr. George called to his wife. Ignoring him, she opened the lid of the trunk and revealed a boy's clothing and toys neatly packed away. Since Nancy knew that Mrs. George had only a little girl, she realized that the clothing probably belonged to a son who had died before the journey. The grieving mother had left his grave behind, but had thought to have something of him with her. Now that too was being left behind.

Mrs. George looked up when Nancy stopped next to her and without a word between them, they wrapped their arms around each other and fought their tears. But the demands of the moment were now ingrained in them, and they quickly dried their eyes. Together they reached out and closed the lid of the trunk, then returned each to their own wagon.

One wagon, a dozen forward of Abe and Nancy, was that of John Belin and his wife Marie. They had never socialized much with those around them, but then not everyone was the socializing type. It was assumed by some that the Belins were too busy, what with five children to look after. There was a girl called Lizzie that was 12, and three energetic boys--Brian, Dean and Glen, aged 10, 8 and 5--and baby Pete only four months old.

Nancy and Effie more than once speculated what it must have been like for poor Mrs. Belin to have started out on the trail after so recently giving birth. After listening to Abe describe his two run-ins with the stern and argumentative John Belin, which Nancy relayed to Effie at her first opportunity, both ladies no longer wondered. It was also commented upon by all the women on the train how much younger Marie was than her husband. A woman who had occasionally looked after the children while Marie washed clothes, said she was 28 and the husband 45. Most had thought Marie nearer 40.

Effie had talked to her several times, and had afterwards commented to Nancy that she thought the woman very worn down by her hard life. Nancy felt unkind for thinking it, but she told herself that although it may have been hard for Marie, she still had all five of her children around her.

They were close to Three Crossings Stage Station, near where Gabe said they would have to cross the Sweetwater's sharp curves through a narrow canyon three times to keep to the trail.

Almost there, Effie came to the Carringtons at the nooning with the news that Mrs. Belin was very ill.

Abe nodded and said that John Belin was complaining to every man who would listen. "He says it's hard on him to have a sickly wife. He chooses to ignore the fact that his daughter Lizzie has taken on most of her mother's chores."

So offensively insensitive was Mr. Belin's whining to the men that several women were surprised that night by considerations from their conscience-stricken husbands.

Never forgetting the presence of the Crows, the Colonel emphasized to everyone a need for renewed vigilance. This was not because the Crows were a warrior tribe, but because they were brilliant thieves who stole stock or anything left unattended with the exuberance and glee of children playing an hilarious game. And they were very good at bending the rules.

As it turned out, the train made no contact with these squat indigenous people because they were moving their village to a better place of hunting. Those on the train saw the village in transit, with the wagons traveling faster than the Crows who were leading their ponies mounded with hides used for their dwellings, and oxen carrying other camp items. Cur dogs slunk silently alongside these large beasts of burden while carrying their own smaller packs, and those who dared bark felt the foot of whomever was nearest them.

Young women adorned in bird skins and beads carried their babies on their backs in colorful cradleboards next to old women in plain garments. These last were herding before them a group of raggedy unwashed children much as they would have a flock of sheep. The men were a mix of those with status and so covered in bear skin or mountain lion robes, and those with little status who wore barely any covering at all. Everyone breathed easier when the wagons were well past the nomadic Crows.

That night at council Gabe included in his fireside ramblings that it was along this route that Bill Cody rode for the Pony Express only three years before. "He once made a run of 320 miles, covering about 15 miles an hour. He'd found dead the fella he was supposed to hand off to, so he had to ride that portion of the route too." This indeed impressed the men, although several boasted that they too could perform such a feat.

The Colonel turned everyone from tales of the past and told the men he had decided they would take the sage hill road away from the river, as it was shorter and would save them a couple of days. Some of the men wanted to go through the gorge as anticipated to soak their dry wagon wheels, but it would mean putting the wagon beds up on blocks and possibly sinking in the wet sand. The Colonel explained that the road around the gorge had been improved, and admitted that he was concerned about making up some of the time they had lost by resting so many times.

Finally arriving at Three Crossings Stage Station, they found it to be only a tiny village isolated in the cleavage of low rocky hills that blocked the view of what lay beyond. The older buildings had mud walls, but the buildings of newer construction had outer walls of logs running vertically as well as horizontally. It gave the overall effect of buildings thrown together with little care, even while yet reassuringly strong.

Abe and Nancy spent a cold night, unable to restock food items at what was only a station for passing stages. At least the animals were watered and the barrels full when they moved out early onto the dusty road to begin threading their way through the sage hills.

It was during the day's nooning that Marie Belin died. News spread quickly and many people gathered for yet another burial. Mr. Belin stood by the grave and clutched his hat to his chest, looking stunned and somewhat betrayed, while his three young sons clung to his legs. Lizzie held her baby brother while tears ran down her cheeks unchecked. Nancy focused her thought on the baby in Lizzie's arms, now destined to never know his mother, or probably even what she looked like. They didn't look like a family to have spent money on a recent daguerreotype of the family.

The next day Mr. Belin declared he couldn't handle so many children and the team too. Consequently, one of the women on the train near the Belin wagon took in five year old Glen and eight year old Dean. Lona was approached by ten year old Brian who offered to help her with chores during the day if he could sleep in her wagon at night. Lona told him she was grateful, and she promised in return to give him good meals.

But Lizzie would give the baby to no one. Instead, she brought him to Nancy and boldly addressed her. "Mrs, I know you lost your little girl recently. I was wondering, if you haven't dried up yet, could you maybe feed Pete here? Mrs. Checo said she had plenty of milk and would put him on tonight after her own has his fill."

The sad thin girl stood before Nancy with her long stringy hair hanging in her face, and her rumpled dress badly in need of washing. Nancy said nothing, and simply reached out for the baby. Little Pete drank as naturally at her breast as if it was what he had always done, and Nancy felt the physical relief immediately. But she also felt an almost spiritual release of the worst of her grief as well.

For the next two days, while Lizzie cooked, mended and washed for her father, the baby was passed between Nancy and two other women who saw to his needs. Each morning Nancy received little Pete into her arms at the back of the wagon, after which Abe watched his wife close her eyes and relax, knowing that she was reliving the last time she had done this for Alice. Nancy only kept little Pete for half an hour, since Lizzie came for him promptly, said a curt "Thanks", then hurried away as though fearful that Nancy might demand to keep him.

At the end of the fourth day a pale Lizzie brought the baby to Nancy, who was sitting with Effie near the fire. Nancy asked her, "Do you feel okay, my dear?" She was concerned the girl was working too hard.

"Dad left on his riding horse during the night." She sighed and added quietly, "He won't be coming back."

"Oh, you poor thing," Effie gushed. "You must be so shocked." Buran right then called Effie's name, and she obediently scurried off.

Nancy looked at the expression on the girl's face and said, "You're not that surprised, are you?"

"No." Lizzie produced a timorous little smile. "I'm more surprised he waited this long."

For the next few days, Abe and some of the other men helped the girl and her brother Brian with their ox team each morning and each night. Brian thanked Lona for her kindness, but stated that he was "needed at home". The men in the wagons fore and aft kept an eye on the little family, but were pleased to see the ten year old quickly become adept at working with the team. Lizzie cooked meals for her little brood, and continued to bring Pete to the three women on the train who were now sharing in rotation the feeding of the baby.

After several days, however, Mr. and Mrs. Checo decided to adopt permanently the girl, Brian and baby Pete. Mrs. Checo's sister and her husband, traveling in the next wagon, took in Dean and Glen. In this way, the children were kept together while their care was shared by the two families. Brian continued to drive their wagon so they could haul water and supplies for the five children.

Nancy did not feel she could ask to continue her feeding of the baby, although she certainly wanted to, and Abe was at a loss as to what he could say to ease the wrench of this for her. He was only vaguely aware that she would soon be in physical discomfort as her milk dried up, but women seldom talked about such things, and like most men of the time he only vaguely understood the process.

That night, lying stiffly beside a sleeping Abe, Nancy's thoughts took an introspective turn. She began by thinking how insular grief is, making one feel like no person ever has or ever will feel agony such as yours. How does one *act* like part of the world, when one *feels* no part of it? After all, this going forward that was being pressed upon her was actually moving her away from all that she had ever loved.

"The further I am from Alice's grave and the last place I saw Harold," she thought, "the closer I am to feeling that I've lost the mother part of myself. Todd is such a young man now, and seems not to need me at all. He turns more often to his father or even the strange mountain men. Everything has changed so much." With these thoughts tormenting her dreams, she spent a fitful night of little sleep.

After Abe retrieved the team and finished hitching them to the wagon, he walked to the back. Nancy was just putting on her chintz bonnet with the foot deep sun visor.

"Nancy! Your hair. Your long hair is gone."

"Don't get all het up about it. It's still down to my shoulders. It's too damn hot for a pile of long hair under these God-awful bonnets." She wasn't sure whether his shocked expression was for her hair or her language, but she snapped at him, "It's just hair! It grows, you know."

Abe walked forward and hollered to the oxen. "Giddup." He tried to forgive Nancy for what she had done, but for the rest of the day he felt somehow betrayed.

Traveling along the Sweetwater River, they were now slowly gaining elevation on the approach to the Great Divide and enjoying a far view of the snow-capped Rockies. Fat prairie dogs sat on the porches of their tunnels and watched without movement as the wagons rolled past. Birds sang from greasewood mounds, and antelope nibbled bunchgrass and when startled ran away with a flare of their white tails. For a change Todd found it only mildly interesting. Instead, he focused on the increasing awkwardness he felt around his parents.

Most people were looking forward to the legendary Ice Slough, and when it was reached, the train nooned there in the shallow of a wide swale in the swampy land. The young boys on the train grabbed shovels and began digging a foot down where they found a layer of ice about five inches thick. This was an occasion of great merriment for the children, and even for many of the adults. Todd, however, hung back and barely allowed himself to be interested.

"Ice?" Effie asked Nancy. "It's summer for heaven's sake."

"Bob said we're at an elevation of about 6,000 feet, and that at one time this area was probably a pond or swamp that was covered in grass. The severe winters here would have eventually frozen it, and as long as its kept covered by grass, it won't thaw even in this heat."

The Colonel sat on his horse and watched the people's delight at this oddity and thought to himself, "Let them laugh for the moment and not think about what comes next." He could think of nothing else. He knew that they would enjoy the assent of the Rockies, the view from the crest, and being relieved that it hadn't been as difficult as some of them had expected. He also knew that when they reached Nevada and the Humboldt River, there would be much suffering. There always was.

Looking in the direction of the Carringtons, the Colonel felt a deep sadness for them. On the other hand, he thought, if the child had been so susceptible to the alkali dust so early in the journey, it was best she died when she did, in an area the parents could remember as beautiful. The dust along the Humboldt would have finished her off for sure, and thinking of one's child left behind in the hell of that vast expanse of alkali crusted sand would be torture. Yes, he thought, there were worse things ahead than any of them could imagine.

When his horse started making familiar nickering noises, he surveyed the ground around him and spotted a coiled rattlesnake in the shade of a large sage. Taking his knife from its sheath on his belt, he threw it artfully and the sharp point hit just behind the head. After a few wild thrashes the snake lay still.

The Colonel retrieved his knife, wiped it on his pant leg, and mounted his horse while muttering under his breath, "Damned bush trout!"

CHAPTER EIGHT
WYOMING
AUGUST, 1863

"I watched a woman in a forward wagon today with interest. Three weeks ago Beth buried her little boy. Today she was offering me a sweet biscuit while her daughter celebrated her fifth birthday with three other little girls. I accepted a biscuit but dared not take a bite for fear I could not swallow. She patted my arm and told me it was okay then turned to the other women. How quickly we women learn how to hide our grief."

Nancy

"As I listen to those who often complain, I realize that most of those who do not are us farmers. What is the difference of walking a day beside an ox moving us west, or behind a mule pulling the plow? I would give much to feel again the optimism and eagerness so prevalent at the start of this journey. If I could bear some of Nancy's grief, I gladly would, even if adding it to my own would bring me to my knees."

Abe

As the Luster train neared South Pass, the Colonel said it was Sioux country and that somewhere in the area there were parties of Crow warriors from the north. If this was not bad enough, a passing stage driver warned them of Blackfeet and Snake war parties in the area. As they focused on the gradually rising and rocky trail before them, they were never without the excruciating tension of dreadful expectation. They saw, however, not one Indian.

The trail had been improved over the last few years by government work crews sent out from the East, but the Colonel wished they had done more, as it was still very rough. Still, the crews had knocked down the worst of the rocky shelves over which travelers in the past had lurched, much to the detriment of their axles. Finally on the high tableland, things improved and they made good time. Morale improved, and most people even began to relax.

None of the travelers had taken Jebb's wild threats against Indians very seriously, and some people had even forgotten them. But while they were in the territory of so many tribes known to be "in a mood", as the Colonel put it, the scouts kept an eye on the irascible man.

Finally within the cool embrace of the Rockies, the Colonel noted how tired everyone was and generously decided to let the wagons circle early while near water, good grazing and the shade of large trees. Soon savory aromas from cooking fires filled the air and people were busy with the routine of evening chores.

Into this domestic scene two young Sioux boys, both about twelve years old, approached the camp on their ponies. They were several years yet from being called a brave, but they sat their ponies with confidence. Their long black hair was held off their face by a narrow band of leather, and their mahogany skin was glowing with health.

Unfortunately, Jebb saw them before anyone else. As the young boys approached, he charged at them while screaming, "Thieves!"

Before either boy could react, Jebb grabbed the nearest one by the leg and pulled him from his pony. As he slammed him to the ground with a loud thud, the other boy turned his pony around and raced away.

"Thief!" Jebb yelled again as he punched the youngster in the face. The boy was far from passive and kicked at Jebb with all his strength, catching him in the stomach and high on his thigh. This only riled Jebb more and he retaliated with a jab to the boy's abdomen that knocked the wind out of him.

As the boy lay on the ground clutching his stomach and gasping for breath, Abe and several other men reached Jebb just as he was aiming a kick at the boy's head. They grabbed hold of the crazed man and tried to pull him away, an effort that got them both bruised. Jebb flailed to free himself while continuing to scream, "Thieves! They're stealing our horses."

Bob slapped Jebb across the face and tried to get his attention. "Jebb, you stupid son of a bitch, stop it! They aren't doing anything of the sort."

Abe helped the boy to his feet while Bob and Herman Crotts held onto Jebb until Harry Jones arrived. After Jebb was dragged off by Bob and Harry to answer to the Colonel, Abe noticed that the usually brusque Herman was shaking.

Abe turned to the Indian boy and brushed the long dark hair back from the youth's face. He was surprised to see how young he was and asked him, "You speak any English?"

"Little," the boy mumbled in a voice that had not yet deepened.

"Why did you come here?" Abe asked gently.

"Sugar," the boy mumbled, rubbing his shoulder.

"You want some sugar?"

The young Indian nodded shyly. Abe smiled at him and nodded as he put an arm around the boy's shoulders and led him past half a dozen wagons to Nancy. The people in those wagons watched the pair pass, every one of them suspicious and tense. The boy saw not a smile among them, and pressed into the side of the nice man who walked with him and who had smiled at the mention of sugar.

Abe announced to Nancy, "It seems this young man would like some sugar, Nan."

Nancy smiled at the boy before turning to her supplies and chopping a small amount of the sweet treat from the loaf. She wrapped it in a twist of paper and handed it to him along with a gesture for him to sit down. He did so, although wary and keeping an eye on the shortest way out of the camp. She wrung out a cloth in the pan of dish water and bathed his face.

"I'm sorry for what that man did to you. He's not very nice."

The boy put a hand to his bruised cheek and nodded. He looked up at Nancy with the recognition of one he could trust, and her heart almost broke. It took all her strength not to reach down and hug him, but knowing such action would be inappropriate, and might even be negatively interpreted, she held back. The boy never took his eyes from Nancy's face while she wiped away the dirt, and when he saw tears in the eyes of this gentle white woman that reminded him of his mother, he stood up and lay his hand on her arm. His face showed alarm.

Without hesitating, she explained, "I had a son about your age. He died not long ago."

However much of her words he understood, he seemed to understand the general meaning and nodded his head. Just then Abe walked up with a rope around the neck of the boy's pony. The boy removed the rope, took hold of the horse's mane and swung up onto its back.

The Colonel joined them with a subdued Jebb in tow between Bob and Chris. The Colonel was still reeling from his confrontation with an angry Jebb who had justified himself while using a litany of inflamed rhetoric and vile language. But the Colonel had rendered him humble by his threat to leave him behind right there in the middle of all the Indians he hated. Now, all the Colonel cared about was how this incident would affect the train's safe passage through the area.

When Jebb saw the boy sitting on his pony, he kept his mouth shut as directed, but he could not hide his harsh malevolent glare. It seemed to Nancy that the look was beyond reason and toward insanity. Finally unable to control himself, Jebb spat out, "Dirty bastard brat!"

Abe barked at him, "That's enough! You won't talk that way in front of the women!"

The Colonel was about to tell the boy to go home when the other boy appeared in the company of three braves, one of them likely the father. Everyone froze where they were, but those carrying guns were a little more aware of where their weapons were in relation to their hands. The boy with the sugar quickly rode up to the men of his tribe.

When the boy who had earlier escaped pointed to Jebb, the Colonel grabbed the still mumbling Jebb by the arm and spun him around. Before Jebb could react, the Colonel punched him in the face, holding little back in the force of the blow. It was a draw as to who was the most surprised--those from the train or the Indians, but certainly none more so than Jebb himself.

The Colonel loomed over Jebb, who lay at his feet. While pointing at the boys, the Colonel demanded that Jebb get up and apologize to them.

"I won't!" Jebb yelled. "They can go to..."

The Colonel leaned down and grabbed Jebb by his shirt front at the same time that he slapped him cross the face hard enough that the impact could be heard over the rising wind. He then muttered something to Jebb that made the old man gasp and turn pale.

"Okay," Jebb nodded. He climbed to his feet, turned to the boys and said, "I'm sorry."

Bob and Chris each took one of Jebb's arms and marched him away. The Colonel walked up to the braves and explained that Jebb had jumped to a wrong conclusion about the boys' intentions and would be further severely reprimanded. The Indian men turned to the boy and he explained in his own language what had happened.

Part of his dissertation included his pointing to Nancy and smiling as he made the gesture of wiping his face. He then showed one of the braves his twist of sugar, prompting the man to almost smile. Instead, he looked at Nancy and gave her a curt nod to which she responded with a smile and a brief curtsey. This last also caused a twitch at the corner of the brave's mouth. Then, without further words spoken by anyone, the boys and the Indians left.

The Colonel walked over to Abe and Nancy. "Thank you for your kindness to the boy. It made all the difference."

Nancy only nodded and returned to the wagon. The Colonel put a hand on Abe's arm as he started to follow her. "I think the thing that impressed the brave the most was when the boy told him that she was so sad about his ill treatment that her eyes watered." The two men looked at each other for a moment before the Colonel added, "I know it wasn't about the Indian kid. I'm so sorry for your loss. I wish there had been something more we could have done about the boy."

He did not mention the baby. Deaths of such young children from accident and disease were common, and were barely noteworthy by those who had seen so much of it over their years spent on the trail.

Abe shook the Colonel's hand and told him, "Yours isn't the easiest of jobs." Then, needing to change the subject, he asked, "What did you say to Jebb that made him apologize?"

"I told him if he didn't, I'd be forced to shoot him."

"And you would have, wouldn't you?"

"I would've had to." The Colonel's quick smile came and went. "Of course, it might not have been fatal."

Abe nodded thoughtfully and walked toward his wagon.

The Colonel later commented to Bob, who repeated it to Nancy, that there were few men he had ever instinctively liked and respected more than Abe Carrington. Nancy had mixed feelings upon hearing this. Her first reaction was to feel chagrinned about how coldly she had recently treated her husband.

This brief moment of self-revelation was followed by a strong urge to justify why she so often felt stand-offish. But she knew this wasn't fair. None of what had happened had been Abe's fault. It probably wasn't even her fault. But was there no one to be blamed?

Nancy couldn't rid herself of her guilt over what she felt was her failure to properly care for her baby. She couldn't bear anyone knowing how Alice really died, in the night and alone. This would later motivate her to tell others that Alice had died when thrown from the wagon, as happened to so many children on the trail. It was considered an event that placed no blame on anyone, and eventually she would think the lie more real than the truth.

Onward the wagons advanced, the barren sagebrush-covered land the same as it had been for centuries except for the deep grooves in the road carved over the years by thousands of wagons. These wheel ruts, some two feet deep, assured the Colonel of being on the correct road, especially considering that they were lined with telegraph poles that followed much of the route.

Nancy commented to the Colonel, "I'm amazed that some tribe hasn't destroyed the telegraph lines by now."

"They've been told the wires reach the White Chief in Washington," he chuckled, "and that if they cut the lines, the Great Chief will instantly know and send thousands of blue coats to seek revenge. During the installation some of the crews met with resistance, but now, since the poles and wire do no damage to the land or the game, they don't need to push the point."

The people on the train watched the river make a wide sweep north away from their road. The meadow through which they moved dwindled down into a small flat of land between the river and a low bluff topped with large rocks, so the wagons were forced to make yet another crossing of the Sweetwater. They did this at St. Mary's Crossing Stage Station and planned to then stay on the north side of the river all the way to South Pass.

They received the latest news of the war at the station. General Lee and his Rebel forces had crossed the Potomac River. To meet this challenge the Union had called to action 100,000 "volunteers". That night at council, Buran spoke aloud what they all had on their minds.

"If we hadn't left when we did, we'd be among those called up." The men that heard this looked at him with solemn faces.

Some nodded their agreement, while others just looked into the fire. But not one disagreed with him.

They were now close to the famous wide and barren gap in the mountains called South Pass. This was the point of the Pacific watershed where they could see the creeks and rivers running west instead of east. While yet a few miles from that point, however, they were confronted with a major split in the trail, and therefore a major decision had to be made.

At council, the Colonel informed the men they would be taking the Lander's Cutoff north toward the old Fort Hall area in Idaho. He explained that there were fewer hills to stress the teams and good grazing all the way. This would help the teams remain in good condition, and better able to avoid breakdowns later during the last and most difficult leg of their journey.

As the Colonel expected, some of the men wanted to continue through South Pass and then cut over Sublette's Cutoff to the old Fort Hall Road. Some suggested then turning west 55 miles before Fort Hall via Hudspeth's cutoff. Others wanted to go southwest toward Fort Bridger so they could renew supplies, even though it would mean several hundred miles added to the wear on the animals. After much patient rebuttal and explanation, and more than a little firm insistence, the Colonel got everyone to agree to the newer Lander's Cutoff.

The next morning they left the main trail, crossing the Sweetwater as it turned north. Near the site of the Burnt Ranch Station, the long line of wagons swung right onto Lander's Road just as the sun rose high in a bright blue sky.

The Colonel had explained at Council that back in 1857 a Federal expedition had taken off from Missouri under the command of Frederick W. Lander, a civilian engineer. He had explored dozens of passes that had over time been considered as shorter routes. The route he recommended to Washington did not go through the popular South Pass, but instead followed farther up the Sweetwater, keeping to the line of an old trappers' trail. Funds were finally appropriated, and in 1858 gangs of laborers had been sent out to clear 44 miles of heavily forested country. This cut off several days travel from the customary route through South Pass to the Bear River and north to Fort Hall.

Chief Washakie and his Shoshone band lived in this area, and Frederick Lander needed the road to cut through the Chief's territory. In the 1850's the Chief was known to be one of the most peaceable Indians any traveler might have the pleasure of encountering, so Lander had easily negotiated for a right-of-way through the Chief's land. In exchange for merchandise given the Shoshone and other tribes, the travelers were allowed through-passage unmolested.

Lander had hired bridge builders from Maine, Mormons from the Salt Lake Valley, and Army drifters. He had also hired men who after backbreaking years of mountain prospecting considered such hard labor easy money. To create the pass, Lander's men moved 62,000 cubic yards of earth, felled hundreds of trees and bridged dozens of small streams. The new road had opened for travel in the summer of 1859 and in the first year alone there had been 13,000 people who had used it.

After crossing the Sweetwater and heading north into the mountains, the Colonel was quickly vindicated when everyone realized that here they had the three prime necessities of their current life: grass, water and wood. All were well distributed on Lander's Road, with the additional benefit that it was free from tolls at the bridges.

After several days, they also realized that this more isolated route had a bleak undertone that gave some of them the willies. Not only did it carry less traffic than the other routes, but some sections of the road were lined with thick forests of large trees that shaded them from the sun. Soon the people were commenting on the many rocky outcroppings that could be convenient hiding places for bloodthirsty Indians and villainous road agents.

Croat made it clear to Abe and Nancy that although the Shoshone Chief had been friendly in years past, there was no guarantee he would feel the same this year. He said this was especially true when so many more people than he had probably expected had funneled through his land on the narrow cutoff. When Abe saw the look of alarm on Nancy's face, he once again felt the urge to strike out at this man.

Crossing the Green River near its source was more difficult than they had anticipated, because although Lander had petitioned the Government for money to construct a bridge at this location, it had never been given him. Due to a recent storm, the water moved swiftly with run-off around large boulders that had washed down from near cliffs.

The Colonel, along with Bob and Chris, rode across where it looked most promising and found that it was not very deep. Wagon beds were raised by means of blocks and they crossed it at an angle so the swift flow could not knock them sideways.

Three-quarters of the way across, one of the Carrington wagon wheels caught on something beneath the water line and was stuck in the swift flow of the current. Abe was mounted on Flame next to the oxen that he prodded forward with a long stick. When he realized his wagon was stuck fast, he was instantly on the edge of panic. Nancy looked out from the front of the wagon at him with eyes wide with terror and his immediate desire was that nothing more happened to upset her. Todd started to climb out, but Abe yelled at him to stay put.

There was nothing for it but to get in the water and see if he could dislodge whatever was impeding the wheels. Croat and Hickly sloshed to his side as he reached the wheel, eager to help before their team blew up from being unable to get out of the water behind Abe's rig. Together they reached under the water to find that a tree branch was wedged between the spokes of the wheel. All three men struggled to dislodge it while the cold water rushed around them, saturated their clothes, chilled them through, and tried to push them over. Although difficult to maintain their footing, with a tug of strength brought on by desperation, they freed the wheel.

Abe tossed the branch into the water so that it floated away from the wagons and made to retrieve Flame. Just as he got his hand on the reins he slipped on the slick bottom and fell into the swift water. While struggling to regain his footing he could feel himself beginning to wash down the river away from the wagons. He gave a strangled shout and vaguely heard screams coming from the wagon train.

Just as he was beginning his negotiations with God, strong arms grabbed him and he felt a rope secured around his chest. Gasping for breath after being dragged from the water, he lay on the muddy bank unable to move. After blinking water from his eyes and rolling onto his side to retch, he realized he was on the opposite shore. Looking up into the dark face of an Indian brave whose body gleamed with droplets of water, he quickly removed the rope from under his arms and saw that the other end had been tied around a tree. Before he could decide whether or not he should replace his gratitude with fear, Chris rode up leading Flame.

The Indian quickly moved away but Chris raised his hand in greeting to the brave that he recognized from the Snake tribe. Abe stood up and looked at the Indian. Not knowing if he would be understood, he said, "Thank you, my friend."

Chris said something unintelligible to the Indian and the brave looked at Abe with surprise, possibly at a white man showing him gratitude, or maybe it was his use of the word *friend*. Abe thought it appropriate for someone who had just saved his life.

While Abe had been on his float trip down the river, Bob had helped Nancy get the wagon across the river. When Abe reached his wagon, he was immediately embraced by a recalcitrant Nancy. She clung to him while repeating over and over, "Oh, Abe, I'm so sorry. I'm so sorry."

Abe did not ask her what she was sorry about, but pulled back from her and said, "I've gotten your dress wet."

"I don't care." She threw her arms around his neck again and added, "I only care that you're here with me."

"Yeah, I'm kind of happy about that too."

She smiled up at him and returned to the practical. "Come on. Let's get the blocks out and dry off anything in the wagon that got wet. And you need to change into dry clothes right away."

Todd, who had watched it all from the back of the wagon while gripped in a terror he had never before known, came up to his father to help with the cleaning. Todd wanted to throw his arms around Abe too, but instead simply told him, "Glad you're safe, Dad."

Abe understood and smiled, gripping his son's shoulder and giving it a squeeze before saying, "Thanks for your help."

While everyone cleaned and rearranged the contents of their wagons, they spent additional time and energy swatting at the irksome mosquitoes that buzzed their ears. While the people could swat themselves and cover their skin, the animals could not, and were soon overcome beyond what the switching of tails could shoo away.

While Todd went to check on the milk cow and their loose stock, Abe climbed inside the wagon and changed out of his soaked clothing. After a few minutes, Nancy joined him in the wagon. Abe was sitting on a small keg while putting on dry socks that Nancy had knitted for him during the odd free minutes she had to herself before retiring for the night.

She collapsed at his feet with her long skirts bunched around her. Wrapping her arms around his legs, she rested her head on one of his knees and after a moment began to quietly weep. Abe put his hand on her soft hair, bare of the bonnet usually covering it, and debated whether or not he should try to comfort her or just let her cry it out.

After a moment, Nancy pulled a square of cloth from her pocket and wiped her eyes. "I'm so sorry, Abe. I'm so sorry."

"For what, love?"

"For all that's happened and how I've treated you. I'm just so afraid."

"Of what?"

"Of feeling...anything."

Abe nodded and looked out through the front drape of the canvas. All around them ranged the familiar sounds of chirping crickets, snuffling horses, and the shouts of people setting up camp. Turning back to his wife, he cupped the side of her face with his hand. "But, Nan, all feelings don't lead to bad ones. Good ones are just what they are, and nothing more. You're allowed to have them."

She turned her head and kissed his hand, then looked up to meet his eyes. "Sometimes, when I feel like laughing, or see something and find it interesting or pretty, I feel suddenly guilty. How am I able to recognize humor or beauty, or enjoy anything?"

"You do because it's who you are. You've always seen humor or irony in situations. Your personality hasn't changed, just your situation."

"You're so good to me, Abe. And I do love you so."

"I know." He leaned down and kissed her forehead. "This is a difficult time in our lives. But it's not the whole of our lives. We'll get through it, and anything else that comes our way too."

Abe's confidence and tenderness worked together to make Nancy feel better than she had in a long time. That night she put forth even more effort than usual to make a good dinner for them all. For dessert, she pulled out the fruit cake stored away for a special occasion and cut them all a thin slice.

While they ate, Todd looked up to see beyond the wagons a brave sitting by a line of trees chewing on something in the dry jerky line, but probably less pleasant. Recognizing him as the man who had saved his father, he stood up and hurried to him. Todd pointed back to their strong fire and made eating gestures, urging the man to join them. When the brave hesitated, Nancy stood up and held out her plate to him while smiling. He slowly walked forward and sat by the fire.

Nancy piled his plate with beans, two biscuits and a slice of fruit cake. When the brave tasted this last, he looked somewhat surprised. His smile as he looked at Nancy said clearly how much he liked it. Abe had only eaten half of his slice, and placed the remainder on the brave's plate. For a brief moment they looked into each others eyes, both smiling and both understanding.

The brave left immediately after eating, but Todd followed him several yards from the wagon. He stood and watched the man disappear into the trees and was overwhelmed with a longing to run after him. Such an unexpected urge both excited and disturbed him, and he quickly returned to his family.

During a short but heavy rain storm that night, the Carringtons huddled in their wagon. This storm meant that when morning arrived everyone needed to once again dry out their wagon, and as the men began this task some of them grumbled at the delay in getting started.

These same men also began suggesting that maybe the Colonel should have listened to them and taken the route over South Pass. The Colonel pulled these few aside and told them to stop fomenting dissention or he'd throw them off the train. They did not complain again.

Nancy could never be sure if she had awakened just before or just after the explosion. Her first awareness was of Abe on his feet in the dim first light of day clutching a gun and looking beyond the circle of wagons, through the trees and toward Smith's Fork of the Bear River. Even so, it took Nancy a moment to realize that the noise had not been Abe's gun that had just been used. Todd climbed out of the wagon, still pulling on his second boot.

"Where did that come from?" Nancy whispered.

Todd said, "I think it was down by the river."

By then men in every wagon were pulling on boots and pants while gathering together their guns, although no one knew what to do with them. The Colonel, along with Bob and Chris, could be seen riding toward a line of trees along the river. It was only minutes before they were heading back, but this time Bob was leading his horse and hustling a man before him.

"Abe, isn't that Jebb with them?"

"I think you're right. What on earth has that son of a bitch been up to now?"

Nancy suggested, "Maybe he was doing some early morning hunting."

"No. The Colonel told us at council last night that it wouldn't be allowed around here. The tribes in the area are already unhappy, and us killing their game could start trouble."

Trouble of course was the polite euphemism for attacking and massacring. Nancy knew this, but wondered if Jebb would care how much trouble he might cause.

The current rotation had the Carrington wagon situated behind the wagon used by the Colonel and the scouts that was always first in line. Bob gathered together Abe and the others nearby while Chris and Harry continued to ride along the line of wagons. They were all informed that there would be no time for breakfast that morning. Instead, they were to load up and get under way as fast as possible. No one complained at this unusual command, knowing it would not have been given if there was not an urgent reason for it.

Abe and Nancy made Todd stay in the wagon while they waited for the Colonel to give the signal to move forward. Nancy moved close to Abe's side and realized that it was the quietest morning start they had ever accomplished.

They had gone less than a mile when they crested a hill and saw waiting at the bottom a line of mounted and elaborately painted Indians facing them. The whole of the space between the side hills was blocked by them. The Colonel, riding his horse next to the lead wagon with Bob at his side, raised his hand as a signal for the wagons to stop. There was no time, or for that matter space among the rocks and brush on either side of the trail, to circle the wagons.

Three Indians broke from the line and rode up the hill toward them. The Colonel also rode forward and they met about 300 feet from the train. Abe and Nancy watched the Indians angrily gesturing and shouting as they pointed toward the line of wagons. The Colonel put up his hands in a placating gesture and nodded his head in what looked like agreement. This seemed to calm the painted warriors. They sat quietly on their horses in a waiting attitude as the Colonel turned in his saddle and waved to Bob to join them. Bob did not look happy, but he rode forward as bidden.

There was a short exchange between Bob and the Colonel before Bob turned and rode back to the train. He rode quickly past the Carrington's position and returned shortly leading a horse carrying a wildly protesting and terrified Jebb. His hands had been tied to the saddle horn.

"You can't do this," he screamed. What protest might have been offered by the others when they realized Jebb was meant as a sacrifice to the Indians, died on their lips when Jebb screamed, "It was just a dirty squaw and her brat."

Bob rode steadily on, past the wagons of horrified people, and toward the Colonel and the waiting Indians. Bob's hand was locked tight on the reins of Jebb's mount until he reached the Colonel, whereupon he handed the reins to him. This made the final act of turning over Jebb to the Indians the Colonel's responsibility alone.

The Colonel immediately laid the rope across the outstretched palm of an Indian who sat his horse straight and proud, and who focused thunderous scowls of rage upon Jebb. The Colonel forced himself to briefly meet the brave's eyes before turning his horse and riding back to the train with Bob by his side. They took up their post next to the lead wagon and waited for the tribe to withdraw. The Indians meanwhile had ridden down the hill leading Jebb's horse that had to gallop to keep up, making it clear they were impatient to get their prisoner to camp. Jebb had given up screaming, quite possibly because he had given up hope as well.

The Indians, however, went no further than the bottom of the hill. While pointedly continuing to block the trail, they built a fire that was soon blazing. There was keen planning in the Indian's actions, for now everyone on the train was forced to be witness to what happened to one who would dare to rape one of their women, and then slit her throat when done with her. Her three year old child, forced to watch, had then been shot between the eyes.

Whether in shock of what was happening, fear of what might happen when the Indians were finished with Jebb, or the extreme heat of the day, those in the wagons were soon sweating profusely. The Colonel, the scouts, and Abe after he was properly instructed, rode the length of the train. The women and children were instructed to stay inside the wagons where they could not see out. The men were told to stay with their wagons and that no matter what they heard, not to react in any way.

That was not easy after the screaming began. At first they heard short cries of shocked pain repeated several seconds apart. Eventually the scream was so drawn out that it seemed there was no space for air to be taken in. It was all of twenty minutes before silence came, and during this time more than one of those forced to listen became sick. Every person on the train old enough to comprehend what was happening would relive those minutes in an occasional nightmare for the rest of their lives.

Not long past noon, the Indians left the area and the Colonel started the train forward. Mothers made sure the children could not see out of the wagons, and only a few of the women dared to look. The men and Lona had no choice as they led their teams past the skinned and charred remains of Jebb, left in plain sight by the side of the road. Their only distraction was their need to control their animals when the acrid stench of death reached them.

That night Nancy asked Abe, "Why didn't the Colonel stop to bury Jebb's remains?"

"He said it was a way to show the Indians that Jebb wasn't really one of us, and that we had no objection to what they did."

Todd noticed the clench of Abe's jaw and asked, "Did anyone object when you rode back to tell them what to expect and not to react to it?"

"Not really. Several started to, but when I told them of his offense, they changed their mind."

Unlike most events shared on the trail, that night at council there were no jokes, no sly references, no suggestions as to how else it could have been handled, and no speculation over what exactly had been done to Jebb. No one ever spoke of it again while together on the trail, and very few times after that.

During the darkest part of the night two days following this horrific episode, Nancy got up from her pallet under the wagon after concluding that sleep was not to be. She walked a short distance from the wagon, her mind crowded with the grimness of Jebb's death, the stress of her own losses, and the general harshness and fatigue of her days. She was overwhelmed by the meanness of life, and her nerves were stripped bare. She longed to hide among the cool vegetation around her where the low keening and wailing of her misery could go unheard, and she could beat on her chest until the ache of her grief was replaced by the bruising on her skin.

At the same time, she kept reminding herself that count-less other women had lost children, husbands, and other family members. They were going about the business of daily living and showing no hysterics. She knew they had to be grieving, but they were also living. "What's wrong with me," she asked herself, "that I'm not always so sure that I want to do that any more? Facing each day is just too hard."

The best thing she had, and that kept her going, was seeing Todd behaving so normally. But her baby girl was gone and buried, and would never be in her arms again. She had also given up the last vestige of hope that Harold would be found. So she slumped to the ground and let the bark of a tree cut into her back while holding to her bosom the bonnet that Alice had so often worn and one of Harold's shirts that she had not as yet laundered. And she wept. When she was afraid her sobs might be too loud, she bit down on the bonnet and buried her face in the shirt so no one could hear.

But one person did. Todd watched his mother's agony from the shadow of a near tree, and wished he too could cry like that. His omnipresent guilt, lurking in the dark recesses of his mind through all he did, now burst into the forefront of his awareness. It filled his chest and choked his throat, just as it did every time he looked at his mother and saw the pain just below the surface of her façade of calm.

Todd knew that the loss of Alice would have been lessened if Harold had been there to comfort her. Harold had always had an intuitive understanding of their mother's needs, knowing just the right thing to say. To Todd, Alice was a sad loss that would heal, but he felt that the abandonment of Harold was a catastro-phe that would alter the family forever. And it was his fault. He should have made sure Harold was safe. He should have gone with him, even if it would have been to also die.

In his mind, all the pain of his mother, and the silent sadness of his father when he looked into the distance without blinking, was his fault. He felt their accusation was not in the way they looked at him, but in the way they avoided looking at him. He had no idea that it was simply preoccupation as Nancy and Abe learned how to cope with loss while also dealing with the pressing and immediate demands of daily life on the trail.

For Todd, a boy almost a man, his frustration was that he could not fix or change any of it. But he thought it his responsibility to at least try to make things better, and after much thought on the subject, he arrived at what he felt was the right solution.

Todd turned away from his weeping mother trying to hide her grief from everyone, and his father who paced continually while on guard duty, and went in search of the mountain man Croat.

CHAPTER NINE
IDAHO
AUGUST, 1863

"I am beginning to feel like myself again, and begin to think about our life in Oregon. Harold and Alice were gifts in my life, and although I had them for too short a time, I hold on to every precious memory. But life, and this train, must go on."

Nancy

"80 days on the trail. Very warm. We're making good time and enjoying steady good grazing. If only we could have it all the way to Oregon."

Abe

The night before, Todd had asked to sleep in the tent rather than in the wagon as he had been doing. Now Abe approached the tent, surprised that his son was not already up and helping load the wagon. On the floor of the empty tent, starkly denuded of Todd's bedroll and sack of clothes, lay a note. Abe finished reading it and caught his breath. For the first time since he was ten and his best friend had been adopted and moved far from the orphanage, Abe fought the urge to collapse on the ground and weep. Before he could give way, however, he heard someone behind him and turned to find Buran watching him.

Buran saw Abe's pale face and overly bright eyes. "What's wrong?"

Abe handed him the note. Reading aloud in a low voice, Buran murmured, *"I have caused too much pain. We all know it was my fault Harold wandered off. I'm a constant reminder to you that I failed to protect him and I can no longer bare to witness the grief I've caused. I have decided to go away with Croat and Hickly. I'll earn my way with them, and will meet up with you at Fort Hall or in Oregon. Please do not come after me. I love you both. Todd"*

Buran looked up at Abe. "Has Nancy seen this?"

Abe swallowed with difficulty and shook his head. "Is Croat's wagon really gone?"

"I passed the wagon on the way here. But their riding horses and the mules that pulled it are gone."

"So they packed out. That means they'll be moving fast."

Fighting through a momentary desire to grab his horse and tear out after Todd, Abe instead took the note from Buran and walked resolutely toward Nancy by the wagon. Buran slapped Abe's shoulder and went to find Effie.

Unsure if he could speak, Abe simply handed her the note. She did not break down or cry. She simply folded the note and put it in the pocket of her apron before bending over the fire and continuing to fry the morning bacon. "Would you mind milking the cow, Abe? Then you can fold up the tent and put it in the wagon. Breakfast will be ready by the time you're finished. We have to be ready to pull out."

"Nan..."

"Not now." She pushed the cooked bacon to the edge of the large skillet and poured in the sliced potatoes left over from the night before. They were the last they would have until reaching a supply depot.

Abe felt a hot surge of resentment and anger hit his stomach, and he wondered how he would be able to eat at all. For a change he was the one who wanted to talk and speculate. Where might they be headed? Where could he and Nancy catch up with them? But mostly he wanted to take out after them and upon finding Croat, beat him into a quivering mass of bleeding parts.

When Nancy saw Abe looking in the direction of Flame, she merely said, "We need to respect his wishes and not follow right now."

"You don't seem surprised, or upset."

"I'm very upset. But in an odd way, I'm not as surprised as I should be. At least we know he's alive. We'll find him."

"What did we do wrong?" Abe lamented. "How could he think we'd be better off without him?"

Nancy shook her head. "Maybe right now he's better off without *us*."

"Shouldn't we talk more about this?"

"There'll be time enough for that later. Besides, no amount of talk will change things."

He did not want to accept her logic, but he had no choice. "You're right. If he's not in the Fort Hall area, it shouldn't be that difficult to track their direction. They're an unlikely looking group. They'll be noticed."

Nancy said nothing. She was pretty sure the three of them would not go in the same direction as themselves. They would probably head west across Hudspeth's Cutoff to the Raft River on the California trail near the City of Rocks, 72 miles south of Fort Hall.

She had studied the maps closely before leaving St. Joseph, and she realized that being on horses with pack mules, this would not be a bad route for them. For wagons, it was a route of great toil without the advantage of time gained as a reward for conquering a series of steep hills and enduring a lack of water for the first 20 miles. But she chose not to share these musings with anyone, knowing that they had to stay with the train and let events play out as they would. Besides, she told herself, Todd will probably change his mind in a few days and back-track to us.

Before the train reached the long flat trail into the old Ft. Hall area, it was necessary that they climb Big Hill. It was the steep ascent that Abe had dreaded since Bob had described it to the men, but he was relieved to find that it did not require extra animals to be hitched on the wagons to get up to the top.

The descent to the valley floor, although slippery, was just gradual enough for them to travel downward without the need to attach drags or winch the wagons down with ropes. It took several hours for them to slowly follow the winding trail back and forth down the steep hill into the valley of the Bear River. With great relief they stopped for the nooning on the flat grassy land of the Fort Hall Bottoms.

The Shoshone tribes in the area of Fort Hall, with its expanding farms and few remaining supply depots, were known to be peaceable. This had not been the case a few months before. Gabe told them that soldiers had massacred hundreds of hostiles during the Bear River Revolt and now a new treaty was in place. Consequently, the Colonel felt it was a good place for the wagons to circle for the night. Water was plentiful and so was grass, and from a small trading post they were able to re-supply themselves with flour, salt, beans, and even potatoes.

Situated on a slight elevation of land less than a mile from the Snake River, back in '49 the fort had been a fur trading post of the Hudson's Bay Company. It had also been an important way-station on the trail that had helped early travelers at a point of desperation in their journey, but it had been deserted in 1855. The wood portion of the old fort had been used to construct a stage station three miles away at the Spring Creek bridge, and now all that remained were a few adobe walls that had survived the elements and a great dissolving flood the previous year.

It had, in fact, been a flood so momentous that during its high point it had created a giant inland sea covering the vast Sacramento Valley. For months this had kept food and other supplies from reaching the eastern side of the Sierra. This historic weather event, and the consequent scarcity of food for both settlers and Indians, was one of the underlying causes that precipitated the Owens Valley Piute War of the 1860's.

At council there in the Fort Hall Bottoms the Colonel reminded the men that they had now completed the second major leg of their journey, having traveled 535 miles from Fort Laramie, or a total of almost 1,200 miles in 85 days. They were a little more than half way to their destination, and even though feeling the discomfort of the heat and not looking forward to the next leg that would take them through fearful deserts, the travelers were for a time filled with the naïve optimism of those who have fared well.

After questioning the owners of the trading post, and even some of the Indians hanging around its porch, Abe and Nancy had to accept the fact that Croat, Hickly and Todd had not traveled through the area. Abe realized the trio had probably headed west on Hudspeth's Cutoff. This meant Todd was on his way to California, and according to his note, he had not anticipated this. Had his role with the mountain men turned from fellow traveler to something more sinister? This became the worry Abe and Nancy discussed as they huddled in the wagon in an attempt to avoid the chill night air.

"When they reach the Raft River Valley," Abe reasoned, "they'll be at the junction in the trail where Hudspeth's Cutoff ends. If we head down to California, we'll pass that junction and be on the same road with them."

"But they'll be on horseback and traveling faster than we can."

"Yes." He took Nancy's hands and held them in his as he looked into her eyes. "It'll also mean that we'll end up in California instead of Oregon."

Nancy lay her head on his shoulder and declared, "Then we go to California. It can't be that bad."

To lighten their wagon even more Abe discarded the mackinaw blanketing and tore out the wooden cupboards along the sides. Nancy tossed out the butter churn and the tent.

Nine miles after leaving the Fort Hall Bottoms, and not far from an active beaver dam, the train crossed one by one over an old bridge spanning the shady banks of the Portneuf River. Soon reached was the wide-bottomlands of the Snake River.

The dark blue water flowed past them, its green margins of short grass ending abruptly at the foot of the brown hills that walled them in. It was a vivid tapestry of blue, green and brown, and terrifying in its limitation of movement. The only way was forward.

Tall rushes crowded the wet areas and the travelers eyed the wet herbage with longing. Several of the families wanted to stay by the river after crossing it, since it appealed so much after the long exhausting day. But the Colonel would hear none of it. He kept them moving, and when they complained he assured them that the mosquitoes would soon make them regret any decision to stay.

Bob also explained that the wet herbage would not agree with the cattle like the dry grasses on the side hills. Many still grumbled, but no one put up much resistance, and they continued on as the Colonel had decided they would. Besides, he had done a good job of instilling in them a fear of the Bannock Indians who lived along the Snake River.

"Odd looking critters," Gabe commented after showing up just in time to get the last of Nancy's coffee. She, however, was not present, being at Lona Hasting's wagon. Gabe explained to Abe, "The Bannocks grow long forelocks at the front of their scalps and then sweep 'em back over their heads to hang down the back of their necks. Good hunters. Used to be peaceable. Not now though."

Abe felt the knot in his stomach tighten. Everyone had heard of the massacre that had taken place in August the year before, and they would soon be passing through the site of that attack. Only eleven wagons had been in that train. Vulnerable by their scant number, they were easy pickings for the 200 Indians that descended on them from the tall rocks. Two other trains had come together with that one after helping to bury the dead, and then had continued on as one train of almost 200 wagons strong. Abe could only imagine how awful it would be to come upon such a massacre. Of course, it would be worse being part of the wagon train that had been attacked, but he almost superstitiously refused to think about that.

Abe finally managed to change the subject to cattle and guns. But when Nancy returned, Gabe seemed eager to leave, assuming that she wouldn't be feeling very friendly toward old single men, what with her kid having left with two of them. Truth to tell, under his beard and old clothes, Gabe was only forty.

As much as Abe longed to talk to Nan about all that Gabe had told him, he didn't want to add to her worry and decided against it. So Nancy surprised him at dinner that night when she said, "Some of the women were telling me about a massacre that happened last year in the rocks up ahead. It's surprising that anyone survived at all."

Abe sighed, once again amazed at the straightforward practicality of women. Why were men taught to treat them as fragile creatures in need of constant protection? He thought of Lona Hastings and how easily she was managing on her own.

He brought his focus back to the subject at hand. "Some of the men were talking about the massacre at council tonight. Then Gabe came by, and you know him and his love of gory details. The Colonel told us to make a show of our weapons and move along as quickly as we can through that area. We're a big train, at least until we get to the Raft River and split, so we shouldn't have any problems."

For several days they passed along the edge of a long, deep and meandering canyon, at the bottom of which coursed the Snake River. Peering cautiously over the edge, they could see far below them a channel cut through ancient lava rock, but only occasional glimpses of the glistening twisting flow of the Snake. While still a mile away, they heard the roar of the American Falls as the water cascaded over a steep rock barrier on its way to join the river below. Gabe was quick to explain that in the early days before wagons had come this way, a boat load of American fur trappers had gone over the fifty foot fall to their death.

Abe's fellow travelers enjoyed swapping tales of what they had heard about the places through which they were passing, especially the more harrowing tales. But once surrounded by the giant piles of boulders and overhanging cliffs where the previous year's massacre had taken place, everyone kept quiet. Even the teams seemed to sense that it would be best to keep their heads down and move forward without balking.

When they reached Rock Creek, they were only two miles past the site of the massacre. All the same, everyone breathed easier and welcomed the rest of an hour's stop. After crossing a small stream, they strained up through several deep gorges cut in the rock. Once on the other side of beautiful Beaver Creek, they circled up among trees and enjoyed the fresh clear water.

As happy as they were to have reached this point in Idaho without incident, it was a sad time for many. In the morning they would cross the Raft River and then separate from one another, most to continue on to Oregon but about two dozen heading to California. Abe and Nancy especially dreaded the moment they would have to say farewell to the Howards. Nancy remembered only too well Effie's disdain for those going to California.

When they approached the Howard wagon after dinner, Buran advanced toward them. "There'll be no good-byes today," he declared. "We're going to California too."

Effie came forward, looking penitent. "We're heading for Placerville on the western slope of the Sierra. Buran heard that it's a busy commercial center and wants to open a shop there."

Abe and Buran shook hands as they grinned while Nancy and Effie hugged in their exuberance. How nice it was to be traveling a little while longer with friends who had shared so much.

"When did you decide this?" Nancy asked Effie.

"We had considered it before, but we rejected the idea when so many people expressed the opinion that we would be hobnobbing only with ruffians." Giving Nancy and Abe a fond glance, she added, "I now realize how silly that was."

Abe said, "We may not end up living in the same town, but at least we'll be in the same state. After finding Todd, we might even consider Placerville too."

The next morning, the train headed out for the last time as one. Then, a few miles later they arrived at the split in the trail, with those going to Oregon turning right. It was difficult saying good-bye to the Colonel, who shook Abe's hand and said, "It's been a great pleasure having you on this trip. Your help and influence was a good one."

"Thank you. We were certainly fortunate having you as our guide. The travelers you take across in the future will be getting the best available."

"Well, I hope so, but it won't be me. I've decided to settle in a little town in Oregon called Eugene. My brother lives there." Again shaking Abe's hand, he said, "If you're ever in Oregon, look me up. At the least, I'd sure like to hear from you once you're settled."

Half an hour later the Colonel, and many of those with whom they had lived for months, rumbled away from them and were soon hidden by a cloud of dust that when cleared by the wind revealed an empty road.

Abe told Nancy of his conversation with the Colonel, but she didn't seem that impressed. "Nice for him, but the rest of the train has him all the way to Oregon. What will we do for leadership?"

"Bob will be with us. He's decided he wants to live in Sacramento. The whole thing will be settled at council tonight."

And indeed it was. That night, the much reduced train organized themselves into a council that now included the women of the train. After a decision that appeared to have already been made by everyone except Abe and Nancy, Abe found himself elected as Captain. Turning to Bob, thinking he would be offended by the decision, Abe instead found him grinning and his hand out. "The Colonel always thought you were a natural leader. Guess others see it too."

Abe's blush turned his ruddy skin dark. "Well, I hope you won't be keeping yourself too far away."

"Don't worry," Bob assured him. "We'll get everyone through."

That night Abe and his fellow travelers slept fitfully, aware that restless Bannock Indians could be within shouting distance.

The next morning the much reduced train prepared to head out under the guidance of Captain Carrington who, before starting through the Raft River Valley, addressed everyone. "We've come two-thirds of the way to a goal. Although there have been losses and tragedy for many of us, Bob says it's imperative that we understand that this last leg is going to be by far the most challenging part of the trip."

"That's right, folks." Bob stepped forward. "The descent into the Big Goose Creek area is the worst you've done so far and the desert crossings will be pure hell. We won't run out of water or supplies as some have done in years past, but the daytime heat and the night cold will be a shock. So be sure your rigs are in good repair. After that, when we get to the desert, feed and water your animals as much as you can when it's available."

From the Raft River to Goose Creek was 65 dusty miles, and it took them five days. They kept to the west bank of the narrow Raft River, only crossing it once, but the road after the crossing was solid and well-maintained in appearance, if somewhat dusty along Cassia Creek.

Their animals lurched over and between boulders and rocks strewn in the confines of what had been promised them to be an improved trail. With everyone worrying about the strength of their wagons, they had to wonder what it had been like before the so-called improvements. The close canyon walls reverberated with the noise of the splashing, rattling wagons and the shouts of men directing their straining teams. Several times a wagon wheel got stuck between small boulders, and the wagon had to be lifted free with the help of the men working together.

As the train traveled through rough mountains with strange steeple-like formations around them, the wagons were shaken and tossed by the rocky trail. A woman in one of the wagons had fallen ill and her husband had prepared for her a soft bed of blankets and quilts. But she was thrown about so severely that she soon begged him to allow her to walk. When he told her she was too weak, she told him, "If I fall, I'd rather be left by the side of the road to die than have to spend another hour beaten blue by my own wagon." He helped her out, and although at first she struggled, after an hour she was feeling almost well again.

After this stressful section of the trail, they arrived at what some called the Valley of Rocks and others called the City of

Castles. After passing through a narrow opening in the tall rocks they entered into a large green meadow of long grass scattered with boulders. Cutting through the center of this green amphitheater was the flow of a clear pure stream. They felt they had been given a glimpse of heaven as their reward for enduring the last hellacious portion of the journey.

Here they camped while surrounded by the immense rocks whose jagged tops poked up almost to the clouds, and that encouraged the game of naming the rocks for their odd shapes. Whether a castle turret or a giant barrel, all were massive and lent a strange and dreamlike quality to their camp site. Carved and painted on these rocks were the names of past travelers, so of course several more were immediately added. The only thing the teams and loose stock were interested in was eating their fill of the cool grass before laying down their exhausted bodies to rest on it.

Leaving reluctantly the next morning, the wagons emerged from the mountains and soon were carefully and gradually descending into the wide green of Junction Valley. Anyone emerging from the Salt Lake Road would confront the strange Steeple Rocks that looked to Nancy like two gigantic arrowheads protruding from a low mound of earth.

Although they told themselves it was useless, Abe and Nancy kept watching for movement on the Salt Lake Road, hoping someone would be there to join with their small train--and who might have seen Todd. In past years when the trail had been much busier, meeting up with those from Salt Lake City had been an important and eagerly awaited event. But on this day, no wagons or pack trains curved up through the canyon.

After another hour of travel, the stock was allowed to graze near a small creek while the people ate their mid day meal. The men could not resist occasionally glancing nervously ahead, and this in turn made the women edgy. Since the 1840's, tales had been legion about the desert, its lack of water and feed, and abundance of alkali dust. It was well known that thousands of animals had died while traveling along the Humboldt River.

Before this, however, they would have to complete the 16 miles from the junction over Granite Mountain and down into Big Goose Creek. In the early 1830's, fur trappers like Joseph Walker and Kit Carson had hunted beaver here. These men of legend were the pathfinders that had established this route along the Raft River to Goose Creek, and then on to Bishop's Creek, which was the headwaters of Mary's River now called the Humboldt. But Kit Carson traveled in the historic tracks of Joseph Walker only part of the way along the Humboldt. Abe's train would go the whole way.

After a tiring but uneventful climb up the steep Granite Mountain, they perched on the summit and enjoyed a sublime view of mountain ridges and blue sky. But they couldn't ignore that they were about to travel five miles down to Goose Creek through a deep green ravine scattered with wild flowers. It had been improved since the early years and a series of twenty foot perpendicular drops had been eliminated, but in some places they would still be faced with the long and arduous job of slowing the wagons with drags and chains on the wheels. Travelers in the past had called this area The Devil's Grave, and Nancy thought it a most appropriate name.

The front of each wagon almost kissed the dirt as it tilted forward and began its downward slide with the wagons dragging branches and heavy chains. Using mules because of their strength and agility, only one team of animals was hitched on to keep the wagon tongue from dragging. Even so, the mules carefully placed their feet as quickly as they could when they felt unfamiliar pressure from behind.

Almost to the bottom, after miles of this torture, a wagon rolled onto its side and slid to the bottom while dragging the mules with it. When Abe realized that the family had been walking behind and out of the way when their wagon turned over, he called out, "Didn't anyone have the reins of the mules when the wagon went down?"

The confused family stared at him for a moment before the man blurted out, "Bob was leading the team from the ground on the other side."

It took a dozen men, but they quickly righted the wagon. Beneath it they found the lifeless twisted body of Bob Cook mashed into the dirt. Abe was overcome with shock and for a moment could not move or speak. Only when he felt Nancy's hand on his arm as she gently shook him was he able to take command of the situation. Nancy walked to a group of women at the bottom of the hill, and with her voice breaking, told them the news. When they began to weep, Nancy found she could no longer hold back her own anguish and tears.

Buran and Gabe picked up the body of their friend and carried it a short distance from the trail. After the last wagon reached the Goose Creek bottoms, a grave was dug on a small hillock of ground covered in wild flowers and everyone surrounded the grave with their sadness freely displayed.

Abe managed to say a few words about how much Bob had meant to them all, and everyone nodded sadly in agreement. When Abe choked and no amount of clearing his throat allowed him to continue, Buran stepped forward and finished the eulogy. Each man who walked past threw a handful of dirt into the grave, while the women dropped in bunches of wildflowers. After the women had returned to their wagons, the men covered the grave with a pile of rocks before they too returned to their wagons. They had miles to travel before the end of the day.

The shock of Bob's death stayed with them as they reached a stream in the midst of a dry sagebrush gulley shadowed by white chalk cliffs that threw dark eerie shadows over the wagons. Exhausted animals lay down as soon as released from their harnesses and the camp was set up around them. But hunger also gnawed at the beasts, and after a short rest they rose slowly and allowed themselves to be led to grass and water.

The dust they had raised while setting up camp hung in the glow of their fires and made the gloom of twilight almost claustrophobic. However, everyone was stirred to action as a sudden drop in temperature presaged a cold thunderstorm that hit the area just as dinner was cooking, drenching the dispirited travelers and extinguishing their cooking fires. After half an hour, it passed on over the ridge. Without comment the resolute women rebuilt their fires and prepared the evening meal. The men checked the stock and found most of the animals that had bolted in the noisy storm.

Finally able to sit down for a few minutes, Nancy rested by the fire as it burned down enough to start cooking. Running her fingers over the tattered hem of her dress, she counted the small holes that peppered it and figured there was one hole for almost every fire tended. She couldn't wait until the time when she could burn the whole dress. It would mean they were finally at their destination.

After a simple meal was quickly eaten, Nancy set aside cooked potatoes for the next morning's breakfast and readied their bed for the night. Nothing altered the routine--not weather, not fatigue, and not even the death of a loved one.

CHAPTER TEN
NEVADA
SEPTEMBER, 1863

"I am constantly amazed at the cleverness and originality of the men when need arises.

Nancy

Exhaustion had become an old familiar friend to Nancy. Each night she greeted it and made peace with it, thinking that if she did then maybe it would not return. But always the next night it was there, mocking her youth and her former assumption that she was a hardy farm woman who was stronger and more resilient than her city sisters. What self-delusion it had been.

All around her were women who had started out barely able to climb in and out of a wagon on their own that now were as lithe as a girl; and those who had started strong and healthy that now had just as many blisters, were just as footsore, and just as dirty as every other woman. The trail was a great leveler, teaching humility as well as pride.

For several days they continued along Big Goose Creek through a dry flat landscape filled with sage, and broken only occasionally by streams that gave them grass and water at days end. It was barely enough of a respite for them to cool off from the relentless heat. But oxen, mules and horses that had been growing increasingly gaunt could eat and fill their bellies at least once a day, even if they were not allowed to linger long enough to fatten. Nor was there time each night for the people to fully rise above the weariness that plagued their every dragging step.

Those driving teams from within their wagons leaned forward and rested their arms on the wood of the wagon front for long periods, and often found themselves nodding off while their experienced mules followed the wagon in front of them. Those who walked next to their oxen dragged their feet and occasionally stumbled, and those who had horses rode a little more often.

If reality had been a pigeon, it would not only have come home to roost, but to mess on the optimism of those on the wagon train. So many children, spouses, siblings and friends had been lost either to disease or accident. Many families had also lost valued possessions and stock to Indians through barter or theft, and almost everyone had dumped along the road something of monetary or sentimental value.

On what was now referred to as the Carrington train, there were no young children in the wagons headed to California, as though only Oregon was fit to receive innocence into its bosom. But there were several young people a few years beyond puberty, and these were the ones who had so often danced at night. Now, they sat together after supper and talked in hushed tones.

This collective sense of loss and fatigue hung over the camp like a damp fog, and Abe was desperate to find a way to raise their spirits. But he could think of nothing

The mood was finally lightened when the Fairlies realized why their sixteen year old daughter Barbara took such long walks every evening. The Carpenters realized at the same time why their son Jason did the same.

The crying by Mrs. Fairlie as she jumped to a conclusion about what they had "been getting up to" on those walks was background noise to Mr. Fairlie's swearing and threats to have the boy hung. Gabe lost no time informing Abe and Nancy that such action had actually taken place years earlier when it was discovered that a boy had lain with a girl.

The crying and swearing by the Fairlies was soon countered by profuse apologies from Mr. Carpenter repeated every few minutes. Although Abe privately felt the girl should bear some of the responsibility for whatever had happened, the boy declared they were only talking and holding hands. After Mrs. Fairlie had a frank talk with her daughter, it was determined that indeed there was no need for a hasty wedding or a hanging. In fact, both parents agreed to let the smitten young people see one another in the presence of a chaperone.

This, however, was evidently not sufficient freedom for Barbara and Jason. Three days later after another wagon train was reported to be only a short ride ahead, each family discovered their off-spring missing along with two horses gone from their loose stock. A note told them they would be waiting in Reno, and married.

The parental reactions ranged between anger at one another and worry about their children, but all finally settled for acceptance of the fact that their families were now to be united. Disappointed that there was nothing more forthcoming from this amusing diversion, the women of the train soon focused again on their own families, much to the relief of their husbands.

As quickly as possible, the wagons passed through the white chalk cliffs and oddly shaped rocks of the Goose Creek Valley. The water was questionable, and the mix of old and recent remains of dead cattle were scattered over the ground. A few still had rotting flesh clinging to the carcass, but most were old bones showing evidence of wolves having gnawed on them.

Gabe told a few of his most lurid stories about these streams, back when they had been polluted with hundreds of dead and dying animals. This led him to recall stories about the many years when cholera and other diseases had decimated the trains. Because everyone listening to Gabe was feeling well, and their stock was in fairly good condition, they were superstitiously uneasy of the land around them. Might not this curse rise up to punish them for the impudence of being healthy?

Whenever the train stopped they now had to deal with what Gabe called Digger Indians, who were actually a composite of two tribes in the area. The women on the train were disgusted by the dirty and greasy appearance of these Diggers, but quickly learned to tolerate them. Everyone was afraid to affront any tribe, no matter their reputation for peacefulness. These nearly naked natives came into the camp at night looking for handouts while making themselves comfortable by the fires and making it clear that they expected to be waited on.

Bob had spoken to Abe about these Indians that he called the Shoshokoes. He had warned that if anyone on the train lost a steer or horse to these people, it would soon be roasted whole to feed their insatiable appetites. The other tribes in the area were stronger, so these impoverished people seldom found large game and were left only with crickets, grasshoppers, lizards, snakes and anything that moved too slowly to escape them. They had learned to prepare it all in innovative ways that propelled it into their stomachs as quickly as possible.

Utes were also in the area. Their name brought forth fear because of their past violent encounters with trains and their ability to steal horses in the night unheard. The Carrington train,
however, was not bothered by them. No, it was the Diggers,
small and seemingly shy, and filthy beyond anything those on
the train had ever witnessed, that quickly became a dreaded
pest. Trappers decades before had shot them for robbing beaver
traps, but this had not unduly turned them against white travelers, possibly because they saw them as porters of food.

Nancy and the other women gave the Indians bread, some
tossing it to them to avoid getting too near. The women whispered in shock among themselves after seeing some of the
Diggers picking lice from their bodies, and then eating the tiny
vermin. Lona suggested they all try to show compassion for
people so desperate. Nancy and the other women, somewhat
ashamed of themselves, agreed. But it was difficult not to show
some degree of disgust.

While the Diggers were in camp, Abe told everyone to keep a
close eye on their loose property. Not withstanding everyone's
attempts to follow this advice, when morning arrived several
people discovered items missing from their campsites. There
was no time to pursue their property, so they traveled on.

When almost through the area, a mule tied to the back of a
wagon jerked loose and bolted, and almost immediately slipped
and fell between two large rocks forming a "V". The frightened
mule brayed and flailed, and somehow managed to end up on its
back and firmly wedged in the rocks. Its owner, a business man
from New York, prepared to shoot it.

"Put that gun away," Abe yelled. "Get some long ropes over
here."

Abe lassoed the mule's head and with the help of three other
men, pulled the animal slowly forward. "Don't relax the pressure on the rope until he's well out or he'll fall back again."

The mule finally curled forward like a pill bug, with the whole
of its body following the drag of the neck. It stood on wobbly
legs at first, but after a few minutes of staggering around like a
saloon drunk, it shook its head and reached down to nibble at
the dry grass.

Abe pressed them to continue on, even past a clearing where
they could have circled early for the night. Some of the men
protested the fast pace Abe was setting, but after Abe pointed

out the moving shadows in the rocks everyone realized they were being watched by Utes and hurried along willingly.

The Utes wanted horses, not scalps, and only then if they could be obtained without much risk. There were too many wagons in this group, and the men wore a display of weapons on their bodies as though eager for a fight, so the few Indians in the rocks let them pass unmolested.

Relieved to be away from the threat of Indians, they were nevertheless not happy to be on a 15 mile dry stretch of trail that led them into more tall rocks. With the only thing in the distance a line of dull gray hills, the people looked across the dry short-grass valley with dread. The wind kicked up plumes of dust from the hills that settled into a canyon that swallowed the wagons into its narrow gullet. Thankfully, once through this passage they were rewarded by the sweet clear water of Rock Spring.

This was followed by Emigrant Spring, trickling over rock and into a shallow pool before flowing into the flats. Here they filled their casks and anything else that would hold water and then cut grass for the animals. They stored it in the wagons and quickly passed on four miles later to Mud Springs. It was much less pleasant. The land was marshy and the deer flies abundant and persistent.

Mr. Carpenter said his brother had written him from this location back in 1853 while on his own journey west. His brother wrote that the carcasses of dead animals crowded the pond edges and the stench of the rot was so bad they dare not linger.

"That accounts for the bones," Nancy commented as she looked at the copious piles littering the ground.

Emerging from a narrow pass through large rocks, they entered into another valley and found it covered with puddles both cool and steaming. A smoky mist of vapor covered the valley floor in the cool of morning, hovering above grass so long and lush that some of the small springs were covered by it.

The Colonel had spoken of this place that some called Thousand Springs Valley, so Abe was prepared. He had the men make poles from branches so they could walk ahead of the wagons while poking the ground before stepping forward. The dwindling number of loose stock was herded directly behind the wagons, and in this way no animal or person fell into these grass-covered pools.

Some of the springs they uncovered were so clear that they could see discarded wagon parts and even an old sheet iron stove at the bottom. It was not the first time they had come across wells or springs that had been fouled by such abuse of water. That it had been done by travelers like themselves made it all the more incredible.

Abe shook his head and said to one of the men next to him, "Amazing that anyone would do this after themselves having felt the torture of thirst."

"I'd like to plunge about a million of these damn mosquitoes in there," Mr. Carpenter complained as he swatted at his right ear.

Some of the men wanted to go left and rest a day or two at wells that were rumored to be a day away. Abe agreed that circling the hills to these wells would avoid the canyon ahead, but he told them of the poison springs that were along that route that Bob had described to him. He insisted they continue on without such a long detour, explaining that the day before he had spotted the dust of another train behind them.

"We need to be the first to arrive at whatever grass may be at the head of the Humboldt," Abe told them, "not getting whatever they leave. If it's a large train, there won't be anything left at all and we'll never make it across the desert."

No one could argue with this logic, so they accepted Abe's decision, even though it was Sunday and some would have preferred to stay put. They were rewarded when they arrived in narrow Bishop Canyon where they found a clean warm spring that the men sat in to rest their sore muscles. When it was the women's turn, they soaked not only their sore muscles but also a few clothes at the same time. Here everyone began contemplating the three-hundred miles of arduous travel along the Humboldt that lay ahead of them.

The rivers so far had either been an abundance of refreshment or had only been good enough for the stock. Although the presence of the Humboldt was fortuitous in giving them any water at all, it would be very limited in its relief. It started meager, ran to a powerful river, and eventually disappeared into a grassy marsh before blending into the Nevada sands.

At places crucial to survival, Abe had been told to expect large patches of marsh grass sufficient to almost satisfy the animals, and he hoped there would also be enough water that they could drain it into barrels. He was only too aware that it was because of an occasional such oasis that the last twenty years of migration through this hellish gateway to an uncertain future had been possible.

At first it was not so bad and their spirits rose toward optimism. The wagons rolled along the base of some high hills, then passed the last peak of the Ruby Range on the way to Mary's Fork coming in from the north. It was a small stream, but it was welcomed by the teams.

When they circled for the night on the north side of the Humboldt, six Utes approached them and offered to trade tiny fish for ammunition. Of course everyone knew that guns, ammo and liquor were things never to be traded. Instead, Lona offered them the last of Pete's tobacco and received in exchange two scrawny fish that she enjoyed that night after searing them in a hot skillet. Two men also offered tobacco, but nothing more.

After the Indians became convinced that nothing else would come their way, they left and crossed back over the river to the south and disappeared. Extra guards were posted with the stock that night and no one slept well as they kept their ears tuned to the sound of movement.

Yet even with all this precaution, a horse was missing in the morning. The guards insisted they had remained vigilant and were exceedingly puzzled as to how the theft had been accomplished. They were also embarrassed because the stolen horse had belonged to one of them. If more stock had been stolen, some of the men would have gone after it, but it had been an extra horse and going lame, so nothing was done about it. It had probably been eaten by then anyway. Abe spent a few minutes brushing dust from Flame's body just so he had an excuse to feel the comfort of touching his treasured horse.

After that the Indians were not seen, but instead eerily felt. Whether this was a reality or only a trick of the imagination, no one knew. Added to this stress, the hot sun seared their blistered skin, the powdery alkali dust billowed with the least suggestion of a breeze, and the urgency of travel weighed heavily upon everyone. Consequently, they ignored the abundance of rabbits in the brush, fish in the river, and even the occasional antelope. Instead, this easy food so near at hand teased their appetites and made a mockery of the hunger brought on by committing themselves to light rations. Water might occasionally be scarce, but Abe was determined they would not starve as some over the years had done.

Passing through the green valley of the North Fork of the Humboldt and near nondescript brown mountains, every night was much the same. The exception was that the brain-melting heat of day was replaced with a cold so sharp that those on guard duty refused to sit or stand in one place for long for fear of freezing. Water in the wash pans froze around any utensils left to soak, and clear sunny mornings were greeted with gratitude even with the knowledge of the heat to follow.

Faced with the rugged gorge of the South Fork, they forded the river at Greenhorn's Cutoff. Ugly yellow cliffs rose up on either side of the wagons and cast a gloom of shadow that brought upon them an edgy mood, while beneath them slick mud tempted several of the wagons to overturn. Then, already exhausted, the emigrants watched the river move abruptly away from the trail into an impassable canyon, forcing them to cross over yet another range of mountains and more dusty hard travel.

They rolled through what had earlier been dubbed Emigrant Pass where the road crossed over hogbacks and twisting swales, with only a vague suggestion of low hills seen in the far distance. It took two long days, and all the while the people ate and inhaled more powdery dust. Those who were prepared for this wore goggles to protect their eyes, but all wore handkerchiefs tied across their noses and mouths. By the time they reached water at Emigrant Springs, both their clothes and their skin were the same color as the pale earth upon which they trudged. At the springs they refilled their barrels, wished they could stay longer, and then continued across the southward bend of the river.

One of the last things Bob had said to Abe was that they would stay on the north side all the way and would NOT cross back and forth, even when it looked like the other side had more grass. Only twice were they severely tempted, causing those with the weakest of animals to argue with Abe over this restriction. Abe told them they could cross if they wanted, but the other wagons would not, and they would be left alone. This brought them in line, although grudgingly.

After crossing a dry lake bed, they passed the cutoff to the steep descent into Gravelly Ford on the south side of the river.

Soon they were suffering not only the weather, the road and the dust, but also an increasing weariness of their spirits. They were in a transition portion of the trail along the river, between the upper Humboldt and the harsh days ahead on the last seventy miles to the infamous Humboldt sink.

The trail curved sharply to the north as they passed between Stony Point to their right and Battle Mountain across the river to their left. In the distance the wavering heat-induced mirages tempted them to believe they were near lakes even while the white barrenness of desert surrounded them. The hard saleratus ground burned through boots worn thin, and when young Mrs. Ashe began to whimper in her misery, Nancy walked with her while holding her hand.

The river nodded off southwest, and since Bob had described this area as only a couple of days before Lassen's Meadow and good grazing, Abe ruthlessly pushed everyone to move along while ignoring the muttered swearing of the men and the great suffering of the women. As his charges looked longingly across the river to a narrow strip of land occupied by the trading post at French Ford, Abe ignored their pleas and suffered their mumbled curses. When Nancy took Abe's hand and squeezed it reassuringly, he swallowed the tightness in his throat and told himself it was from thirst.

The sun on the white sand was blinding and as Nancy walked beside their creaking wagon, she squinted her eyes and pulled the deep brim of her coal-scuttle bonnet further down to shade her face. She had placed two of the bonnets in the wagon in a cloth pocket sewn to the underside of the canopy, and had the day before given one to a woman who had none and whose face was blistering in the sun.

But no matter what anyone did, they had cracked lips and a nose that often trickled blood. Alkali dust and hot sand invaded and irritated all the sensitive places on the bodies of man, woman and beast.

Nancy arose one morning to discover her beloved milk cow dead by the wagon. Why it decided to die right then when it had shown no distress of illness, Nancy would never know, but it would haunt her for days. They left the loyal cow where she had fallen, knowing that the Indians would soon have a feast day, but unable to do anything about it.

Finally they reached the tule meadows north of the big bend of the river where the Little Humboldt River flowed into the main stream of the Humboldt. Their respite there was only for one day, but the animals were able to eat and drink and lay in cool grass, and the people did the same. The women washed clothes, knowing it would be the last time for over two weeks.

Abe had grown fond of his oxen and he was proud that all of them were still healthy. Yes, they were gaunt, foot sore and red of eye, but they did not appear as bad off as some of the other teams.

All along the way, whenever an ox had died, Abe had cut off long strips of its hide if the owner did not himself do it. Now he showed them how to cut squares of the hide and tie them over the hooves of their severely foot-sore animals. After spending hours cutting as much grass as they could fit into their wagons, they filled every barrel and pail and bottle with water.

That night at council, he told the men, "I know you feel like you have an abundance of everything in your wagons, but from what I'm told, we can't begin to imagine the difficulties ahead. So I'm putting us all on short rations. Whatever we would normally eat, we'll now eat half of that. And we'll drink less water too, even though we'll want twice as much as usual."

When some of the men started to object, he raised a hand and stated firmly, "If any of you decide not to listen to me, and run out of supplies, you'll be on your own. Don't expect the rest of us to save you." But as he walked away, he knew that if it came to that, others *would* help. It was the cooperative spirit that had gotten so many across the country for so many years.

On they went, along a river determined to sink away into the hot white sand that sucked at wagon wheels and burned through worn boots. The animals were saved only because of the leather socks they wore, their feet protected from the hot sand and rocks that resembled the cinders of ancient fires.

The Humboldt now became a sick oozing wound of a river separated from them by a steep white bank that curled like proud flesh. Here the river had for years trapped any heavy animal that slid down its banks in the hope of slaking its thirst or eating the sparse green grass at its edge. When the steer, horse or mule was unable to get back up the steep bank, it eventually died at the water's edge and the river was at some points nothing more than a swill of rotted carcasses. The travelers were often plagued for miles by a stink that choked in their throats.

Thankful that they had water enough for themselves, the people still had to clamber down to the river to bring back buckets of water for their animals. Little green water snakes darted around the buckets that the men lowered into any water that moved swiftly and was furthest from a carcass. Abe and the other men held their breath as much as they could, breathed shallowly when they could not, and clawed their way back up the bank. Men at the top helped them up while they tried desperately not to spill the water in their buckets.

Nancy filtered the water through muslin before offering it to their oxen, and defiantly claimed that they appreciated the effort. Abe couldn't argue the point, since he did the same for Flame while fretting about the horse's loss of weight. At night they fed the teams a ration of the grass they carried in their wagon, along with dry willow branches from the scattering of trees near the river, but it was never enough. The oxen would begin bellowing just before first light, and Nancy was not the only one brought almost to tears out of pity for animals that had so faithfully served them for almost 2,000 miles. For themselves, they ate only enough to take away the worst of the hunger.

When they were a half day from the Great Meadow, they reached a slough of cool water that tasted only mildly of alkali. To their surprise, they also found a reservoir built in such a way that the water of a small stream constantly trickled into it. This water was the last of any decent quality they could expect for the next sixty miles, and again they filled every vessel.

Early the next day they came across two wagons that sat by the side of the road. The wagons held two couples composed of a brother and sister and their spouses, all in their twenties and one couple with two children. They had all been cast off from a larger train a few days before, and what little food that had been left with them was almost gone. But much more critical was their lack of water.

Everyone from Abe's train came forward with a little of their cherished supply of water while Nancy made them plates of donated food. The children, not much older than eight, turned their begrimed faces up to her and whispered, "Thank you."

Abe waited until they had all eaten every crumb on their plates before asking them what had happened.

Ben Wilson explained in a low voice. "We refused to leave my wife in the desert to die. They were afraid of Mary, and insisted that we should leave her by the road, or all leave the train."

Ignoring the brutality of such a decree, Effie spoke up in a voice that made obvious her fear. "What's wrong with her?"

The man hesitated, then looked down at his tin mug of water rather than meet anyone's eyes.

His brother-in-law, Martin Franklin, answered for him. "My sister's gone insane, or just about."

Ben spoke up then. "No, she hasn't. She's just given up, that's all."

Jeannie Franklin said, "The captain of the train and some of the others were real religious. They saw Mary's behavior as a curse from God."

"Was she like this when you started?" Nancy asked.

"No," Ben answered. "Mary's younger sister died two months ago. Then our oldest girl died a bad death, and shortly after that Mary lost a baby in child birth. She hadn't cried since our girl died, so I thought she was doing okay."

Martin's wife gave Ben a look of naked disgust, but he was oblivious to it. Nancy followed his glance into the wagon where his wife sat on an old straight-backed chair. Her thin body was as rigid as that of the chair, and her pallor as pale as the canvas top that protected her from the sun. The food brought to her by Lona was untouched on the box next to her. Mary Wilson, her hands tightly clasped in her lap and her eyes closed, was so still that her breathing was barely discernable.

Ben murmured, "Recently she's become convinced that she's watching our two other children slowly die, and I think she's trying to go before they do. She'll be okay once we get to Sutters Fort. Her parents are there. But first we have to get across this damn desert."

While Effie got them another biscuit, Nancy and Lona went into the wagon where they bathed Mary's face. After a few minutes she opened her eyes, and although she still didn't speak, they got her to eat a biscuit and swallow a little water. Still, she never once looked directly at them.

"I think her husband was right," Nancy said. "She has given up."

Lona nodded. "How can we bring her out of it?"

"I think I know a way." Lona stayed with Mary, gently brushing her hair and talking in a soothing voice. Meanwhile, Nancy cleaned up the children, Dorothy and Dennis, who she realized were twins. They were bright and naturally cheerful, and responded immediately to having a full stomach and their thirst quenched. When their faces were clean and their hair combed, Nancy brought them to their mother.

"Mommy," little Dorothy whispered, "we've had food and water. We're not hungry any more and these people are really nice." Her brother nodded and smiled.

It was probably the first time in weeks that either of the children had been unafraid or not hungry, and it showed in the enthusiasm of their tone. A few minutes after they spoke to their mother, she looked up and stared at them as though willing herself to focus. Finally pulling her gaze from the children who watched her intently, Mary slowly turned her head and looked up at the women next to her who smiled at her so kindly.

When she turned back to her children with recognition in her eyes, the children stepped forward eagerly. Mary wrapped them tightly in her arms and murmured their names over and over. When she began to cry, neither Nancy nor Lona tried to stop her. They understood only too well her need.

CHAPTER ELEVEN
NEVADA
SEPTEMBER, 1863

"We are approaching the 40 Mile Desert. There is an overwhelming urge to shrink from it and turn back to the dry scrub that is so familiar. This desert goes beyond the definition for barren into realms of unearthly. A breeze blew past that sounded like the sob of some lost soul, and in this place I can well believe it."

Nancy

"How am I to get all these people across safely? Why did this responsibility fall to me? I can only hope my best efforts are good enough."

Abe

Now longer by two wagons, the train reached the great meadow of the Humboldt and found all the grass they could want. They turned the animals out to freely feed while everyone filled their wagons with armloads of grass. When they thought to stop because of their fatigue, they recalled the pitiful bellows in the night from their hungry animals and crammed into their wagons even more.

Abe and the other men smiled as they watched their wives and daughters making daisy chains with the long blades of grass while sitting in the cool of it surrounding them. Nancy had been the first woman to do this, but she was quickly joined by those who also longed to spend even a few moments in the pursuit of something pleasant.

Just before leaving the area early the next morning, Abe rode out to scout further from the wagons than he had the previous day. That was when he found the new grave. A leather saddle-bag partly buried in the sand at the head of the grave had words roughly scratched into its surface:

Barbara Fairlie
Accident took my beloved
August 1863

Abe was stunned into immobility, and several minutes passed before he could force himself to ride back to the wagons. After informing Nancy, the two of them went to the Fairlie wagon to break the news of Barbara's fate. He and Nancy attempted to console the devastated parents while also reassuring the agitated Carpenters about their son. But at the same time, Abe knew he had to keep to the schedule by getting everyone underway.

As they passed young Barbara's grave, the train stopped briefly to allow the Fairlies a few moments there. Lona brought her daisy chains of grass and laid them on the grave. While doing this she spotted a note protruding from under the saddlebag serving as a headstone. It had been written by Jason Carpenter and simply said, "I will be in Reno." Lona hurried to the Carpenters to give them the message.

Every monotonous mile along the length of the Humboldt River to Humboldt Lake was the same whether traveled on the north or south side of it, but the Carrington train remained on the north side where the trail was firmer. The scenery, if it could generously be called that, was about as much of nothing as was possible. For several days the people and the animals walked upon miles of unforgiving hot sand that was crusted with bright white alkali. If ever anything had grown there, it had been scrubbed off by nature to leave hundreds of white crusted acres so flat it looked to have been ironed. It was certainly unwanted by any living thing.

For a diversity of challenge they discovered that while the bright glaring days were blistering hot, the black nights were shockingly cold. After taking advantage of the little grass produced along the lake's margins, they began to mentally prepare themselves for the 40 Mile Desert beyond the infamous sink.

At council the night after they passed a shallow lake formed by the dwindling river, Gabe told the men, "There're caves on the south side of the lake where Indians have lived for hundreds of years. When one of their elders dies, they place him on a reed raft and take him into the middle of the lake. Then they place rocks on the raft until it sinks."

Not that anyone wanted to drink the sudsy, evil looking water, but after that they were even hesitant to give it to their animals. Forced to do so, they were relieved to find there were no ill effects from it.

At this point they were faced with another split in the road. To the right was a trail that passed through a short stretch of desert and continued to the Truckee River, then on to Reno. After that, people could stay or choose to continue on to Sutter's Fort and the northern mines.

Mr. Carpenter came to Abe and told him, "We're going to cut off toward Reno. The Fairlies are coming with us."

"Do be careful. You'll be traveling alone."

"We have no choice. That's where Jason is." He glanced back at their lonely wagons that had both suffered a number of recent emergency repairs. "I don't think we can take another major crossing of a desert. Thankfully the Truckee River is closer than the Carson. We do thank you for your help this far."

Abe was not comfortable about the man's decision, but he had to admit that if there had been word of Todd in Reno, he would have deserted the train and gone with them. Soon everyone was watching this fragile duo pull out of line and roll down the road away from them. As Abe waved a final time, he pondered the quixotic nature of a trail that brought people so suddenly together and just as suddenly pulled them apart.

At the south end of the lake they encountered a natural dyke made of mud. The long brown ridge, about a half mile long and thirty feet high, forced them to the south end of it where they could most easily go up and over at its lowest point. Some on the train thought this was the infamous sink, but the water of the lake flowed through a wide break near the center of the ridge and went on for several miles as a slough of wet that begged the sand to accept it and produce something worthwhile. But the only thing the stubborn desert would allow was a broad marsh that teased with promises of feed, yet yielded nothing but stagnant sumps and sickly dark marsh grass.

When the desert had enough of this jest it sucked up even that bit of moisture and laughed out its dry hot breath upon the Carrington wagon train. Here was the actual sink, and it gave them no easier an experience than any other set of travelers that had passed through this area over the past twenty years.

Just before the river had disappeared completely into the maze of sloughs, swampy mud, and marshy meadow there had been a little grass and water that allowed the animals some relief. This was fortunate because barely past the sink they had their next challenge by Nature gone amuck. A maze of large sandy knolls, some as high as five feet and topped with greasewood, confounded their progress. The area before them reminded Abe of a field where a farmer had left his harvest of bound wheat behind, although the drifts of sand around them made that image difficult to hang onto for long.

Looking down as she walked, something everyone did if they wanted to stay upright, Nancy mused to herself, "How can the land look so firm and flat, and yet to the body seem such a torture?"

Nancy looked up briefly and noted that her friends were spread out, each having to assess for themselves the easiest course for their wagon through this awkward terrain. At a brief rest stop, Nancy had an epiphany and climbed into the wagon to look for the moccasins she had received in trade for two stale biscuits. They were well made and for the rest of their time through the desert, her feet were cooler and more comfortable than they had been for weeks. When the brush scratched her ankles, she wrapped them with the strips of hide Abe had taken from dead oxen along the way.

The first sight of the 40 Mile Desert caused a recoil of shock that brought Nancy to a standstill. She could not refrain from mumbling, "Yeah though I walk through the Valley of Death." Even after the last twenty days of stark conditions along the Humboldt, nothing had prepared the people for this. There would be no vegetation here, no water, and no shade.

They began two long days of almost constant movement through flat alkali sand the color and consistency of coarse flour poured over black volcanic gravel. This sand was gathered up by the spokes of each slowly moving wheel before it fell back down to the parched desert floor, only to be taken up again by the next wheel. Nancy would never forget the sound of the salty crust crunching beneath the wheels of the heavy wagon as she walked next to it mile after mile.

The alkali dust that rose in the air gathered in their throats and made them raw, and soon they were seldom without the metallic taste of blood at the back of their throats. What the straining, weary and thirsty animals endured was evident by the oxen's low bellowing, the nickering of the horses and an occasional pleading bray from a mule. The misery was relieved only once by a cluster of small wood-sided wells filled with bad tasting but drinkable water.

Low red mountains slunk along the trail as though unhappy to see more people invading their miserable desert, while hills further away were a hazy blue only slightly darker than the washed out sky. A small hill nearby was merely a mound of brown rock that had barely enough dirt in the crevasses to maintain a scattering of insignificant scrub, but there was no vegetation for the teams. When night came they still continued on and were grateful for twice being allowed an hour of rest. As they walked, the people chewed on the jerked beef of oxen and buffalo, and it served to bolster their energy for another few miles.

Nancy thought often of the Wilsons and hoped they were faring well at the back of the line of wagons, where they insisted on traveling in appreciation for being taken on by the train. Nancy worried that the stress of this portion of the desert would adversely affect Mary Wilson.

Mary had recuperated well in the company of other women, regular meals and plenty of water. However, it was the continued good spirits of her children that served more than anything to fire a renewal of life in her. After Ben Wilson received a hesitant suggestion from Abe, hugs from her husband were more frequent and this seemed to speed her recovery even more. At the end of each day Mr. Wilson did all he could to help around camp, even starting the cooking fire for Mary. Thankfully, the children were old enough to take care of themselves with only a little assistance.

Mr. Wilson's sensitivity was more willingly given than Nancy had seen from many of the men on the trail, most of whom refused to alter the role they had played their whole lives. There were exceptions, of course, but Nancy found it interesting that when women were forced by circumstances to take on men's duties, they exhibited pride and even enjoyment in their new tasks. The reverse was never the case. Even when the woman's

chores were done willingly by the husband, it was usually accompanied by an air of apology or complaint to the other men.
Such attitudes aside, the men acknowledged that Gabe made
"damn fine" biscuits.

Just past the mid point in the 40 Mile Desert, when their water was nearing a dangerous deficiency, Abe saw ahead the dust
of a wagon headed their way. Excitement and relief abounded
when it became clear that it was a water wagon sent out from
Fort Churchill on the Carson River to assist them. The water
was costly, but it was welcome at any price, most especially by
the teams.

"How did you know we were here?" Abe asked the soldier.

"A rider came in saying he had seen your dust when he was
your side of Ragtown. You should get there tomorrow. But you
look in good enough condition that we weren't really needed."

"Oh, please don't think that," Nancy told him. "The animals
are in great need of water."

And indeed, everyone on the train gave most of the gift of this
unexpected water to their thirsty animals. Without a team able
to pull another day, their wagon would end up abandoned in
the desert. The soldier, his wagon now lighter and pulled by six
strong mules, was quickly out of sight as he returned to the fort.

At council that night, which still included the women, one of
the men brought up Fremont's report of the region. He alluded
to Fremont's description of "a rich alluvium beautifully covered
with blue grass, herd grass, clover, and other nutritious grasses;
and its course is marked through the plain by a line of willow
and cottonwood trees."

One of the men suggested, "Maybe he was describing a thirst
induced dream he had one night."

Abe shook his head in disgust. "Then again, the meadow at
the start of the Humboldt came close to that."

"Yes," Lona spoke up uninvited, "but he made it sound as
though grass and trees were all along the way." Although most
of the men had read the published report while preparing for
the trip, they couldn't hide their surprise at her knowledge of
it. Lona drew herself up to a picture of wounded dignity and
responded sharply, "I too can read."

Gabe intervened. "He probably saw a wet early spring just
past. That would make for a lot of green along the river and out
into the desert even. If there was a heavy winter followed by a

quick hot spring like in '52, the flooding of the river makes the way along here so muddy that teams sink in over their heads and drown in the mud pits." When he heard someone snort, he added hotly, "I was told by someone who'd been on such a wagon train that a wagon got stuck and nine yoke of oxen could barely pull it out. It was that bad."

"Trains have known for years what it's really like here," Abe said. "But I'll give you that those back in the '40's were ill prepared for what we've gone through."

Buran said with wonder, "Even with the preparation we did, the small well we encountered, and the water wagon too, it's been the hardest thing I've ever done. Or ever hope to do."

Everyone nodded. They did not discount the hardships, the losses, the deaths, or how much distance lay ahead, but they were also very aware of the hundreds of miles they had survived. Many who had traveled the trail before them never got the opportunity to make that claim.

After traveling most of the night beneath the illumination of a full moon, they hit Destruction Valley at dawn. Although everyone had enough water if they were careful, they were out of feed for the animals again. The last of the carefully cut grass had been fed them the night before and their constant bellowing tore at the hearts of even the staunchest soul.

Some of the women mixed a little water and flour, cooked it barely through and fed the cakes to the oxen, since they would take it willingly. The horses and mules were not so easily satisfied, but thankfully they were also less noisy about their misery.

The axle on the wagon of the Mattes family, pulled by four mules, was discovered to have broken. There was no time to repair it, so the family's goods were distributed among two other wagons. Those wagons then hitched on the mules belonging to Mr. Mattes, and this compensated for the extra weight. Left behind in the sand with the wagon were the tools that Mr. Mattes had planned to use when he joined his brother's wagon repair business in Minden, Nevada. No one missed the irony of this.

Although the harsh desert night had brought a bitter chill to their situation, the dawn introduced them again to the blistering heat that drained the little traveling community of energy. When they rested near salt wells filled with water unfit for consumption, they gave the teams some of their precious water reserves to keep them from rushing the bad water. Several of the men tried to cool themselves by saturating their clothes in the well water, but when it evaporated it left a crust that had to be scraped off.

That night, Abe gave everyone an hour of rest before pushing them on in the light of the waning moon. The horse and mule teams were left in harness and the oxen yoked together. The animals slept where they were, most staying on their feet but a few laying down together in a cooperative spirit seldom seen among them.

Nancy dozed fitfully while Abe sat looking into the dark. He knew they had been very lucky during their grueling passage so far, but the sand was getting deeper and they were still a dozen miles from the Ragtown settlement near the Carson River. There was a little water left but no feed for the animals, so Abe dared not give the people or teams more time to rest.

He looked around at the hundreds of rusting and deteriorating items lying on the sand. It was only a fraction of what they had been passing for miles, and he thought of the hundreds of women who had wept as they left behind their treasures in the burning sands of this stark arid landscape. Looking at the rusting iron tools and plows, rotting barrels and even guns, he also thought of the men who had been forced to leave behind the physical inventory of a new business in a new land.

The driving stock was of the greatest concern now if the wagons were to get through. One family already had replaced a dead ox with a milk cow that had surprised everyone with how well she traveled with the oxen. Abe felt deeply the heavy burden of his responsibility to these people and prayed they would all make it at least as far as Dayton, Nevada. For himself, he just wanted to find Todd in one of those places, and dreaded what it would do to Nancy if they did not.

Abe asked himself, "How much pain can a woman take?" He assumed that his grief, although intense, could not be as bad as that of a mother. If that seemed logical to him, it was only because he could mask his feelings better and had so much responsibility laid upon him by those who trusted him that he had little time to brood. But there were always those moments just before falling asleep. Then he found it impossible to completely block the tight grip of pain he felt at his core when thinking about his children and how much he missed them. Sleep was a blessing, not only because of its restorative properties for the body, but also because it gave surcease from the torment of the mind.

The next morning, under the pink dawn of a cloudy sky, they passed the remnants of hundreds of horses, oxen and cattle that past travelers had left behind either dead or dying. Their bleached bones covered the ground, and forced everyone to confront not only the horrid reality of their predecessors, but also the fragility of their own current situation. Their gratitude for their own fortunate circumstance was not enough to override their imaginations, or gentle their nightmares.

Five miles from the Carson River the oxen lifted their heads, smelled the air and bellowed a different tune. Soon the horses and mules did the same, and while still a mile from the water every animal reacted to basic instinct and found hidden energy to move forward faster than they had for weeks. Within sight of the river the oxen began to trot, and Abe called out to everyone that no one should try and stop their teams. It would be futile, and anyone trying would be in jeopardy of being run over.

The parched and exhausted creatures rushed forward, passed between cottonwoods and clumps of willow that lined the bank of the river, and stopped only when the cold water hit their hot bellies. The animals buried their faces in the water and began drinking, still yoked together and attached to the wagons. Water! Good clean moving water!

People caught up with their teams and also waded into the river, men and women together without reservation. All soaked their clothing with abandon and splashed water over their heads. Some of the men threw their arms around the necks of their teams before splashing them with the cool water. Other men sprawled in the shallows and let the water flow over them.

Flame was immediately led into the water and while the horse drank, Abe washed the dust from his fur. Nancy waded in up to her knees and filled her cupped hands with the clean water and gulped several hands full before bathing her face. Finally climbing up the bank, she wrung out her wet skirt and looked up at the sky as the breeze picked up. She listened to the rattle of leaves in the old cottonwoods whose roots trailed into the water and then spontaneously stepped forward to wrap her arms around one of them. She laid her cheek against its rough cool bark, let out her breath as one who had been holding it for weeks, and let flow her tears.

Other women also wept as they stood in the water, sat on the shore or rested against a tree. Some wept in grief for the loss of dear ones, some at the memory of treasured possessions strung out across the plains and the desert, some at the sheer relief that the worst was over, and some just because exhaustion had overcome them. Abe later shyly admitted to Nancy that a few of the men had wiped from their cheeks more than just river water.

When Nancy saw a lizard dart from one rock to another, she realized that it had been many days since she had seen any such sign of life. Here rabbits dashed about as the people disturbed them from beneath bushes, and looking up she saw a hawk perched on a branch at the top of a nearby tree. The men talked about hunting again as they filled the water casks, and this sign of normal life resumed made Nancy want to cheer.

That night everyone slept as soundly as if they had been drugged, since most had not slept for almost 36 hours. The next morning Nancy stood in the shade along the Carson River, facing a day of heat and sweat after moving away from its shore. But she told herself that after they found Todd they could settle down somewhere, and the thought of that gave her renewed energy.

Not far from the river the train approached Ragtown and everyone sighed with relief. That is, until they saw it up close. Although a supply depot of sorts during the rush, it now served more as a saloon with a small trading post adjacent. Beyond it was a scattering of shacks, a lean-to with a forge, and a dilapidated hotel. Throughout the area the bushes were draped with men's clothing drying and flapping in the breeze.

Nancy walked next to Abe as he brought their wagon to a stop and signaled everyone behind them to do the same. "Why do you think they call it Ragtown?"

Abe glanced first at the clothing covering the bushes then at the men milling around the saloon porch. "Because everyone here looks like a dirty rag?" Then he looked closer at his traveling companions and added, "We sure do."

While Abe remained with the wagons, Nancy walked to the trading post. Before going in, she looked back at the rag-tag caravan of wagons that remained in a line, ready to move on again after a bit of rest and the addition of supplies. Every man, and Lona by herself, was disconnecting their team preparatory to leading them to nearby grass and water.

Relieved of the stress of focusing only on the trail ahead, Nancy took the opportunity to remember these wagons at the start of the trip when they were freshly painted and their white canvas tops sported jolly slogans. She recalled how muscled and sleek the animals had appeared, and how full of eagerness the people had been to get underway. Now, after 2,000 miles, what paint that was left on the wagons was chipped and faded.

But it was the animals that saddened her most. All were gaunt and so obviously exhausted that it would not have been surprising to see any one of them collapse and refuse to rise up again. She knew that trains of the past had tried to save their flagging animals by sawing off the back of the wagon and leaving only a cart, all in the hope of lightening the load.

There at Ragtown, many of the travelers over the past two decades had even made the decision to abandon their wagons and continue on by using their teams as pack animals. The rusting iron portions of these wagons were still in evidence in the sand. The wood portions had been scavenged to build the trading post and bar, the two privies in the back, and several shacks.

Gabe told Abe and Buran that in the early years of the migration, men would swap out a broken wagon part for a better one recently abandoned. Abe thought to himself that the Colonel's train had no such need, then caught himself and with a smile thought, "*My* train has no such need."

This introspection was interrupted when a freighter, his huge rig parked near the wagons, passed Abe on his way to the saloon. As the teamster wiped the sweat from his face, he mumbled, "Jesus! It's hotter than a whorehouse on nickel night!"

Abe laughed and determined to remember what the man had said so he could share it with Nancy later, knowing it would make her smile. Regardless of all they had been through, he felt blessed to still have his Nancy.

In the ramshackle building that was the trading post, Nancy walked over to the far corner of the room. A small piece of cracked mirror hung on the wall above a large white crockery pitcher nestled in a matching cracked bowl, and both sitting on a small brown table with wobbly legs. She looked into the mirror and saw staring back at her a hag with red eyes, split lips, skin as dark as a desert miner and as dry as a lizard. Removing her limp, dust-encrusted bonnet, Nancy gasped at her filthy matted hair.

Abe appeared behind her. When he took off his hat, his appearance was much the same as her own, except that he had a thick scraggly beard and a white band of flesh along the top of his forehead where his hat usually rested. He shook his head and enunciated clearly, "Je-sus Kee-rist!"

The unexpected humor of his reaction struck Nancy so sharply that she laughed out a short explosive bark that surprised them both. Abe marveled at the strength of her character and the depth of the courage in her to face life as something to live rather than just endure. His chest almost swelled with the strength of the love he felt for her.

But he only said, "I think we'd best put our hats back on and hide in their shadows until we can get to enough water to bathe."

Nancy smiled at his reflection in the mirror and lowered her voice. "Do you think we smell as bad as we look?"

"Who knows? The loss of the ability to smell may be the only benefit of all the alkali we've inhaled."

The first few people to approach the proprietor, a tall man whose dark face was a network of wrinkles, got all the supplies they requested, although everyone on the train was able to get flour, salt, and cured beef. Those who could afford them even purchased melons.

"Hey, Sam," a disheveled old man hollered at the clerk. "I think you'd better check your rooms at the hotel. I just found ole Bill in his bunk."

Sam shook his head in disgust. "He still dead drunk?"

"Nope. Just dead."

"Hell!" the trader sighed. "Well, I'll go fetch him out when I'm done here."

Pointedly ignoring this exchange, several people lined up near a large jar of sour pickles. They wasted no time biting into the sharp juicy flesh, cherishing the tang on their tongue after such a long time tasting only flavors bland, salty and greasy.

Also on the counter was an old cigar box filled with loose tobacco next to cigarette papers and a tin mug full of loose matches. It was free to customers and a few of the men rolled a cigarette that they inhaled with a reverence usually reserved for things religious. Considerately taking only one helping each, they all agreed that this trading post was as good as the best they had seen across the country.

Nancy looked with eagerness at a wooden bucket by the door filled with cool water. A dusty freighter that smelled much the same as his mules, but with an additional pungency only too human, stopped next to the bucket. When done drinking, he wiped his mouth on his sleeve, plunked the tin mug that was tied to the handle back into the water and left. Nancy passed the bucket without stopping.

For those with money to spare, there was plenty of liquor available in the saloon. A few of the men visited the rickety building, but they returned quickly after the burn of the alcohol hit their cracked lips.

At council that night it was decided that for the next few days on their way to Dayton they would travel the south side of the Carson River. It would mean the crossing of two large areas of sand and sage to avoid the curves in the river, but the water would be close enough that they could return to it at night.

Abe gathered everyone together and spoke to them from his heart. "I know how tired you are. But you're almost to Dayton where you can get all the rest you need. You must think of nothing else. In only hours the desert will be behind you."

Some of he men thought he talked a lot of nonsense. A man just did what was expected of him, that's all, and no need to make a fuss about it. But they soon were on the move again, heading southwest along the Carson River. After an hour in the cool of the river bottoms, they began moving at a faster pace than they had thought possible of themselves that morning. But even when their pace slowed to a tired trudge after hitting the sand hills, no one complained.

They were near Fort Churchill, situated in the scrub not far from the river like an adobe mirage backed by brown rolling hills. Three stagecoaches passed them before moving over Sam Buckland's toll bridge at the river, racing past his station and surrounding maze of corrals, and continuing on over the hill to the fort that served as a way-station for the stages.

Within sight of Sam and Eliza Buckland's log cabin, Abe's train circled near the river in a short grass meadow spreading out from the lush riparian edges of the river. The Carringtons and their friends luxuriated in all the grass now available for the teams and rejoiced as the animals ate their fill before lying down to sleep. The river offered as much water as had earlier filled their dreams and they wasted no time filling their barrels.

Nancy looked at the cool green landscape and the lovely old trees, and wondered at the great good fortune of those original seeds that had chosen such an ideal spot to put down roots. But then, she also wondered the same about the people at the trading posts, stage stations and ranches they had passed all across the country. This ability to survive in the face of adverse conditions, in nature and in humans, was something that Nancy would ponder for the rest of her life.

They heard rather than saw the soldier's life beyond the near hills. At daybreak the next morning they could hear the sound of reveille echoing across the hills from the Fort. Within minutes the bugle sounded again, only this time with a different staccato tune, and Gabe said this was the stable and water call. This was followed by the call to breakfast and half an hour later came fatigue call. Sick call signaled for ill men to be marched to the post hospital for treatment, but if they were found actually to be a malingerer, they would be sent to hard duty.

Throughout the day the Carrington train rested in the cool shade while the sound of bugle calls accompanied their chores. The women washed and mended clothes, cleaned the wagons, baked bread and roasted coffee beans. The men greased wagon wheels, chopped wood, and doctored their animals.

That afternoon two soldiers with fishing poles joined some of the men from the train, along with Lona. They lined up along the river bank and settled down to wait for a nibble on their lines. The First Sergeant, a comely young man called Ron, caught the largest fish and enjoyed the bragging rights. But Lona caught the most fish and reveled in the chagrinned looks from the men. As she walked back to the wagons, she held her string of fish in the air and several of the women applauded. Lona bowed from the waist and laughed all the way to her wagon.

That evening some of the soldiers came to Bucklands for a drink, and others to play cards and lose some of their $13 a month pay. Still others came just to watch and get away from the post. Their dress was similar to the blue uniforms worn by the Union soldiers and was the reason the Indians referred to the soldiers as "blue coats".

With plenty of water and food for themselves and the stock, and Dayton only two days travel away, Abe and Nancy allowed themselves the hope of seeing Todd soon. Abe pointed in the general direction of Gold Canyon over the hills to the north and announced to his fellow travelers that if anyone wanted to reach the silver mines of Virginia City, it would be through that canyon. Four wagons left the train the next morning, one of which belonged to Lona.

That a woman in her early thirties would willingly venture alone into such an infamous mining camp, greatly surprised everyone. Whenever someone questioned her as to what she intended to do there to earn her living, she flashed a smile and reassured her questioner that she would be fine. She told Sally Ashe that she was going to stake her own claim, but her enigmatic smile was such that it led Sally to report to the other women that Lona was only joking. It was with awkward well wishes that Abe and Nancy bid Lona good-bye the next morning.

Later that same morning they all left the soldiers behind and set out for the supply and mill town of Dayton. By March of 1870 Fort Churchill would no longer be a fort, but only a small supply depot. Sam Buckland would purchase for $750 the wood, windows and hardware that had composed the stables, blacksmith, forge house, bake shop, ice-house and the family quarters. With these supplies Sam would build a large two-story white house to serve as a way-station next to the river bridge.

The last wagons that had started out together as the Carrington train now passed through the lush welcome of the lower end of the Carson Valley. The sun shone golden on fields of wheat surrounded by blue sagebrush, and long green grass waved beneath the protecting shade of tall trees along the river. Abe's people filled their lungs with the sweet scent of meadow grass, the tang of sage, and the sultry riparian blend of rotting vegetation and wet mud.

They passed cattle in pastures that hosted bees droning loudly while visiting late summer wildflowers. The oxen answered the soft bellowed greetings of their bovine cousins grazing in pastures. Large black and white magpies called from fence posts where they chastised those passing, and local ranchers waved at the passing emigrants from the fields where they were harvesting their crops. It was for everyone a time of euphoric joy as they embraced the civilized sights and sounds and smells.

That night they gathered just outside Dayton and everyone cooked large dinners of whatever they had left, knowing that better and fresher supplies were now easily at hand. Women exchanged some of their concoctions with the other families, and the men wolfed down the largesse while swapping stories and opinions. Already the shared ordeals and shocks of the journey were taking on the proportions of good tales to be told and retold.

Gabe joined Abe and Nancy for dinner and brought along his own bread. He dipped it into Nancy's bacon dripping gravy and declared, "Ma'am, you make the best dope of any woman on the train." He sopped up the last of the gravy with great satisfaction.

Nancy laughed at him and wondered how many families had shared their meals with Gabe. At least he often brought something with him to contribute to the meal, and many had received some of the results of his hunting.

The next morning their wagons entered Dayton. They were eagerly met by mercantile and saloon keepers, blacksmith Silas Cooper, restaurant cooks, Hurdy Gurdy House madams, mill workers, and much of the general population of 1,600 citizens. They felt as though they were being welcomed home, and were just a little overwhelmed at the outpouring of friendliness from these citizens.

They were offered the best of what everyone had available, and made to feel like their arrival was a blessing to the town. Abe wondered if it had been a long time since a train had come their way. Townsmen jogged ahead of the wagon train to lead them to a large field where they could easily form a circle to enclose their stock. Abe was told the field was across from the camel compound on Pike Street, and although finding this an unusual comment, he followed the men to the site.

After positioning their wagons, they set the teams and loose stock to grazing within the circle. Many of the people then visited the complex of corrals at the Leslie Hay Barn, since no one wanted to miss an opportunity to see the strange animal called a camel. For the past few years they had been used to haul salt, wood and other mining supplies to mines and mills at Gold Hill, Silver City, and Virginia City.

Most of the men then visited the saloon where local men were still talking about the recent hanging, witnessed by 2,000 people from near and far. They were quick to explain that the event was court ordered. Meanwhile, some of the women took the opportunity to put stew and bean pots to simmer over long-burning hardwood fires. They also agreed among themselves that they deserved a meal in a cafe that night.

While this was taking place, Abe and Nancy found the Sheriff and asked him about recent strangers in town. He had no happy information for them on that front, but he suggested that it was more likely that Todd and his companions would have continued on to Carson City, saying, "It's a considerably larger town, and if three men want to blend in, it'll be easier there."

With hope still alive, Abe and Nancy joined some of their friends at a boarding house dining room. The women enjoyed for the first time in months eating a meal they had not cooked over an open fire while hot grease splattered the hem of their dress. Conversation was remarkably devoid of the hardships, losses and incidents already experienced. Instead they focused on that portion of the trip that still lay ahead of them, and especially enjoyed talking about the lives they hoped to establish when their destinations were finally reached.

The camp shut down for the night and Abe looked at Nancy soundly asleep beside him on their pallet under the wagon. Abe was not sleepy and he could hear a man and wife nearby discussing whether or not to stay in Carson or continue on to Sacramento. They evidently came to a decision because soon the night was filled with the chirping of crickets, the buzz of mosquitoes, horses nickering, a coyote yipping in the hills, a woman softly crying in a near wagon, and two men playing checkers. Gabe, who was growing progressively subdued as they approached California, was reading aloud from a Bible.

In the clear perspective of a moment infused with memories of their life in Missouri and the trials of the last five months, Abe thought to himself, "What a vast difference between a romantic notion and a battle-scarred reality."

CHAPTER TWELVE
CALIFORNIA
SEPTEMBER, 1863

"This morning I could see beyond Dayton the peaks of the giant bulk that is California's Sierra Nevada. Its promise looms somewhere between our current hardship and our future uncertainty, but travel is made more bearable by the knowledge that we are soon to reach our destination. Try as I might, I cannot hold back the hope that we may find Todd in Carson City. Am I setting the stage for the tragedy of disappointment?"

Nancy

"I dare not tell Nancy my misgivings, but I don't think Todd will be in Carson. But at least it is a real town. Civilization, security, law and order, and plenty of everything a tired traveler can desire. At last we are beyond months of gaunt want."

Abe

Carson City lay a short distance northwest of the trail, but only four wagons planned to head in that direction. One of them belonged to Abe and Nancy. The rest of the wagons, including that of the Howards and Gabe, were to continue on the main trail toward the old Mormon Station known as Genoa, fifteen miles east of the California line. There the travelers would rest for a couple of days before climbing over the Sierra on the narrow but recently improved road south of Lake Tahoe, staying on it all the way to Placerville and Sacramento.

Before they parted from one another, however, everyone approached Abe where he stood in the shade of a large willow. They thanked him profusely for his wise leadership, and more than one person commented that they had managed to remain confident of surviving the ordeal simply because Abe was so certain that they would.

Nancy stood a few feet away watching the parade of people fulsomely express their appreciation to her kind and capable husband, and felt enormously proud. She also felt more than a little ashamed of herself for not having more often shown him as much affection as would have made the carrying of so much responsibility more tolerable.

Effie approached and Nancy turned aside to hug her friend and shake Buran's hand. Each assured the other that they would meet again some day, all the while knowing it was a hollow promise, but gratefully for the reassuring words filling the awkwardness of the emotional parting.

Nancy watched Effie walk away, expended a heavy sigh, then walked to Abe's side as the last few people came forward to say good-bye. When Nancy slipped her hands around his left arm and smiled up at him, Abe was so flummoxed at this public display of affection that he barely acknowledged the last handshake.

Gabe came up to them and offered his hand. "Hope everything turns out well for you."

"And you," Abe told him. "What do you plan to do? Stay in Sacramento?"

Gabe looked at the ground for a moment, then looked up to face them straight on. "My full name is Gabriel Hawthorne. I was raised in a seminary in New York and left when I was twenty to explore the country. Now I've done enough of that. I'm heading to the coast to join an old friend who's a priest at a mission."

"Well, I'll be hornswoggled! You're a priest?"

"Yes and no." Gabe grinned as he noted Abe's surprise. "I was ordained, but I never served. Maybe I can be of service now. I feel I'm ready."

Nancy was the first to recover. "Best of luck to you, Gabe. It's been a great pleasure knowing you."

Gabe chuckled. "Well, interesting anyway, I hope."

Nancy smiled. "Yes, you've been that."

"I hope I didn't bore you too often."

Abe laughed. "I can honestly say none of your stories were boring."

Gabe chuckled again, then became serious. "May God keep you safe and help you in your quest." He made the sign of the cross over them, and then walked away without further comment.

Finally, all the wagons had departed, leaving the Carringtons and the two wagons of the Wilson family to continue their journey to Carson City. Alone by their wagon, Nancy told Abe, "I'm so proud of you for getting us here. I know the Colonel and Bob would be too. Maybe someday we'll be able to find out where the Colonel is and write him about our travels." After a moment's hesitation, she added softly, "And let him know about Bob if he doesn't already know."

Abe smiled and slipped his arms around her waist in a spontaneous burst of enthusiasm. "Ah, Nan, what a great idea." He kissed her hot cheek and stepped back, not wanting to crowd her if she was not ready for more affection. "Now what say we get ourselves to Carson and see what we can find out."

"Why," he thought to himself, "did I dare not finish the sentence with *about Todd*?" But the dubious hope of success lay too fragile between them, and like the ephemeral mirages they had seen in the desert, Abe knew this goal too could just as easily disappear.

Almost to Carson City, the four wagons passed the busy mill town of Empire City. Nancy admired the cemetery perched on the crown of a hill behind the town. Most of the rectangular graves and large monument markers were surrounded by fancy iron fences to keep out the wild animals, and Nancy thought it a lovely if somewhat lonely resting place.

Carson was a booming town of close-packed whitewashed buildings and wide muddy streets filled with drovers on horseback doing their best to avoid the large freight wagons. The overriding noise was that of shouting teamsters urging their long lines of mules down the muddy main street using every swear word known to man in varying colorful combinations.

In the center of the town was a large open plaza, the center of the town's activities, and accented with a tall staff topped by a flag flapping wildly in the rising wind. The plaza was surrounded on three sides by businesses fronted by hitching rails and wooden sidewalks filled with rushing people who all seemed to be heading somewhere important.

Nancy stood next to their wagon at the edge of this busy open square and watched men nearby haggling over the sale of a horse, two freighters shifting the load of goods in their wagons, and a man at the nearby stable yelling at a green broke horse as it resisted his mounting it.

Mary Wilson came to Nancy to say good-bye. With a tear hovering at the corner of one eye, she said, "I can't thank you enough for all you and your husband did for us. I'll never forget your kindness."

"Oh, Mary, I'll never forget you either."

Without further conversation, they hugged briefly before Nancy watched Mary return to the Wilson wagon. Ben helped his wife climb inside, and with the Franklin wagon following behind, they headed down King Street toward the Sierra Nevada beyond the near hills. Gabe had already passed from town on his way to Genoa where he planned to sell his wagon and change to a pack train for his travel over the mountains.

While Nancy entertained herself watching the various activities around her, Abe began his search for Todd. After getting no satisfaction from the town's Sheriff, he began a desperate trek from one saloon to another. This promised to be a lengthy proposition, considering that there were at least a dozen such drinking emporiums in the town and the sidewalks were packed with people. Nevertheless, he asked anyone who would pay him attention if they had seen the motley trio of two weather-beaten mountain men and a clean-cut young boy.

Half an hour later Nancy noticed a woman standing in front of a two-story boarding house across from the plaza. It looked like a nice establishment with its newly whitewashed siding and lace curtains showing through gleaming windows. The petite elderly lady, somewhere close to sixty, stood at the top of the three steps leading to a broad covered porch occupied by four empty rocking chairs.

A crisp white apron covered the length of the woman's dark print dress, and the up-sweep of her thick gray hair was held up by a thin black ribbon. After a moment's hesitation, she adjusted the tiny wire-framed glasses on her nose, lifted her skirts and walked gingerly across the muddy road. Nancy stood fanning herself in the meager shade lent by the wagon's shadow and watched the woman approach.

"Hello. I'm Mrs. Lee. I couldn't help but notice you."

"Nice to meet you. I'm Mrs. Carrington."

"Are you waiting for someone?"

"I'm waiting for my husband to return. He's in town looking for someone."

"It's warm and the wind is kicking up. Why don't you come inside and have a cool drink while you wait. No one will bother your wagon, and anyway you can see it from inside."

Nancy gratefully accepted the kind invitation and after entering the boarding house, the two women exchanged sociable platitudes about the weather. Nancy politely admired the comfortably furnished parlor and Mrs. Lee quickly enchanted Nancy with her easy chatter as she shared little stories related to her accumulation of books, paintings, and china items on shelves.

Soon Nancy was explaining that she and Abe had been on the trail for the last four months and were uncertain where they were going to settle. After handing Nancy a glass of cool sweet tea, Mrs. Lee left the room. When she returned she had thrown a shawl around her shoulders and was in the company of four men who she introduced as her current boarders. The men filled two of the small leather settees forming the conversation area near a polished black parlor stove awaiting the first cold day of fall.

Nancy and Mrs. Lee sat on straight-backed chairs on either side of a small table and faced the men who could barely hide their eagerness to meet Nancy. After introducing themselves with great formality, the men quickly dropped their reserve and excitedly plied Nancy with questions about trail conditions, Indian activities, buffalo hunts, and where everyone on the train had "hailed from".

When their questions began to turn to personal reminiscences of their own travels, Nancy tactfully mentioned two mountain men that had been on their train. Her description startled Mr. Garcia and Mr. Huerta. The latter stroked his long beard and said, "I saw two men of that description here in town while I was in one of the saloons."

"Only they had a young boy with them," Mr. Garcia added.

Trying not to show too much interest, Nancy said, "Oh?"

Mr. Huerta chuckled. "He was about sixteen I'd say. They brought him into the saloon and bought him a whiskey. He drank it down, but it almost choked him blue."

All four of the men laughed, perhaps remembering their own first burning swallow. But it was rage Nancy felt burn in *her* throat. She bit her tongue as she was tempted to tell them that he was just fifteen.

Kathleen Haun

Mr. Huerta continued talking. "But the kid was smart. I thought he would ask for water, but he covered himself well and said, 'I'd rather stick with lager.'"

The men responded with admiration coloring their laughter. Mr. Garcia said, "Yeah, you couldn't help but admire his pluck. I offered to buy him another but he said he'd rather have a pickled egg, so I bought him one from the jar on the counter. When the two men with him got into a game at a near table, I asked the kid what he was doing with their kind."

Nancy impatiently prodded him. "And?"

"He said they weren't so bad, and that they were headed for Genoa. I asked him if he had folks or family there. He just shook his head and said he had family but he couldn't be with them right now. He looked so sad that I bought him another egg, patted his shoulder and let him be."

Nancy fought the desire to reach out for the hand that had so recently touched her son. Before she could do anything so fanciful, the man rose up, stretched his back, and walked away with the others after they bid her good day.

Mrs. Lee refilled Nancy's glass. "Men," she commented with mild disdain. "They always miss the subtleties. Honey, that was your boy he was talking about, wasn't he? Is that who your husband is looking for in town?"

Nancy looked into the intelligent eyes of Mrs. Lee and nodded slowly. "He ran away with those men after a family tragedy that he blames himself for allowing." Nancy grabbed Mrs. Lee's hand. "It wasn't his fault, and I thought he knew that." Without hesitating, she told Mrs. Lee the details of Harold's disappearance and added that her baby daughter had fallen out of the back of the wagon.

"Life is seldom easy, is it? Especially when it comes to the dying of those we love." With a sigh, and obviously remembering her own experiences, Mrs. Lee rose from the settee and walked over to a mirror on the wall. Her long elegant fingers tucked several strands of loose gray hair back into place before she said, "I've been thinking lately about my younger days when I lived in the East. I was quite the popular belle back then. Was here too when I arrived with my husband. He died a month later. My second husband was a miner who died in a cave-in six months after we wed." With an effort at irony, she ran a hand over her wrinkled cheeks as she added, "A lot has changed since then."

Nancy's appreciation of the woman's humor fought with her ingrained politeness, and she said nothing.

Mrs. Lee continued, more to herself than to Nancy. "In my mind I'm still young and beautiful with a beau waiting on the porch." She sighed. "But I'm not. Never again will there be a man who wants to dance with me, or who'll admire my brown eyes." She looked out through the front window at the town full of men. "And I'll never again feel strong arms wrapped 'round me in the night." She looked at Nancy and smiled before summarizing her present life. "I'm old, you see."

Nancy walked to her side and turned her so they were both looking into the mirror. "You think you look old. I *know* I feel old. But we're both handsome women, and I think we can expect a few more dances in our futures."

Mrs. Lee laughed. "Oh, my dear, you're very kind." She removed her delicate wire-framed glasses and reached down for the corner of her shawl. After rubbing the lenses clean, she set them once again on her pert nose. "I know I'll never again be courted, or gallop a horse across the prairie, or dance all night, or nurse a babe at my breast."

"Yes, but..."

Mrs. Lee laid a hand on Nancy's arm. "It's okay. Those things had their season."

"Does anything take their place?"

"Oh, yes." She smiled with a confidence borne of years of productive and satisfying living. "Hopefully one gains the grace of patience, and has the joy of many sweet memories. Then eventually comes the courage of acceptance, and with that there's the release of regrets and old resentments." She smiled fondly at Nancy. "And that's really quite nice."

Nancy smiled back, thinking of any number of things she currently resented very much. "Yes, I imagine it is."

Breaking the gentle spell of the moment, Mrs. Lee walked back to the settee and sat down. She arranged her skirts so they fell gracefully around her legs and picked up her glass. "But for you now, you need to catch up with that boy of yours in Genoa."

Nancy looked out the window at the plaza and their wagon. "First, I need to find my husband."

Just then a dispirited Abe walked up to their wagon and looked around obviously puzzled. While he untied Flame and led him to drink from a nearby trough, Nancy gave Mrs. Lee a quick hug and hurried to join him.

"Where...?"

She cut him off and rapidly told him of her conversation with Mrs. Lee's boarders. "We've got to purchase a few supplies and get the wagon to Genoa."

After a moment's thought, Abe said, "We're traveling too slow. I think it's better to continue on by stage."

"But our things," Nancy lamented. "And what will we do with the wagon and team? And Flame?"

Mrs. Lee joined them and Nancy introduced her to Abe. When Nancy told Mrs. Lee of Abe's plan, the woman said, "You can sell your wagon and stock to the blacksmith down the street. Ask for Hank. There are plenty of buyers coming through that he can resell it to, so he'll give you a fair price. As for your personal things, you'll only be able to take about 25 pounds each on the stage, so pack carefully."

The sale of the wagon and its contents, and the purchase of space on the last stage to Genoa, took them only three hours. Nancy rummaged through the dented cooking utensils, crumbling food items, tools, and camp paraphernalia, and realized how little they had that was of any value to them now. She took Alice's bonnet and Harold's shirt, a light quilt she had made when a young girl, the lace fan her mother had given her, her clean under garments and one good dress, and her journal. She walked away from the rest. Abe took only his personal effects, his trail diary, and Flame's curry brush.

After packing it all into two new valises, they walked to Clugage's Stage Depot with Abe leading Flame. While waiting for their departure, they stood in front of the new Ormsby House with their stuffed bags at their feet. They felt a bit naked by the absence of possessions, but yet also oddly free. Abe held tightly to Flame's halter and lead rope that would be used to tie him to the rear of the stagecoach.

Soon they were compressed into the interior of a coach with four men, as well as three more on the roof, and Flame tied on behind. Barely settled in their seats, the stage jerked forward and they departed from Carson City amid the whistles of the driver, a cloud of dust and the rattle of chains.

The colorfully painted stage was little more than a red box on large metal-rimmed yellow wooden wheels, and given bounce by long folded strips of leather beneath called thoroughbraces. The interior consisted of narrow benches facing front and to the rear that were thinly padded and covered in worn brown leather. On the wall opposite the door, under a window with a leather rolled shade, there was a small seat that could be let down to accommodate another passenger if needed. The Carrington's valises, holding the sparse residue of all they now possessed, were tucked securely in the large leather boot slung from the back of the stage. The coach was pulled by three matched pairs of brown well-muscled steeds that seemed to enjoy their job, and Nancy thought it cozy and even luxurious. Why would she not, after riding for months behind the backside of an ox in a cramped bouncing wagon, or walking while covered in sweat?

They arrived in Genoa three hours later. It was a tiny neat town developed around a large log building used as a trading post that had originally been a small fort. The only outpost in a long narrow valley, it sat at the bottom of pine covered Sierra Nevada foothills that towered above the western edge of the town. Near where the stage let them out were several small wooden and rock houses, a tavern, and a general merchandise store. They walked toward a boarding house proudly displaying a respectable vegetable garden and a dinner bell hanging by the door that was rung each day at noon and sunset.

They passed the first Catholic Church in the area, built two years before, and Nancy noted a priest standing on a path between an iron gate and the church doors. He had a neatly trimmed beard and was dressed in a hooded long brown robe. He also seemed to be watching them with an unusual intensity. Nancy stopped and turned toward him, exclaiming, "It's Gabe."

The priest's arms were folded across his stomach, but he raised one hand slightly in a wave of greeting, smiled softly and turned to walk inside the church. Abe said, "I guess he decided to stay here." Looking at the clean streets, the well-maintained buildings, and the beautiful landscape, he added, "I can see why."

Soon they were settled into a room so small that the bed barely fit inside it and with walls of thin fabric over studs that gave the illusion of privacy. After depositing their bags on the bed, they found the old United States Indian agent, whose job it had been to find passage east for widows and orphans of Indian massacres. He told them he remembered seeing the trio, but had not talked to any of them and knew nothing of their current whereabouts.

It was while eating in the dining room, enjoying a meal made sumptuous by the addition of fresh vegetables and hot bread, that a man cautiously approached them.

"Are you the folks looking for a young man traveling with two older fellas?"

"Yes." Abe wiped his mouth and stood up. "Have you seen them?"

"I think so," the tall bearded man told them, the lines around his eyes deepening as he smiled. "Can I sit down?"

"Oh, please. I'm sorry. We're the Carringtons."

"My name is John Thomson. Some people call me *Snowshoe*." Abe and Nancy eagerly shook his hand. One of the men on the stage had told them about this 36 year old man who, since January of 1856, had been carrying the mail to and from Placerville on the western side of the Sierra when even mules couldn't get through the snow. He did this on homemade wooden skis that most people called snowshoes.

"It's a pleasure to meet you. You're kind of famous around here, aren't you?"

John laughed. "Well, I like to think I'm appreciated. I don't know about famous."

"How heavy are your packs of mail?" Abe asked.

"Oh, anywhere between 50 and 80 pounds. But I don't carry anything else except a little food."

Nancy resisted the temptation to kick her husband under the table as she cut into their conversation. "What about the boy you saw?"

"It's hard not to remember him," John said, "seeing as how he stood out next to the other two. The boy told me they were heading over the Sierra to old Hangtown. He thought he'd leave the others and get a job, since he'd heard there's a lot of businesses there."

"Hangtown?"

"They're calling it Placerville now, but it's earned the other name."

"How did he know about the businesses there?" Abe questioned.

"Don't know," John responded, "but he's right."

After they parted from John Thomson, there was no need for discussion about their next move. When the next stage left going west over the Sierra, they were on it and again Flame was tied to the back. Their destination was the old mining town of Placerville, now a supply center for the mines and cities on either side of the Sierra.

But whereas the trip from Carson City to Genoa had been uneventful and comfortable, this was a trip they would remember always. They were given long white dusters to wear over their clothes and the driver read to them a list of things to keep in mind while on this trip.

The driver, a Mr. Hank Monk, told his passengers, "If you're not headed to Placerville or Sacramento, you're getting on the wrong stage. There'll be no strong pipes or cigars on this trip since there's a lady on board. Don't complain about anything at the stations or I'll leave you behind. If you need a rest stop between stations, rap on the wall behind my seat. When I tell you we're leaving after a stop, you'd better be ready or I'll leave without you. Some of the road will be narrow and pretty scary for some, but if you scream you could kill us all." He looked pointedly at Nancy and she just as pointedly looked back at him. He smiled and said, "Okay, folks, get on board."

With this pronouncement, Mr. Monk nodded to each of them in turn as he stood by to help them into the coach. Nancy noticed that his eyes were dark and intense, and could tell that the man would brook no argument. His neatly trimmed, short-cropped beard set off a mouth that showed a determination to say as little as possible, but promised that if he did speak it would be meaningful.

Once underway, there were breathtaking mountain views around every curve. The road was little more than a narrow cut on the side of a mountain with steep drops down to gorges carved by a river at the bottom that rampaged over huge tumbled boulders. Nancy looked down from her seat by the window to find this terrifying view directly beneath where the coach overhung the road edge. She did not do it again.

She did breathe often and deeply the cool fragrant breezes that filtered through the dense forests of soaring red-barked pines. Nancy felt an odd sensation of excitement for new adventures as she looked up through the dark green trees to the most brilliant blue sky she had ever seen. In that moment, deep within her soul there began the first stirrings that would some-day lead to once again feeling whole.

Near Woodfords a long train of three freight wagons, chained together and pulled by eight pairs of large mules, headed down the road toward them. The muleskinner was riding the left mule directly in front of the lead wagon, and was holding the jerk lines that ran all the way down the row of mules to the leaders. In this way, the teamster could give a few short jerks on the lines and the team would move to the right, or he could pull back steadily and move them left.

The wagons they pulled were huge: five feet deep and seven-teen feet long. The first of the three carried three tons of goods, the second 5,000 pounds and the third held 3,000 pounds. To control all this weight on down-grades, brake levers were mount-ed on the side of each wagon with big shoes on the rear wheels. One of the men on the stage said the rig was probably a Washoe Wagon made in Placerville out of the strongest hard woods avail-able. The other men nodded their heads in agreement, whether or not they knew what the man was talking about.

Hank Monk pulled the stage into a widened space to let the huge rig pass, but even so, no more than two inches separated the wagon and the coach. After that the road widened, but the stage passed through an almost constant cavalcade of people, most of whom were heading toward them. Some walked, some drove wagons, some led pack trains, and others rode horses or mules. One of the passengers said most of those on the road were probably heading to Virginia City.

Rest stops were welcome but brief. The coach passengers were offered nondescript meals at some stations and nothing but water at others, but at each the horses were changed for fresh teams and Abe watered Flame as well. The sharp chill of night in the high Sierra invaded their comfort at the home sta-tion where they spent the night.

Nancy wrapped her heavy shawl around her shoulders and stood outside on the porch. The canopy of sky above the trees was almost white with the density of stars seen through the crisp clear air. The beauty of the view caused her to wonder at the fact that she remembered so few such skies while crossing the prairies. Of course, dust had hung in the air and the high clouds of thunderstorms had been frequent, but Nancy also wondered if the hardships and tragedies had kept her from noting the beauty of the nights. Nancy sighed and went in to bed. The inn was near a creek rushing over and around a series of boulders, and the sound of it was to Nancy a symphony of musical notes that lulled her to sleep.

Unknown to the Carringtons, they had followed much of the route of the Pony Express riders of 1860 and '61. The last of the long series of relay riders had ridden through Hope Valley south of Lake Tahoe, turned north through Luther's Pass up to Echo Lake by way of Johnson's Pass, and then west toward Placerville. Here the route ended, having begun in St. Joseph, Missouri, as had the Carringtons. For eighteen months these brave young men had raced back and forth across the country with the mail until replaced by the lines of telegraph wire that followed much of their historic route.

At Strawberry, situated at the foot of a huge flat wall of granite and surrounded by tall narrow pines, they found awaiting them a good meal that cheered them greatly. The inn was a rambling building with a tall false front on the original building, but over the years other rooms had been added onto it so that it now looked like many small individually roofed buildings hastily shoved together. When it had first been the small way-station owned by a Mr. Berry, he had tried to pass off straw as the more edible hay. Once caught at this, he immediately became known as "old Straw Berry". Eventually his stage stop was referred to as the inn at Strawberry.

The size of the trees here were a shock to Abe and Nancy, even though in the East both had seen many forests. These western trees were over six feet in diameter and towered well over 200 feet above them. So fresh and vital did they appear that Nancy pressed her hand to the bark of one soaring giant, almost expecting to feel a pulse. She of course found no such thing, but she did feel oddly reassured.

At one of the stops they saw their first hairy black tarantulas when a gleaming family trooped across the road with their luxuriant hair glowing in the sun. Nancy recalled Mr. Monk's admonition and tightly pressed her lips together. The lizards with spiky hides and horned heads were a fascination enjoyed by those who had never seen them before. The men watched

Nancy show only calm interest in the unusual creatures that crawled and respected her lack of squeamish response.

Her resolve, however, was tested when they spotted two rattlesnakes that were larger than any seen on the plains. The snakes made haste along the road edge before disappearing into the underbrush. The passengers several times walked around more scorpions than made any of them comfortable. However, there were also cute squirrels that chattered from the drooping branches of trees, and colorful birds that darted among the greenery while chirping and bickering. Larger wildlife was glimpsed too--marmots, raccoons, bobcats, coyotes, and two grizzly bears.

One passenger went off for a walk in the woods after requesting a stop. An hour later he sat in the corner of the coach scratching a growing red rash on his arms. When Mr. Monk saw it, he laughed and explained about poison oak. "Just be glad you didn't squat in it." After everyone stopped laughing, Mr. Monk told them, "In the old days, prospectors 'round about here had to deal with it before they knew what it was. One fall, some fellas I know tossed the bright orange branches on a fire to clear the way to their diggings. The smoke about killed 'em. As bad as dysentery and scurvy put together, which were frequent enough visitors. But this stuff swelled 'em up and itched 'em enough to die from."

Mr. Monk, a highly respected and experienced whip who had driven teams in the Sierra for years, directed the passenger to wash his arms in the cold water stream nearby. He opened a metal box that he had taken from under his seat and offered a bar of soap to the man, saying, "Stop scratching or you'll make it worse."

The man ignored the soap and glared at the driver as he reached his fingers to his wrist where he scratched with stubborn determination. Hank shrugged and everyone got back into the coach.

Fifteen miles from Placerville they stopped briefly at Pacific House; a mile later they barely hesitated at Bullion Bend, where it was rumored that some years before thieves had buried as yet undiscovered loot from a stage holdup; and two miles later they enjoyed a longer stop to eat at Sportsman's Hall, named after the *sports* or gamblers that had plied their trade here during the rush.

The open ground around the building was crowded with canvas covered freight wagons piled high with food and equipment destined for miners in Nevada. The building inside was crammed with freighters, travelers and gamblers who crowded around small tables or lined up two deep at the bar. Abe purchased two meat pies and a large glass of lager and brought it outside to Nancy who stood next to Flame where he was tied to a hitching post. They ate while standing under a tree dropping golden leaves onto the ground around them. Next to them was a huge maze of wooden corrals filled with horses and mules used by the freighters, and from which Abe dragged some hay for Flame.

The stage had traveled beneath rattling aspens and willows, pines and tamarack, but the stage now began heading downhill through open terrain scattered with scrub. Travel suddenly became much faster, as this length of road through the mountains had gradually been improved since its construction in 1852. Nevertheless, Nancy later described the route as miles of tedium broken by miles of terror.

An hour later, after a short stop at Five Mile House, they traveled on to Placerville. The town was spread out along the course of Hangtown Creek where it ran through the narrow valley in neatly maintained channels. During the rush a little over a decade before, the creek had been diverted to fill the ditches that fed the pans, rockers and long toms of the hopeful prospectors. Now, the mountain slopes lining either side of the wide ravine bristled with young second growth pines, willows and aspens. The town seemed both threatened and embraced by these tree covered hills.

Looking out the window of the stagecoach from the road that sloped down to the town, Abe and Nancy's modern view was quite different from those days of the rush. Gone were the tents and canvas-roofed log shacks, brush huts and shanties, and the helter-skelter log town that had developed from that. In 1856 the town had suffered catastrophic loss by fires in April, July and August of that year.

Many of the commercial buildings had been rebuilt with brick, and the homes of wood and stone. Nancy admired the two and three story buildings facing each other across a wide main street, its muddy length disappearing into the distance where Nancy hoped to soon follow it. Why did she suddenly feel so adventurous? She almost asked Abe this question, but decided she couldn't expect him to understand something that she herself could not.

Their stage entered the town from the east and slowly moved down the wide and crowded main street. The Carringtons were amazed at the number of tall brick buildings, fancy wooden two-story businesses with wide porches covered in wood or canvas, rock-sided hotels with ironwork frets and carved corbels, restaurants with crisp clean curtains showing at the windows, saloons with covered porches and benches beneath their front windows, and a street edged with neat wooden sidewalks. There was construction underway in almost every block, either enlarging what was or creating new.

It had been during the rush that miners had first hit this area like hungry locusts settling over a sprouting field. But the crop here had been gold, and the men (there were no women present) called their town Dry Diggings, a somewhat popular name for such primitive mining camps in California during the rush. The shacks had been shared by as many as a dozen men and were separated by muddy streets just wide enough for a wagon or a pack mule.

There had also been little ordered thought given to where the men placed their hovels in the camp, since the main goal of each miner had been to be as close as possible to their diggings. No one had been concerned with constructing a lasting town, and in fact, little time was spent on anything but looking for gold. Eating, drinking, gambling, and occasionally sleeping were the only luxuries while working to strike it rich.

Everything necessary to reach that goal was expensive, and after a new prospector arrived, it could take him a month of profitable work to obtain all the tools he needed to continue. Just a pick, pan and shovel could cost him $50 or more; a cradle to wash the rock or the lumber to build a long-tom ranged from $200 to as high as $800; basic provisions were $1 to $2 for each item; woolen shirts sold for $50 and boots from $25 to $150. If he desired a mule, that could run him up to $400.

Rubbish had been piled in heaps wherever there was room, and sometimes dumped into an abandoned mine after it was determined there was no payable yield. The mining towns of the Sierra Nevada were wild and no one used words such as *civilized* or *refined*. When there was occasionally a minister in camp, he had been more interested in his diggings than sorting out the souls of his fellows. And then the sporting women had arrived, and the men had another reason to spend their money.

While denuding the hills of timber during the rush for riches, after the easy placer diggings had been exhausted, the men dredged the creeks and power-washed mud down hillsides into once crystal clear rivers. They killed anything edible that moved, and when they discovered that coyote meat only triggered their gag reflex, shot them for sport and their hides. When desiring more than meat, they dug up plants for their edible roots and left nary a one for future replenishment. All of this was done with no regard for how it impacted the few native tribes that had not been earlier exterminated by the first miners to reach the area. The miners were simply too busy with the present to think about the future, and too accustomed to their own supremacy to think of anyone else's needs.

By 1863, however, the miners had mostly rushed on to new excitements, although there were always a few putting forth die-hard effort in the hills around the town. Signs of past efforts were evident on the hillsides in the form of small abandoned pits next to heaped piles of rock and rubble. Many of these pits dotted the dozens of dry creek beds tucked in the ravines wrinkling the hills around the town. Abandoned mines could be next to a newly built substantial home or even in its back yard.

A few mine owners were successful enough to keep local men employed and themselves prosperous, but most of the local miners had been enticed away from the El Dorado County mines to Virginia City in Nevada, Monoville south along the Eastern Sierra of California, and Aurora just over the border in Nevada. If one desired to go from the coast over the Sierra to these eastern mines, or west to Sacramento from points east, most of that traffic had to pass through Placerville.

Abe and Nancy alighted from the stagecoach near the Cary House built in 1857 by William Cary. Standing on the sidewalk they faced a three-story brick structure with an iron-railed balcony running the length of each floor of rooms that overlooked Main. Beyond the large double doors standing open before them was a lobby of rich wood, crystal chandeliers and large upholstered sofas. The promise of calm refinement pulled them into the splendid building, but first Nancy had to wait for Abe to stable Flame. Abe soon entered the lobby of the Cary House and joined Nancy at the counter.

The heavy door of the hotel shut out the muddy street filled with long lines of freight rigs driven by dirty and loudly swearing roughnecks, small wagons hauling supplies to outlying ranches, riders on nervous horses finding their way through the traffic, strings of heavily loaded pack animals, and noisy cattle being herded through the town while leaving behind their filth. Also shut out was the hollow rattle of footsteps on the narrow wooden sidewalk that echoed the booted footsteps of miners, freighters, drovers, policemen, politicians and merchants.

These men shared the walkways with ladies in high-necked wool or fashionable chintz dresses in subdued tones to whom men nodded or tipped their hats. There were also bold women with painted faces whose colorful gowns plunged at the neck to reveal uplifted mounds of naked flesh, and to these the men smiled with familiar recognition.

After checking into one of the Cary's seventy-seven small but clean rooms, they washed themselves with hot water in the bathroom provided for those staying on their floor. Other items they needed were brought to their room by a formally dressed porter who introduced himself as James Derham. Abe's face was soon shaved smooth for the first time in months, and both enjoyed the feeling of freshly pressed clothes over clean skin.

Nancy slipped her arm through Abe's and they walked downstairs, ready to launch themselves upon Placerville. Abe opened the door of the hotel with a flourish and stood aside for his wife. Once on the sidewalk, Nancy looked around at the tantalizing number of shops with wonder. Across the street she could see a hardware store, a news agent's shop, a saloon and a restaurant. There was a long line of businesses stretching down the street in both directions and she could almost hear them calling out to her invitations to visit. She longed to explore their full shelves, piled tables and racks of goods, but instead she forced her thoughts back to the present. "Now what do we do?"

"We eat," he declared. Abe carefully led Nancy across the street between a break in a line of wagons and into the restaurant. Sitting down at a table covered with a white cloth, Nancy ran her hands over the fabric while breathing out a quiet sigh.

They accepted a menu from a smiling woman in a black dress covered in a long white apron, and Nancy felt almost as though they were on a date. Excited in spite of her eagerness to begin their hunt for Todd, she asked Abe, "What shall we have?"

"No damn rabbit!" Abe told her with force.

"Right." Looking down at the menu, Nancy added, "But I'm having a problem with everything else on the menu too. Ox-tail soup is a little too reminiscent of our recent travels."

"Fried bacon is on here too," Abe mumbled in disgust.

Nancy looked at the other items on the menu. "Bacon and beans. I guess we've been eating better than we thought all these months." They shared their first companionable laughter within recent memory, and both felt a surge of appetite in spite of the limited menu.

"Roast grizzly seems interesting," Abe commented. "But I think I'll have the beef steak with a potato, then the rice pudding with brandy peaches."

"I'll have the 18 Carat Hash and the same desert."

They ate with enthusiasm and enjoyed every bite. Nancy savored being waited on as much as she did the food. When they finished, they walked outside and looked to their right to where the street was divided by a wedge of buildings. At the point of the V was the plaza where the two streets met at a point and one large building.

All around them moved a milling throng of people that were part of the 5,000 living there. Abe suddenly stepped forward to grab the harness of a carriage horse nervously tossing its head while a shopkeeper loaded packages wrapped in brown paper into the back of the smart black rig. A handsome older woman dressed in severe black watched nervously from the sidewalk, but after calming the horse, Abe turned to her and offered his hand to help her in.

"Thank you, young man. My husband was so good with the horses, but I'm just learning." She took his hand and allowed herself to be assisted before gathering up the reins. She nodded her head in acknowledgement and joined the moving throng toward the eastern end of town.

Turning back to Nancy, he found her smiling at him. "My hero."

Abe blushed. "I couldn't let the horse hurt itself." Nancy merely smiled and slipped her arm through his, urging him to escort her along the sidewalk.

The next day they breakfasted early and then set out to familiarize themselves with the town. No bare space had been allowed between buildings, and they passed many set smack up against the next. One building even had a new gas light in front of it that was the first in the town.

"We can't live in the hotel for long," Nancy commented as they stood in front of the town's large hardware store, peering curiously through the window. Household goods filled shelves that rose from the floor and reached to the ceiling. Nancy sighed at the abundance of goods and realized they needed almost everything on those shelves if they were to create a real home.

"We'll find a boarding house as soon as possible," Abe told her, "or at the least rent a room in a house."

A passing stranger overheard them and said that a friend of his had moved out that morning from the Nevada Hotel on Broadway in Upper Placerville. When they found the hotel on the east end of town, proprietor Burton rubbed his bleary eyes and scratched his bulbous nose, then sadly informed them that the room had already been rented.

To their good fortune, and that of Mr. Burton who liked the look of the couple, a young man in a stiff boiled shirt and a carefully brushed black suit chose that moment to check out. Before his key had fully come to rest on the counter, Abe placed his hand over it and told Mr. Burton, "We'll take it." When the man hesitated, thinking of his long waiting list for rooms, Nancy spoke up and offered to clean the room.

Mrs. Burton, overhearing the offer, stepped forward from behind her husband where she had been sorting messages and said, "Welcome to the Nevada." Any woman who was willing to clean her own room endeared herself to Mr. Burton's overworked and harassed wife, Izelda.

While Nancy busied herself with broom, bucket, and a stack of clean linens for the bed, Abe returned to the Cary House to retrieve their things. After his return, Nancy quickly found her husband more in the way than a help, and encouraged him to begin his canvassing of the town for word of Todd.

Abe's hopes were high and he carried with him for the first time a strong expectation of finding his son and bringing him to his mother. It was important to him that Todd realize there was no need to feel guilty about Harold. He carried enough of that for everyone. After three hours Abe returned to Nancy with the news that the three had been in town, but were now gone.

"One man said that Croat had announced they'd be back soon with freight from Sacramento and heading with it to Virginia City."

Nancy fought her disappointment, then told Abe, "At least we know he's well and that we're in the right place." Small blessings, she reminded herself, are still blessings.

They stood in the middle of their tiny home and took inventory. Other than a double bed, there was only a dressing table and a cloth-covered folding screen in the corner. Behind this was a dark wooden chamber pot chair that when the solid seat was lifted, revealed another seat with a hole in it and a chamber pot boxed in below.

Having made a list of provisions, they spent several hours in town shopping and the remainder of the day creating as much of a home as could be managed.

Three crates stacked on their sides back to back with three more served as both storage shelves and a table, with room for two new straight-backed chairs. A row of hooks on the wall held their clothing since there was no wardrobe in the room. They pushed the bed into the corner to allow more room to walk, as well as space for two ancient overstuffed chairs on loan from Izelda Burton.

Abe lay in bed that night watching Nancy as she draped a small tablecloth over the crates before setting an oil lamp in the center. Her new long white wrapper hung open showing the thin matching gown and Abe could see the outline of his wife's trim body as she moved around the room in a flurry of cotton muslin.

Finally Nancy stopped fussing with the room's furnishings, and much to Abe's delight sat down at the dressing table. Watching her remove the pins from the coils of her hair, he smiled when the thick tresses tumbled below her shoulders as though relieved to be free. With a smile he realized that it had grown several inches since she cut it.

Nancy was not unaware of Abe's eagerness for her to finish brushing her hair and come to bed, and smiled to herself. Finally taking pity on him, she slipped the wrapper from her shoulders, rolled down the wick on the lamp until the flame was extinguished, and then slipped into bed.

Later that night they realized the grim reality that the Nevada Hotel was a stage office for those departing for Sacramento and points beyond. Loud talking, boisterous laughter, occasional cursing, and the clomping of heavy boots sounded as though coming from under the bed. The ruckus stopped just past midnight but began again at first light, and Nancy fervently hoped for better accommodations in the near future.

Abe wasted no time in searching for a job. After several unpromising interviews, he went to the main building of the Zeisz Brewery. Located at the foot of a small tree-covered hill near the east end of town, the brewery was an imposing square brick structure with a narrow covered porch running the entire perimeter of the second floor. There were several smaller out buildings, and room for the wagons that hauled the brew. Men swarmed the area, but one took the time to tell Abe where the owner usually ate his lunch.

Finding the boss at the Stoney Point Saloon, Abe introduced himself to a tall thin man with a full beard and hooded eyes. After he explained that he was new in town and was looking for a job, he was told to sit down.

"I'm Jacob Zeisz." He squinted at Abe for a long moment, as though assessing something he saw in Abe's face, then wiped his mouth with a napkin and asked, "What can you do?"

"I can handle men and animals, and drive wagons. I can read and write, so I suppose I could do clerking if I had to."

Mr. Zeisz chuckled. "Well, I don't think any man should do only what he has to, so how about driving one of my delivery wagons? You look strong enough to hoist a barrel without falling to your knees."

Abe indeed found it easy to heft the wooden barrels to his leather padded shoulders, and he quickly memorized to what area in each saloon he was to deliver the brew. Mr. Zeisz took to Abe's cheery demeanor that was as readily offered at the end of the day as it was at the beginning, and before long they were often seen together enjoying drink and conversation after the ten hour workday ended.

Although wondering if Buran and Effie Howard had actually settled in the town, neither Abe nor Nancy knew how to find them. As it turned out, Effie and Buran were friends of the Zeisz family. In fact, Effie had made it her mission to become friends with every wealthy and influential family in the town. It was while the Howards shared a meal with Mr. and Mrs. Zeisz two weeks after the Carringtons' arrival that Abe's name came up in conversation.

The next day Buran wasted no time finding Abe on his delivery route. Effie meanwhile arrived early enough at the Nevada Hotel that Nancy was still cleaning up after their breakfast of hard rolls and coffee. After squeals of delight at once again being with an old friend, they settled down with more coffee and caught up with one another's lives since parting near Carson City.

"You'll love it here in Placerville," Effie announced with certainty. "The people are friendly and hardworking, there's not too much lawlessness, and the shops are full of everything your heart could desire."

"It's also a beautiful location. How's the weather in the winter?"

"They say the snow isn't too bad." She made a face. "I'm not eager to find out what that means."

"Well, we won't have too much longer to wait. The leaves have all turned and are dropping. By the way, how's Charlie?"

"He's doing very well in the school here, although he's not much of a student as it turns out. Not like ..." Effie stopped, turned bright red, and covered her mouth with her hand.

A little stung by Effie's thoughtlessness, Nancy nevertheless smiled graciously and said, "Not like Harold was, you mean."

"Oh, I'm so sorry." Effie had the grace to mean it. "I shouldn't have brought him up."

"No. It's quite all right." Nancy's hand trembled slightly as she took a moment to pour them more coffee from the china pot on the table. "I'm learning to remember him without it leading to tears. Maybe it's time I learned to talk about him too."

"Maybe." Then Effie hesitantly added, "But we'll do that only between ourselves. People can be so judgmental about some things."

Nancy changed the subject, because although she wasn't sure what Effie meant, she did know that she wasn't ready to pursue the issue further. Later that night, however, she realized that Effie had been alluding to the fact that some people would feel that a *good* mother would not have let her son wander off to the point of being forever lost. Some might even be critical of Abe's decision to continue with the train rather than stay behind to continue looking for Harold. But Nancy also wondered if it was really Nancy's reputation Effie was concerned about, or her own if she claimed Nancy as a friend.

A week later Izelda, mindful of her husband's absence from the boarding house, whispered to Nancy that she knew of a small cottage for rent. "It's only half a mile from the brewery on a narrow road called Cedar Ravine. I know that a young woman like you can't be happy here. You'll be wanting your own home."

"That's so generous of you."

"Oh, not really," Izelda smiled and lowered her voice. "We'll rent your room in no time."

"Well, I'll be sure to thank your husband for the gracious generosity we've been shown here."

"Maybe you don't have to say anything to him about my part in your leaving." She surprised Nancy by winking at her.

Nancy fell in love with the small white house the moment she saw it. Her enthusiasm, however, did not carry into the interior. It was a simple rectangular building with no interior walls, and the unpainted side walls were roughly finished.

Abe's first comment was, "What the hell? Did the owner get interrupted?"

"Someone probably shouted 'gold' and that was it."

"Yeah," Abe agreed, "it's that kind of town, isn't it? But seriously, this is nothing more than a rough cabin. It can't be any wider than about fifteen feet. At least it has a wood floor."

Unwilling to accept defeat, Nancy pointed out, "The kitchen is here though."

This was an overstatement, although there was a small two-eyed black iron stove, a pierced tin-fronted pie safe for food, a water barrel with spigot on a small blue dry sink, and a narrow wooden table separating two wobbly cane-backed chairs. A long iron rod was suspended from the ceiling by wires minus a curtain that would separate the back twelve feet from the rest of the cabin. A bed of surprisingly good quality was pushed against the side wall in this space.

While Abe showed his doubt, Nancy began a creative discourse of ideas from an imagination quickened by the aching desire to once again have her own home. "We'll whitewash the walls and I'll get fabric for window curtains, and a long drape to divide the bedroom at the back from the rest. And more hooks for the wall for our clothes," she told him. "I can line a couple of crates with left over fabric to hold our under clothes."

Abe caught her enthusiasm. "I guess I can get some wood to strengthen and enlarge the table so you'll have a work space. And at the same time I can make a couple of tables for the front area."

"And soon we'll have other furniture for the parlor."

"Is that what we're calling the front of the cabin?"

"Oh, Abe, soon it won't be just a cabin. It'll be our home." She turned to him with a radiant smile.

Abe made no other criticism. Instead, he went into town and gave the landlord $10 for the first month's rent.

The house took up most of a small plot of ground located on a street off the south side of Main between the business section and Upper Placerville. Cedar Ravine was a narrow shady lane that followed a creek separating the road from the front yards of the few homes in the area. The Carrington's cottage was set back among large trees where the sound of the creek's singing waters could still be clearly heard. It was one of the reasons Nancy was so delighted with their new home. She cared nothing for the fact that this creek had once been the source of over a million dollars in gold.

Nancy enjoyed the approach of fall. No matter where she walked, she could see dark green pines upon the hills that cast their shadow upon aspens and willows as they shook loose luminous yellow and gold leaves. The wind sent them tumbling across the forest floor where they mixed with the thick spongy carpet of pine needles accumulated under the trees.

The swiftly flowing creek carried many of the bright leaves downstream like a flotilla of tiny boats. The vibrancy of the fall views and the crisp air was freshening to flagging spirits and hard working bodies alike, and the townspeople began to anticipate, and bet on, the first snowfall of the season.

By the time Nancy had transformed the sparsely furnished cottage into an inviting home, Abe had cut and stacked a large pile of wood against the house under the porch overhang. They were already burning it not only for cooking, but also for warmth in the late autumn chill.

Nancy gradually made the acquaintance of her neighbors, and enjoyed the friendliness of their greetings that generated in her a delicious feeling of inclusion. She especially enjoyed her walks through the town when she had time to explore the many shops and observe people arriving on the stages. Trying to guess who would be staying and who would be moving on was a game she invented while resting on a bench at the point where the triangle of plaza buildings met.

Although Nancy never would tell Abe, she viewed with fascination from a distance the colorful and noisy Chinese District at the far west end of town. When she reached this area, she knew it was time to make her way back. She would then pause across from the Cary House and try to picture Horace Greeley standing on the balcony.

He had visited back in '59 when he was running for President of the United States and she had many times heard the story of how stage driver Hank Monk had terrified the prestigious personage on his trip over the Sierra to Placerville. The story was, of course, always accompanied by the addition of the orator's own flourishes of imagination.

But she never shook the underlying feeling of tense expectation as she waited for word of Todd, or hoped to see him on the streets. That was why she spent so much time in town by herself. Unknown to her, Abe also carried with him a constant grip of tension. He never forgot that it was primarily up to him to catch word of Croat, Hickly and Todd before they arrived and then passed out of town again.

But winter arrived and the snow piled up, and by the end of January of '64 they had to accept that the trio had not returned to Placerville. They reassured each other that they would probably see them in spring when the passes were again clear.

Meanwhile, Abe and Nancy settled down to endure their first winter in the Sierra, and soon they were only too well aware of how much snow could visit the area even in a drought year.

CHAPTER THIRTEEN
PLACERVILLE, CALIFORNIA
1864 – 1865

"At last, a home of our own. I hadn't realized how much I missed such domestic order."

Nancy

"I stood across the street from our little white house this morning watching Nan sweep the porch clear of snow, and I remembered her words when I first showed the house to her and apologized for its small size. She said, 'What does it matter? There's only the two of us.' The ability to wound with words—how easy to do without intention."

Abe

Nancy and Abe managed to establish a life of near contentment, but underlying there was always a tense expectancy that suspended any sense of certainty about their future. Would Todd be found soon, or at all? Was there something more they should be doing to find him?

Only the beauty of the mountains and the welcoming nature of the townspeople helped Nancy bear the burden of this, and brought her a degree of peace. But when trying to describe in a letter to Elsie what it was like to live in the heart of such a regal granite beast as the Sierra Nevada, she quickly realized how feeble a thing words can be. How does one describe the emotional reaction that attends spending ones days surrounded by lush forests, deep blue snow-fed lakes, soaring peaks only a few would ever conquer, and dramatic glacier-carved canyons?

Even Abe, the most practical of men, felt the subtle allure and struggled to understand the solution of the Sierra's seductive nature. The miners thought the answer lay in releasing the mountain's gold, the freighters and businessmen thought it could be found in profitable commerce, developers sought to exploit it by expanding the towns, and politicians in manipulating its growing population. Each discovered amid success or failure that the Sierra's mysterious enchantment cannot be definitively resolved.

Although she quickly realized it was not the cause of either the rise of fortune or the loss of it, she still felt it a privilege to be living there. With so much capriciously taken from her, she concluded that she was allowed to live in such a special place more by the quixotic nature of life than earned right.

Although Abe and Nancy met many diverse and friendly couples who had been there for years, it was the men from work with whom Abe drank and visited most frequently. These men enjoyed talking about the people they had known in the town in earlier years, and Abe enjoyed being a new audience for them. The men's favorite watering hole was Fortunato Baldrini's Saloon on the south side of Main across from the courthouse. Abe liked his lager cold, and this saloon was near the old mine shaft where the previous winter's ice blocks were kept after they were cut from the frozen streams and lakes. There was always room there for a keg of lager for Mr. Baldrini.

Some of the men liked to drink at the Herrick House, but it always seemed to invite grisly reference to when it was the Jackass Inn next to Elstner's Hay Yard. It was there that the old oak known as the hanging tree had stood, and although the tree had been cut down, the stump was still in the basement of the Bye & Steward Grocery. While Abe found the men's jocular references to the town's infamous past off-putting, Nancy's more ironic humor might have appreciated that in the next century the building would become a bar brazenly named The Hangman's Tree.

During an evening of camaraderie with his friends, they were talking about the rumor that someone had purchased the lot where the Cedar Ravine Blacksmith Shop stood. It had for years repaired the colorful Concord coaches and big freight wagons that plied their trade between Placerville and Virginia City, and both vehicles usually returned loaded with Comstock riches destined for Sacramento and the Pacific Coast.

Bored with rumors, one of the men stated, "I first met Philip Armour at that shop. Nice redheaded young man. He arrived here in '52 with little in his pockets, established himself as a butcher, and left in '56 with enough money to go back east and start a meat packing plant."

"Lots of enterprising young men here, now and in the past," Juan Hernandez told them. "Just hope we don't lose them to Washoe."

"Yeah. Men like ole Mark Hopkins," Leroy, the oldest of them, declared. "He'll make something of himself someday, you'll see. He came here with a load of goods he brought from San Francisco. Now his grocery store is one of the most popular."

"Is he the one always talking about trains?" Abe asked.

"That's right," Leroy told him. "He says there'll be trains coming over the Sierra someday." Everyone laughed at such an idea, but at the end of the decade they would no longer be laughing, and they would be remembering *ole Mark* with renewed pride.

"One of the most ambitious men I've ever met was John Studebaker," Shorty Joe commented. "He saw a need for wheelbarrows during the rush and figured out a way to build 'em cheap. He had a shop on the corner of Main and Bedford, what goes up into the fancy homes, and sold 'em as fast as he could turn 'em out. I hear after he left here he started a good wagon business. He sure likes things with wheels." Everyone laughed at that, but little did they know that someday, when automobiles would be chugging through Placerville, many of them would be carrying the Studebaker name.

After the talk turned inevitably to the war, one old man told them that General William T. Sherman had been in Placerville back in '48. "It was still Dry Diggings back then. He was part of an official inspection of California gold camps out to prove if the rumors of gold were true or not. He even took samples back to Washington. That's when the news spread about the gold discoveries here."

"Yeah," one of Abe's friends agreed, "but it took until the next year for men to start pouring in from the East. Men from Mexico and South America beat them here."

Abe sat up straighter and exclaimed, "And because 1849 was the year that the first rush of men arrived in the gold country, they were called Forty-Niners!"

"Just gettin' that, are you?" Leroy smirked.

Abe colored and laughed along with the others. Before anyone could say it, Abe himself commented, "Don't forget, I'm from Missouri."

"That's right," Shorty Joe said. "I forgot ole Abe here was a puke."

And again they laughed. But they slapped Abe on the back and bought a drink for their friend who was slow to take offence, and could even laugh at the derisive name for Missourians. All were familiar with the popular belief that those from Missouri were a bit slow and a little rough around the edges. Abe laughed because he knew it wasn't true.

Nancy was proud of the way she had fixed up their little house, knowing the town was so crowded that some men slept in tents among the trees. She had quickly disciplined herself not to compare it to their old farm house, not so much because of the difference in the dwellings as the images of the children that would then arise. Most of these were of events filled with what she now thought of as her naïve expectation of happiness.

The lingering rawness of her losses disallowed the perspective of recognizing that beyond the tragic death of their children, good fortune had actually accompanied their journey west. Difficult and exhausting their days might have been, but there had been no decimating illness on their train, no starvation, and no Indian attack. Now they were settled in a modern town full of accommodating people where Todd was likely to return, and had a comfortable home and steady employment. It would take many years, but eventually Nancy would put all this in perspective, and she would wonder that it took her so long.

Christmas was a somewhat somber affair for them. They participated in the decorating of the town's tree at the Plaza and sang carols with others on Christmas Eve night, but agreed that the house was their gift to each other. Nevertheless, Nancy brought Abe's breakfast to him while he was still in bed, and Abe borrowed Mr. Zeisz's sleigh and took Nancy for a ride beneath the stars.

One of Nancy's morning activities that first fall, and throughout the winter that followed, was the same. After Abe left to go to the brewery just before dawn, Nancy would throw another log into the stove, wrap a shawl around her shoulders, and sit by the window in the small platform rocking chair that Abe had built for her. Sitting where she could see those passing, but they could not see her, gave her a sense of being part of the world without having to actually be out in it.

In the dawn light she watched men and women heading into town as they started their day in the shops, court buildings, saloons, and businesses. Some were on foot, some in wagons or light rigs and others on horseback, but all moved swiftly whether or not the road was covered in snow.

She looked forward each time to the emergence of the pines in the early light, first as black silhouettes against a pale sky and then against the sun's warming glow that quickly added hints of green to the view. This early hour was a rare quiet time in the town. The saloons were mostly empty of drinkers and gamblers; the Hurdy Gurdy women were resting from the previous night's excesses; and muleskinners and jejus slept soundly in boarding houses or tents while their freight wagons and stages were parked where their teams could sleep on fresh straw.

Nancy found a strange contentment in listening to the nearby prowling coyotes as they howled and yipped, and quieted the town dogs that desperately avoided drawing attention to themselves. Then, a quarter hour before the sun hit the tops of the trees, the forest would come alive with the dawn chorus that is the avian world's coordinated pronouncement that another day has arrived. With the sun glistening off the snow, Nancy enjoyed taking inventory of the night's visitors by looking at their tracks in the white fragile crust.

Always too soon this brief interlude passed. With light came the crow of roosters, and soon to follow was the noise of life being lived by those who could not avoid it. In winter the teamsters attached blades to the locked wheels of their rigs and small round snowshoes to the feet of their mules. But when eventually the snows were too deep for even these efforts, the passes closed and all freighting stopped until spring.

On a morning in March of 1864, after waking earlier than usual, the warmth from the rising fire in the stove finally reached Nancy in her rocking chair and she shivered. Soon the heat under the coffee pot would set it to boiling and the aroma of coffee would fill the house. That would be Abe's signal to get out of bed, although it was his day off and he might decide to sleep longer.

Nancy was finally at the stage of her adjustment that she could admit that she missed the loss of their companionable intimacy, once so taken for granted between them. But her frequent dark moods and bouts of depression during the long restriction of winter had brought them to a point of delicate and mostly subdued interaction. She had no delusions about her responsibility for this decline in their intimacy, but most of the time she just could not generate the interest to care.

More than once she marveled that although she was familiar with the physical pain of grief, she had never expected that there was such a similar ache that went with isolation. Their neighbors here were cordial, but she had made no close friend other than Effie, who had become so busy with her socializing and community work that the two women seldom saw one another.

Nancy often thought of Elsie and wondered what she was doing back in Missouri. Byron was too old to be conscripted into the army, but the war was no doubt impacting them, and Nancy longed to be assured of their safety. Although she wrote to Elsie often, she knew it would take almost a year for her letters to reach Missouri and a reply to make its way back to California. Elsie's letter would travel by stagecoach via Atchison on the upper south fork of the Platte, and then through Latham, Colorado, 60 miles northeast of Denver, before finally getting over the Sierra to Placerville. And that was only if Elsie paid first class postage of 10 cents each half ounce. Otherwise, her letter would go by ocean steamer from New York via the Isthmus of Panama. Oh well, she thought, I'm learning well how to endure loneliness.

That she did not immediately consider turning to her husband for companionship was not unusual. She often felt blame and recrimination toward him, even while knowing she was being unreasonable. But then, she felt the same for herself.

How long will it be before I once again feel joy, Nancy asked herself. She felt a flush of sudden amazement, for worded that way, the question intimated that it was only a matter of time before she *would* feel such an uplifted emotion. Maybe there was after all the possibility of a life accepted, and maybe even seasoned with moments of pleasantness if not happiness. That thought was followed by instant contrition, as though desiring to be happy was a betrayal of the memory of her children, and once again she was tempted to back off from the effort to move forward. However, this time she forced herself to take a more subjective look at her life.

"Two of my children have died, and my third has run away from me. That is the fact. Will my living in the black abyss of grief and anger change that? Haven't I been punished enough?"

She remembered a conversation with one of the older women on the wagon train as the woman prepared to continue with her family to Oregon. Mrs. Rader had stopped packing long enough to tell Nancy, "Don't blame yourself, my dear. Blame the trail. Your losses can be counted among hundreds of others that have haunted every mile of this trail for years."

"So my life reduces down to a mere statistic?" she had snapped at the woman.

"In a sense." Mrs. Rader was unfazed by Nancy's tone. "Or you can think of your family as part of the history of progress that's opening up the West to the rest of the country. How broad our sense of life, or how narrow, is simply a matter of how we choose to think of it. Hopefully, someday you'll be ready to make the choice for a life larger than your loss."

At the time, Nancy had been angered by the woman's words. Now she began to see the wisdom of them. Then, as reason does when allowed to follow its course, it brought forth the question, "Would Harold want me to be so unhappy?" She knew without question that he would have been the first to reassure and encourage her.

Nancy looked out the window when she heard the whinny of a horse and saw a wagon loaded with goods covered by a large tarp. The town had returned to its routine busy life, full of opportunities and promise, and for the first time in a long time Nancy felt that her days too might have a promise within them.

After a few moments she moved the coffee pot off to the side of the stove and went into the bedroom. She removed her shawl and her robe, and climbed into the bed beside Abe. When he felt the warmth of her press against his back, he rolled over to face her. She smiled shyly while running her hand down his cheek, then kissed him gently on the lips. Both were hungry for affection and reassurance, and with an abandon they had not felt since newly married, they reached out for one another in the gentleness of dawn.

With the arrival of each stagecoach and wire from the east came word of the war. Sometimes the tone in the saloons was jubilant because it looked like the Union was persevering, and at other times more subdued cheers were due to the Confederacy winning a battle. They had heard upon their arrival in town that in July of 1863 Lee's army had been whipped, that Vicksburg had fallen to the Union, and that gold prices had fallen along with it. The status of the war was something discussed in saloons and private homes, but the price of gold was discussed everywhere.

One occasionally heard someone referred to as *a Sesesh*, which should have merely meant someone favoring secessionist views, but it was quickly taking on the meaning of being a scoundrel. This did not sit well with Southern sympathizers, but since there were many more Northern sympathizers in the town, they could only mutter among themselves. Of course, there were always those who chose to react with their fists, but that only got them a trip to the doctor or the jail.

By the early summer of 1864, General Grant was commander-in-chief of all the armies of the United States, and had passed the Rapidan River with 100,000 men and 40,000 more under his immediate orders. He had been met by Lee with only 30,000 men. At this point, the status of the war was decidedly in favor of the Union.

In June of 1864, local interest was sparked when the Union ship *Kearsarge* sank the Confederate cruiser *The Alabama* off the coast of France. In the Owens Valley, Confederate miners had named the hills in which their mines were located *the Alabamas*, much to the chagrin of the miners loyal to the Union located just north of those hills above Independence. Consequently, when the Union miners heard of the sinking, they promptly called their small mining town *Kearsarge*. In time, the town of Kearsarge would disappear from the map, but the giant boulders of the enigmatic Alabama Hills would remain forever.

At the beginning of November, 1864, with the leaves falling quickly in the cooler temperatures, Abe decided to escort Nancy to breakfast in town at the Cary House. It was crowded, but James Hayes, a waiter friend of theirs, seated them at the first available table. A man standing nearby approached and asked if he could join them, saying that he was in a hurry to eat something before catching the Overland Stage in front of the hotel. They invited the man to join them and he held out his hand. "I'm William Brewer."

A man of average height, he was thin in a way that spoke of fluent movement and hidden reserves of strength. Although his hair was cut very short, his dark beard was full and his mustache luxurious. Straight thick brows anchored intelligent eyes that observed the world with an ironic if keen observation. His high cheekbones and long aquiline nose gave him an aura of aesthetic distinction, and Nancy longed to see what he would look like without all the facial hair.

"What are you doing in Placerville, Mr. Brewer?" Abe asked.

"Oh, please, call me William."

"Thank you," Nancy told him. "We're Abe and Nancy."

"You live here?"

"Yes. A little over a year now. It's a wonderful town."

"I can see that. Wish I could stay longer, but I'm heading to Virginia City. After that I'm going east to teach agriculture at Yale University."

"Oh, my," Nancy exclaimed, obviously impressed.

"Yes, it's quite an honor," Mr. Brewer smiled, "and a big change of life for me after tramping around the West. I've been working with Josiah Whitney for several years. He's California's Geologist. We're doing a geological survey of California. Last summer I was in Yosemite Valley."

"How wonderful. I hear it's the home of the Yo-so-mite tribe."

"Yes, but we didn't see much of them. It sure was dry. The grasses were mostly brown instead of green."

Abe nodded. "Yes, we're in a terrible drought here. I'm told it's pretty unusual though."

"Even so, the canyons and meadows of Yosemite Valley were some of the most magnificent places I've ever seen." After a few minutes of wistful reminiscence and artful description, Brewer added, "Last August I was hiking with Frederick Law Olmstead. A few years ago he was in New York landscaping acres of land for a public park, but now he's the superintendent of Fremont's Mariposa Mining Estate. There's talk of making him Commissioner of Yosemite and the Mariposa Big Tree Grove there."

"Where did you hike with him?" Nancy asked.

"We climbed up from Mono Pass on the eastern side of the Sierra to the top of what we named Mt. Gibbs after Professor Gibbs of Harvard."

"How did you get here to Placerville?"

"I spent the winter in San Francisco and took a steam train from there to Sacramento. From there I traveled by stage."

As they ate their breakfast, they continued to listen to Mr. Brewer's tales of his travels and explorations. Both of them were enthralled, and in later years would take great pleasure in relating to friends the fascinating morning they spent with a man destined to be a famous Western personage.

California's long and harsh drought of '64 came to an end with a few rain showers, but everyone was eager for good snowfall. It was this snow that each year melted the following spring to fill the streams and rivers flowing east and west. This water would always be of vital importance in determining the amount of water available to the cities of Southern California.

Throughout that year, Nancy forced herself to attend Effie's parties and ladies' teas. She even reciprocated with several luncheons. This made Effie happy, and among the women Nancy met, there were a few who were especially friendly and who responded warmly to Nancy's overtures. They came together for canning of shared fruits and vegetables, for shopping and an occasional café lunch. Nancy began to relax and enjoy being part of the town's feminine society.

On April 11, 1865, Lee surrendered at Appomattox and the war ended. Telegraph lines hummed across the country, and soon flags flew from every window, house top and balcony. Banners were painted and hung between buildings over Main Street. Brass bands played loudly every piece of music ever written that was near being a celebration of American pride and patriotism. Celebrations and parties commenced, and many gallons of liquor were consumed in the making of toasts. Those who had previously talked against the Union were suddenly claiming to have been for it all along, as much to avoid fights as to fit into the celebratory atmosphere of their community.

Abe and Nancy attended their share of parties, but far fewer than most people, and Effie lost patience with Nancy and told her so. Abe bent his arm at the saloons more than he had ever done in the past, and paid the penalty each following morning.

Two days later, with celebrations over and hangovers on the mend, everyone felt the need for news with an urgency that had no precedence. The presses of the Mountain Democrat that usually published every Saturday, printed the news as fast as they received it over the telegraph wires. When the wires were silent, with no actual news to fill their minds, the people resorted to rumors. This resulted in tensions that channeled into arguments and brawls. Abe and Nancy remained apart from the fray, but watched it with fascination. They were simply happy that the war was over and that they were enjoying a new closeness in their relationship.

Then, with the war over for only a matter of days, the revelry came to an abrupt stop. On Saturday, the fifteenth of April, a telegram arrived from San Francisco informing Placerville that President Lincoln, who most considered beloved or at least respected, was also hated by others. And one of them had shot him. It had taken President Lincoln nine hours to die of his head wound.

On the same night Secretary Seward, his son and a servant had been attacked in the Seward home and it was uncertain at first if the Secretary would live. Everyone in Placerville wondered what was happening to the country, and to be sure that nothing of an untoward nature happened to *their* town, all saloons and businesses were requested to close at dusk.

Placerville, like most other towns, cities and villages across the country, took down the gaiety of banners and put away their musical instruments. Instead, the town was draped in black and white bunting and smaller American flags. The overriding sound was the new fire bell tolling slowly throughout the day at the top of its wooden tower.

Many of the saloons closed out of respect, but those that did stay open at least silenced their pianos and closed the gambling tables. The tone of those drinking was unusually somber, and even those who had been pro-South were shocked that something like this could happen to such an esteemed and important person. People felt it important that proper decorum be maintained, and a rumor started that anyone showing disrespect for the fallen President would soon wear a hemp collar.

Women wept openly, and men who had shed not a tear through physical pain or loss of loved ones, now were unmindful of the droplets on their cheeks. When their wrath mixed with their grief, some men became voluble with imaginative promises of what they would do if they could lay hands on the evil one who had laid low their great leader. Other men found themselves so overcome with the shock of loss that they had nothing to say for the first time within anyone's memory.

Voices on the street were subdued and the only business conducted was that of necessity. No man was seen without a black band upon his arm, and women dressed in funereal dark colors. The banks were closed to avoid a run in the midst of wild rumors, and the courts were adjourned. The noise of construction was silenced, ore wagons and freight teams deserted the streets, and soon a quiet descended upon the town unknown there before. It was broken only by the constant dirge of bells tolling from church towers and the flag flying at half mast on the tall pole on Main Street as it snapped smartly in the wind. The busiest places in town were the newspaper offices of the Mountain Democrat and the Placerville Daily News, whose papers now sold out before they could be delivered down the street.

On the Wednesday following, Placerville and the near towns joined together to pay their respects to the fallen President. Before the speeches could begin, a procession started from the Methodist Episcopal Church on Main Street. It was composed of first the Placerville Union Brass Band, and was followed by the military with arms reversed escorting an empty hearse with pall bearers. Then in order came the judiciary, the City and County officers, fire communities, the Masons and other such organizations, citizens on foot, colored citizens on foot, and finally the citizens in carriages. They left Main at Coloma and continued to Mill Street where they turned onto Main in Upper Placerville and then passed back down Main to the lot fronting the Methodist Church. Not once did decorum and propriety of behavior waver.

The only incident of note was when part of the seating set up for the public collapsed under a young man from Diamond Springs. When it was determined that his leg was broken, the crowd quickly collected $100 that they thrust into his hands, and order was restored. There followed hymns, scripture readings, a sermon, and a benediction. Only a few people mentioned the city elections the day before that had passed off quietly.

The avoidance of amusements continued through the next few days, and only a minimum of commerce took place. People instead followed the steady flow of telegraphed reports about the President's embalmed body on its way by train to the Oakridge Cemetery in Springfield, Illinois. The fact of his being the first president to be embalmed fascinated the people, but they knew it to be a common practice during the War. Each side had embalmers traveling with the troops so they could be treated and returned to their families for viewing before burial.

By May of 1865, the passes over the Sierra Nevada were once again free enough of snow to allow traffic through from the east. Placerville's citizens ended their mourning and got on with their lives. Freighters filled their wagons and headed out to the mining towns east of the Sierra crest, and westbound traffic passed through on its way to Sacramento and the coast.

One of the miners in Virginia City had spent the winter trapped behind walls of snow that might as well have been concrete and brick. Gary Rosen emerged from this isolation of winter only to face the prospect of now working in the hot steamy underworld of the mines. There in the deepest shafts men worked mostly naked for fifteen minute shifts broken only by short breaks to drench themselves with ice water lowered in buckets. After due consideration of this, Gary reached the conclusion that he was not cut out to be a miner. Instead, he decided to return to his job as a clerk in the comfortable refinement of Placerville.

Immediately upon his return, Mr. Rosen found Abe and brought him the news of having seen Todd in one of the silver mines. He was sure it was Todd, because Croat and Hickly were also working there, and he had recalled Abe's vivid description of them. But the older men hated the hard work, and talked loudly and often about how they were going to quit and begin freighting as soon as they could save enough to purchase a rig.

Abe brought the news to Nancy and together they wasted no time making their plans.

CHAPTER FOURTEEN
VIRGINIA CITY, NEVADA
JUNE, 1865

"What a fickle thing is hope. It flirts with one's emotions and then laughs and runs away, leaving in its place only a sad emptiness."

Nancy

"Looking back on my search, I see it as a quest not unlike those who sought the Holy Grail."

Abe

Abe secured his well-stocked saddlebags and bedroll behind Flame's saddle while Nancy stood on the porch, tense and drawn, and wary of feeling anything akin to hope. She wanted to say something to show faith in Abe, but try as she might she simply failed to think of anything beyond, "Please, please, bring him back." Realizing this would only put more pressure on him, something she was sure he was already feeling, she wisely kept silent and tried to straighten her wobbly smile.

As though understanding, Abe turned to her and said, "I'll do what I can. You know that."

Putting forth more effort to look confident, she told him, "I do know." She looked at her husband and saw him for the handsome man he was. After clearing her throat of its tightness, she added, "You be careful now. I hear Virginia City is a wild place."

"I'll be careful."

"And send me a telegram when you get there."

He nodded, hoped the telegram would convey good news, and raised his foot toward the stirrup.

"Abe?"

He looked at her. "Yes?"

"I do love you, you know."

He smiled, and for a moment was unaccountably happy. "I

know."

He wanted to sweep his pretty wife into his arms and tell her how much he loved her. He wanted to reassure her that he would bring home their son. He wanted to stay home and wait for Todd to return to Placerville. But more than any of these, he did not want to raise her hopes unrealistically high.

As he rode out of town, Abe recalled his conversation with Gary Rosen when he had arrived fresh from Virginia City. During their conversation in the Oasis Saloon, Gary had been sure there was a boy of Todd's description with Croat. After all, it was hard to mistake the description Abe had painted of Croat and Hickly. Poor Todd, Abe thought, he was probably wondering when he was to be rescued.

Abe was relieved that it was a pleasant summer day wherein he would not have to deal with waist-deep snow or boiling heat. On his way to Washoe, he planned to follow a route laid out for him by friends in Placerville who had peppered their descriptions of what he would see with personal tales that he now recalled. He also remembered the unnervingly long list of places, things and people they had told him to avoid.

It would be a hard ride of 117 miles to the booming mining camp first known as Virginie. This name came from one of its colorful early characters, J. Finnimore, who had died back in '61. Now, after several years of magnificent prosperity, the town called itself Virginia City.

Abe was not alone on his journey, even if it seemed that a large number of the wagons, mule trains, mounted riders and foot sore walkers were approaching him from the opposite direction. This on-coming line of animal and human flesh was dirty, tired and dispirited, and Abe wondered what had brought them to such a sorry state. But the recently paid freighters with empty wagons were happy enough, and were headed to Sacramento for more supplies needed in the Nevada mines.

Those people moving along with Abe were all eager and in a hurry, many passing him with a swiftness that would soon wear down their steeds. Abe was astonished at the number of men traveling on foot and a few even pushing wheelbarrows. No matter their mode of travel, all had with them a blanket, a coffee pot, a satchel of personal belongings and another of food. The most unusual of his fellow travelers was a San Francisco dandy who rode a fine thoroughbred and wore a suit with a silk vest and a top hat. Abe figured that he was either a gambler or a lawyer. It was known that Virginia City had more than its share of both.

Abe passed a man limping along valiantly on crutches made from branches, but who was in the process of accepting a ride on a freight wagon. A Mexican with a pack on his back and accompanied by an energetic black dog herded a small flock of sheep, and the crowd moved aside for three drovers on large horses herding a dozen steers toward the hungry miners on the hill.

While a few optimistic men cheerily sang as they rode along, others simply glared at anyone so foolhardy as to look in their direction. Most men simply focused on breathing in the high altitude while making as much rapid progress as they could.

Abe looked at these strangers and wondered at their origins. He knew that most had passed through Placerville after having steamed across San Francisco Bay on large river boats that had disembarked in Sacramento, forty miles west of Placerville. Those with a substantial grubstake had purchased a horse or wagon, while those with less money in their pockets had set out on foot.

But the one thing those moving forward with Abe had in common was the vitality and brashness of youth. It was a youth that had as yet not known the disappointment of the vanquished, and who could not imagine anything less than a future as a silver king.

Those men who had experienced the thrill of the catch looked longingly at the many springs gurgling at the side of the road, a few of them trickling across the trail under bridges before falling over the steep wall of rock that edged the road. Looking up, Abe realized he was surrounded by abrupt granite walls of shockingly dangerous steepness. Crossing a bridge, Abe looked down at the creek beneath him that plunged into the narrow rocky defile carved by the American River roaring far below. Flame stepped off the bridge and Abe moved them further away from the perilous drop-off edged by telegraph poles linking the towns east with the home he already was missing.

After miles of fighting the dust of the curving road through pine covered mountain slopes, Abe came to a six mile stretch planked with three inch boards over the deepest of the soft dirt. Not long after this he crested the western flank of the Sierra

Nevada where he was surrounded by a dense red-barked forest. The old growth pines were so tall that the sun reached the forest floor only as dim rays slanting toward the earth between the stately green giants. Some of these trees were anchored in what seemed like solid granite, where over a hundred years before a tiny seed had found a soil-filled split in the rock and had there put down its roots.

By mid afternoon the red dust of the trail covered Abe's hat, his clothes, and Flame. It had also invaded Abe's eyes and lined his nose, and his throat ached as he longed for a tall glass of cold liquid. When he stopped to let Flame drink at a stream, Abe finally made liberal use of his handkerchief and took a pull on his canteen.

It was then he became aware of the balmy scents of warm pine, and the red and blue wildflowers that swayed in the breeze along the side of the road. Black and gold bees drank hungrily from the flowers in competition with yellow butterflies, and birds seen and hidden celebrated with song. Quail ran between the scrub, their tiny legs a blur as they streaked to find cover before a hawk screaming overhead could pin them to the ground with its rapier talons.

Yet as grand and pleasant as was all this summer abundance, there remained blankets of snow on secluded areas of ground always in shadow. It was a reminder to those born of the mountains, and a warning to those from more temperate climes, that if they timed their return too late in the fall they might not make it back at all. Some winters saw fifty feet of snow accumulated in the passes.

The men on the trail with Abe cared only for the present. All that mattered to them was getting to Washoe and digging out their fortune. At the least, they wanted the opportunity to receive the generous $4 a day standard wage set for those who worked in the mines. Some figured a few months working in a big mine would support them while looking for their own rich deposits, although men returning from the hill had laughed at the idea that new independent mines could be developed.

Those returning told the hopefuls to be prepared to sweat in a mine or work at a trade like sweeping floors or mucking out stalls. The men rushing to Virginia City barely listened, but they had no idea how expensive it would be to support themselves, or how alluring would be the saloons and gambling halls, or how friendly some of the women.

The first night brought Abe to Pete's Tavern, where he was informed that the accommodation consisted of space on the floor for his bedroll, although he found little room between the dozens of men already there. The landlord, evidently too busy to shave the brittle stubble on his face or change his stained clothing, waved his arm in the direction of the room's corner and said, "There's a wash basin over there." Abe noted the gray water in the tin pan, the broken piece of mirror on the wall over it next to a length of string tied to a common toothbrush, and decided he was clean enough.

After spreading his bedroll in a shallow depression in the earth beneath the low branches of a large pine, he slept well and rose early. He grabbed some grub from the landlord and continued a journey marked with beautiful views, and just enough danger to keep boredom at bay.

A number of pack trains passed him, each with a dozen or more large mules tied to each other and straining to carry heavy packs full of Washoe silver. Was it from the Ophir Mine, or the Gould and Curry Mine, or the Mexican or the Central? Wherever it came from, it was on its way to the smelters in San Francisco, and eventually would be minted into coin.

Long trains of mules moved down the hill behind him. Small bells hanging from an arch of metal over the mules' collars created a tinkle of metal that whenever heard, allowed those on the trail to move aside before being run down. Abe pushed Flame against the mountain wall so another such team could pass, yet was still twice raked by packs on the passing mules. Only the reliable temperament of Flame kept them both from more serious harm.

A mid day campfire warmed Abe and a dozen of his fellow travelers, including a man with red-rimmed eyes and sagging jowls who was returning from Washoe. The man told them, "I don't have much to show for my year on the mountain, but it's enough to buy my patient wife a new dress and myself a little store. And I'm damn lucky to have enough for that."

"You didn't want to stay longer?" someone asked. "I mean, so you'd have more to bring back with you?"

The man shook his head. "I've had enough of that place. There's too much shooting, too much arguing about the war, and too much loneliness. The only law there goes to the man who can pay for it. More money is being spent on judges and juries than development of the mines. And no one seems willing to admit there's a decline in production." Some of them exchanged a glance, but no one interrupted him and he continued. "President Lincoln, God rest his soul, sure seemed to like Washoe, and those on the mountain mostly liked him. He got the House of Representatives to vote in an Enabling Act so Nevada could draw up a State constitution. That's how Nevada became a State year before last, you know. Lincoln knew that Nevada would give him the necessary few votes he needed to pass the Thirteenth Amendment and end slavery. So you know the Secesh fellows tried to keep Nevada from becoming a state, and that caused some tense times in the town."

There was a long moment of silence. For most, it was the first time any of them had thought of Virginia City in any context but the making of money.

The man's brow furrowed and his voice lowered. "If you guys were smart, you'd turn around and go back to where you come from. The mines are about as deep as they can go unless someone invents a way to go deeper. But first they'll need to find a way to pump out all the water and muck that's been collecting at the bottom of the shafts. Mr. Sutro thinks he has a way, but no one listens to him. No sir, it's all coming to an end."

The men walked away from this nay-sayer, not a one of them willing to accept as truth what the disgruntled stranger was telling them. Maybe he just didn't know what he was doing, or was lazy, or had worked the wrong mines. *They* would have a better experience.

By the end of the third day Abe arrived at Strawberry, recalling his last stop there with Nancy on the stage to Placerville. God, how he missed her already! He pulled his thoughts away from her and made sure Flame was bedded in the open corral with good hay to eat. He then made his way to the sprawling building and a welcome fire in the large fireplace. It was ablaze with logs not much shorter than a man, and they produced such heat that most of the room's occupants seemed to have chosen the side furthest from it.

Abe was satisfied with a plate of decent baked beans and bread, strong coffee, and a space on the floor in a corner where he could be alone with his thoughts. A few men gave him a cursory glance, decided he was not going to be up for cards, and then ignored him. A stage pulled up in front and disgorged six more people into the noisy throng. Much of the talk around him centered on gold and silver, but most of those fresh from Nevada talked about fortunes lost and plans of starting over on the western slope of the Sierra.

There was only one treasure Abe wanted to find and it might require a rescue. He thought of the gun in his pack wedged between his back and the wall, and not for the first time wondered if he could actually kill a man. Then he thought of Croat and felt his anger rise. It mixed with his guilt over what he thought of as his failure as a father and how that had led to Todd leaving with Croat. Yes, Abe thought, I will indeed be able to pull the trigger if that's what it takes to bring Todd home.

Abe's attention was drawn to an old freighter who was playing at one of the near tables. Tucked into his cheek was the largest wad of chewing tobacco Abe had ever seen, and somehow the man managed to get the brown juice of it propelled ten feet into a spittoon without missing his target. He performed this interesting feat with such regularity that Abe thought he could probably set his pocket watch by it.

Before he realized it, Abe had fallen asleep where he was. The last thing he heard was a group of freighters arguing about which of them had traveled the most treacherous trail, who had hauled the heaviest load last season, and who owned the biggest mule.

The next day Abe was glad of his resolute determination to find his son, because anything less would have turned him around and headed him back home. A terrific hail storm passed through the area just as he prepared to cross the summit, forcing horse and rider to find shelter under an overhang of rocks or be pelted into a mass of bruised flesh.

For an hour the steel gray sky was rent by lightening while trees swayed and thrashed, and branches snapped and dropped unnervingly close. The noise of the storm deafened him. He held fast to Flame's halter to keep him from bolting, and only the fact that he had wedged the horse between large boulders allowed him to succeed. The storm ceased as abruptly as a stage play when the curtain falls, and he was finally able to continue his journey.

Not far from Meyer's Station, and with the gray storm clouds still ominously looming overhead, Abe passed a huge wall of bare gray granite close to twenty stories high and several hundred feet wide. It stood as a reminder to all who saw it that they were traveling through an area of superlatives—megalithic rocks, cataclysmic weather, monumental peaks, rampaging rivers, and plunging drops into cavernous impenetrable ravines.

Then the sun broke through and the deep shadows were filled with bright golden light. A gentle breeze brought Abe sweet floral scents and the perspective that he was after all simply passing through a range of mountains. He continued over the 7,300 foot summit on a road that emerged from the confines of the mountain to reveal a vista filled with the beauty of Lake Tahoe.

Nestled at the bottom of a huge broad valley with side hills covered in trees thick as nap on a green rug, Abe looked down into sapphire blue water mirroring the white clouds filling the sky. Abe found it difficult to turn away from such beauty, but he had a goal and he couldn't afford to allow anything to delay him.

There was another summit Abe had to cross, but this time there was no lush valley on the other side to encourage him on. There was only a broad view of a harsh and desolate desert filled with miles of gray sagebrush and white sand. Abe remembered the journey west when their stage had passed through this scrub over practically the same route. Then, however, there had been the Sierra's cool promise ahead of them. Now, he could only see low mountains in the far distance that had once been broken by ancient volcanic fury and beyond these a desert scorched by those ancient blasts.

Abe felt a shock as strong as if he had never before seen this broken and barren land. A friend in Placerville had shown him a cutting saved from The San Francisco Bulletin of May, 1860, written by the paper's correspondent Almarin Paul after his visit to the area:

> **The fag-end of Creation. The Almighty had some great idea when He planned Washoe, but halfway through He forgot. It was never finished. His creative power was exhausted. All that He had left was mineral. Regarding it of the least benefit to mankind He held onto it until He reached Washoe, then He emptied His lap.**

With the image of Todd ever before him, Abe was not going to be intimidated by anything he had heard or anything he now saw, and he rode on. In the far distance he could see his goal, a huge gray imposing mountain rising from the hot sand and sage at its feet as though wanting to distance itself from such unimportant plainness. It seemed to be gloating, "Don't I, after all, host millions of tons of shining glittering silver and gold after which men lust?" Such was the character of this mountain, especially when first viewed from the harsh desert below, that one was tempted to consider it alive with its own demon thoughts.

Abe shook his head and nudged Flame forward, sensing that the horse mirrored his own desire to turn around and return home. "Not yet, boy. Not yet."

After descending 3,000 feet to the Carson Valley, he crossed the Carson River bridge, rode through dry acres of desert scrub broken by a gully churning with the run-off of a recent storm, and eventually climbed another 2,000 feet of hills. He arrived in Carson City with an overwhelming sense of relief.

Abe rented a tub at a bath house, washed off six days of grime, scraped his face smooth, and changed his underwear with greater enjoyment than he ever thought possible. He wondered what Nan would have thought of his deplorable condition, but did not allow himself to think too long of her. What if he failed to find Todd?

Abe inquired at Mrs. Lee's Boarding House and found that the kind elderly lady had moved to San Francisco. The current landlord told Abe that she had married a man of wealth who had fallen in love with his gracious and attractive landlady almost immediately upon meeting her. Since the boarding house was full, Abe walked away to find another. He couldn't wait to tell Nancy of her friend's good fortune.

Fortunate to get a space in any boarding house, Abe was eventually shown to a room that he was required to share with only four other men. He allowed himself a good dinner and climbed into bed between relatively clean sheets. However, his slumber was not totally without interruption. The wind that had started in the afternoon as a hat-chaser, by midnight was a full-out storm of riotous noise. The boarding house walls and ceiling creaked under the stress of the wind, and sand mixed with small rocks pelted its exterior. Thankfully, by two in the morning the wind suddenly stopped and he fell soundly asleep.

After a large breakfast, Abe retrieved Flame and saddled him once again. "Okay, boy, it's on to Dayton. Then we'll tackle the mountain."

He rode past hot sulphur springs with jets of yellow steam rising in the air, over red earth that smelled of tar, and through acre upon acre of dry sage. The coyotes resting in the shadows of the sage were gaunt, their diet limited to half-starved jack rabbits and lizards. As the sun rose higher and the discomfort of the heat mounted, the smell of the sage grew so strong Abe wondered how he had ever before found it pleasant.

Nick's Tavern the sign read. But it was just another place where Abe could shove into a crowded room of freighters, miners and gamblers, and fork over two bits for beans and coffee. Desiring to be away from this tired and volatile gathering of human flotsam rushing toward Virginia City, Abe ate his meal in a few gulps and left hurriedly. Once more he chose to sleep in the corral with his horse.

"The last day of travel," he told Flame the next morning. "Halleluiah!" But he sang no jubilations as he climbed the steep rocky defile of Gold Canyon toward Devil's Gate where one could not miss the sign that hung across the road between high walls of jagged yellow rock.

"DEVIL'S GATE TOLL ROAD – 50 cents – PASS ON AND UP"

Everyone around Abe was eager to pass through the narrow canyon slicing through the hills that otherwise blocked their progress, but first they had to pay the toll. Abe stayed in line and waited his turn to pay. A long building with a sharply pitched roof, and more like a barn than a house, took up most of the only flat ground to his left. The covered front porch was a haven for men with mugs in their fists leaning back in old chairs while sharing rumors. Abe resisted the urge to tarry there in the shade and instead mounted Flame before passing through a canyon so steep and narrow that the wagon in front of him could barely squeeze between the tall stone walls.

The road through Gold Canyon wound through rolling hills that made Abe feel that maybe he was intruding where he was not welcome. Only a few small pines and bushes were scattered over the rocky terrain, while the holes of coyote mines dotted the hills in such a way that it reminded Abe of the prairie dog villages seen on the trail.

The hillsides of the canyon were a crowded display of timbered frames over mine openings, clusters of heavy iron stamps pounding ore, wooden shacks held together with rags and newspaper, and wind-shredded tents. Men climbed up hillsides and slid down steep gullies, probing with bursts of industry into the yellow folds of dirt.

Jostled on every side by men finding their second wind in their eagerness to reach Virginia City, the throng that included Abe passed Eilley Orrum's Gold Hill Boarding House. A man next to Abe said the house had taken on many improvements since Eilley had gained her wealth and become Mrs. Sandy Bowers. He also said that she had occult powers and had helped her husband find the fortune that was now declining due to her spending excesses.

Abe led Flame by the halter as they climbed higher and the yellow-brown hills folded around them. The high elevation taxed his breathing and forced him to stop often. This gave him the opportunity to look up and around at the swarms of men clambering over the hills and gullies like ants disturbed. He felt like everyone around him had a purpose unknown to him, and was rushing to fulfill it before someone could keep them from it.

Gold Hill was a small collection of buildings on either side of the main road. Men at a brewery were loading barrels onto large high-sided freight wagons heading a mile further up the steep winding grade to Virginia City. Abe was reminded of his powerful thirst for something cold and wet so he stopped briefly at the rock-fronted Vesey Hotel. He purchased a mug of lager in a bar so small there was no room for tables, then took his glass outside and sat in the shade of the porch near the hitching post where he had tied Flame. After watering the horse at the common trough, the refreshed pair headed up the hill.

At the top of the canyon, happily free from the cloying reaches of its gloom and crowds, Abe finally found himself looking down on the outstretched arms of Virginia City's streets. He was 6,200 feet above the sea, and 2,000 feet above the Carson plains, but the mountain still rose another 1,662 feet above him.

The citizens of this city had not settled for a scattering of rude multi-purpose shacks for their town. No, this was a proper city of substantial buildings laid out in long rows like center cut ribs of beef. Three tightly packed rows of hefty buildings made up the long spine of the city, with a few less meaty rows running parallel on either side and with narrow connecting ribs off of those.

Entering the town on "A" Street, at the end of which was the Ophir Mine, Abe could see several other narrow streets running parallel to his right. As he walked down the steeply terraced slope, he crossed through several streets and ended in the heart of the town. Each street had a share of the city's hotels, boarding houses, warehouses, markets, livery stables and business offices. Beyond these were small homes and at the far outskirts of the town were the brothels, blacksmiths, cemetery and larger mines.

"Well," he thought, "if this is heaven as some claim, it certainly has a lot of buildings."

He continued through the town and passed fancy hotels, restaurants, two theaters, reading rooms, assay offices, hardware stores, a tobacconist and stationery shop, and a Fulton Market. There was also a newspaper in town called *The Territorial Enterprise* that had recently boasted the sharp wit of an editorial writer with the colorful pen name of Mark Twain. Abe heard someone say that Twain had been forced to flee the town because of an illegal duel. They declared that this was, after all, a civilized town with laws and rules. Just note the doctors, lawyers, courthouse, Wells Fargo Bank and Express Office, and the large number of three story brick buildings.

Of course, for those not caring about civilized behavior, there was also an amazing quantity of saloons offering liquor, fancy women, and gambling of all the kinds known to man. If that was not enough to occupy a man's time, there were rows of cribs housing the common prostitutes. These were tiny shacks only large enough to hold a single bed and a small wash stand. Those professional women who were of long standing in the town, and known to the wealthier inhabitants, had invested in the mines in the early years and were now either retired or owned fancy parlor houses.

Abe noticed immediately that there were no trees on any of the earthen folds of gullied hills swirling around the town. The need for wood to build or burn had left upon the land only bunch grass and a few scatterings of spiny cactus. Although the outlying larger houses had picket fences, no trees cast shade on the homes they enclosed and no lush plants filled flowerbeds. A few scraggly vines or rose bushes sometimes grew near a front door, but this only managed to call attention to the forlorn aspect of the property.

Looking up through the town to the top of what was now called Mt. Davidson, Abe saw at the peak a giant flag pole and an appropriately over-sized American flag. Its stars and stripes whipped about in the strong breeze, and whether one's heart lay with the Union or the recently fallen Confederacy, no one was left to forget that the war had been liberally funded by the wealth that came out of this mountain.

The pounding of the stamps in the mills echoed through the town but it was almost drowned out by the rumbling of ore wagons, the shouts and curses of a hundred teamsters driving rigs heavily laden with supplies, and the sharp crack of bullwhips. Gunfire popping in alleys gave accent to the larger explosions of dynamite in the mines. Occasionally Abe passed the raised voices of heated political debates and other arguments taking place on the sidewalks among diverse members of the population.

Abe shared the sidewalks with a mix of silk-hatted businessmen with neatly trimmed beards, miners whose faces were smeared with dirt and who wore tattered overalls, drovers in dusty chaps and felt hats who had recently been on the trail, muleskinners wrapped in deer skin jackets, and travelers fresh off the stage in rumpled suits.

Most of the women hanging on men's arms were the painted and flirty type. They carried small ruffled parasols in bright colors and twirled them coquettishly. Those few females who were wives of the successful wore decorous gowns of calico in demure patterns with high collars. Their parasols had few flounces and remained over their heads to block the sun and nothing more. However, Abe was surprised to see that both classes of women greeted one another with polite smiles and nods as they passed.

The town was filled with more than a suggestion of obvious wealth. Men in new suits whose soft hands had never held a pickaxe smoked big cigars while lounging on balconies overlooking the street below. Their bellows and guffaws hung on the air as they greeted each other with the latest joke, discussed stock prices, or shared news from the East. But only a few men bragged about the current production in their mine.

This was the grand magnificence of Virginia City, discovered only six years before. Stock was sold in feet of a mine, rather than in shares, and in 1863 while Abe and Nancy had trudged across the country, stock in the Gould and Curry had soared to $6,000 per foot. The Ophir had reached $4,000 a foot, and by the end of that year, 64,433 tons had been taken out so fast that the mill in Six Mile Canyon had been unable to cope, forcing the building of 15 additional mills.

To work all of this on the Comstock, and supporting those who dug and milled and hauled it, were 25,000 people. In Gold Canyon there were another 9,000. All had to be housed, so boarding houses flourished along with hotels, many of which were more like barracks than places of fancy leisurely rest, although there were a number of those too. Homes of wood, stone and brick, along with huts of brush and canvas covered the outlying hills. However, because of the pressure to get the silver out so fast, millions of dollars would be lost in the tailings.

As impressive as it seemed, Abe thought there was an odd false note to it all. Even in the saloons, with their loud music and raucous laughter, he felt an underlying tone of desperation and shuddered as he thought what it must be like there in the winter. With snow piled up on the surrounding mountains, all travel in or out would be blocked by an impenetrable barrier of snow in the canyons. Abe shook his head and thought, "No wonder Gary left when he had the chance."

The reality was that these thousands of people were in constant need of food and drink, clothing, animal feed, timber, and the mundane things of life like buckets, buttons, hair oil and medicine, not to mention everything needed to run a mine. It had all been freighted to them across the Sierra Nevada. Although there were passes through Downieville and around Donner Lake, most of the supplies had come over the same route followed by Abe.

Between 1860 and 1865 the Placerville Road had carried over 5,000 freight and ore wagons. Fifteen thousand draft animals, along with 2,000 teamsters and hostlers had been employed to do this hauling. Every day 120 tons of freight had passed into the town and every year the Comstock had paid out $12 million in freight charges as well as $1.5 million in tolls.

Abe had been told that the Pioneer Stage Company brought

100 people each day to the town, maintaining twelve Concord coaches with six horses each, and generating $1 million in fares. Looking up as one of these colorful coaches passed him, Abe watched the driver in his long leather duster and lemon yellow gloves pulling back on the reins. There were nine people inside with baggage on top of the stage and in its boot, and more similarly crowded stages would soon arrive behind him. The drivers saluted one another as they passed.

This coaching fraternity was a close-knit bunch, a clutch of feisty roosters that knew how to take care of themselves and their passengers, and who didn't hesitate to draw down on anyone who might offer interference. It would be almost twenty years before they would discover that a hen dressed as a rooster had been in their midst for years--a driver they currently called friend and who they acknowledged as one of the best whips anywhere in the mountains.

As the agitated passengers of a dusty coach alighted in front of the stage depot, Abe gathered from their excited conversation that they had been held up by a masked shotgun-toting bandit. One of the passengers seemed much less upset than the rest. To the surprise of the other passengers, he pulled out his shirt, reached into his pants and removed a flat money belt that rattled with silver dollars. Tucking his shirt back into his pants, he commented, "Oh well, such holdups are only to be expected."

The glare of resentment that the others aimed at him showed them to be less philosophical, but Abe felt that he had just received a valuable lesson.

CHAPTER FIFTEEN
VIRGINIA CITY – AURORA – BODIE
SUMMER, 1865

"I miss Abe terribly, but at the same time it begins to feel like the town belongs to me. And I to it."

Nancy

"I always knew I could be stubborn, but I never knew to what extent. And I now know what it takes to finally push me to the breaking point."

Abe

Abe made sure Flame was comfortably settled in a stable then walked north up the steep incline of Virginia City, surprised at the sprawling scope of the town and how it felt more industrial than domestic. There were substantial buildings behind the false front facades, some even three stories high. Many were protected by black iron bars over windows and sheets of iron used for doors to protect the wealth earned by those who were not willing to have it plundered by the dishonest, or the desperate.

Second floor balconies surrounded by railings of black iron, and furnished with small tables and chairs, were decorated with pots of bright red flowers that hung from the balconies and swayed in the breeze. Abe stopped for a moment to press his nose to their muted scent.

Civilizing influences were evident all along the length of the main street, including gas lights that illuminated the wooden sidewalks and even the interior of some shops. A wooden sidewalk extended the length of the street on both sides and was in good repair, and men with small carts shoveled up the animal droppings from the street.

Dozens of saloons lured thirsty men to step inside both day

and night. The best were run by men in pressed suits and freshly boiled shirts sporting new collars and cuffs fastened with studs of precious stones. Inside they looked more like private clubs than saloons. Gold leaf accents abounded, gleaming brass footrests ran the length of the dark wood bars, huge mirrors reflected the sparkle of crystal on the tables, and artfully painted murals or the best flocked papers covered the walls. Many saloons had portraits of Lola Montez in her dancing dress, or Ada Menken covered in a sheer gauze costume while strapped to the back of a black stallion and looking pleadingly up to heaven. Oh, how the men loved it when the Menken appeared in their theater!

As he walked through the town, Abe found himself entertaining strange and random thoughts. "Chaotic, unstable, pretentious, glittering, tormented, unrealistic, relentless, and wonderful." He stood at the top of a hill and looked back on the town. "Just think, all this shabby splendor sprang forth in a geyser of irrepressible entitlement when the mineral Gods favored the fortunate few with incredible wealth."

Abe felt the temptation to be drawn into the glamour and excitement of the place, but he never lost sight of his reason for being there. Considering the massive crowds of people and the layout of the town, he was beginning to think finding Todd a more difficult task than he had anticipated.

The first places he approached were the mining offices where a couple of foremen remembered the trio, but claimed not to have seen them recently. Oddly, no one with their names had been recently on payrolls, leading Abe to wonder why they would have used false names.

Piper's Old Corner Saloon, The El Dorado, The Howling Wilderness, and The Melodeon were only a few of the fancy watering holes and gambling parlors Abe visited over the next several evenings. During the day he went into stores, newspaper offices, livery stables, boarding houses, restaurants, business offices, and mining shacks.

Leaving each time with "no" ringing in his ears was a repeated assault on his optimism. Abe more than once swallowed hard and took a deep breath, stoically refusing to acknowledge even a hint of the disappointment that fought to take over his resolve. Instead, he told himself that in the next place he entered there would be someone who had talked to one of them enough to give him a clue as to their present location.

His eyes continually scanned the crowds of people milling around him, and each time the whistle blew at shift change he stood outside a different mine. Whenever a tall young man approached, his breathing quickened until he could see if it was Todd. It never was.

A lesser man would have headed to one of the saloons for liquid solace, and the thought did occur to Abe more than once, but he needed all of his faculties sharply in focus. Nothing could be allowed to get in the way of finding his son. Hour after hour he held himself together with a stubborn determination that nevertheless disavowed too much hope.

On the morning of the fourth day, Abe stepped into one of the smaller saloons on Main Street. He had skipped it until then because it was always so crowded and raucous that no one paid him any attention, but on this morning there were only about a dozen drinkers at the bar. It was the bartender here who told Abe that the trio had been there only two days before and that the man called Hickly had spent considerable time at the faro table. Abe cursed the fact that he had so narrowly missed seeing Todd, and went in search of the faro dealer. He found the table at the back of the saloon next to the stairs that led to the second floor.

Abe approached the faro table with its layout of thirteen cards, all spades, painted on its surface. The open-faced dealing box was there ready to hold the cards face up for the first gambler to approach. Abe noted that the chair on a raised platform to the dealer's right was empty, but knew that later, when the saloon was full of gamblers, the seat would be occupied by a lookout that could keep an eye on the play.

Abe focused on the man standing next to the table. "Good afternoon. I'm Abe Carrington and I'm looking for my son. The bartender said he was in here recently."

"Hi. I'm Herbert Smith, the dealer here." Mr. Smith was in his early twenties but had the bearing of a man who had seen enough of the world to never be surprised by anything it could present. Abe noted his above average height and broad shoulders, his meticulously groomed short mustache and thick dark hair, and the perfectly pressed suit showing a gold silk vest between the folds of the fine wool jacket. When he leaned against the wall next to his table his jacket fell open and Abe noted a small turning-barrel six-shot Pepperbox in a holster under his arm.

Smith gave Abe close scrutiny as he lit a small cigar. "You don't look old enough to have a grown son."

"He's just seventeen." Abe told him the basics of what had happened to his son.

"That's rough." Mr. Smith picked up a deck of cards and shuffled them from hand to hand with rhythmic ease. "I did see a group like that. It was late afternoon just before the shift change at the mines. One man played here while the other drank at the bar. They were dressed like any miner, but the older one at the bar had a fur hat like you don't see much any more. The young man was dressed in overalls like the miners wear, but he didn't have the build of a kid. Working in the mines will muscle up a fella fast."

"What did he say?"

"He didn't say anything the whole time he was here, just sat at a near table and watched the man playing. I think he was trying to learn the game."

"How did he look?" Abe asked anxiously.

"Not all that clean, but definitely healthy, even robust. He ate some bar food and when the old man found out he barked at him. But he paid willingly enough. I did wonder why the kid had no money of his own."

"Did the boy look like he was scared?"

Smith considered a moment. "No. That never occurred to me. More like he was bored."

"Do you know if they're still in town?"

"I wouldn't know. I didn't see them again after they were in here."

"Did you hear them say anything that might indicate where I can find them?"

Smith shrugged. "I've talked to a lot of people since then."

"I know, but please try to recall."

A few minutes passed as Smith cast his mind back. "At one point the older man with the fur hat came up to the man at my table and watched him play. Then out of the blue he told him they needed to get out of town. The man who was gambling said why not head to Aurora. They didn't say anything more than that."

Abe thanked him profusely and walked out to the sidewalk where he found space at the end of a bench in the shade of the building's overhang. The sounds around him were those of any large mining town. Men nearby shouted curses of impatience while trying to get through the crowds, wagons creaked and groaned, mules brayed while the freighters swore at them, and the shift change whistle cut through the air.

But the sounds emanating from the hills that wrapped around the town were strange to him: the echoing thud of heavy iron stamps crushing ore, the throaty rumble of dynamite blasts deep in shafts, the pulsing pound and rattle of heavy machinery, and the hissing of steam pumps overworking to empty shafts of the constant seep of water. The noise irritated Abe just enough to keep him from falling into a sullen cast of mind that threatened to overcome him.

"So," he thought to himself, "Todd isn't here after all." Looking desperately for something positive, he settled for, "At least he's well."

He found the telegraph office and sent a message to Nancy with this mixture of good and bad news. He also told her that he was going to Aurora by stage. Only this stage line wouldn't allow Abe to tie Flame to the back, because it traveled too fast to assure his safety.

It hadn't been an easy decision, but Abe reasoned that a stage pulled by six horses could go faster than one horse carrying a man and his gear. He was not, after all, a Pony Express rider--under twenty and light of frame. He said as much to the man at the livery who was willing to buy Flame and his tack for more than enough to cover Abe's fare to Aurora.

"Ah, those were the days," the man recalled with a grin as he watched Abe feed grain to the horse he had just sold, and that now he was brushing with long slow strokes. "The Pony Express riders came through Dayton, and in the beginning some of us would go down the mountain to watch 'em race on by. Hell of a time, it was."

The man wanted to talk further, but Abe didn't trust himself to speak. He clenched his jaw, gave a last scratch to Flame's nose, and resisted the urge to throw his arms around his neck. Instead, he shoved the grooming brush into the man's hand and hurried from the large barn. Hearing a familiar whinny behind him, Abe's mind raced through the last five years of images of himself and Flame, stopping at the picture of Todd riding the horse for the first time out on the trail. Abe gritted his teeth and picked up his pace.

"Abe?"

"Lona!" Abe fought the urge to raise an eyebrow as he noted the glow of rouge on her cheeks, the red stain on her lips, and her yellow low-necked dress. It took him a moment to grasp the fact that Lona was a *sporting woman*. His mind rejected the harsh but accurate word prostitute.

Lona's laughter as she watched Abe's reaction was highlighted with throaty sexual undertones, but she was totally without embarrassment. This was so unlike anything Abe had heard from her before that he was struck speechless.

"Dear Abe," she chuckled. "Why don't you escort me into the saloon over there so we can talk?"

When they were seated and sipping, Lona asked him, "How's Nancy?"

"She's fine. We're living in Placerville now." She listened intently as he brought her up-to-date with their lives.

"I thought I saw Todd about a week ago," she told him. "But then I assumed it was a flight of fancy."

"Where was he?"

Lona looked down at her drink and said, "You may not want to know."

"Yes, I do." Then he realized why she might be hesitating and said, "Not with you! He would have recognized you."

"No, no. I saw him come out of a crib just off Main."

She watched his stunned realization that Todd had tasted the pleasures of the flesh, and knew that Abe still thought of his son as more child than man. "Maybe what made me think it wasn't Todd was the fact that he moved not like I remember him, but with assurance and confidence. I know his leaving you the way he did must have been a torture for you and Nancy, but frankly it may have been the making of him."

"But he's only seventeen," Abe protested.

"Nancy told me you were younger than that when you two married."

Abe grimaced. "Yeah, but..."

"Oh, for God's sake, Abe. Don't say you were different."

Abe changed the subject. "Why did you used to speak so formally?"

"Oh, that." She smiled and took a swallow of her drink. "I often still speak in that manner. See?" She laughed at herself. "It's a habit I gained from studying books on etiquette." Her smile vanished and she turned to look out the window as she spoke. "When Pete met me, I was only fourteen and doing what I'm doing now, only in much less refined and profitable circumstances. He took me in, cleaned me up, educated me, and then determined that I would make him a proper wife. Gratitude and some degree of fear prompted me to accept."

"Fear?"

"He wasn't always a gentle man." Her hand brushed her cheek with a slight wince of memory.

"We heard him yelling at you several times."

She snorted her disdain. "Oh, that was the least of his ill treatment. He felt our childless state was God's punishment upon me for my wicked past and that he, being married to me, was also being punished." She stopped and looked down into her drink. "He liked that word, *punish*."

Aghast, Abe asked her, "He was often physically violent with you?"

She looked up into Abe's red face and smiled softly. "Oh Abe, it gives me such joy to know that there's still a man in this world that can be shocked by such a thing. Yes, he hit me often."

After a moment, he said, "Then his dying the way he did, when he did..." He left the sentence hanging.

"Shall we just say that it was an unfortunate tragedy? But fortuitous for me."

He put his hand over hers as it lay on the table next to her glass. "Yes, fortuitous. But is this the life you really want?"

"For now," she shrugged. "I've got quite a nest egg and it's growing."

"Really? From just the money you earn doing...what you do?"

Her smile returned. "No. From time to time I buck the tiger in the saloons."

"That means faro, right?"

"Right. Herb Smith, a dealer here in town, taught me."

"Yes, I met him. Nice to you, is he?"

"Yes. Very nice."

The sudden blush to her cheeks pleased Abe when he realized that Lona was not so jaded that she had stopped hoping for love. "So what do you plan to do with your nest egg?"

"At some point I plan to open a lady's clothing emporium. I get along quite well with the *good* ladies of the town. I know all their pet charities and give generously."

Abe laughed, amazed at her self-reliance and wisdom. "Well, if you ever decide you want to get away from here, come to Placerville and we'll introduce you as a distant cousin or something."

"In other words, if I don't mind denying who I am so I can spend my days in *proper* society," she teased.

But Abe answered her seriously. "Yes, that's it exactly."

"Dear Abe." She smiled tenderly at him. "It's a kind offer, but I like it here. There's an atmosphere here that appeals to me, and I think I'd miss Virginia City if I was long away from it."

"Well, the offer's always open."

"Go look for your son." She smiled brightly. "And don't worry about me."

She walked with him to the stage and watched him climb inside. Just as the coach rolled forward, she threw him a kiss accompanied by a wink. Seeing the other men smile, Abe was glad no one in the coach knew him. But the ache in his heart right then was not for Lona, and he dared not look down the street at the livery stable.

The stage was a swift one and soon Abe was traveling south through Nevada's Sweetwater Valley and past the Toyabe Mountains. They stopped briefly at the Sulphur Springs station, which featured a nearby round tent packed with gamblers and rough drinking men. The previous station keeper, also a Justice of the Peace, had recently murdered his wife there and everyone was talking about it.

The stage passed over the Walker River bridge, crossed through miles of desert scrub, hesitated at The Elbow stage station, and passed down Pine Street into the booming town of Aurora. Abe pushed through the press of people around him and made his way along the sidewalk while listening to the off-key music escaping from a number of busy saloons. He stopped at each one to ask after Todd, with no results.

It was easy for Abe to find his way around the town because

Pine, which was the long central business section, ran parallel to Spring Street, which led east to a hillside dotted with straggly pines and cedars near Willow Spring as it flowed through a narrow meadow. The other street names left no doubt as to the reason for the town's existence, since they were named after the local mines or mills: Bullion, Silver, Juniper, Cedar, Mono, Winnemucca, Del Monte, Antelope, and Wide West.

He was impressed with the elegance of the Exchange Hotel, the decorative Real del Monte Saloon, and a surprising number of tall brick buildings. They were all on the one long central street, with the shorter streets branching from it. Abe barely had time to take in this much of the busy town before falling exhausted into bed at a crowded boarding house. He shared the room with ten other men stacked like cord wood upon bunks lining the walls.

To Abe, Aurora was just another desert mining town, one of over a hundred that sprouted in the sagebrush when times were good and then shriveled back into the scrub when the ore played out. It was surprisingly larger than he expected, but its only purpose for existence was still that of supporting the local mines. The number of businesses necessary to support the miners had grown in keeping with the rate of rich ore bodies being discovered, but he could tell that already the mines were playing out and soon men would be looking for greater "excitements" elsewhere.

When discovered in the early 1860's this had been an area of meandering quartz veins that varied in size from an inch thick to as wide as 80 feet. The rich veins ran through volcanic rock, and had to be hacked out with sharp picks or blown out with unstable black powder. After the ore was hauled in large wagons over the steep hills to the mills, it was crushed beneath the 700 pound feet of the stamps and then run through amalgamators that used mercury to separate the gold from the rock. After the gold was melted down in red hot forges and poured into molds, it was freighted to the Carson City Mint or hundreds of miles further to San Francisco. Few of the men involved in all of this lived healthy or long lives.

The first dwellings had been dugouts in the sides of gullies, the walls lined with stacks of mortarless rock and the ceilings nothing more than stretched canvas and brush, with the best beds being a pile of straw sandwiched between rawhides. Most of these had been replaced by either simple shacks or nicer adobe houses, many of which were now crammed with men using them as boarding houses.

Many thought Aurora an exotic name for a town stuck out in the high desert of the Esmeralda Mining District, 7,400 feet above the sea. Aurora was a Roman goddess, but the name also shared the same Latin root as aurum or gold. Most miners thought this too highfalutin' to be the origin of the town's name and claimed it came from the Aurora borealis that sometimes played above the town. Still others claimed that one of its first claimants came from Aurora, Illinois. It was a favorite debate that was never settled.

But Abe thought about none of this. Over and over he asked himself if Todd was somewhere in this busy town longing for his father to rescue him. Consequently, Abe slept poorly that night and was up early the next morning.

It was Sunday and he forced himself to eat a quick breakfast of brown bread and beans at J. Marchant's Bakery. After washing it down with a large amount of strong coffee, Abe emerged to stand on the front porch from where he could see the stubby pinion pines scattered over the hills surrounding the town. He was surprised at the presence of so many general merchandise stores, there being over a dozen, but he called in at every one of them. He then inquired at the hotels and all of the twelve boarding houses. By this time he was more surprised than disappointed, so sure had he been that he would easily find Todd in Aurora.

In the process of visiting the saloons, he barely avoided three barroom fights. Quickly leaving the last of these noisy watering holes, out on the muddy street he encountered a loud argument between two men that was drawing a crowd eager to take sides. By the tone of the shouts surrounding the combatants, it was obvious that the verbal confrontation was going to evolve into a street brawl. Abe extricated himself from the excited throng and moved on as quickly as he could.

The explosion of a gun behind him propelled Abe into an alley. When he peered around the wall, it was to see the other people who had been in the street running for shelter. When the area cleared, Abe saw one of the men who had been arguing prone in the mud with a bloody hole in his back. A man wearing a badge and holding a gun in his hand was ushering the other man before him.

Late in the afternoon, Abe's inquiry at the Sazerac Saloon brought a positive response from a pretty blonde saloon girl called Rose. She wore her hair piled on her head and too much makeup on her face, but her smile was genuine. Having lived in Aurora almost from its beginning, Abe could tell that she still enjoyed her job and the men she met. They certainly enjoyed her, even if at twenty-five she was almost too old. Rose smiled up at Abe, leaned back in her chair with her breasts thrust forward, and slowly scanned his body from hat to boots.

When Abe described his search for Todd, she realized he wasn't a potential customer and leaned forward to rest her arms on the table. After a moment she decided to admit that she had seen the young man just the day before. "He called me ma'am and said my eyes reminded him of his mother. Not many men would say something as sweet as that."

Abe couldn't hide his irritation. "He's only just seventeen. You couldn't tell?"

Genuinely caught off guard, Rose said, "I just figured he was really clean shaven. He was nicely muscular." The edge of her mouth twitched as she recalled that when they had been alone, he had been as proficient as any more mature man she'd ever known, and in less of a hurry. She forced her attention back to the present, and chose to offer no details of her encounter with Todd.

She didn't have to. Abe was good at reading people's expressions. He clenched his jaw and asked her, "Did he say anything about where he was headed?"

"No. As it turned out, the two men with him got into an argument with a miner and they took it outside."

Rose related the details of the fight with evident relish, ending with the fact that Hickly had been knocked out early in the scuffle and not long after Croat took a knife in the shoulder. "The wound wasn't too deep, but it did need some sewing."

A nearby man in overalls walked over while clutching his glass. His bearded face and his hands had not been washed since his shift had ended in one of the mines. "I was there," he told Abe. "The kid put an end to the whole thing by displaying a rifle. The hard rock miner they were fighting didn't much care anyway. He'd drawn blood and was happy about it, so he left."

Rose nodded. "The doc was at his claim in Bodie. No one was sure the miner wouldn't return to settle more of the score, so after they roused the guy that had been stunned, the kid talked his friends into going to Bodie to find the doc."

It was late when Abe left the saloon and he was exhausted. When almost to his boarding house, he was jostled off the sidewalk by a swarming crowd of people rushing past. The street was filled with men and women yelling, "Stage comin'." All around him was a mass of bodies in a tangle of excited expectation of the last stage of the day. When the dusty coach stopped in front of the Express and Post Office, it was greeted by miners in overalls, men in suits, the good women and the less than good women. They all followed the driver and his packages inside where they formed a noisy crowd around the delivery window.

Abe watched from across the street where he waved away a swarm of gnats attracted to his hot body and the flickering lantern light in the window behind him. After a few minutes, he slowly turned away and headed to bed. He didn't belong with this crowd of eager people intent on a unified purpose. He was just a wanderer--disconnected from those around him, unsure of the future, and grounded only by his immediate needs.

Abe knew he had to get to Bodie as soon as possible if there was to be a chance of catching up with Todd. Early the next morning he purchased a ticket on the first stage out of town and crowded in with seven other men and their gear. He tried not to think about what he would do if Croat's nomadic movements once more kept him from his son.

The stage jerked forward and headed northwest. As it passed St. John's Cemetery on the hill, one of the men on the stage commented to no one in particular that there were almost 80 individuals buried there, most from disease and accident. "But," he added with pride, "well over a dozen died by violence."

Five miles from town they passed the Real del Monte Mill where the coach bounced in the ruts of the road, tossing those within the coach so roughly that they fell against each other. Righting himself with some embarrassment, Abe looked out the window. Through the rising dust he could see the two story tin-roofed Gothic mill, as well as the smaller brick structure of the Antelope Mill. At the height of production, these brick and granite mills hosted 120 steam driven stamps. The large number of stamps indicated that an impressive amount of ore had so far been taken from the mines.

Heading south with Bodie Creek to their left, it was not long before all the men tied bandanas across their faces as protection against the fine dust that filled the air. It also reduced the sharp pungency of the hot sage to a pleasant scent, and allowed enough comfort that Abe enjoyed looking out the window.

The road was a good one, and soon they had crossed into California. Abe commented that he thought the cliffs and rocky outcroppings gave the route a confining and dangerous aspect. The others had barely finished nodding in agreement when a shot rang out and pinged off the frame of the coach. The stage came to a skidding stop amid the protesting screams of the horses.

A muffled voice called out for everyone to get out of the coach and the passengers quickly obeyed. With hearts racing and mouths dry with fear, they lined up and raised their hands in the two-handed salute that was expected. Abe couldn't believe that he was about to be robbed, but he was more irritated at the loss of time than he was the loss of the coins he carried in his pocket. He had earlier put most of his money into a flat leather belt under his clothes, having taken the hint from the man in Virginia City.

The lone bandit flourished his gun in the face of each passenger before demanding his valuables. Although his lower face was covered with a dark blue bandana, and his black hat was pulled down low, his eyes were left to bore into those of each frightened man with a most menacing stare.

Abe reached slowly into his pocket for his money and at the same time noticed that the smell of the man was peculiar. It produced a sharp picture in his mind and when he looked more intently into the bandit's eyes, the man stepped back as though jerked from behind. He quickly stepped forward again and grunted to Abe, "Give me your money."

Abe put the coins into the man's outstretched calloused hand. While the man poured these into the leather saddlebag draped over his shoulder, Abe told him, "Why shouldn't you take my money? I've already lost what's most valuable to me."

The bandit hesitated a moment, then took a step back and

commanded them all with a curt, "Get back inside." As the men clambered into the coach, the bandit added with a strong emphasis, "Go on to Bodie." Abe, last to enter the coach, knew that the bandit was speaking this directly to him.

When everyone was inside, the driver yelled at the horses and they proceeded on their way. It then occurred to the driver that the bandit had not asked for the strong box, and he wondered what could have distracted him.

They soon reached Fogus's Quartz Mill. It filled most of a narrow canyon formed by steep rock walls but with enough room for a peaked roofed stone mill with three tall chimneys spewing out a smoky discharge that covered the area with a dirty cloud.

A plump smiling woman stood on the porch of a simple wooden cabin across from the mill. After wiping her hands on her apron, she waved to the passengers. "Come in, come in. The food's hot and there's plenty of it."

The cabin's unexpectedly clean and homey interior was a delightful surprise to these men who had last seen a real home months before. A meal was laid out for the passengers on a long table covered with a canvas cloth, and each of the men removed their hat as they moved to the table. The wife of toll keeper Haskell smiled at each one of them as they passed her, and they felt very welcome. The lady of the house had lately been dabbling in watercolors and had prominently displayed her art on the walls, creating a domestic coziness that made Abe wretchedly homesick.

While they ate, they told Haskell about the hold-up. He said he would warn the eastbound stage when it stopped there later in the day. Abe thought it would do little good now that Hickly knew someone had recognized him.

The team had been changed by the time they finished eating, and the stage was soon passing through twisted volcanic hills, between shallow gullies running along both sides of the road, and past several small ranches tucked into the flats between the side hills. Here a little hay had been planted and natural grasses had been encouraged to grow long. This grass was in fact the most valued commodity being taken from the area, as it was the main feed in Bodie and Aurora.

One of the small spreads was the Bodey Ranch, owned by brothers John and Ben Hasslet. They sold hay at the ranch for

$40 to $60 a ton and were doing well. They had recently added a stable made of logs and the sign on it read *Bodie Stables*--the spelling change that would go down in the history of the town beyond.

While traveling through other open and flat areas, the stage passed cattle grazing on rich grass fed by springs trickling down the walls of bluffs that backed these lush pastures. Another was filled with tall rows of corn and yet another had been planted with potatoes.

A man with a short neck and a long beard across from Abe said, "Aurora and Bodie get some of their produce, meat and dairy from the twenty or so ranches at Mono Lake. The Big Meadows area brings in some stuff too, especially dairy. It makes scurvy a thing of the past."

A large muscular man heading to Vining's Rancho to work in the mill there, said, "The timber mill at the Rancho brings in lumber for the buildings of Bodie and Aurora. But Aurora's mines are playing out. That means the demand for building materials will be declining too, so I may not have a job for long." No one knew what to say to that, and silence followed.

Finally the stage passed through a stretch of incredible desolation where the only vegetation was dry sagebrush and bunch grass, and little of that. The dry white hills were wrinkled and folded and lifeless, and the only sign that humans had ever set foot on them was a dozen deserted mine shafts. This was the travelers' introduction to Bodie, and the message was as clear as a printed sign: *Life here is harsh and most likely whatever you think you will find here, you will not.*

Abe knew they were almost to their destination when he saw the reddish color of Bodie Bluff jutting above a line of hills covered in mine openings. Each one had a small pile of tailings next to it, indicating it was either new or abandoned early. Mining was profitable for someone, however, as three small buildings were under construction up on the bluff.

Then, at the foot of the bluff, Abe saw the barest of towns. The only difference between the weathered homes and the ramshackle businesses was the presence of a small sign outside the mercantile, the livery, and the two boarding houses. The saloons needed no pronouncement of their purpose.

Less than six years had passed since William Bodey and Black Taylor had made the first discovery of gold just east of this barren flat of land. In 1860 the Bodie Mining District had been organized, and in 1863 Leland Stanford and F. T. Bechtel had purchased thirteen claims and organized the Bodie Bluff Consolidated Mining Company. It was a short-lived venture and it had been sold in August the year before to a New York merchant group that incorporated as the Empire Gold and Silver Mining Company. They were now working their new investment with high hopes.

Unfortunately, three years later these hopes would give out. Before that Mr. Fogus would also cast his lot into Bodie's mix of hopefuls and would bring his mill to Bodie at a cost of $45,000. He too would eventually sell out, although in his case it would be due to $450 in delinquent taxes. Little did Abe know that the short time he spent in the town was a period of determination by a few to keep alive a dream that would only in the next decade profit many.

Now it was home to only about 40 people living in a dozen wooden and stone shacks, a few dugouts on the hillsides, a scattering of canvas-topped hovels, and battered tents restaked almost daily due to the winds. These makeshift dwellings huddled together for protection against isolation and the hardships of daily life. This close proximity was especially important when winter hit, as the snow's depth was often measured in tens of feet. Most people left the area during the winter, but that did not mean the population missed dealing with snow. A storm could hit Bodie even in summer.

Since no one was waiting in Bodie to board the stage, the driver barely hesitated and Abe was forced to jump out while holding onto his bedroll and pack. The stage continued over the hills toward Bridgeport a good twenty miles northwest of Bodie where it would then turn around and head back to Aurora over the newly improved Aurora Road. After the dust cleared, Abe found himself standing next to a newly constructed shack that served as the Wilson Butler Blacksmith Shop.

A precocious little girl of about four, her long brown curls bouncing as she ran, came up to the door of the blacksmith shop and yelled, "Uncle? You hungry?"

Behind the child hurried a woman who was out of breath and carrying a small covered basket. "Helen Anne! I told you to stay with me."

The child looked up at her mother and smiled. "I'm sorry."

Abe thought that he had never seen such a delightful little girl and felt a stab of regret grip his heart. At that moment the muscled blacksmith, sweat gleaming on his naked chest, walked out into the daylight and picked up the child.

"I am indeed hungry," he told the little girl in his arms. "Do you have my lunch?"

She reached out and gave a quick yank on his long square-cut chin whiskers. "No. Mother does."

The man turned toward the woman. "Hello Elizabeth. Sure glad to see you."

"No, you're not," she told him with a smile. "You're glad to see the basket of food."

The man kissed her cheek. "You're a good sister."

"I'll be glad when that wife of yours gets to feeling better."

Abe walked away from this common domestic scene, refusing to give in to the wash of loneliness that tempted to envelop him. Instead, he turned toward the hills and thought, "So that's Bodie Bluff." He looked up at the sloping barren mountain and the few mines located there. To its right was High Peak, also barren and pocked with the small openings of shafts. Over the yawning mouth of each vertical mine opening was a wooden framework centered at the top with a block and tackle. Several men tended to each apparatus and hoisted buckets of rock from deep within the earth.

Above all the people, mines, structures and hills glared a canopy of dark blue sky packed with boiling white thunderheads. Hoping any storm would hold off until he had located Todd, Abe turned his attention to the small wooden town that fought so valiantly to hold on until hit by the lightening strike of prosperity. He followed a spring at the end of Browne Street, then turned around and returned to the base of the Bluff. As he walked, he stopped several men and asked after Todd, but they shook their heads and kept on walking.

Although Abe had heard exciting rumors of Bodie's possibilities even as far away as Placerville, he was amazed at how few inhabitants clustered at the north end of the large meadow near Bodie Bluff. Even so, not far away the Empire Company's brick two-story Gothic 16-stamp mill was under construction. This mill was quite a change from the arastras that were more commonly used by miners, an inventive arrangement of stones laid out in a circular trough and used for crushing ore.

Abe pictured the few he had seen. In the center of the stone-curbed circle was an anchored post to which was attached a long pole that swept out over the rim. A mule or ox could be attached to it, and as the animal walked it dragged a 100 pound stone over chunks of wet ore. Eventually the ore became almost a paste and could be mixed with mercury, to which the gold adhered. When water was let in full force from a stream, the muddy water was washed away and the heavy amalgam of mercury and gold would settle to the bottom where it could be retrieved.

Abe stopped to talk to two gentlemen who were watching the construction of the new mill and who introduced themselves as Judge McClinton and Dan Olson. They said they were recovering enough high-quality ore from their mine to make the effort of building a mill worthwhile. Abe mentioned that he would like to see the arastras he'd heard about, and they told him he could find them to the west over the hills on Rough Creek.

Dan Olson said, "You'll find the creek at the bottom of a deep canyon cut by the water. We use the water power to wash the ore. It's effective, but an arduous haul for the wagons."

"That is," McClinton cut in, "when the roads aren't too muddy or completely closed by deep snow." The two men laughed at this as though such difficulties in their lives were a secret joke. Abe was duly impressed with how harsh life was for miners there in Bodie.

The two men proclaimed that the current laconic state of Bodie was just the beginning of a huge up-turn of prosperity and a great town to support it. That history would prove them right would not have surprised them, but that it would not happen for another eleven years and that the town would become infamous for its violence, *would* have surprised them very much. Judge McClinton would over time become only too aware of this.

Abe was introduced to Ramon Sanchez who, accompanied by his wife Laura, had recently been hired to supervise the completion of the mill's construction. Wondering how Mrs. Sanchez had felt when she saw the barren little town for the first time, Abe was quickly diverted from such contemplation by the rumbling of his stomach.

It was at the new Empire Boarding House and Saloon, built for the workers of the Empire Mill, that Abe was given a bed by landlord William O'Hara. Mr. O'Hara was a personable colored gentleman of generous proportions who also served as night watchman at the Empire Mine. He had recently accepted a deed to the Bunker Hill claim, owned by miners Peter Essington and Lewis Lockwood, in exchange for their unpaid board and a loan he had given them. That made Mr. O'Hara also a mine owner.

Abe wandered around the town until after dark, but no one had seen Todd. As he walked, everything he had been told of Todd's travels and behavior ran through his mind, and he ended by asking himself, "What's wrong with this picture?"

Emerging from the recall of blurred images and confusing conversations, Abe came to a stop in the middle of the street with the sudden realization of what it was that had been bothering him. His son was *not* hoping to be rescued from his current situation. He was, in fact, making decisions that would make it more difficult for him to be found.

Abe sat down heavily on an upturned barrel just outside the blacksmith shop and fought to order his thoughts. Whether Todd was dealing with guilt, a misunderstanding of his parent's feelings or something more nefarious, Abe didn't care. He had to see Todd and explain to him how much he was loved, and that he and Nancy very much wanted him to come home.

Abe decided it was time to find the doctor who had treated Croat. As he walked between the buildings, soft white dirt rose around his legs and was carried on the air like smoke from a dying fire. Before he realized it, the buildings were behind him and he stopped to scan the area in which he stood.

What a desolate place, he thought, noting that there were more Indian encampments on the sloping hills to the north than there were people in the town. To the west Abe could see where the narrow ribbon of Bodie Creek pooled in a reed-lined marsh at the lower end of the bluffs and hills. A dozen years later the marsh would be gone, drained to feed a large steam powered mill. In place of the marsh would eventually be a network of roads and buildings, and the home of two people Abe would consider his dearest friends.

Abe returned to the Empire Boarding House. Its construction was better than most of the town's weather-worn buildings with their gaping slits in siding stuffed with newspaper and rags. The front porch roof sagged a little from the weight of the last heavy snow, but otherwise it looked very sturdy. Inside, there was almost as much dirt as outside, although most of it had been swept neatly into corners. All six tables were occupied, but there was plenty of standing room at the bar and the rotund landlord greeted him with a welcoming smile.

"Mr. O'Hara, I could sure use a glass of lager."

"Call me Billy." He poured the foaming liquid into a glass mug. "So how do you like our town?"

"I like it fine. Appears to have a lot of potential." Abe took a swallow of the surprisingly cool liquid and asked, "Can you tell me where I can find the doctor from Aurora?"

Billy laughed shortly. "You don't have far to look. He's at that table in the corner. He's the one with the hat that used to be white."

Turning around, Abe saw a small man in dusty old clothes drinking at a table with four other men. Abe approached them, introduced himself, and was invited to drag up a chair. The doctor indicated the other men. "This is Ben and Elijah Butler, and this is their father Daniel. Dan and Elijah just arrived back in town. They were off fighting in the war for awhile."

Abe vaguely noted the faces sporting an array of beards, mustaches and clean cheeks and gave them all a friendly nod. But he wasted no time with small talk. Turning to the doctor, he asked, "Did you recently treat an old man traveling with a boy in his teens?"

"Why?" the doctor asked sharply.

"I'm sorry." Abe took a deep breath and tried to be less direct. "The boy is my son, and I'm trying to catch up with him. He went off with this man Croat while we were on a wagon train coming West."

"He didn't seem to be with him against his will," the doctor noted. "He could have gotten away pretty easily while I was stitching up the man's shoulder."

"He's not a prisoner. He's with him because he wants to be." Then, feeling on the defensive, he added, "But that doesn't mean he wouldn't want to see me."

The doctor shrugged. "Well, it's nothing to me either way. Anyway, I don't think your boy is with him now."

Alarmed, Abe asked, "What makes you say that?"

"I saw the kid talking to some Indians on the edge of town. They'd just returned from some big fandango down at Mono Lake."

"And after that?"

"Didn't see him or the Injuns again."

Ben Butler spoke up. "I saw the man you call Croat. He was getting into a stage headed to Bridgeport, but he was alone."

At first Abe was too puzzled and shaken to say anything. Billy O'Hara noted this and came over to the table. "Would you like a stronger drink, mister?

"No, thank you." After thanking the other men for their information and kindness, he walked out onto the porch. While his temples throbbed, he stood there trying to think about what he should do next.

He heard Billy say to the doctor, "Do you think we should have told him that the kid looked more in charge than the old man? Or that he had a strange haunted manner about him?"

"Maybe that was normal for him," the doctor answered. "Naw, we did the right thing."

Abe wandered over to the blacksmith where he discovered that it was run by Wilson Butler. Recognizing the family resemblance to the men he had met earlier, Abe told him, "I met your brothers and father at the boarding house."

"Oh, yeah? You planning to settle here?"

"No. I'm looking for my son." Abe then repeated a brief explanation of why he was looking for Todd, this time adding what the doctor and Ben Butler had told him.

Wilson nodded. "Yeah, I saw the man you call Croat leave on the stage. But the kid left town earlier with some Walker River Piutes that had been in the area for awhile. Maybe he was sold to them."

"Walker River?"

"Yeah, south of Carson. Big reservation there, spread out along the river north of the lake," he said. "They were probably visiting relatives 'round here. But they were heading toward Bridgeport. I'd look in that area if I were you."

"Yes. Thank you." Bone weary and disappointed that his journey was still not at its end, Abe kicked a rusty can lying in the road and exclaimed, "I'm going in a damn circle!" Not knowing what else to do, he decided to have dinner and try to get some sleep.

The food at the boarding house was unexpectedly good, and he gratefully settled down to enjoy an expensive but excellent steak, fried potatoes and fresh bread. Billy gave him an apple for dessert and it was such a surprise that he *almost* allowed himself to feel joy. But he told himself that until he arrived home with Todd, he would not allow himself such an uplifted emotion.

Abe had convinced himself that finding Todd would make up for the loss of Harold and Alice. It helped him believe that it would someday be possible to be free of his guilt when thinking of them, even though realizing it was an unrealistic way of coping. He chose to hang onto it anyway because it was the only thing he knew to do.

As he climbed into one of the bunks in the sleeping room back of the bar, he heard behind him the shouts of several men as they entered. All were exceedingly drunk and they continued to be very loud. Although it quickly became apparent to Abe that the five other men in the room's bunks were able to sleep, between the shouting from the bar and the incessant pounding of the stamps, Abe doubted that there would be any rejuvenating sleep for him. After two hours he accepted the pounding of the stamps but could not rise above the shouting and laughing in the room beyond the curtain where the miners were playing cards.

Finally he put his boots on, gathered his pack and bedroll, his gun and his dignity, and walked purposefully toward the front door. He caught Billy's eye and held it with a glare of disgust. Billy started to come forward, but then shrugged and poured a drink for one of the revelers at the poker table. Abe took this as an act of acquiescence, considering that he had yet to pay for his bed.

"Hey, where you goin'?" One of the men at a table stood up and blocked Abe's way to the door. The man's bushy black beard was flecked with food and tobacco juice spittle, and his eyes were more red than brown.

Rather than answer the man's question, Abe made to move around him. "Excuse me."

"I don't wanna." A smirk split the belligerent man's face as he stood his ground.

"Mike," one of the men at the table barked, "it's your turn to deal."

"Be right with you. I have a bug to squash."

Although evenly matched in size, they were not in that moment matched in temperament. The resentment Abe felt toward Croat, the build-up of frustration each time he had just missed finding Todd, feeling himself victimized by Hickly, the years of guilt and suppressed grief, and his rage at a life that had not turned out as he had planned, all coalesced into that moment.

Abe took a step forward and shouted into the man's face, "Get out of my way you son of a bitch or I'll rip off your arm and use it to smash your God damned filthy face into bloody pulp!"

The stranger drew back and took a second look at this man who he had thought was going to be a timid victim, but who had suddenly changed into an eager combatant. Mike let himself be pulled back into his seat by one of his friends.

Abe burst through the door without closing it, and was all the way to the stable before he stopped shaking. He finished the night in the livery stable on straw shared with two mellow horses. When in the morning the hostler found him curled up in the corner and roused him by the boom of his laughter, Abe quickly climbed to his feet to explain.

"It's okay," the man told him, still chuckling. "You out of money?"

"No. Out of patience." He explained what had happened at the boarding house.

"Yeah, sometimes it can get pretty rowdy when the miners decide to let off steam."

"I'd be happy to pay you for the accommodation," Abe offered.

"No need. You didn't eat any of the hay did you?" He laughed again before asking, "Would you be wantin' to buy a horse?"

"When does the stage to Bridgeport get here again?"

"In two days."

"Then I guess I need a horse."

"It's a good thing ole Thunder there didn't step on you then. He's a good horse. Only seven years old."

Abe ran his hands over the horse's legs before opening the animal's mouth to look at his teeth and found that the upper jaw teeth had begun to indent. Abe turned back to the man and asked, "How old did you say he was?"

"Oh, that's right. He's a little older than that."

"Yeah. Still, he seems sound."

After the deal was struck, which included a saddle and tack, the hostler saw him hesitating in the door of the barn.

"Problem?"

On a hunch, Abe asked, "Did you see an old man here in town traveling with a young man? The older one would probably have been wearing a fur hat."

"Yup. A couple days ago. Young man with a rough lookin' cuss with a fur hat."

Abe felt the pulse in his neck give a kick. "That would be him."

"Who were they?"

"The young man is my son."

"Well, when I saw the young 'un last he was with some Indians. They were headed over the hills toward Bridgeport."

"Were they Piutes?"

"What else would they be around here? Someone said they were from Nevada. We got another tribe of northern Piutes here. The older fella took the stage headin' to Bridgeport by his self."

"Wilson Butler said he thought Croat might have sold Todd to the Indians."

The man shook his head. "I'd think that would be pretty unusual for 'em. Besides, it makes it sound like they was taking the kid as a prisoner. He didn't act like that at all."

"How did he act?"

"Kind of eager to be gone. I heard him tell the older fella, 'I don't owe you anything now.'"

"He must have meant his indenture to Croat for taking him along."

The man shrugged and said, "It sure seemed to me that the kid was making his own decisions."

Abe frowned. "If he thought being with the Piutes better than being with Croat, he must not have been treated all that well."

"He didn't look mistreated." The man hesitated, then said, "One other thing. There was a young Indian girl in the group that was about your kid's age. She was real pretty and she kept stealing looks at your boy."

Abe sighed. "He's at that age."

"Yeah, well, if it was me I'd ask around the Big Meadows area for this here Croat. The Indians'll probably go around."

"Maybe I should go direct to the Walker River Reservation."

"And do what? The Indians in the area won't help you. In fact, if they think you're after the boy, it might be dangerous for you. The Owens Valley Indian wars are still active to the south."

Once more Abe left one town to head toward another. And once again, although he was not sure he could endure arriving at another dead end, he knew he had no choice.

CHAPTER SIXTEEN
BRIDGEPORT
SUMMER, 1865

"My thoughts so often went to my dear wife as I rode on to Bridgeport. I wished instead that I was heading home."

Abe

Although Nancy continued to write in her diary from time to time, it was less often than when they had first arrived in town. With Abe gone, she thought about picking it up more often, but had faced the realization that she needed to participate more in the town's activities. She would, however, only allow herself such pleasure after her chores were completed, and *efficient* was not a word much used in the 1860's household.

Each morning when Abe was home, once the fire was built and going strong, the breakfast could be started and his lunch packed. But even with him gone, the dishes had to be washed in water heated on the stove, the dry sink wiped out, and the kitchen floor swept. After this, if the weather allowed, the small rugs were beaten on the clothesline out back and laid back down before the furniture was dusted or polished with bees wax. Bread had to be baked as needed, and vegetables harvested from the garden.

Chopping wood and hauling it inside to be stacked by the stove was a task done every other day. Before supper could be started, the fire had to be brought to life and then the meal prepared, cooked, eaten and again dishes washed. This alone took close to three hours. Preserving or drying fruit was done throughout the fruiting season to support them during the winter. Sewing, mending, making candles in the tin molds, canning vegetables, and straining rain water through muslin for hair washes, were tasks done as needed. Now that Nancy no longer saved the wood ash to make soap, and instead purchased it in town, she felt like a fancy lady.

Monday wash day was the exception to all of this. After building the fires under the wash tubs in back of the house, there followed the boiling of the white clothes in strong lye soap and bluing. The colored clothes were soaked in milder soap, but all clothes were rubbed on the washboard before either could be rinsed and starched. In the west women wore only one or two petticoats which not only made for easier movement but also an easier wash day. After passed through the rollers of the mangle clamped to the side of the rinse tub, each item was carefully hung on the clothesline and brought inside while damp to be plied with a series of heavy black flat-irons kept hot on the top of the stove.

All of this took most of the hours between a light early break-fast and an even lighter late supper. Often the ironing could not be completed until the next day, so clothes were sprinkled with water and rolled tightly within toweling so they would be damp enough to be ironed dry the next day. Bedtime was always wel-come.

Even with all of this activity, after two weeks Nancy felt a loneliness that was unexpected. It was then she discovered again the comfort that writing in her journal afforded. She al-ways opened it to a fresh page, and never reread any earlier writ-ten portions. She mostly wrote about Placerville, and in later years would think of these weeks of waiting for Abe and Todd as a pleasant pine-scented interlude between life's intrusive chal-lenges.

As Nancy cleaned her house, her memory rambled through numerous events, conversations and impressions. The first was that of Effie arriving in town from the Howard's house on Bedford Avenue north of town. Effie always sat proudly in her shiny roll top black rig pulled by a large gray horse groomed to perfection. From this vehicle she would wave to those she felt worthy of her attention and nod to those who wanted to be one of the chosen few.

Nancy tried to quell her envy every time she saw the rig since she and Abe only had a spring wagon and when they used it, Abe rented two horses at the livery. Nancy looked forward to the time when they too could own a rig and a carriage horse, since Abe would never hitch his precious Flame to anything. She smiled as she recalled how he had pampered Flame when they were on the trail, making sure he had the best grass and even several times sharing his water rations with the horse.

Her thought moved on to her last trip into town when she had delivered to Abe the lunch he had forgotten. She had watched with fascination as freight had arrived at the newly built Wilcox Warehouse next to the brewery. The stone building was constructed using hydraulic cement, an air-dried mud compound that ensured the building would be so sturdy that it would not fall to wind, flood, or fire. A dozen huge wagons had lined up to off-load their supplies, and Nancy realized there was something reassuring about watching strong men labor and sweat.

She was glad Abe enjoyed his work at the Zeisz Brewery. The wages were good and he said the men he worked with were pleasant company. Abe was certainly more muscular since he had begun hoisting all those barrels, and Nancy smiled at the picture in her mind.

While delivering the lager, Abe had made sure he got to know well the bartenders and regulars. They were soon wondering why Abe was so eager to find two old mountain men who looked as peculiar as the ones he described, but even more they wondered why Abe always added the phrase "and anyone with them". But the men liked Abe, as he bought his share of drinks after work, and his wife occasionally sold fruit pies with a flaky crust that made eating them the nearest thing to physical satisfaction outside of a brothel. So if it made Abe happy, they agreed to keep an eye out for the men.

When finally someone had brought Abe the news he wanted, his friends had been flummoxed when it resulted in Abe's almost immediately leaving town. Mr. Zeisz had a little more knowledge about why his employee and friend had left as abruptly as he had, but he kept it to himself and assured Abe that his job would be awaiting his return.

Nancy was fascinated with Placerville, having learned how quickly it had grown since the days when it was called Old Dry Diggings at its start back in 1848. Aware that the title *Old* or *Ole* was often applied to places and people as an indication of respect or affection, Nancy surmised that the rushers had been very fond indeed of any place that had given them as much gold as this area was purported to have yielded.

She had noted early on that a number of houses of ill re-
pute were established in the town, one even on main near the
courthouse. These were owned and operated by women, as were
a number of popular businesses that included a livery stable,
dairy, brewery, lumber mill and book store. When the Sole
Trader Act of '52 had given single women the right to own property in their own names, many women had lost no time taking
advantage of it. Enterprise benefited the whole town, and easily
overcame traditional roles or prejudices.

Abe had explained to Nancy that this egalitarian attitude was
very different from the town's early days. Back then opinions
of right and wrong had been rigid and justice sometimes took
the form of floggings, brandings on hip or cheek, or the ultimate
punishment of hanging. This last actually occurred no more
often in Dry Diggings than in surrounding communities, but
this one chose to promote its reputation by changing its name to
Hangtown. It made ruffians think twice before causing trouble.
Of course, when the good citizens realized that their community was no longer just a mining camp, but was prosperous and
permanent, they rejected their past and changed the name to
Placerville, based on the placer gold that had originally drawn
people to the area.

Nancy often thought that the fires of '56 might have destroyed
much of the town, but the new and improved Main Street was
certainly a smart way to welcome the traffic that passed through.
The Carringtons were continually impressed at the many businesses and hotels under construction. Not to be outdone by
buildings in larger cities, the most modern improvements of the
time were installed.

After the Miner's Home at the west end of town had become
the Ohio House Hotel, each floor had gained a bathroom with
hot and cold running water. It was almost as luxurious as the
Reunion de Francais Hotel that had a flat roof holding a water
reservoir lined with brick and cement.

The Round Tent Store had gone from a round canvas tent
filled with miner's supplies in 1850 to a round wooden structure.
This had burned in '56, but had afterwards been replaced with a
brick building that extended out into the street and enticed each
passerby to enter and browse simply by the impressiveness of
its facade.

On the south side of Main there was also the Empire Theater with seating for 1,500. Traveling theatrical groups were welcomed, local ladies used it for their charitable causes, and politicians held their meetings and did much of their campaigning within its generous proportions.

People had always been eager to spend their money in Placerville, whether a prospector with a full bag of dust, a hardrock miner with a pay slip, a freighter just paid for his goods, or a traveler newly arrived from across the country. Consequently, there were a number of fine clothing stores, cafes, mercantile shops, fancy hotels, and a reasonable number of saloons.

During the period that Nancy and Abe lived in Placerville, Main Street was a modern reminder of the era's progressive ideas. It was lined with telegraph poles made from tall tree trunks that edged a Main Street loosely paved with crushed gravel. Adding to the town's refinement were five churches and a synagogue, several barber shops, the J. Vantines Bathing Saloon, Messrs. Armstrong and Gage's Grocery and Paint Store, the water-powered presses of the Mountain Democrat, a shop billing itself as "a book store and periodical depot", and Pettit's Drug Store. To keep the town lawful and safe, there were two policemen, a Marshal, a large number of lawyers busy at the courthouse, and a volunteer fire department.

Of course there were also the societies necessary to any up and coming town: Masons that met "on the Monday of or next preceding the Full Moon of each month"; the Odd Fellows; the Temperance Order (Upper Placerville Division Sons of Temperance and the Independent Order of Good Templars); the Hebrew Benevolent Society; and the El Dorado County Medical Society.

Placerville was proud of its established city government of Mayor, Tax Collector, Marshal, City Attorney, Road Overseer, and Justice of the Peace. In 1850 an act of the Legislature had created El Dorado County, and in 1857 Placerville had become the County Seat as a reward for transforming itself into a modern center of civilized behavior. The town's pride in its history and contribution to the settlement of the West, was so great that its early pioneer ambiance would persevere beyond even the next century.

Nancy's reminiscences and sweeping of the floor were interrupted by rapid and determined knocking at the door. When she opened it, she was surprised to find a deputy sheriff standing there.

He touched the front edge of his hat to show that he knew he was talking to a lady. "Sorry to disturb you, but some men attempted to hold up the Express Office last night. They got away, but someone said at least one headed toward this end of town." His dark eyes watched her reaction carefully as he asked, "Have you seen anyone around here that looked out of place or like they were trying to avoid being seen?"

"No. No one." But her thought had immediately gone to Charlie Howard. She had seen him very late the previous night on a strange horse racing down Cedar Ravine, and it had struck her as odd that he had been heading away from town. The only things in that direction were tree covered hills, valleys and canyons. But she said nothing about this to the deputy.

"Well, keep an eye out," he told her. "Someone who saw the three leaving the Express Office said one of them looked to be a kid."

"Really? Some father bringing his child with him during a robbery? That doesn't seem likely."

"Yeah, I know. Witnesses can't always be relied on. But I think he meant more a young man than a child." He started to walk away, but then changed his mind. "You alone here? Where's your husband?"

Not wanting to appear vulnerable, she said, "He's due back any minute."

"You have a gun?"

"Of course."

"Well, keep it handy."

After he left, Nancy brought out Abe's Henry repeating rifle and located the ammunition. He had taken his hand gun with him. As she made sure a cartridge was in the chamber, there was another knock at the door. Thinking the deputy had something else to say, she hurried to the door but took the rifle with her. Effie stood before her holding a covered dish. Her black rig and grey horse had been tied to a tree at the side of the house.

Nancy propped the rifle by the door and stepped aside to let Effie enter. "Whatever you have in that dish, it sure smells good."

"Oh, it's just left over cobbler. It's an excuse to stop by." Effie pushed Nancy aside, tossed her short cape onto a chair and continued into the kitchen where she put the bowl on the dry sink with a clatter. She pulled out a chair and sat down without being invited.

Nancy sat opposite her and said, "You seem agitated. Is it about the attempted robbery last night?"

"Oh, don't be silly." Effie waved her hand with impatience. "I don't care about that stuff. There's always an argument in a bar or the theft of something going on. No, I'm angry at Buran and upset with Charlie."

"Why?"

"Charlie came in very late last night. Well, early this morning actually. Said he was pitching pennies with some boys all night. You know how against gambling Buran is."

"No, I don't know."

"Well, he is," Effie snapped at her. "He got really angry. When Charlie sassed him, he smacked him across the face. He's never done that before. Charlie has sassed us both a lot lately, but I still think Buran over reacted."

"What did Charlie do?"

"He stomped outside and didn't come back for several hours. When he did, he apologized and said it wouldn't happen again. But I think he only said that to throw us off. I don't like the kids he's keeping company with at all. They're older than him and not very nice."

"What kids are they?"

"I don't know." Effie looked embarrassed. "He always meets them somewhere and won't bring them home."

Nancy hesitated, weighing the consequences of telling Effie about the deputy's visit, but a child's future was too important to be ignored. "Are you sure they're kids?"

Effie frowned at Nancy. "What do you mean?"

Nancy shook her head and got up to pour herself some water from a pitcher on the counter. She made sure one of the lemon slices floating in the pitcher to purify the water was also in her glass. "Would you like some water?"

"No."

"Why don't I put on the kettle for tea?"

"Not for me. What do you mean about his friends not being kids?"

Nancy sat down again at the table. "Sometimes boys get a hero worship for some older man who acts like a pal, or gives them attention they're not getting at home. Sometimes they don't choose wisely."

"Like Todd did with the mountain men," Effie recalled aloud. "Charlie hung out with them too. He thought them intriguing." She snorted her disdain.

"Are there men like that in town now?"

"Yes. Charlie has mentioned some drovers that talk of recently herding cattle along the old Santa Fe Trail."

Nancy said with resolve, "I don't want to be offensive, Effie, but a deputy came by and told me a kid had been seen with two older men last night. They were all running away from the Express Office. He said one headed in this direction. And I saw Charlie racing past going south about that time of night."

"It couldn't have been him!" she retaliated immediately. "He was home."

"Effie, you just told me he wasn't." Nancy put her hand on Effie's shoulder. "This isn't a time for blind defense of one's young. This is too important for that."

Effie rose up to protest, then sat down again. "I really don't know, do I? But I'll certainly be talking with him. Thank you, Nancy. I'm so rattled that I can't think straight."

The next time Effie and Nancy crossed paths in town, Effie mentioned casually that the drovers had left town in a hurry and that Charlie was spending more time with his father. Since the robbery attempt had not been repeated, the incident was soon forgotten. Nancy felt that Charlie had just missed taking a wrong turn into a life of crime, and hoped that she had played a small part in that by her willingness to speak up even at the risk of a friendship.

As the calendar turned over to September, Nancy finished her many chores, donned her bonnet and wrapped her good shawl around her shoulders. She walked down the hill toward town with a basket holding three apple pies destined for The City Bakery. The money she earned from this occasional baking was what she spent to furnish their house, and she was very proud of her contribution to their growing prosperity.

The evidence of fall soon to arrive splashed the hillsides with shades of yellow. The oranges and reds would follow when the colder night temperatures settled in. After that the snows would blanket the town and fill the canyons while freezing the creeks and lakes. Everyone was quick to say the snow was not bad in Placerville, and this was true when compared to the snow in the high Sierra, but Nancy fretted over Abe's return. A stop at the Placerville-Humboldt Telegraph Company office brought no relief of her anxiety.

As Nancy walked down Main toward the hardware store, she caught a wave of the hand from a friend of Abe's lounging on one of the upper balconies of a two story business. She returned the wave just as Mrs. Kritz emerged from the shop next door and followed Nancy's look up at the balcony. She tossed her head while uttering a loud "Humph!".

"Good morning," Nancy greeted her.

"Have you noticed," she began by way of greeting, "that men always seem to have the time to sit on balconies for hours? They smoke and observe the passing throngs below while their women are at home working." Mrs. Kritz waited for no response, but turned on her heal and walked down the street continuing to mumble under her breath.

Nancy smiled and entered the magnificence of the hardware store. She wandered the narrow aisles, unaccountably pleased by the hollow echo of her shoes upon the narrow planks while inhaling the rich smells of leather, candle wax, soap, and coal oil that surrounded her. Shelves from floor to tall bead-board ceiling lined the long cavernous room, and rolling ladders were strategically placed to afford access to the eclectic assortment of items even on the highest shelves.

Goods were piled on tables, crates stacked in corners, and large barrels crowded the floor space. On the front counters there were so many decanters, jars and displays that scant space was left. There was little anyone could desire that they could not find it in this store.

People also used the popular store as a place to visit and exchange news. The men gathered together by the tools and mining equipment to swap their stories and latest rumors, and the women stood among the house wares while visiting and sharing bits of gossip. On this visit Nancy was approached by two women she had met at one of Effie's teas, and they spent several minutes conversing about local events. Mrs. Hall and Mrs. Elder lived near one another in Upper Placerville, and were seldom seen in the town without the other.

"So Nancy," Mrs. Hall asked, "do you still like living on Cedar Ravine? It's a long walk into town."

"It's only a mile," she enthused, thinking back to the 2,000 miles she had mostly walked across the country. "We're not that far off Main Street, and it's a lovely day."

They discussed a dance at a church, a fundraiser for the volunteer fire department, and the price of items at the shops. Nancy found herself enjoying the sociable time spent chatting with such nice ladies and wondered why she didn't allow more time for such pleasantries.

Mrs. Elder broke into this thought by commenting, "My husband said Abe has left town."

Nancy hesitated amid a confusion of what she could say and felt her cheeks grow warmer. "He's in Carson City on business."

Sensing that Nancy preferred to impart no further details, Mrs. Hall changed the subject to the latest shipment of fabrics at one of the merchandise stores. This did not mean that Mrs. Hall was willing to ignore the subject. No, Nancy knew both ladies would not only question their husbands, but would also more keenly keep their ears alert to any gossip about the Carringtons.

The enjoyment of the visit had palled for Nancy. She made a brief excuse, paid for her purchases and hurried from the store. Angry at herself for not handling the situation better, she could picture the two women standing together speculating about what they would sense as a secret. Nancy clenched her fists and played with the image of herself walking up to them with perfect poise to inform them that it was none of their damn business, and if they didn't like that, it was too bad. But she kept walking and did not turn back.

After filling her basket in various shops, Nancy walked quickly toward Cedar Ravine. When almost home, she finally ceased feeling like she was fleeing from danger. From the edge of the road she took a moment to admire their little white house glowing in the sunlight filtering down between the tall pines surrounding it on three sides.

When the cabin had been constructed, the owner had built a little bridge over the flow of the narrow creek. It was just wide enough to accommodate a spring wagon and as she walked across, Nancy realized that she could easily block access to the house from the street by barricading the bridge. It was a comforting thought, even while she knew she would never do it.

Nancy continued to feel that living in Placerville was a privilege. She sometimes felt that people were only being tolerated by the mountains that looked down on each person and determined whether or not they would be allowed to stay, and what condition they would be in when they left. That night she snuggled in bed beneath the comforting weight of blankets and listened to the whispering of the breeze in the pines, the gurgling of the creek, and the gentle croaking of frogs before relaxing into contentment.

Abe decided to follow the newly improved toll road from Bodie to Bridgeport. He was told that until recently the route went from the head of Rough Creek and across Table Mountain, but in winter this had been a treacherous place to be caught if snow arrived unexpectedly. The new toll road, built by a consortium of Bridgeport businessmen, routed Abe from Table Mountain on a road that went east three miles to the head of Aurora Canyon and down its mouth eight miles and west one mile to the bank of the East Walker River with Bridgeport in the near distance.

Approaching Bridgeport, Abe followed the narrow road through lush meadows that had lost the bright green of summer and where cattle grazed the rich brown grasses. In the far distance to his left he could see the tall jagged peaks of the Sawtooth Ridge of the Sierra, and to the west of that the bulk of the Sweetwater Range. In the center of this vast and open valley, Abe discovered a small freighting and supply town that presented itself as a New England transplant.

Both the horse and Abe were hot and thirsty, and both looked longingly at the wet marsh to the left of the bridge. Not for the first time Abe felt a stab of regret at having sold Flame, but reminded himself that at the time he had thought the speed of taking the stage imperative to finding Todd. He sighed deeply and urged forward the less spirited Thunder.

Entering the small village of whitewashed wooden buildings, shacks, tents and even a few canvas-topped wagons, Abe pulled up to assess the buildings situated on the near side of the East Walker River.

The buildings of the town's first effort to establish itself were to the right of the bridge just before crossing, with Weaver's Hotel the most prominent near a blacksmith and livery. The small Indian encampment beyond was quiet, with only a few women and children moving between their brush dwellings. Abe assumed that the men were out hunting, and as he did with everyone, wondered if they had any awareness of his son.

Thunder's iron shoes sounded hollow on the dirt-packed log bridge when Abe continued over the narrow river, although there was little to cross over to on the other side. Abe continued down the wide wagon road that sliced east and west through the young community. He passed a line of freight wagons carrying supplies to the towns of Aurora, Dogtown, Poverty Flat on Rescue Creek (later Lee Vining), the miners on Green Creek, the last hold-outs at the Monoville diggings, and the ranches near Mono Lake. The supplies brought to the town had recently been on the trail from Carson City after arriving from San Francisco's ports.

Because of such traffic, Main Street had two livery stables, a large blacksmith and wagon shop, several warehouses and two mercantile businesses, along with several saloons and two hotels. Behind these businesses, both along the river to the north and at the edge of the meadow to the south, were the small whitewashed homes of its citizens.

The town's judge, having no courthouse in which to hold his trials, was as usual using the upstairs of one of the small hotels. Abe noted the large number of horses tied to the hitching posts in front of the hotel and wondered at the popularity of the trial.

After a quick meal, Abe decided that it would make sense to ask about Croat as well as Todd. Toward that end, he decided to start his inquiries with the town's Sheriff.

"If the Indians don't want to be spotted, they won't be," Sheriff Seth Sneden told him. "If your son is with them of his own free will, it looks like he won't do anything to imperil them either. I do have an idea though. They might send him into town for supplies."

"What would they pay with?"

"The tribes make a little money selling fish or rabbits to the households. Some of the local Indian women work in gardens. They don't need very much, but they like coffee, sugar, tobacco and fresh vegetables. Even a tribe out of the area might want some supplies."

"So I should question the shopkeepers?"

"I would. Some won't sell to those from outside the local tribe, or at least to those who've made themselves unpopular 'round here. So for the Indians to have an Anglo to do it for them would be an advantage. But if I see him, I'll sure tell him you're looking for him."

"Will you let me know if you talk to him? In case he doesn't contact me himself?"

"Sure." He made a note of how to contact Abe in Placerville. "Uh, one thing."

"Yes?"

The Sheriff hesitated, then said, "That old guy you mentioned. Croat? I think he's here in town."

Abe felt a coldness settle over him. "Where?"

"I don't want any trouble," the Sheriff warned. "I can see where you want to talk to him, but don't let it go any further than that."

"Where is he?" Abe asked again.

Sneden sighed and told him, "Try the saloon by the bridge. If he isn't there, try the other one."

Abe said nothing else, but merely walked out and headed to the saloon where he found Croat alone at the far end of the long bar. He watched Croat tip a bottle of cheap whiskey into a glass and toss the contents down his throat in a single gulp. Abe walked forward until Croat sensed someone so close on his left side as to practically touch him. It took a few seconds for Croat's bleary eyes to focus and another few for him to recognize Abe, but when he did, he jumped back. His hand immediately disappeared under his hide jacket.

Abe knew Croat was going for his knife. With a swiftness that startled Croat, Abe reached out for the whiskey bottle on the counter, bashed it on the edge of the bar, and held the jagged gleaming ends toward Croat.

"I don't want to fight you, Croat," Abe told him in a low voice. "I'm just here for information. Put both hands on the bar where I can see them, and I'll do the same."

"How can I trust you?" Croat asked.

Abe's color deepened. "Well, you can sure as hell trust me more than I can trust you. And you know it."

Slowly Croat did as suggested. Abe put the broken bottle far to his left, but not so far away that he couldn't easily reach it. When the bartender started toward them, Abe raised his hand to stop him. "Nothing's going to happen. The Sheriff knows I'm here with this man." The bar man nodded and walked away.

"I don't know where your kid is," Croat told him before being asked.

"That's a lie. Don't do it again, or I'll cut you."

Croat had never heard Abe talk like this. But he had enough common sense to realize that he was dealing with a desperate father.

"Okay, but all I know is that he left me in Bodie and went off with some Injuns he'd met."

"The ones from the Walker River Reservation?"

"So you know that?"

"Yes. Why did he do that? Had you mistreated him?"

Croat started to turn toward him, then remembered to keep his hands on the bar. "Hell, no. He came with me because he wanted to learn how to survive in the wilderness." He snorted. "Not that there's much of it left now. Anyway, he was a good traveler. Didn't talk much, but he watched and listened, and we got fond of him."

"How come Hickly isn't with you any more?"

"We had a parting of the ways."

"Do you know what he's doing now?"

"Do you?"

Abe heard in Croat's tone something that signaled that it wouldn't be wise to pursue that line. Instead, Abe returned the conversation to his son. "Did Todd give you any indication of his intention to find us?"

"No. But he knew you were looking for him."

"How did he know that?"

"Some guy from Placerville was asking about us when we were working in Virginia City. Todd assumed it was on your behalf. That's why we didn't stay there."

Abe said nothing, shocked by the fact that Todd had known for that long that his parents were looking for him.

The wily Croat realized this and turned to Abe. "Hard to accept that your kid don't want nothing to do with you?"

Abe might have let the words pass, but not the sneer that celebrated them. Abe did not, however, reach for the broken bottle. Instead, he reared back and with the weight of his entire body behind his arm, punched Croat on the side of the head with his fist. Croat went down like a tree felled in a forest. Abe didn't wait to see what condition he was in, but instead went back to the Sheriff and told him what he had done.

Sneden shook his head and tried unsuccessfully to hide a smile. "Okay. Let's call it self-defense. But I think you should get out of town. Which way you going?"

"North I guess."

"Okay. I'll go check on him. If he's still alive, I'll tell him you rode south."

"Do me a great favor and don't tell anyone about my son."

"No one's business but yours."

"Thanks."

Although there was as yet no improved wagon road going straight north along the Walker River, Abe retrieved Thunder from the livery and followed a narrow track over the hills. Late in the afternoon he found himself eighteen miles north of the Sonora Road in the small hamlet of Centerville, two years later to be renamed Coleville. He spent the night with a rancher who accepted overnight travelers, even while building his cabin at what he called High Mile Ranch. Alex Goens commented that night that he had seen a small party of Indians with a "skinny white man". Trying not to sound too eager, Abe asked him for more information.

Alex told him, "All I know is that they went east after a short stay by the river."

Abe considered traveling on in that direction, but "east" was too vague. Instead, he went to Carson City and checked in with the Sheriff. He was sympathetic, but he had heard nothing.

Depressed and not knowing what to do next, Abe walked through the town and finally ended up on a rutted road between plowed fields. Before he realized how far he had wandered, he had reached a farm house with a large garden on one side and a corral of six horses on the other. One of them was a sorrel quarter horse.

As soon as Abe walked up to the fence, the horse threw his head up, emitted an ear-splitting whinny, and trotted over to the fence. He stuck out his chin to be scratched and Abe was only too happy to accommodate.

"He seems to know you."

Abe turned around and saw a man with long gray hair walking up to him. "I'm sorry to be trespassing." Abe quickly offered his hand. "My name's Abe Carrington."

"I'm Stan Harding."

"I was out walking and didn't realize how far from town I'd come. Then I saw your horses and ole Flame here."

"Flame, huh? You the guy who sold him in Virginia City?"

"That's right. One of the hardest things I've ever had to do, but I needed quick cash for stage fare. I've been looking for my son and I thought I could catch up with him in Aurora."

"Did you?"

Abe shook his head. Instead of saying more about that, he told the man, "I had Flame here since he was a colt. Broke him, trained him, and brought him across the country from Missouri with our wagon train in '63."

"You must miss him then."

Abe could only manage a nod. After a moment, he asked Mr. Harding, "You wouldn't be interested in selling him, would you? I can give you the horse I bought in Bodie and $25."

"Bring the horse by, and we'll see."

Abe wasted no time returning to town and bringing Thunder to the ranch. After the man carefully examined the horse, he said, "Make that $30 and you have a deal."

Transferring his saddle and tack to Flame, Abe gave Stan's hand a vigorous shake and walked Flame down the tree-lined avenue toward town. Several times Flame nibbled Abe's shoulder, causing him to laugh out loud. After tightening the cinch and before mounting, Abe gave a quick glance around and threw his arms around the horse's neck. With the softness of Flame's fur warm against his cheek, Abe felt better in that moment than he had in weeks.

As he settled in the saddle, he murmured, "Let's go home, boy."

To avoid the traffic on Johnson's Cutoff, he traveled instead down through Hope Valley, spent the night at Woodfords in the corral with Flame, and then continued on toward Volcano. Before reaching it, he cut off to the right on the road that would take him northwest and more directly into Placerville. All along the way, leaves of yellow and orange tumbled across the road and the crisp air made Abe glad of his jacket.

Abe's return home was not the jubilant celebration he had hoped it would be. He would never forget the look on Nancy's face when he opened the door and she realized he was alone. Nancy herself thought she had been prepared to see Abe arrive without Todd, but when she felt the sick lurch in her stomach, she knew she had only been fooling herself.

Abe followed her through the parlor to the small kitchen and found her at the dry sink peeling a carrot with more energy than the task required. She had turned away in time so that her face was hidden from him, but the depth of her disappointment radiated from her like heat from a stove. She managed to say, "It's good to have you back. I missed you."

Abe stood awkwardly behind her, but refrained from laying his hands on her shoulders. He longed to feel the warmth of her in his arms, but his spirit couldn't absorb more rejection.

"I'm sorry, Nan. I went to Carson City, Virginia City, Aurora, Bodie, Bridgeport, Centerville and back to Carson City. I checked at each town and the stage stations in between. He remained just ahead of me, even though I was always close."

"Do you know if he's well?"

"Yes, he is. And in charge of his destiny it looks like."

"What do you mean?" She dropped the vegetables and turned to find him sitting at the small kitchen table.

"This a new table cloth?"

"Yes."

"I like the red and white checks."

She poured him a cup of coffee and while he gulped it down, she brought him a large piece of apple pie.

As he ate, Abe told her the details of his travels and ended by describing Todd going with the Indians. "Everyone I talked to gave me the impression that it was his idea."

She received the news the same as she would have a slap across the face. "You mean he knows we're looking for him?"

It was then that he told her about his encounter with Croat.

"Oh, Abe. You could have been hurt."

With obvious pride, Abe said, "Yes, but I wasn't. Croat was."

Nancy felt herself smiling. "Yes, you did a good thing there."

"I wonder if I hurt him," Abe chuckled. "I hope so."

After a few moments of silence, each of them alone with their thoughts, Nancy said, "So Todd knows where we are." It was an admission that her maternal yearning screamed to deny, so when Abe nodded, Nancy said, "If he's free to move about, then he can come here to see us at any time." She frowned and looked carefully at Abe. "But if he *wants* to find us, why hasn't he?" Then, with the color draining from her face, she declared, "Oh, my God, Abe. He's actually avoiding us."

"Nan..."

"Why do you think he dropped his association with Croat and took up with Piutes? It's the surest way of not being found."

"You're reading a lot into his decision to go with them."

She shook her head. "I appreciate your trying to spare me from the unpleasant reality that our son wants nothing to do with us. I'd rather face the truth, whatever it is."

"You have to remember that he thinks we blame him for Harold's disappearance. He's carrying a big burden for such a young man."

Nancy glared at him. "Man? He's a boy!"

"Not from what I've been told. Both in looks, attitude and behavior he's declared that he's now a man. We'd best remember that. And there's another thing."

"What?" She braced for the pain she expected but was not sure she could bear.

"There's a pretty Indian girl in the group he's with."

She took in the information, and then smiled. "He *is* becoming a man."

"By the way, I saw Lona in Virginia City."

"How is she? What's she doing?"

He couldn't keep the twitch of a smile from his lips. "Well, evidently she's doing what she did when Pete met her."

"Working in a café or shop?"

"No. She's a prostitute."

Nancy felt her jaw drop down and only closed her mouth with an effort. "No!"

Oddly satisfied with her reaction, Abe told her Lona's story.

"Well!" Then she laughed. She laughed until her eyes flooded and her stomach ached. Just as Abe began to fear for her mental state, Nancy got herself under control.

"Nan, are you okay?"

"Better than I've been in a long time. There's something about all this that sort of puts things in perspective. We really never can tell about people. Or life, for that matter. About the time one thinks its going to be one way, it veers off in a completely different direction."

Abe smiled. "Makes our time on this earth interesting, doesn't it?"

"It certainly does." Then a thought occurred to her and she sobered. "Oh, Abe. I really do think our suspicions about Pete's death might actually be true."

He nodded. "I'm afraid so."

After a moment, Nancy told him, "I'm sorry you had to sell Flame for nothing. You must miss him terribly."

"About that." He then told her about his finding Flame and bringing him home. "I put him in a stall at the livery before walking home."

Taking a deep breath, she stood up and said, "I'll fix dinner."

Abe decided to hold back what Lona had observed of Todd, and what the saloon girl in Aurora had suggested by her saucy smirks. He went to the window and looked out at the lengthening shadows of the trees along the creek.

Behind him, Nancy sighed again and said, "I just wish we were watching Todd mature. It's happening so quickly."

She noticed the muscles of his shoulders tighten, and realized that maybe he hadn't needed the burden of that last comment. Nancy stirred the stew in the pot that simmered with enticing aromas and after a long silence, turned to Abe to ask a question. He was sitting in her rocking chair by the window, dozing with his chin on his chest.

How tired he must be, she thought, and I didn't give him a very warm reception. Why do I keep acting like this is somehow his responsibility to fix? I'm the mother. I should have been more vigilant with the children in the first place, yet he's never once acted as though he blames me.

She knelt by the chair and gently placed her hands on his shoulders. When he jerked awake, she kissed him on the cheek. The tenderness and intimacy of the gesture surprised Abe more than if she had kissed him passionately.

"It was a valiant effort, my dear," she told him in a soft voice. "I think it's time we accept that our children are gone, each in their own way. God sees over two and Todd sees over himself. Someday he may choose to make contact. You talked to enough people that he knows where we are. He'll track us down when he's ready."

"True."

"And maybe, because of the pretty girl, he's looking forward to finding out what it means to be a man." She looked at her husband with a mischievous smile. When a light blush colored

Abe's cheeks, Nancy laughed and so did he. They were both feeling the exhilaration of relief that comes when life has been accepted on its own terms. It was enough that Todd was well and happy.

Two weeks later, with a cold evening approaching and the sound of dry leaves crunching underfoot, Effie and Buran Howard arrived for dinner. The Howards had quickly become successful members of the community, thanks in part to Effie's social aspirations. Buran's clothing store, decorated so comfortably by Effie, had an established clientele of the best families in the town. Buran had wisely stocked his store with quality goods, and it had brought in quality customers. Effie had joined every club and organization run by or open to women, and invitations to her luncheons were high on every woman's wish list. This night Effie had a pie in hand.

Although Nancy eschewed Effie's social climbing, the two women had still remained close, even if not seeing one another very often. They had a shared history, and Effie found she could relax and be her old self with Nancy. Both couples had been so busy since Abe's return that this dinner was their first opportunity to come together for a visit.

During dinner Buran asked, "Did you hear about the fire in Virginia City?"

"No." Abe felt an unexpected proprietary anxiety. "Was it bad?"

"End of September a fire started at the Fountain Head Restaurant and burned from Union Street to below Sutton Avenue. Someone said it was as far as D Street east and A Street west."

"Damn!" Abe pictured the area of businesses and homes. "That must have been costly."

"About $400,000 the paper said."

"What a shame."

"They'll rebuild," Buran stated with certainty. "They always do. The fire back in the summer of '63 was worse. It burned most of the business section from A Street clear down to C Street."

"I didn't see anything of that when I was there."

"That's what I mean about rebuilding. By the way," Buran asked Abe, "did you get a look in any of the mines while you were there?"

"Only one, and just briefly. But they're all pretty much the same."

"Did you see the Deidesheimer square set cribbing they're using to shore up the shafts?"

"Yeah. It was very impressive. More importantly, it's cut way back on cave-ins and loss of life."

"They say it's become the standard for deep mines around the world since '61."

Both women looked bored and Effie could not repress a yawn. Abe laughed and told Buran, "I think we should save talk about mining until we're in a less social setting."

Buran agreed and they changed the subject to events occurring in the town. Knowing that Abe had not brought Todd home, the Howards noted that Nancy still seemed in good spirits. When the pie had been cut and placed before them, Effie could stand it no longer.

"Am I allowed to ask if you have any word of Todd?"

Abe shrugged. "There isn't that much to tell." He briefed the story of his search before concluding with, "The last I heard, he was headed to Nevada in the company of Walker River Piutes."

Effie's hands went to her face. "Oh, dear. I've heard that Indians kidnap white children."

"Not this tribe, Effie," Abe corrected her.

Buran spoke up. "Thankfully he wasn't part of the tribe killed recently by troops looking for cattle thieves."

Abe started to change the subject, but Nancy asked, "Was it bad?"

"Very. It was just an Indian fishing party, but the troops over-reacted and killed 'em all. Men, women and even some children."

"How awful," Nancy gasped. Effie looked at her in surprise, obviously not seeing the same degree of tragedy in the story.

Nancy stared back with surprise at the heartlessness Effie's response indicated as Buran continued. "Chief Winnemucca's youngest was among the children killed. He can't be happy with whites right now."

Effie commented, "Even Todd's youth can't help him if he gets caught among Indians when troops are set against them."

Nancy spoke up. "Todd is hardly a child now. He's a young man, and evidently he went with the Piutes voluntarily."

Both Buran and Effie stared at her with disbelief clearly written on both their faces. "Why would he do that?" Buran asked. "To escape bad treatment from Croat?"

"From what I can tell, Croat wasn't that bad to him," Abe told them. After describing his encounter with Croat in Bridgeport, he concluded, "Todd met those particular Piutes, was accepted by them and liked them. He then decided to stay with the tribe."

"I can't believe he would want to *live* with them, though," Buran persisted.

"Several men told me there was a young girl with them that was very pretty." Abe and Nancy exchanged a smile. "So maybe that had something to do with it."

"A white girl captive?" Effie asked eagerly.

"No. An Indian girl," Abe clarified.

Again Effie and Buran stared. "He wouldn't consort with a Piute woman, surely," Effie barked. It was said as a statement of fact and left no room for argument, and barely room for comment.

Nancy and Abe looked at their friends in astonishment. It then occurred to them that although they had made allowances for the fact that Todd was at least safe, such broad-mindedness might not be possible for everyone. They were forced to face the reality that others might be angry that Todd had chosen to live with Piutes, especially while stories of the Indian wars continued to reach them from the Owens Valley of the Eastern Sierra.

Effie asked, "You don't think he'll bring her here do you?"

Wondering why she had to point out the obvious, and unable to lessen the sharpness in her tone, Nancy told her, "I have no idea. But if he does, at least I'll be able to see my son again."

Effie had the grace to blush. "Well, yes, but people wouldn't be very accepting of them."

Buran added, "People might think he was a white Indian like we heard about on the trail."

"Meaning a white living with Indians?" Abe asked.

"No, I mean those whites who dress as Indians and are reported to have massacred dozens of homesteaders."

Abe gawked at him. He found it difficult to fight his way through the wide range of irate emotions he felt at hearing his friend say such a thing.

Nancy barely managed to keep her temper in check as she said, "Oh, Buran, he isn't going to lead a raid on the town! Or torture and kill people like those you refer to. He's probably only living with them for awhile and for the adventure of it. I'm sure that when he comes home, he'll have left all that behind him."

Effie looked down at her plate and mumbled, "One can only pray that's true."

The subject was quickly changed, with few other subjects to follow. Buran and Effie left almost immediately after dessert.

CHAPTER SEVENTEEN
PLACERVILLE
SUMMER, 1866

"I have discovered that what one sees when eyes are finally opened is not always attractive."

Nancy

The first hint that something was amiss occurred to Nancy when she realized that within the previous two months Effie had held two luncheons and three teas, and she had received not one invitation. Over the harsh winter, even at Christmas, she had not thought this too unusual, but it was summer now and at this point Effie was usually well into her social season. In the past, even when Effie had known that Nancy could not or would not attend, she had still offered her the courtesy of an invitation.

Nancy had too much to do to worry about such things, and assumed Effie had just given up on her. Summer meant the preserving of vegetables, cleaning more deeply than winter allowed, airing the mattress, and sewing new clothes. Finally, however, the need for supplies brought Nancy into town.

The groceries and heavier things needed at the hardware store would be boxed and waiting for Abe to pick up in their spring wagon pulled by a new pair of horses. Of course, those purchases of a more feminine nature Nancy would get for herself from the stores located at the Plaza at the west end of town. It would mean a long walk, but she would never ask Abe to pick up a package containing her under clothes or other intimate items.

It was a warm day and even though wearing her lightest summer frock, Nancy felt the effects of the long trek. After entering the Union Building, and while waiting in Bill Henson's shop for him to retrieve Abe's repaired boots, she set her basket on the floor at her feet. Pulling from her purse the silk fan with ivory sticks, she energetically fanned the air in front of her damp face.

Just as she was thoroughly enjoying the effects of this, Effie entered the shop. After greetings were exchanged and polite comments on the weather completed, Nancy commented casually, "I hear your luncheons have lately been well attended."

Effie kept her back to Nancy as she looked over a pair of abandoned lady's boots now for sale. "Oh yes, very." She turned to face Nancy and without taking a breath, told her, "So many women want to attend. Of course, I only have just so much room in my house. Knowing you're not particularly fond of such gatherings, I knew you wouldn't mind not being invited."

"Really?"

Effie kept her face carefully arranged into a practiced cordiality. "Of course. You've always been so generous in attending, but I certainly wouldn't want you to feel you must do something you would prefer to avoid. By the way, my Charlie is going to Heald's Business College so he can run the business with his father. It's so nice having a son so close to his parents."

Nancy was well-versed in the polite verbal code of women, and had not missed the underlying message in Effie's words. She hesitated only for a moment before saying, "It must be so comforting to have a son you can be proud of and who has never done anything to cause you worry. Such perfection in one's offspring is so rare."

Effie glared at Nancy, hating the fact that she knew about Charlie's near scrape with the law. Nancy glared back.

"All children cause concern for their parents from time to time," Effie sniffed, "but most don't do anything to completely ostracize themselves or their parents from society."

"That's true. Of course, the transgressions of some children stay hidden, especially if they have someone to intercede on their behalf." Nancy reached for Abe's boots on the counter and when placing her coins in Mr. Henson's palm, realized that he was avoiding her eyes.

Although Nancy thought her conversation with Effie had come to an end, Effie exchanged a glance with Mr. Hanson before addressing Nancy. "Is your son still off on his adventure?"

Nancy turned to stare at Effie. Mr. Hanson later told his friends at the saloon, who listened with fascination, that he had briefly thought the exchange might turn into a hair-pulling brawl. "I've never seen a woman express such loathing in a single look as Mrs. Carrington did. She drew herself up and told

Mrs. Howard, 'Your comment is a reflection of your sensitivity. Good day.' Mrs. Carrington left with as much dignity as any woman I've ever seen."

Mr. Hanson had no idea that Nancy had been near to tears at the obvious snub. At The City Bakery, Mr. Lacey noticed Nancy's state of agitation and was especially gracious and accommodating, which acted to calm her. However, just as she reached the sidewalk and before the door closed completely behind her, she heard him say to his partner, Tom Hogsett, "I think the busybodies are spreading rumors."

"Nasty cats!" Tom replied. "And she's such a nice lady, too!"

"Was that about me?" Nancy puzzled to herself as she walked away.

Walking past the hardware store, Nancy came upon Mrs. Elder being helped out of a smart black rig by her husband. She greeted them with a cordial, "Good morning."

Both husband and wife looked startled, and for a moment Nancy thought they were going to hurry past her. But they returned her a polite if somewhat curt greeting before they made haste to enter the National Restaurant.

Nancy determined not to pay any attention to the odd behavior of these people, and entered the drug store on the plaza to purchase a new hair brush. It was actually more an excuse to admire the perfumes and fancy articles that had before always brought her such delight. Today, however, as she stood before the jewelry case, she found the sparkling gems much less tempting than expected and after nodding to Mr. Morrill the druggist, she decided to return home.

On her way, she passed Mark Levison outside his men's clothing store just north of the courthouse. He was talking to a distinguished older man whom she had seen with him before. They had always tipped their hats to her when she encountered them, but this time they hurriedly retreated into the shop amid whispered exclamations just as Mr. Bigilow, the cook at the Orleans Hotel, walked purposefully down the sidewalk toward her.

Nancy breathed out her tension when she saw that he was smiling in the way he always had. "I just wanted to repay the five dollars I borrowed from your husband." He removed a small handful of coins from his pocket and held them out to her.

"Why don't you wait until you see Abe?"

"No, I'd rather do it now. Don't like being in debt to anyone." He handed her the coins, stepped back and tipped his hat to her, and walked away. The whole of the two minutes they had been together Mr. Bigilow had spent the time darting his eyes around as though concerned with who might be watching.

Nancy had never been so relieved to reach home, and this time she spent no time enjoying the approach. Instead, she hurried inside and waited anxiously for Abe's return. As soon as he walked in the door, she laid out her day to him in all its confusing detail.

He listened without comment through the whole dissertation, not mentioning how lately some of the men at work had cooled toward him. He had not reacted to it with undue concern, but he had still thought it odd. Then, after a week of being excluded from after-work sojourns to the local saloons, men had suddenly ceased their conversations when he came near. It was only when he overheard one of the men use the term "Indian lover" that he had realized what it was all about.

Abe had been quick to confront Buran. "Did you tell people about Todd living with Indians?"

"You didn't tell me not to." Buran had attempted to give the appearance of innocence, but it had come across as hollow when he refused to meet Abe's gaze.

"I didn't think I had to," Abe had snapped at him. "I trusted you to have enough common sense to know better than to spread it around."

Buran had bristled at that. "I only told one person."

Abe had shaken his head and said, "That's all it takes."

Buran had looked chagrinned. "I'm sorry, Abe. I didn't think. I was just so shocked at the whole disagreeable idea."

Abe had looked at the man he had once called friend and shook his head again. "No, the mistake is mine. I thought you'd understand the circumstances, but you're not the same man I met on the trail. You used to be a person of character."

It was the last time they had spoken, and Abe felt the loss of the friendship more keenly than he would ever admit to anyone. So as he listened to Nancy tell him about her confrontation with Effie, her frigid reception in town, and other snubs over the past few months that she had dismissed until now, he understood only too well what it was all about.

"It's because of Todd," he told her without preamble.

"I suspected that was Effie's problem, but how could that be back of the other snubs?"

"Buran and Effie didn't keep their knowledge to themselves. And the real facts have probably been warped and exaggerated in the retelling."

Nancy was too well aware of the society in which they lived to doubt what he was saying, but at the same time, she did not want to accept it. "Are you sure?"

"Buran admitted it to me."

Gesturing helplessly, she said, "It's not like we want him with the Indians."

"No. And if he had been kidnapped against his will and was trying to escape, that would be different too. What they can't accept is that he *wants* to be with them."

Her sigh was so deep as to be almost a shudder. "So they wonder what kind of parents we must be that our son would want to live with Indians instead of us."

Abe looked at her and nodded, wishing he could make it otherwise, but respecting Nancy too much to lie to her. "Nan, give them time. If we act like nothing is different, maybe after a little time passes they'll do the same."

"I suppose that's possible."

So they proceeded through the summer in much the same way they always had, only now with little social interaction. And indeed, by fall most of the men had softened their posture and only a few refused to drink with Abe. The conversations at the brewery had also returned to normal and it seemed as though Abe's son was no longer a topic of interest to the men who knew Abe well.

The women, however, were not so quick to let the subject go. They fanned the flames of what they considered at the least a shameful deception, and at most a scheming betrayal of their friendship. Only a few of the oldest women, who were not often seen in society, seemed willing to treat Nancy as usual when they encountered her in town. Several of these women even went out of their way to be kind to her, always stopping to chat about gardening or cooking, or even the changing weather. Nancy wondered if it was because they were too old to care about the rules of society, or if there was some incident in their pasts that made them sympathetic to someone being ostracized.

Through the holiday season, the winter to follow, and the entirety of '67, Nancy convinced herself that this was enough female companionship and kept herself busy at home. Her garden was expanded, her journal entries were more detailed, the hills to the south along Cedar Ravine were explored, several rugs were hooked, a table cloth was crocheted, and the larder was filled with enough preserved items to support three families through winter.

By late spring of 1868, the town experienced the last of the snow on the streets and the streams thawed. But the hearts of the town's women had not. The longer the women shut her out, the more the men of the town seemed determined to balance this by focusing their attention on Nancy whenever they saw her. Nancy and Abe were amused by this effort to make up for their wives' lack of charitable behavior. What started as greetings accompanied by smiles and tips of their hat slowly evolved into a few moments of light conversation.

However, instead of this helping the situation, the men's actions only fanned the flames of the women's resentment. They put it about that Nancy was an outrageous flirt and that every woman should watch her husband more carefully. That Effie, or any of the other women Nancy had ever thought a friend, did not take umbrage with such statements was a hurt so deep she had to recast it as anger in order to cope with it.

After some introspection, Nancy realized that her anger was not about the loss of friends as much as it was the sense of being robbed of the special joy that living in Placerville had always given her. The mountains no longer romanced her, the birds no longer sang just for her, and the sunrises were not as wondrous.

Abe spoke to several of the well-intentioned men and tried to explain how their misdirected kindness had fed into the women's appetite for gossip and revenge. The confused men of course backed off their attentions, but it was too late. The women had determined to put Nancy in her place, and they made it clear to anyone who would listen that Nancy's son preferred to live with Indians rather than her, and that Nancy approved of her son "turning Indian". Unspoken was the accusation, "How dare this woman challenge the sanctity of motherhood. Doesn't she realize that white women have the responsibility of producing the next generation of American citizens?"

In the eyes of many at that time, citizenship should not be open to include the Irish, the Chinese and especially not the Indians. Mexicans were acceptable because someone had to do the hard labor and after all the state had at one time belonged to them. The Basque, German, French and other nationalities were tolerated as long as they contributed to the community in which they lived. Such thinking allowed people to feel tolerant and generous of spirit, while holding firm to the beliefs that everyone had "their proper place".

Living under the critical and disapproving eye of her peers taught Nancy a unique self-sufficiency and an inner reliance on what she knew to be right rather than popular. This gave her a calm demeanor and authoritative bearing that riled the townswomen even more, as they felt she was not showing the proper degree of shame. Nancy knew that if she did, even if they knew it to be an act, they would probably allow her a degree of acceptance. She refused to play that game. Abe said nothing, but he was very proud of her.

Then he came home one day to find Nancy sitting in the rocker by the front window clutching a damp hanky and her eyes red from weeping.

"Nan, what's wrong?"

Sitting in the cottage she loved so much, she thought of the flower boxes under the windows now full of new plants and the vegetable garden ready to produce an abundant crop. She looked at the new gingham curtains she had proudly sewn herself and recalled to mind the sunny yellow paint she had planned for the bedroom. Then, swallowing with difficulty, she turned to Abe and declared, "We need to move from here."

"Yes," he agreed reluctantly. "I think so too."

He chose not to ask what had happened that day to bring her to such a conclusion after so long and so well tolerating people's attitudes. He only knew that it had to have been most unpleasant. Nancy never told him, but for the rest of her life whenever she saw a man spit into the dirt she would clutch her skirts and move quickly out of range.

Neither one of them needed to discuss all the reasons why moving was the best decision. They lived in a society that was accepting and tolerant of much in the way of differences between people. It was also a society that refused to forgive or accept many things, especially if it was something perceived as a threat to the fabric of their carefully ordered society.

Abe and Nancy were also aware of how many people while traveling to the Far West had been negatively impacted by Indians, whether on the plains or the territories west of the Rockies. Many had not forgiven the Indians their "thieving ways", while others had either experienced or heard numerous stories of brutalities toward emigrants. Other people simply resented the terrified months they had spent traveling in sick dread of attacks that never came. Consequently, any white man who admired or respected a tribe enough to choose to "turn Indian" and live with them was considered to be of the same caliber as they considered the Indians. He must perforce be despised, or at least mistrusted. By association, the family who produced such an "aberration of humanity" must also be considered suspect.

It would be many years before the general population would come to realize that the Indians also had a point of view. Generations of native people would keep alive stories of how their ancestors had often been misunderstood and mistreated by emigrants who shot at them unprovoked, and who slaughtered their life-supporting game for mere sport. They would describe how many tribes were decimated by diseases brought by those in wagons. They would tell of soldiers who had herded them like animals from their ancestral lands for hundreds of miles over mountains with no regard for the welfare of the women and children, the old or the sick. They would describe being forced onto reservations that were barren, with infertile land and no game, and no better than waste dumps.

The elders would tell grandchildren about the Government that had consistently broken its promises and treaties when it wanted more land for settlers and their cattle. They would tell the children stories of government sponsored Indian agents who had regularly stolen allotments of food intended for the reservations, not caring that the children were starving. They would tell of tribal villages filled with only women and children that had been burned to the ground and everyone in them massacred by Army troops. Eventually whites would hear of all this too, and eventually some would even care enough to be outraged.

Abe and Nancy knew none of this at the time, and only cared that their son was safe and evidently happy. If he was not, they reasoned that he would have come looking for his parents.

Abe informed their landlord of their decision to leave town. Although the man gave voice to regretting Abe's decision, he did a poor job of masking his relief. Abe wondered how long it would have been before the man found a convenient excuse to evict them.

Abe made up his mind to keep this last insult from Nancy. However, that night when he watched her eyes looking around the parlor as she started a sentence with, "Maybe we could wait...," he stopped her and told of his conversation with their landlord. Nancy merely pressed her lips together and nodded, then forced herself to smile as she asked, "Have you thought of where our next adventures will take place? And how we'll get there?"

"Yes. We should go somewhere that Todd might find us," Abe reasoned, "or where we might even spot him in town. I've been thinking about the places we already know he's been, but also where a young white man living with Indians in Nevada will be talked about by both whites and Indians."

"So, my dear, do we go to Carson City or Virginia City?"

"No. Too many there might remember why I was hunting for him. If the Indians become aware that Todd is being sought, they could abandon or harm him in fear of reprisals. Or they could hide him in such a way that we would never find him."

"So where do you suggest we go?"

"I was thinking of Bridgeport."

"Won't people there know about our relationship to the white man with the Indians?"

"I don't think so. The Sheriff there is the only one who knows why I was looking for Croat, and he promised to say nothing. Anyway, he's no longer the Sheriff there. Some guy named Zackary Tinkum is. Everyone else, if they remember me at all, will assume it was something personal with Croat that got settled."

"And the town isn't far from the Nevada border."

"Right. Freighters arrive from the north all the time. They might hear something specific about the location of the white Piute, since I'm told there are many Walker River tribes and they're spread over almost 300,000 acres. Piutes living around Bridgeport could possibly be related to those in his tribe. They're all part of the greater Northern Piute family."

After a moment, Nancy said, "Then it's to Bridgeport we go."

Abe began filling their light spring wagon with supplies and household items. He was deeply touched when Mr. Zeisz gave him two more large horses, saying, "You'll need a good team going over those mountains, and these two know how to pull together. Use them as the wheelers."

"I can't afford more animals," Abe told him. They had just enough money to set themselves up in Bridgeport after paying the tolls on the roads on their way there.

"I'm not selling them to you. I'm giving them to you."

"Oh, but I can't..."

"Yes, you can," Mr. Zeisz told him, putting a hand on Abe's shoulder. "It's been an honor having you work for me. I could always trust you, even with bank deposits. And you often worked an extra hour without complaint, or pay for that matter. That deserves a bonus. But I consider you a friend first. I'm only sorry you feel you have to leave here."

Abe was overcome with gratitude. "It's just become too difficult. I could probably rise above it, but my poor wife has been through enough heartache. I can't ask her to put up with the shabby treatment of the women, or expect myself to keep silent one of the times someone snubs us."

"Yeah," his boss nodded, "stuff like that means a lot to women."

Remembering those who had turned their backs on him in the saloons, Abe could have told him that it evidently meant something to some of the men too. Instead, he thanked his friend for his generous gift and brought the new horses to the stable where he kept Flame and his own two wagon horses.

Early in August, not long after sunrise and before many people were on the sidewalks, Abe drove their wagon out of Placerville and headed west toward Sacramento. They were not long on the trail when the mail arrived in Placerville on the noon stage. One of the letters in the canvas pouch was from Missouri. Elsie had written to inform them of Byron's passing. It had taken five months for the letter to reach Placerville. Since Abe and Nancy had purposely not left a forwarding address with the post office, Elsie's letter was put in the dead letter drawer of an old oak file cabinet. It was one of many that had little hope of ever again seeing the light of day.

Abe had decided they would travel south on the western side of the Sierra Nevada through the mining towns of El Dorado, Plymouth, Amador City, Sutter Creek, Jackson, Mokelumne Hill, San Andreas, Angels Camp, and Jamestown before heading east to Sonora and then over the Sierra to Bridgeport. It would mean many weeks of travel, but they would have no worry of getting water, supplies or feed for the animals.

If leaving Placerville had been emotionally difficult, their journey south in the warmth of summer was at least not physically arduous. The weather was mild and the wagon was in good repair, so Abe allowed them a leisurely rate of progress, although the possibility of early snows in the mountains was never forgotten.

Once they reached Jamestown, they spent three days resting and enjoying themselves. They were so taken with the quaint village that they even discussed staying there. However, it was too far from Nevada and there was no reason to believe that Todd would ever go there, so they continued on to Sonora. Here the Carringtons rested a day and refreshed their supplies.

The next three days were spent traveling east to Strawberry Flats where they acquired more supplies at the stage station. Since it was by then nearing fall, they also asked for information about the road conditions ahead. Early storms that brought down the first several feet of snow, and that eventually reached forty feet, were not unusual along the Sonora Road. It would forever be only a seasonal connection over the Sierra.

When emigrants had taken this route in the late 1840's, it had been nothing more than an old Indian trail widened into a dirt track by the first explorers who used it. In the 1850's, after traveling 2,000 miles from the East to get to California, the condition of the road was not going to stop the early emigrants even if it meant they had to dismantle the wagons and carry them over in pieces. Thankfully, since 1861 the road had been gradually improved by a number of construction crews, each contracted for a particular portion of the road. That summer the Sonora Road had been closed until July due to snow, but the Carringtons traveled over it without undue delay, and only occasionally saw patches of white in deeply shadowed crevasses.

Even with the recent improvement, it was a steep, twisting, occasionally rocky road, and the horses pulling the wagon had their work cut out for them. Several times Abe and Nancy had to work together to clear the road of rocks that had rolled down from the mountain walls or branches fallen from the trees overhanging the road. Their reward was spectacular views from their mountain perch of far-reaching grandeur and beauty.

They stood at the edge of many a sheer precipice that edged the road and looked down into deep canyons many miles long filled with Alpine meadows covered in thickets of red-barked pines tossed with giant boulders. The cliff faces several times presented waterfalls that plunged down into gorges filled with bushes bright with red berries and prowling bears.

At one such stop, Abe commented, "Places like this sure put one's life in perspective." He smiled and put his arm around Nancy's waist, inordinately pleased to feel her move closer and press against him.

As the narrow road followed the ridges along the Stanislaus River, they often traveled with other people. Of those not traveling by stage, there were men walking or riding, with or without a string of pack mules.

Abe and Nancy were enormously grateful for the stage station at Strawberry Flats run by Major Lane and the one at Niagra run by J. W. Brightman. They obtained fresh milk, meat and even a few eggs. The conversations at these way-stations covered a wide range of topics. At both facilities there were groups of men discussing Nebraska, admitted to the Union just the year before as the 37th state, and everywhere they stopped men talked excitedly about President Ulysses S. Grant and Reconstruction in the South. Virginia, Mississippi and Texas had been restored to their position as Sates of the Union, but not Georgia and this caused much speculation.

There was also excitement about the national census just completed and how this could help California. Completion of the Pacific Railroad caused speculation among the freighters who wondered if it meant more freight to haul, or less.

After following a small tributary of the river, Abe and Nancy ascended to the crest of the Sierra Nevada before dropping down sharply along its eastern scarp. This landed them at Indian Valley, settled by the Leavitt family as a stage station and ranch. Here they rested a day before traveling twenty miles on a portion of the road that was narrower, steeper and more twisting than so far traveled. It challenged not only their wagon but also their courage.

Finally reaching the junction with the Mono Road, they stayed the night with Mr. Mack at The Junction House. While Nancy lay on a bed that was delightfully comfortable and wrote in her journal, Abe took advantage of the hot tubs filled by a natural hot spring. His muscles had never felt so relaxed and not sore. After that it was a fairly easy trip south over the newly improved Mono Road to Bridgeport.

The day was bright and cool as the Carringtons neared the town from the north. The worst of the scorching summer heat had passed and yellow was beginning to tint the abundance of cottonwoods, aspens and willows along the river and creeks. They forded the rocky West Walker River and were grateful for a shallow flow because of the late season. This dangerous crossing completed, they relaxed and settled into an appreciative enjoyment of their surroundings.

The road followed the edge of the leaping white water of the river as it crashed over its rocky bed and curved through a narrow canyon with boulder strewn walls, then ushered them through miles of scrub that slowly gave way to lush meadows of brown autumnal grasses. Although they approached from the north, following the curve of the road around a small hill, they entered at the west end of the town.

They had been told that Bridgeport was also easily reached from by a natural pass through Bridgeport Canyon that had been traveled by native tribes since ancient times and now connected the area to the Mono Lake region. The broad sweep of Big Meadows was backed by the Sierra, and in the opposite direction by trackless and heavily forested hills. The bulk of the Sweetwater Range completed the closure of the valley and Nancy embraced the atmosphere of isolation, and protection.

Abe felt a happy rush of recognition as they approached the small town that huddled in the heart of what was called Big Meadows. Abe turned toward Nancy to express his delight and saw that she was looking around them with evident enjoyment as she saw the fields filled with cattle and horses. He chose to let her find her own sense of belonging and said nothing.

Nancy was enchanted by the ranch houses and barns surrounded by white slab fencing situated far apart over the hundreds of acres of short grasses. The cattle and dairy cows grazed contentedly amid a network of meandering streams that turned the land into more of a marsh than pasture.

In the early years, the local Piute tribes had clustered in villages in the mountains and near the junction of the Sonora and Mono Roads, the Big Hot, Travertine, and Buckeye Canyon. These and other locations were far from the settlers that carried guns wherever they went and from whom the Indians felt they needed protection as the town slowly expanded.

With its growth dependent on the large number of mines along the Eastern Sierra, the town was fortunate to be so close to the mines of the Mono Diggings, Dogtown, Bodie and Aurora.

Even the earliest settlers had not lacked the basic necessities of life. Water was abundant throughout the year, and due to the hot summers and extreme winters, the grasses grew quickly to take advantage of the short growing season.

This rich grass supported large herds of cattle, dairy cows, and even some sheep, although most ranches also grew hay. The Chinese raised vegetables in their village at Clark Canyon and on the edge of Warm Spring Flat, and sold them to households in Bridgeport. Whatever else the townspeople needed to sustain commerce and homesteads was freighted from the Carson Valley, while the beauty of the landscape served to sustain their souls until a church could be built.

They also developed a cooperative spirit that accomplished whatever was necessary to enhance or secure the town. When the spring snow melt overflowed the creeks, they built canals that crossed Main to drain the water and foot bridges over the drainage. When they needed better access to other towns, they cleared the sagebrush and rocks and opened up wagon roads. When they needed to assure security with the local Piutes, they met with them and came to mutually agreeable commitments that rendered both the town and the tribe secure. When children were born, the women came together to assure a safe delivery until Doc Sinclair and his family moved to the area. When people died, Amasa Bryant donated part of his land for a cemetery on the north side of Main.

For social interaction they had their lodges, saloons, stock auctions, local rodeos, Fourth of July celebrations, quilting circles, town Christmas tree and caroling, and occasional dances and picnics. So dedicated to the town's prosperity, and so proud of its beauty were they, that 150 years later many of their descendents would be living there--some on the same land and some even in the same houses.

As Abe and Nancy drove their exhausted team toward the town, they were met by the refreshing smell of cut hay and the more pungent but not unpleasant odor of the grazing herds. Flame raised his head and whinnied when Abe stopped the wagon. Nancy admired the first of the homes situated on the edge of the pastures, the near end of the house almost covered with long vines of hops now turning bright autumn colors. Further evidence of fall was the impressively large wood piles stacked near back doors of businesses and homes, and in any bare space nearby.

Nancy felt the yearning of the homeless to have a place of her own again, and longed to once again sit by a warm stove in her small platform rocker--the only piece of furniture taking up room in the wagon--and listen to the sounds of the meadow awakening in the early morning.

As Abe commanded "Giddup" and the wagon started forward, a large family of quail flushed across the road and disappeared into the scrub. Nancy smiled at their comical run, hop and fluttery flight back into the scrub. Watching her, Abe knew he had made the right decision in coming to Bridgeport.

CHAPTER EIGHTEEN
BRIDGEPORT, CALIFORNIA
1868

"No longer are we cloistered among trees and walls of granite. We are instead adrift in a sea of grass and open space, at once exposed and protected, but still within sight of Sierra peaks."

Nancy

Only a half mile long, Bridgeport was a shock to Nancy after the many brick buildings, numerous shops and throngs of people in Placerville. Her sense of being thrown into pioneer living was not helped by Abe commenting, "The town sure has grown."

Most of the small settlement, less than a dozen years old, was huddled on the west and east sides of the Walker River. The bridge connecting the two areas was just wide enough for a freight wagon, and because loose stock was often herded across the river, a wide trail had over time been worn into the sloping banks near the bridge. The narrow river sent out uncountable stringers of water that crisscrossed the valley, and it was instantly obvious to the first time visitor why the 50,000 acre grassland had been called Big Meadows.

When the town had been declared the County Seat of Mono County two years before, one of the oldest buildings, the American Hotel, had served as the courthouse. Its close neighbor was a frame blacksmith shop that shod the freighter's ox and mule teams, after which they were turned out into the surrounding expanse to graze until needed. There was also a butcher, the Kingsley Inn, a small hotel owned by Louis Ladd, and several small cabins.

The first settlers owned miles of ranch land spreading out in every direction from the town. At Daniel Waltze's Empire Dairy, the cows grew fat on the rich grass and gave unusually large quantities of milk. The mountain canyons of the Sawtooth

Range had been found the ideal locations for saw mills where men brought the timber they cut in the foothills.

The clusters of old wagons and tents that had been present during Abe's '65 trip had disappeared. There were now several dozen structures on the west side, including another blacksmith shop near the river, three saloons, the Bridgeport House Hotel, Bryant's Store, and dozens of homes both on Main and back of the businesses.

Two houses in the center of town belonged to the Parrish and Kingsley families, who in 1866 had been united by marriage. The Parrish house was situated next to Kingsley's house on the south side of Main, along with 160 acres behind it. Joe Kingsley, known from earliest years as "the old man at the bridge", had a few years earlier sold his farm and dairy property to his son. The purchase had included the house on Main along with his wealth of 18 milk cows, 12 head of cattle, several hogs, and a flock of chickens. Second generation pioneers were already taking over and developing the town.

Nancy loved the look of the slab fencing that enclosed the pastures and homes. These fences were whitewashed along with the wood houses, and the result was architecture reminiscent of a New England village.

It had all started in the late 1850's when George Byron "By" Day, the Whitney brothers and a man named Green, came to the wide valley and saw its potential for raising cattle and growing hay. Others were quick to follow and soon Joe Kingsley arrived and built the first inn, followed by N. B. (Napoleon Bonaparte) Hunewill and his family.

N.B. had amassed a considerable fortune when placer mining on California's Yuba River back in the late 1850's, and after floods destroyed a mill he had built outside San Francisco, he moved his family to Aurora. When he realized that the most needed commodity was wood and that it came from the Big Meadows area, he built a saw mill near Buckeye and Robinson Canyons.

The first mill in the area had been established in 1861 by Z. B. Tinkum's Tuolumne Mill Company located at the foot of the twin lakes ten miles above the town. By the time Tinkum decided to sell out in 1865 to Sewell Knapp, the industrious Mr. Tinkum's holdings consisted of two sawmills, a shingle mill, a lath mill, and a nice home. He was now the town's Sheriff.

When Abe and Nancy arrived late in 1868, some of the other people they met were ranchers John Dawson, Sol Townsend, George Ault, Jim Barnes, Nat Luce, John Murphey, Dan Waltze, Jack Severe, Sidney Huntoon, and West Towle. Doc Sinclair was hoping to expand the few sheep he had into a sizeable flock, while still tending to the town's medical needs. Meanwhile, Rebecca Poor gave the growing number of children their basic education in her home.

One of the largest spreads was owned by one of the earliest arrivals. In 1863 Amasa F. Bryant had built a small 16 X 24 foot store east of the river, but in 1866 when he moved his store to the west side of the bridge, he turned it into a two story merchandise store with a residence on the side. The balcony across the front of the upstairs created the porch roof below, and was held up by four substantial posts that also commonly supported the leaning of men clustered to discuss current events.

In 1868 Mr. Bryant owned not only the store but also an adjoining ranch of over 160 acres that spread north between the town and the river. It was home to his wife, son and daughter. This versatile gentleman also served as Postmaster, having worked in the Boston postal system before heading west. In 1881 he would donate land for the site of a white Victorian Courthouse. Over a hundred years later this stately building would be the historic hub of the County Seat's downtown that would still be only a half mile long and wide.

When Abe and Nancy arrived, they found no rooms available at the American Hotel or the Kingsley Inn, no boarding houses available, and no houses to rent. So they pitched their small tent next to their wagon on the north side of town near the river where they had a sweeping view of ranch houses, barns and corrals nestled in a part of the meadow lower than their perch near the town. These were the sprawling ranches of Bryant, Stewart, Hughes, Murphey and Moorman.

Nancy set up a cook fire and Abe went into town to "get the lay of the land around here". When he returned three hours later he smelled of lager beer and was smiling broadly, eager to inform Nancy that just to the north of where they were camped was a small plot of land for sale by Mr. Bryant. It was on his land that they had unknowingly set up their camp.

"It's only four acres, but we can do a lot with that much land."

"Can we afford it?"

"The price is cheaper than I would have thought." He looked down at his boots. "He's very welcoming. I think he took pity on us when I told him some of our story. And I accepted his offer." When Nancy looked stricken, Abe quickly added, "I guess I should have talked it over with you first before accepting."

"No, no, that's fine. But how much of our story did you tell him?"

"Oh, that." Abe put a hand on her shoulder and gave it a light squeeze. "I merely told him and some others that were with us in the saloon that we'd come across the country by wagon train and had lost our baby girl. I told them that we're looking for a peaceful place to make our home."

Nancy thought that clever, as it would certainly be noted as unusual for a couple their age not to have had children.

"They called one of the men N.B., but his full name is Napoleon Bonapart."

"He had imaginative parents."

"He told me how he and his wife Esther came around through the Isthmus of Panama to San Francisco not long after they were married."

"When I meet Esther, I'll have to ask her to give me her version of such an adventure. It must have been quite an ordeal."

The town may have been small, but the hearts of the people in it were big and the Carringtons were eagerly accepted. The women especially were happy to have another to add to their number. When it was discovered that Abe could drive a large wagon and its team, he was approached with work by two sawmills and N.B. Hunewill. He decided that rather than hire on full time with anyone in particular, he would freelance his many skills. That way he could take whatever jobs were available, that paid him the most, and that would still give him time to work on his own home.

Abe immediately purchased the wood and nails for their house and hauled it to their new property. Nearby Nancy set up camp around a large tent loaned them by Mr. Hunewill. On the ground inside was a straw and horsehair mattress next to Nancy's rocking chair, a couple of small rag rugs, a crate with a lantern on it that served as a table, and two camp stools.

They were comfortable emotionally if maybe a little less so physically, but that didn't seem to matter all that much as they rapidly made friends. Each day they went into town so Nancy could shop, or to share a cup of coffee between Abe's jobs. Abe regularly had a drink in one of the saloons, claiming it was simply to make a connection with the locals, but Nancy couldn't hide her smile each time he said it. Sometimes Abe and Nancy walked the length of the town just to be seen, and they never came back home without having made a new acquaintance.

In this way the news of Abe's purchases and his plans for a house spread quickly through the small population. At the crack of dawn the day after Abe began work on a wood and stone foundation, there arrived at the Carrington tent a number of men armed with tools. With them came several of their wives and the Hunewill cook, Mrs. Vaughn, all carrying baskets of food. Among the men who were known to be expert carpenters were Peter Nye, Jesse McGath, Hiram Leavitt, Sam Hopkins, Patrick Hughes, and Michael Whalen. All had businesses in town or ranches in the meadow, but they took the day off to help this newly arrived couple get settled before winter crashed down on the area.

Nancy made sure there were beans generously laced with molasses cooking on the open fire, much as she had done on the trail, as well as a pot of coffee hanging from the cross piece over the fire. She was assisted by Esther Hunewill, a friendly and outgoing woman only a few years her junior who talked happily about life in the valley. She took for granted that Nancy too would love living there, it being beyond her imagination that anyone could feel otherwise.

Nancy watched Esther's young son Frank happily carrying nails and small tools to the men, and found herself thinking that it should have been Todd helping them. But it was because of Todd that they were there in Bridgeport in the first place, so in some odd way she did feel his presence.

By dark that night there was ready for the Carringtons a small square house with a raised wooden floor. It had a steeply pitched shingle roof that extended down over the front to cover the narrow porch and over the back to shelter the wood that would later be stacked near the door off the small storage room.

The interior walls were not yet finished, but the framing was ready for three walls to separate it into an entry parlor, a bedroom to the left, a kitchen beyond the parlor and the storage room to the left of that behind the bedroom. There was a partial wall blocking the left half of the kitchen from the parlor, which was a request from Nancy that the other women backed her on. No woman wants her unwashed dishes apparent to a visitor entering her home.

In fact, it was this collection of experienced cooks that pushed for the completion of the kitchen instead of the interior walls. Nancy almost wept as she surveyed the large dry sink with a row of shelves above and a long work counter on either side. Abe promised that when he had the time he would make for her two hanging cabinets as well. There was also a pierced tin-fronted pie safe that Mr. Bryant had removed from his store's inventory and hauled with him in his wagon. The right side of the kitchen as seen from the parlor was prepared for the installation of a large stove so that when the new stove arrived from Carson, it could be situated between the kitchen and parlor to keep both rooms warm. A small table and four chairs were tucked into the back corner of the kitchen not far from the stove.

Over the next week Abe and a few of his new friends completed the interior walls, installed the stove and vent pipe, and built a bed frame with a network of ropes to support their horsehair mattress. They also dug a root cellar and lined it with straw. Esther and Eliza Bryant brought Nancy a small settee and two end tables, and with the addition of curtains at the windows across the front and Nancy's handmade rag rugs, the house soon had the feel of a cozy home.

Whenever Abe was paid for a job of work, he and Nancy added something new to their collection of donated furniture, dishes, cooking utensils, and linens. By the time the winter chill was numbing their toes, they were ensconced in comfort and warmth. Nancy and Abe invited everyone they had met and everyone who had helped during the construction to a chilly but festive picnic, and although some of the women insisted on bringing food, Nancy provided most of it. Her pies were commented on with great enthusiasm.

The winter of '68 hit suddenly in the middle of December. Although everyone said it was a "mild winter", Abe and Nancy were not used to temperatures near zero and a *minimum* of two feet of snow for weeks at a time. It was for them a miserable few months, especially for Abe who had to be out in the elements while working.

Abe and Nancy's first Christmas in their new home was festive yet simple. Abe, By Day, and N.B. took a large wagon into the mountains near the first of the twin lakes and brought back a pine tree so large that it overhung the back of the wagon by several feet. Using timbers and much assistance, they propped it up in front of the saloon that had been recently purchased by John Dawson. When finished, Abe and the others rewarded themselves by taking advantage of the tree's location and each accepted a drink from those who were grateful they had been spared the work of obtaining or shoring up the tree.

Soon the women were decorating the large pine with strings of popcorn, branches of holly berry, and dried fruits. They discussed their plans for the coming holiday season, which included the baking of cakes and savory dishes to be shared at a series of pot luck dinners held in the homes of family and friends. For the dozen or so children of the town, the women sewed clothes for the girls and their dolls, and the men made toys and games for the boys.

Abe was concerned that Nancy would be stressed and sad, but at the party in the American Hotel where the presents were given to the children, the joy of their reactions seemed to please Nancy, and Abe relaxed. After the children had received their gifts, a boy of ten hesitantly walked up and stood before Abe.

With both hands clasping an old felt hat in front of his chest, the boy said, "My dad told me you made my wagon. Thank you. It'll make my chores a lot easier." He looked around to be sure no one else was close, then added, "My dad is the best with horses and mules, but he's not very good at building things."

Abe carefully hid a smile and told him, "Well, Charlie, being good with animals is much more important. If the wagon ever needs repair, you just come to me."

"Thanks, Mr. Carrington." Charlie crammed his hat back on and hurried off to join Frank Hunewill and the other boys by the punch bowl. Watching him, Abe suddenly had to swallow twice to remove the lump in his throat, but he was content as he looked around the room, and less depressed than he had feared.

Nancy watched the little girls in the room dancing and playing with their dolls, and wanted to run from the room in tears. Sensing her distress, Esther, Eliza and several of the other women surrounded her and began relating humorous stories

about themselves and their years in the meadow. Soon they had
Nancy smiling, and eventually even laughing.

They told her about the time one of them lost her wedding
ring during haying at the Day ranch. The next morning after
the men had moved on to help at the next ranch, the women
and children had crawled around on their hands and knees for
hours until it was found.

They told her about Esther and Eliza spending hours in the
Bryant kitchen squeezing the juice from bushels of grapes so
they could make jelly. After eating their lunch outside on the
porch, they returned to the kitchen to discover that the Piute
woman that worked for the Bryants had thrown out the juice
and meticulously placed all the skins and seeds in the waiting
glass jars.

They told how some of the men would get together to haul
wood or other goods to Aurora, but would then spend the night
with friendly company before heading back to town. Of course,
none of the women present claimed *their* husbands would ever
do such a thing. It was, however, a joke among them that the
men never considered that their wives knew about such things.

They told her their reactions the first time they saw one of
the Piute women reach into the bosom of her clothing and remove a little leather pouch full of fat. Mrs. Day told her, "They
wipe it all over their face. It keeps their skin soft and free from
the chapping effects of the winter cold. As gross as it looks, I
think they've got a very good idea there."

That reminded Esther Hunewill of something that happened
just before the previous winter. The Piute lady who came to
do the mill worker's laundry boiled the men's wool longjohns.
"When they dried, they looked like doll clothes! The men were fit
to be tied," she laughed. "One of the freighters coming in from
Aurora had a few pairs with him destined for Bryant's Store.
While the hands waited for him to get more, some of the men in
town loaned them their extra pair."

The women talked over each other in their eagerness to describe Mr. Bryant's old crooked-horned ram chasing the children who tried to swipe the melons from his vegetable patch.

Nancy shared the story of the man on the stage afflicted with
poison oak. They all giggled when she quoted Hank Monk telling
the man it was a good thing he hadn't squatted among the vines.
She also told them of cooking and other domestic mishaps they

could all relate to, and laugh about. Although all the stories that day brought laughter, Nancy and her new friends had already shared a few luncheons where they had described the hardships of their travels to Bridgeport, the loss of loved ones, and other intimate details of their lives. But it had not escaped the notice of the women that Nancy never gave any specific locations or dates when talking about the events she referred to in *her* life.

Abe heard the women laughing and when he realized Nancy was one of them, he suddenly felt himself grinning. Her pleasure or pain always affected him more than he would ever admit to anyone.

After they arrived home from the Christmas party and had climbed into bed, Nancy said to Abe, "You know, it occurred to me this evening that life not only 'moves on' as people say, but that it moves on as we choose it to be. I think our lives are more governed by our attitudes than we might realize."

"There's that philosophical bent of yours," he teased her.

"But I'm right," she responded, poking him in the side and making him laugh.

"I know you are."

He wrapped his arms around her and she nestled against him, completely relaxed and feeling just a hint of contentment. "I like it here, Abe. These are nice people and it's such a beautiful valley. I'll be happy to settle here."

"Me too." And in such a state of mind they fell asleep to the serenade of the coyotes that patrolled the edge of the river not far away.

The next day, with the smell of the sagebrush fires drifting on the air from the Piute village near the bridge, Abe and Nancy watched some of the town children skating along the narrow channel of the frozen river. Others flopped onto their sleds and whizzed down the gentle snowy slopes toward the flats along the river.

Abe was there because he had been hired to help cut ice. Along with several other men, he ventured out where the river was wider and they could cut the blocks. Abe then drove the wagon to the ice house in town where he helped store the blocks in drifts of saw dust from the mills. The townspeople would be using this ice well into summer to store milk, eggs and cheese.

As the snow melted and the ground thawed, and with remnants of snow still streaking the meadows, blades of grass immerged that each morning grew an inch longer. Gardens and fields were tended, the buzzing of sawmills was heard on the breeze, and freight traffic passed through town spurred on by the shouts and whistles of freighters hauling supplies to the local businesses and the mines to the south.

The saloons filled with thirsty hard working men who talked of rumors coming out of Carson about Reconstruction in the south, the hard winter in the high Sierra, and the big 1,200 pound grizzly the cold had driven down into Bloody Canyon south of Mono Lake. The forges glowed hot at young Patrick Hughes's forge as freighters arrived in town and needed their oxen shod, and when time allowed, Patrick turned out hand-forged iron tools for the men and kitchen implements for the ladies.

Trials were once more held in the second floor rooms of the hotel where curious citizens packed in to watch. Stages arrived with mail and packages that had piled up at the Carson City and Reno post offices during winter. It was a busy start to 1869, and no one was more eager for the new year than Abe and Nancy.

Spring meant the ditches and canals had to be dug out and reinforced so the snow melt could pass through and around the town. All the men, and even the older boys, began this task as soon as the ground had thawed enough to allow their shovels to penetrate, but before the ground was too muddy. The men then turned their attention to herding home their cattle from winter ranges in time for the birthing of calves.

Spring for the women was a routine of domestic chores. Mattresses were aired in the sun, blankets were washed and hung on lines for several days until dry, cupboards were wiped out with vinegar and hot water, heavy coats were wiped down and carefully stored in trunks, clothes were boiled outside in large kettles instead of inside in small ones with the inevitable steaming of windows, lye soap was made, candles were dipped and stored in the cool of the root cellar, vegetable gardens were dug and seeded, and the hop vines around the houses were cut back to encourage lush new growth.

When it came time to socialize, women gathered over cups of tea and quilting frames. They arrived with jars of yeast starter to exchange with their hostess so the supply of both would be freshened. Some of the women had insisted everyone in their family be dosed with sulphur and molasses to ward off the diseases of spring or as a restorative after the severe winter. Those women who did not subscribe to this were often roundly chastised by those who did, but it was given and received with good humor.

Nature too set about its spring chores. The lilac bushes were blooming, the current bushes set their buds, the quail and grouse dashed through the meadow and people's yards looking for seeds, coyotes and wolves howled to reinforce family groups, and rabbits leaped over one another in their mating rituals. Eventually calves and foals and lambs were born, and bragged about by proud owners.

Abe and Nancy planted their vegetable garden with joy after the hard work of rooting out the sagebrush. Two heavy boards were hammered together with the long spikes extending through the wood so when they were dragged by the wagon horses, the sagebrush was pulled up enough that a shovel could finish the job. After that the horses pulled the smooth side of the boards over the land so that Abe could then plow it. Flame watched the activity from his partially roofed corral, no doubt happy not to be pulling the plow.

Even though Nancy and Abe worked long hours, they found time to participate in the routine of the town and they soon became known as "the nice couple from Missouri." Most thought them a little quiet perhaps, but still decent people who were good-natured and quick to help others when needed.

The women knew the Carringtons had lost a little girl when she had been thrown from a wagon while they were on the trail. That was not an unusual circumstance. The age of the child, when they had crossed and other details were not readily forthcoming from them. It would have been a display of bad manners for anyone to inquire further, so even though many remained curious, the Carrington's were simply accepted as presented.

By early summer the men had finished the ditches and dumped into the water a dozen carp to eat any growing algae. Wildflowers burst out in colorful swaths across the meadows and were enjoyed by the grazing cattle and dairy cows, as well as Piute women who sold bunches of them to the hotels and housewives.

Children also returned to school for classes held now in the Dave Hays home by his wife Alice. In 1876 she would become the first female Superintendent of Schools in California.

The hot sun of summer encouraged the rapid ripening of the vegetables in the gardens, and Nancy was proud that she had grown enough produce for their current use with enough left over to preserve or dry for the winter to come. Three hogs, a small flock of chickens and a cow completed their homestead.

Life took on a rhythm of men's work outside, women's work in and around the home, and social events both segregated and shared. Their lives were filled with the local events of the time, in which they participated as much for the enjoyment of their community as for the possibility of hearing rumors of a white man with the Piutes. Consequently, Abe and Nancy quickly became known for their interest in Indians. They explained this interest as that of people who simply wanted to know all aspects of their new community, and again the townspeople accepted this at face value.

In Bridgeport, as in the other towns along the Sierra, men gathered at their lodges on a regular basis. Abe was invited to join the Masons and the Independent Order of Odd Fellows. All excluded the women, who thought nothing of it, as they had their own activities where men were never seen, such as quilting circles, luncheons and teas. It was a balance of divided interests that gave each group something special that was theirs alone, and a place where they could feel understood and accepted by those of the same gender.

They did, however, both enjoy the square dances in the summer under the stars where couples waltzed, performed the schottische and the polka. Those who knew these dances taught those who did not, and were backed by a violin, a banjo, and a clarinet.

The highlight of summer was the Fourth of July celebration. Saplings were cut and brought into town where they lined the street, a tradition brought to California by European miners and common in California mining camps. The special day started with literary readings by children and adults in the morning, a deep pit barbecue at noon, races and games of athleticism in the street in the afternoon, and a grand ball in the evening where everyone wore their best clothes.

Summer haying was a task in which everyone participated, including the women and the older children. While the men gathered to cut and bale the hay at one ranch after another, their wives gathered in the kitchen of each successive ranch to cook the food that kept the men working at top speed. There was no competition to this, only cooperation, and in this way the entire community prospered.

It was during the spring and summer that the Piutes came into town for work to earn money for tobacco and whatever else they had learned from the white man to enjoy. Abe spent more time in the saloons hanging around with the locals than he would have otherwise, so he could hear another of the many rumors that were circulating through the area of a white man living with the Indians. Except that by 1869 he was being referred to as "the white brave".

In answer to their curiosity, Abe and Nancy were given much information about the Piutes, most of whom lived to the north around the hot springs near Fales Station and in Buckeye Canyon. Unlike the Owens Valley Piutes to the south who had been at war with the miners and settlers from 1862 until 1867, the Indians of the Big Meadows area had never seemed particularly unhappy about the settlers coming into their valley. However, in the early 1860's when they had realized their game was being killed, they had become afraid of the power of the new arrivals and had moved higher up into the mountains. There they had felt safe and yet could keep track of the movements of those in the valley.

The early settlers in Big Meadows had been smart enough to realize that the tribes living in the mountains would have greater hardships, and reasoned that this might eventually result in enough desperation that the tribes would feel the need to retaliate. Consequently, as the winter of '63 had approached, some of the men brought blankets and food into the mountains, leaving them where they knew the Indians would find them. Sure that they were being watched, the townsmen also laid their guns on the ground while they unloaded the supplies.

After that, any time they saw an Indian they would lay down their guns as a sign that they meant no harm. Eventually, By Day was able to talk to Captain Jim, chief of the Charlie Creek Indians. He also gave him a gun for hunting. Soon after that,

By Day and Captain Jim agreed that the Indians should gather for a meeting with the whites at Big Hot north of town.

At this meeting, the men from the town had piled their guns into a heap on the ground and the Indians had piled up their bows and arrows next to those. N.B. told Abe that he and West Towle, By Day, Bill Elliott, and Dave Hays had raced a group of Piutes to the stacked weapons.

"We agreed that whichever group reached them first could choose the pile they wanted to keep." N.B. smiled at the memory. "The Piutes won and they chose the guns, of course. After that we all shook hands, declared ourselves friends, passed a sacred pipe, and consumed a feast we had brought from town."

As people talked about the Indians and their culture, Nancy listened in an attempt to understand why her son would be content to adopt their ways. She especially enjoyed descriptions of their native foods which she was surprised to find so varied. Of course, what they ate depended on the time of year and the vagaries of the weather, and the list took advantage of anything edible that walked, crawled, flew, swam or grew out of the earth.

This gave them pine nuts (and the caterpillars on the trees) and grains; wild onions, rhubarb and native rice; seeds of Huki, bush sunflower, grass and rose hips (stored in grass-lined pits); tubers and roots of taboose, tule, bulrush and swamp grass; and buck and elder berries, currents and choke cherries. For meat there was rabbit, deer, pronghorn, gopher, lizard, quail, grouse, mountain sheep, duck, Mono Lake worms (fly pupae), and fish. They also ate a potato-like root found at the base of the Mariposa Lily that grew in great abundance east of Bridgeport. From this eclectic combination they produced soup, mush, and bread. The food was seasoned with salt from the alkali marshes, and much of it was dried and stored for survival of the long harsh winters.

For this storage, the women made beautiful baskets, woven mostly of willow, but also grasses, rushes and pine needles. Each was fashioned to its use. Some allowed air within and some were so tight as to be able to hold liquid, especially when lined with pitch. Flat baskets were used as dishes upon which to eat, while others were cupped for scooping fine seeds and grains or even beads used in ceremonial garments, and some were large for carrying burdens. Reeds were specially woven into cradleboards (hoo-pa) to hold babies upon the backs of mothers.

Made by the grandmothers, the design designated the child's gender: a line or arrow for a boy or *nat-se*, and a diamond for a girl or *tse-u-za*.

Their lore and legends were woven into the designs of their baskets from an image held in the creative mind of the weaver and never laid out for others to see until the item was finished. Occasionally a woman (*mahala*) would offer one of her baskets for sale in town and Nancy managed to purchase several of them, never knowing that a century later these baskets would be considered treasures coveted by museums and collectors.

With all the Carringtons learned about the Piutes in general, they learned nothing specific about Todd. There were, however, a growing number of rumors about a white man living with the Indians somewhere in Nevada. One rumor said he had married a shaman's pretty daughter; another rumor claimed he was a warrior who had earned the title in battle against whites (although another said it was against tribes from across the mountains); and yet another said the white brave was a great trapper and hunter who had brought prosperity to his adopted tribe.

Abe and Nancy listened carefully to them all, but gained no information specific enough to help them make contact with their son. All of their gradually acquired knowledge did help them begin to glimpse why Todd might enjoy living as a Piute. What they could not accept was that this might be more than a temporary circumstance.

In June, Abe helped the ranchers brand and castrate the calves. It was hot, dirty and exhausting work, but the celebration when it was over was great fun for the town. However, Abe and Nancy both agreed they were glad to be a farmer rather than a rancher.

In October the ranchers weaned the calves born in the spring, and in November helped ready the cattle for herding south to warmer winter ranges. It was good that they did this, because the winter of 1869 was more severe than the one previous, and it was a challenge for everyone.

Snow piled up around the buildings and it was a daily trial to keep a space around the house wide enough for access to the wood pile and the ladder against the roof. Abe climbed it each morning and reached with the rake to pull down the night's heavy accumulation from the roof.

The mills in the foothills were shut down for fear of avalanches, and often many days would pass when Abe had no work. Even more days would pass where Nancy had no women with whom to visit, which she sorely missed. Although everyone made a concerted effort to gather at Christmas, it was a less exuberant affair than the year before.

The town welcomed the spring of 1870 with elevated moods and a comfort felt in bones that were thoroughly warm for the first time in months. Mills were cutting wood again, and people were congregating on sidewalks.

Thomas Magilton had recently acquired the mill of I. P. Yaney that had been in operation since the early 1860's. It was about four miles east of Fales Hot Springs on the Sonora and Mono wagon road, along with a shingle mill, and here he offered Abe good money to work. It was a tempting offer after the long winter, and although it necessitated that Abe live at the station, he accepted the offer. At the end of three weeks, Abe decided that he would rather work closer to home even if it meant making less money. He would not admit that he missed Nancy too much to stay longer.

Meanwhile, although mining continued in Aurora, it was much reduced. Bodie was holding on, and a few more people lived there at the beginning of the 1870's than when Abe had seen it. In fact, Bridgeport women had found great interest in the news from Bodie that Rodger and Marietta Horner had in April of '69 produced a son, the first child born in Bodie.

Marietta's sister, who had been the first woman to live in Bodie, was Elizabeth Butler Kernohan. Abe told Nancy that he had seen Elizabeth and her little girl Helen Anne when he had been in Bodie. Elizabeth would later marry Almond Huntoon, brother of Bridgeport's Sidney, and after Almond's death, she would marry Jesse McGath who the Carringtons knew only as a rancher and expert carpenter. But Bodie was still a sleeping giant in 1870, with its future as a colossus a few years away.

Mining and milling was developing in the Dunderberg area south of Bridgeport, and because of this, an organization of toll road companies were building roads that webbed the area and connected the mining districts. The promising Castle Peak mines were active near what is now known as Dunderberg Mountain, and many claims were being filed. The whole area around Bridgeport was attracting an influx of people who needed supplies, livery stables, blacksmiths, wagon shops, and places to spend the night.

Thus began an incredible prosperity for the ranchers of Big Meadows. They bred stock horses and mules, the dairies provided for the locals and miners, and some vegetable farming began taking hold. The Antelope Valley area north was especially profitable in its farming, and much of its apples, pears, berries, wheat and honey found buyers in Bridgeport. Raising sheep finally caught on, and lumbering continued to be an important enterprise. Already in 1868 and 1869 the local steam driven saw mills had cut 400,000 feet of lumber and 330,000 shingles, and although mostly for local use, the mills found new customers at the ranches developing around Mono Lake.

In the summer of 1870 Abe stood on a new portion of wooden sidewalk and watched an ox being shoed at the blacksmith shop. Men lead the animal beneath a tall gallows frame outside the shop, encased its body in straps, tied together its rear legs, and then hoisted it into the air amid indignant bellows.

Abe shook his head and chuckled. "Now that's efficiency!" He turned away and entered the cool of the saloon. Sitting quietly at a small table in the corner, he sipped a glass of lager and let his mind wander where it wanted to go. After his thoughts had traveled through the events of that day, they began on those events of the past year, and eventually skimmed across the span of time that brought him up against their wagon train's gathering at St. Joseph.

It was there that he remembered most his boys' laughter and excited chatter. He never talked to Nancy about what he felt he was missing by the loss of his sons, or the ache he felt when thinking of little Alice. He always assumed she felt these losses more deeply, and concluded that if his grief was so painful, then hers must be almost unbearable. He did not yet understand that talking to Nancy about his feelings could make a difference, not only for himself but also for her.

So occupied with his thoughts was he that he was unaware of the men at the bar until he heard the phrase "...the white brave near Carson City." Abe was immediately at the speaker's side, demanding, "What did you say?"

The stranger faced him with a raised brow. Realizing the man was trying to judge the intent behind Abe's sharp tone, he forced himself to smile.

"I'm sorry," Abe chuckled. "My wife has become so damned concerned about a white child she heard was with the Indians that she drives me nuts with questions. But I can't ever give her answers."

The man nodded as he shook Abe's hand and said his name was Marcy. "I know how women are about kids. Got three of my own. Kids that is." When he laughed, Abe managed a polite chuckle in response. "But this ain't no kid with the Indians. It's a white man. Young, but definitely a man."

"How old do you think he is?"

"Oh, about twenty."

"Where did you see him?"

"In Carson City. He goes there regular to buy tobac and medicine for the Injuns too shy of town or who don't know the lingo. Guess he still likes some real food for himself too, 'cause he does some work on the ranches occasionally."

Several men made no pretense of their curiosity and one asked, "Does he go into the saloons?"

"No. Guess he could 'cause he's Anglo. But he doesn't."

"What does he look like?" Abe asked him.

"Tall, long brown hair, not as dark as a Piute but not all that pale either. Dark eyes like an Indian though. I know 'cause I spoke to him a couple of times. In fact, he asked me to bring some rabbit skins to Bryant when I told him I was coming here."

"So you'll be seeing him when you get back?"

"That's right. In fact, I'm leaving here in the morning."

Abe casually asked for a drink, trying to appear as though he had all the time in the world. "I have business in Carson. Lonely ride and I've been putting it off. If you'd not mind the company, I'd sure like to ride along with you."

"Hell, I don't mind. Glad to have the company."

"Good. I'd best get home and let the wife know." He downed his drink too quickly and fought to catch his breath.

Marcy said, "I'll meet you out front of the new Dave Hays store at six in the morning."

Before the sun was high enough to begin the day's heat, the men were riding along the torrent that was the Walker River. Continuing past Fales Hot Spring, they finally reached Coleville where they spent the night. Abe found Marcy good company, although the man never explained whether or not this was his first or last name. He did tell Abe that he had come across the country by wagon in 1853, and as Abe listened to descriptions of the dangers and deprivations Marcy had encountered, he realized how fortunate his own crossing had been.

Marcy spent most of the night in a saloon, while Abe nursed a lager for over an hour and went to bed early. The next day's ride was very quiet while Marcy suffered his hangover, but Abe didn't spare him the fast pace he set for them. Just south of Gardnerville they cut across the west fork of the Carson River and traveled north to rest and eat in Genoa. Marcy had recalled that he wasn't scheduled to meet with the "white brave" until late the next afternoon, so they decided to spend the night in Genoa before continuing early the next morning.

When they arrived in Carson late in the afternoon, Marcy went immediately to a large mercantile store. Abe followed him to the storeroom but stood back in the shadows among a stack of barrels. Marcy walked further into the room without noticing that Abe was no longer behind him.

At the far end of the long narrow room, an Indian stood with his back to them while looking out a small window. His long straight hair hung just below the back of his neck, but it was how tall he was that Abe first noticed. He was dressed in snug denim pants, a vest of deer skin that left his muscular arms bare, and moccasins on his feet.

Marcy asked, "White Elk?"

The Indian turned and presented himself with a calm confidence. His prominent jaw called attention to his face, but there was about his mouth a softness that was balanced by a strong brow line over dark eyes that fairly glowed with defiance. A brittle hardness radiated from him that told of a life that was more often a challenge than a reward, and made anyone approaching him move carefully out of his way.

Abe's first thought was that if he had not known this man so well as a boy, he would never have recognized him now. In that moment Abe realized he would never know all that his son had experienced that had made him the man he now was. Todd's unbraided brown hair was parted down the middle, hanging loose and tending to fall forward when he looked down. He spoke in a low voice, as though not wanting to call attention to himself, an Indian habit that Abe had noticed many times before in various tribes across the country.

To Abe, it was mostly the difference in his son's body that underscored the change. Standing before him was a man with broad well-developed shoulders, powerful forearms, athletic narrow hips and long muscular legs. His bare chest and hard well-defined stomach showed where the vest of tanned hides didn't quite meet.

Stepping into the stream of light from a small window, Abe said, "Hello, Todd."

"Dad!" His smile was joyful and his face softened so that he looked more boy than man. Abe felt a tremendous wave of relief.

"Dad?" Marcy yelped.

"I'm sorry I didn't tell you," Abe told him. "I've been looking for him for a long time."

"I'll be damned." Then Marcy asked, "No one knows about him in Bridgeport?"

"No." Abe looked at Marcy with obvious alarm and in his sternest voice told him, "No need to tell anyone about this. It's a private matter."

"Damn right!" Marcy handed Todd the money from the sale of his rabbit skins, opened the door of the storage room and mumbled, "I need a drink."

Father and son, face to face for the first time in seven years, looked at each other for several seconds without speaking. Abe finally broke the silence. "Your voice is so deep now."

"Yes. I've changed a lot." With a gentleness that reminded Abe of Nancy, Todd asked, "How's Mother?"

"She's fine. She'll be wonderful now."

Todd walked closer to his father. "My leaving must have caused you much pain. I'm sorry for that. Until I had my own son I never realized..."

"You have a son?" He was surprised at how angry he felt. It was one more thing deprived him, and he had to swallow hard to calm himself.

"Yes. He's only two months old.""

"Your wife?"

"She's Piute."

"Yes. That much I assumed. But..."

"Dad, I'm not going back with you." His face hardened and once more took on the defiance Abe had noted earlier. "I can't leave my family and they would never be accepted into your society."

"But it's your society too."

"No. Not now. I've changed too much. And I don't want to change back."

"So we're to be deprived not only of you but also knowing our grandchild?" The hurt in Todd's eyes made Abe instantly repentant. "I'm sorry, son. But these years haven't been easy for us."

"Again, I'm sorry."

Abe changed the subject before their time together was ruined. "What's your son's name?"

"Andrew."

"That's my middle name."

Todd smiled and said, "I know."

Abe cleared the sudden constriction in his throat and asked, "Did Croat and Hickly treat you okay?"

"Most of the time. At first I found the pace we traveled difficult. I was tired, hungry and uncomfortable most of the time."

"Oh, Todd, I..."

"No. I was glad of it. It felt right." When Abe frowned, Todd added, "It worked to take away a little of the guilt I felt at letting Harold go off by himself."

"I guess I can understand that."

"The guys also taught me a lot of things about surviving in the wild. They taught me to hunt..."

"I taught you that when you were ten," Abe objected with considerable heat.

"Yes. But they taught me how to kill bear, and how to trap beaver. And I learned about using native plants to abate fever and heal cuts."

"Is that why you stayed with them?"

"We ran into a lot of tough men, and Croat taught me to fight with a knife." Todd ignored Abe's gasp. "It took me over a year to begin to feel that maybe I didn't need their protection."

"You were only sixteen, after all."

"And we'd been in enough towns that I thought I could make my own money, but I lacked the confidence to set out on my own. Later, after some time in Virginia City, we went on to Aurora where Croat was stabbed in a fight. I realized then that I'd had enough. After they had a row about something, Hickly decided to stay in Aurora while Croat and I went on to Bodie. That's where I made friends with some Walker River Piutes. They were in the area for the Mono Lake gathering during the harvest of *ko-cha-bee*."

"The what?"

"A food we eat. You don't want to know more." Todd chuckled and went on. "There were games, gambling, and dancing. I loved it all and felt very much at home with them. And for some reason they were very welcoming of me."

"So you went off with them?"

"That's right. And I'm not sorry for the decision I made. I can't be, when I know how good my life has turned out."

"Isn't it a hard life?"

"Sometimes. But it's a very free life too. The rules are clear, and I've been accepted by the tribe because of my contributions."

"Who makes the rules? The Chief?"

"No. They were made by the great unknown power. We find its order in all things--animals, rivers, even rocks. That's why it's so important to respect the earth."

"Does the tribe respect you?"

"I've earned their respect."

"How did you do that?"

Todd sat down on a barrel and Abe followed suit. "I was put through an initiation that proclaimed my entrance into manhood."

"You weren't hurt, were you?" Abe had heard strange stories of painful tests by tribes across the country.

Todd laughed shortly. "No. It wasn't easy, but it wasn't torture. It was simply a combination of blessings, prayers, a plunge into the cold river, an uphill run of several miles repeated over several mornings, the schooling of their ways, and then a hunt where I gave the animal I killed to someone else. That, and other things I did, earned me their respect." After a moment's hesitation, he added, "That's something we both know I'll never be able to have in white society now."

Abe didn't argue. He knew Todd was right. "I've never seen a Piute dressed like you."

"These clothes are for when I come into town or when the Indian Agent visits. We don't care much for clothes. Rabbit skin robes give us warmth in winter, but when it's hot, men require little more than a breechclout and the women a short buckskin skirt."

"Where's your home, then?"

"Northeast of Walker Lake. We're referred to as the 'trout eating Piute'." He flashed his smile again. "It's a good reservation and not strict about our leaving for awhile, as long as we return."

"That doesn't bother you? Being on a reservation, I mean?"

"No. Not on this one. It's fairly run, and we have what we need to be happy." Todd walked to the window and opened it wider, inhaling deeply. "A storm is coming."

"But the sky's clear."

"Yes. But I can smell the storm's breath. And last night's new moon lay on its back."

In that moment Abe realized his son was an Indian after all. His anguish and frustration in the face of this sudden realization made him blurt out, "No one need know about your past. If you come back with me now..."

"And wear white men's clothes and cut my hair?" Todd moved closer to his father, putting a hand on Abe's shoulder. "And am I then never to think again of my wife and child?"

Abe had never before been so close to tears of frustration, and resolved never again to scoff at a woman reacting in such a way. Sensing Abe's distress, Todd hugged him, something he had seldom done as a child. Todd then stood back and looked boldly into his father's face. "I love you, and I love Mother. I'm responsible for a lot of pain. I know that."

"Your mother and I never blamed you for Harold's disappearance. It's important that you know that."

"But I blamed myself." Todd grimaced and shrugged. "I realize now that I over-reacted. No, I meant I'm sorry for the pain of leaving you when I did. I can't change what I did in the past or all that you might have felt these years, but you must make Mother realize that I'm happy now."

Abe nodded. "Yes. Okay. I know I have to return alone."

"I want you to realize that I didn't leave because I didn't love you both. It was just something I had to do."

After a half hour of telling his father more details about his life since leaving with Croat, Todd said, "You can at least tell Mother that someday I might come to see you."

Abe must have flinched or in some way have reacted, because Todd asked, "What is it?"

"We lived in Placerville for several years. We then moved to Bridgeport."

Discerning that there was more to the story, Todd waited. Abe hesitated only a moment before deciding to be forthcoming. "People in Placerville found out we had a son that had chosen to live with Indians. They were very judgmental. The women were particularly hard on your mother."

"Would the same thing happen in Bridgeport?"

"I don't know."

Todd shrugged, "Then why risk it?"

"I think your mother would rather see you and take that risk."

"Maybe. But it's one bit of pain I can spare her."

"How can I get word to you if I need to?" Abe asked him.

"The shop keeper here is a friend and knows how to keep a confidence."

"So you do keep a foot in the Anglo world?"

Todd smiled. "Well, more like a toe, but I do like to know what's going on in the area, if not the country. It could make a difference to the welfare of the tribe."

Abe was impressed that Todd related everything to his tribe. It showed how completely he had assimilated into his new life, and it confirmed to Abe that Todd was right in staying where he was.

CHAPTER NINETEEN
BRIDGEPORT, CALIFORNIA
SUMMER, 1870

"I had no idea how many emotions could wash together at the same time. It has taken me several days to define each one and learn to reduce them all to something I can manage."

Nancy

Nancy took one look at Abe as he walked into the kitchen of their house and said, "You found him, didn't you?"

"Yes. But he's not with me."

She merely nodded.

"You're not surprised?" When she shook her head, his frustration bubbled to the surface. "Damn it! Talk to me!"

Nancy poured him a cup of coffee before leading him to the kitchen table. "While you were gone, I got to thinking. If he wanted to be with us, he would be. He's obviously happy where he is. So, no, I'm not surprised. But I'll admit I was hopeful of being proved wrong."

"Well, you're right on all counts. By the way, we have a grand child."

"Really?"

This had obviously not occurred to her, and Abe grunted with satisfaction. "Yes, a boy, Andrew."

"What does Todd look like? Would I recognize him?"

"He's taller than when we last saw him, and his shoulders are broader. He's much darker too, probably from being outdoors so much. And his hair is very long. I think he would be considered handsome by women."

"I imagine his wife thinks so," she chuckled.

"He told me about the time he spent with Croat and Hickly. When they left the wagon train, they cut over to Salt

Lake City where they resupplied. They went on to Placerville and Sacramento, and then headed to Virginia City where they worked in some of the mines. It was hard work and Croat hated it. After Croat and Hickly lost most of their pay gambling, they decided to go to Aurora." Abe hesitated before adding, "He tactfully refrained from telling me that he wanted to get away before I found him there." When Nancy said nothing, he continued, "After getting into the fight in Aurora, Todd and Croat went to Bodie to find the doctor while Hickly stayed in Aurora. Todd thinks there was some kind of falling out between the men, but he's not sure what it was. When I told him Hickly had turned to robbing stages, he didn't seem surprised."

"And then Todd decided to leave Croat."

"Yes. While talking to the Piutes who live on the hillsides above Bodie, he met a family of Walker River Piutes who were visiting. There had been a big fandango at Mono Lake and some of the northern tribes had attended. The southern tribes were afraid to travel because of their off and on troubles with the settlers. That's when Todd met the girl. He wouldn't tell me her Piute name, but said that in English it's Sandra. They had an immediate attraction for one another, and her father was surprisingly okay with Todd joining them."

"And eventually he married the girl and now they have a child."

"Yes. He said it wasn't easy at first fitting in with the tribe, because not everyone was happy with him being there. They thought he would bring them trouble. But he proved to be a hard worker, and good on the hunt. It also helps that he can go into any town for supplies and blend in if he wears his 'white clothes' as he calls them. He can also negotiate with the reservation's Indian agent, who evidently is a pretty good guy."

Nancy got up to finish preparing their dinner. Keeping her voice even with an effort, she asked, "Now that he knows where we live, will he be coming to visit?"

Abe took a long time answering before saying, "I don't think so, Nan. He knows why we left Placerville and doesn't want to cause the same thing to happen here."

Nancy nodded with resignation and said little throughout dinner. After clearing the table, she went for a walk down by the river. There, in the silence of the gathering dusk, she leaned against a tree and allowed herself a good cry. When she was done, she blew her nose and returned to the house to finish the evening's chores.

Life continued in much the same manner as it always had. Abe, having been able to visit with his son, felt the contentment of a man who had achieved an important goal. Because of this, he went about his daily work with a new enthusiasm.

Seeing this, Nancy felt an unreasonable resentment. She wanted it to be enough that Abe had told her in detail about his conversation with Todd. He had responded to her repeated requests for more details with unforced patience, and had respected her intelligence enough not to embellish after several tellings just so she might have more to cling to as she slowly accepted the situation. He took care each time to repeat that Todd's first words had been to ask about his mother, and his last to send her his love.

A month later the women assembled at their first meeting to plan for the holiday celebrations and the making of toys for the town's children. The heat of summer challenged their imaginations, but it was necessary to begin months ahead in order to have everything completed by Christmas.

The ladies assembled in the dining room of the American Hotel with greetings that ranged from polite to warm, exchanges of gossip, and obligatory comments on the heat.

It was not until the end of the luncheon, served by the proprietor and several of the ladies present, that Mrs. Huntoon called the meeting to order and discussions began. It was also at that point that Nancy could no longer ignore the fact that the atmosphere was a bit strained. This was especially true whenever she voiced a suggestion, volunteered for a project, or offered an opinion. Although everyone listened politely, most offered no comment and she was then promptly ignored. When a couple of the women started to respond to her ideas, they were cut off by another and the discussion was guided in a different direction. Nancy might have made excuses, or waved it away, if she had not already been down this road.

As soon as lunch was over, Nancy made the excuse of other plans and prepared to leave. Several women looked relieved, several seemed confused at what they sensed as undefined tension, and several more looked down at their laps in embarrassment. The fact that no one tried to stop her or even feign regret over her early departure hurt Nancy deeply. But it was the three haughty women who looked at her with pursed lips and raised brows while waiting for her to leave that prompted her anger.

At the door Nancy turned back and said to the assembled ladies, "I would like to make one suggestion. It is foolish, if not an act of narrow-mindedness, to accept the prejudices of others. This is especially true of mothers who should know better and are gathered together to celebrate the innocence of children. You're promoting isolation among women who need one another in situations where men won't suffice, and it means the loss of valuable nurturing friendships."

Those women who were obviously confused, and who didn't understand to what she referred, began to speak. But when they looked at the older women with their set faces and hard eyes, and who had for years been accepted as the arbiter of social conscience, they turned their gaze from Nancy and held their tongue.

Seeing that conformity was to be chosen over moral courage, Nancy turned from the assemblage of women. She flung open the door and marched through it with her head up, unconcerned whether or not the door slammed behind her, which it did.

When Abe came home, he heard Nancy weeping and rushed into the bedroom to find her lying across the bed with her face buried in the quilt.

"Nan! What's wrong? Are you ill?"

Slowly sitting up, she blew her nose on a delicate linen handkerchief before taking a shuddering breath. She reached for the glass of water Abe held out to her and took a big swallow before whispering, "They know."

"Who knows what?"

"The women know about Todd."

Abe fought the sudden roiling nausea in his stomach, and his ruddy cheeks became even more so. "How do you know?"

She told him about the meeting, then asked him, "Did you tell anyone?"

"No, of course not. I think N.B. suspicions, but he's said nothing to me and I don't think he would to anyone else. The only one who knows for sure is Marcy, the guy I went to Carson with. But I haven't seen him in town."

"Still, he must have told someone who brought the news here."

"I guess he could have." He reached out and drew her to him. She huddled in his arms with her head on his chest, feeling like a child who had fallen and skinned her knee. He kissed the top of her head and said, "I'm so sorry. I should have handled it better so this couldn't happen."

Nancy drew back and placed her hands on either side of his face. "Don't you for a minute blame yourself for this. Maybe after people have time to adjust to the idea, we can get back to the way things were."

Abe nodded, but he was doubtful. As it turned out, he had good reason to be. Over the next few weeks, not only did many of the women continue to ostracize Nancy, but a few of the men showed open hostility toward Abe. He found this surprising since the town had a peaceful coexistence with the local Piutes. But after thinking it through, Abe realized that it was a negotiated peace, not an acknowledgment of equality.

A month later Abe and Nancy lingered at the table after dinner, slowly sipping their coffee and deep in their own thoughts. With grim determination, Abe said, "We need to move."

Nancy nodded. "I know. I don't want to wait any longer for people to change."

"Some of the men won't play poker with me, or stand at the bar near me. I tried to discuss the situation with them, but they wouldn't have it. It's only a few men, but it's still unpleasant. I imagine it's worse for you."

Nancy shrugged, not wanting him to know the degree of her hurt. "There's nothing holding us here really. Todd has made his choice, and we can get word to him about where we're going."

"Where should that be?" Abe asked her.

"Heavens, I don't know." She controlled the tears just back of her eyes. "We'll have to think about it." She patted his hand lying on the table by his coffee cup and said, "At least we have each other."

Abe smiled and moved around the table, ready to put his arms around her. Before he reached her, she stood up and walked to the sink, saying, "I'd best clean up the kitchen."

Abe stood where he was and watched her fill the kettle from the water barrel. Why was she once again pulling away from him? Did she blame him for not making Todd change his mind and come back with him, or for their again having to leave a town?

But Nancy felt no blame. She did feel that to share affection right then might weaken the anger she had adopted in order to mask her hurt. It was easy right then for her to mistake cool reserve for strength.

A few days after they made their decision to leave, N.B. and Esther arrived on the Carrington's porch in the early evening. There were two bottles of lager in N.B.'s hands and a small cake in hers.

"Come in, come in," Abe enthused as he stood back for them to enter.

When Nancy saw Esther, her delight was evident. Esther Hunewill was a few years younger than her popular husband, but she was liked and well respected throughout the community. Unfortunately, she had not been at the meeting in the hotel or things might have turned out differently.

After they were seated around the kitchen table, the men with their lager and the women with cups of coffee, N.B. cleared his throat. "Mrs. Parrish told Esther what happened at the lady's meeting at the hotel."

Neither Abe nor Nancy responded.

Esther's cheeks grew red. "I think it's just disgraceful, and I told her so too. I'm so sorry."

"You don't have any reason to apologize," Nancy told her. "And I think some of the women would have been more accepting if it wasn't for their fear of being ostracized if they didn't side with the most opinionated."

N.B. sighed and his long aquiline nose almost quivered with indignation. "Isn't that always the way?"

"Some of the men aren't much better," Abe asserted. "I've cleared room at the bar and had several backs turned to me."

"Who did that?" N.B. demanded.

"It doesn't matter. I don't blame them. It's just the way life is."

N. B. asked Abe, "You know how it got around?"

"No."

"Well, I do." He sat back and stretched out his long legs. "A freighter came to town, got drunk and bragged that he knew who the 'white man with the Piutes is'. He laughed about it being the son of a local here in Bridgeport and no one knowing it. I tried to stop him, but he told everyone that the name of the father is Abe something. And, well, you're the only Abe here."

The women retired to the parlor to sit on the sofa under the front window where the last of the summer light caught their hair and made it glow. As the sun dropped behind the mountains, Nancy got up and lit the coal oil lamp on the end table.

Showing keen insight, Esther turned to Nancy and said, "You must feel rather deflated and left out, what with Abe having been able to visit with your son. I know I'd be very dispirited. Will he be coming here to see you?"

Nancy looked closely at her questioner, trying to detect fear or repulsion, but saw only curiosity and eager hope reflected in Esther's face. "No, he won't. We left Placerville to come here because this same thing happened there."

Esther gasped. "Oh, Nancy, how awful for you. And missing your son so much on top of it. It seems so unfair."

"Yes," Nancy nodded, "but like Abe said, it's the way people are. There's nothing we can do about it, but we don't have to live with it either."

"No. I don't suppose you do."

"I hear N.B. is looking to buy some meadow land."

"We talk about it all the time," Esther said. "He wants to raise cattle and I want a larger house. I'm tired of the cabin at the saw mill and our little house here in town. Frank wants to help his father more, and he loves the idea of our raising cattle like so many others."

In the kitchen N.B. was telling Abe, "I sure wish there was some other way to handle this instead of your leaving."

"So do I, but I talked to Bryant yesterday and he's agreed to buy the house. It was his land to begin with anyway."

"How much did he give you?" After Abe told him, N.B. whistled softly. "That's a really good price."

"I know it is. I think he feels bad about what's happened too."

"Abe, there are men here who have a problem with the Indians, but most of us don't. So why do you have to leave?"

"Those men who do care can make life hard." Then he looked into the other room.

Following Abe's glance, N.B. sighed and simply said, "Women. So when are you planning to leave?"

"As soon as we figure out where to go and can pack."

"You know the Owens Valley Indian wars are over. If I was you, I'd head south to that area."

"What's there?"

"Mining mostly, but also cattle and some agriculture that I think will develop eventually. The towns there supply the mines and the ranches, and get their supplies from Carson via Aurora. The county seat of Inyo is a small town called Independence because it's near Fort Independence. Bishop Creek is a larger town and about 45 miles closer to here."

"What town is the furthest from here?"

N.B. grimaced. "As far as a real town, that'd be Lone Pine. Olancha, about twenty miles further south, is only a freighter's stop."

Abe turned in his seat and hollered in to Nancy. "Hey, Nan, how does going south to a town called Lone Pine sound to you?"

"I like the name. It seems to apply to us." She turned back to Esther and asked, "Do you think you and N.B. might some day get down that way?"

"I don't know. Maybe." She shook her head and sighed. "Probably not."

"No, probably not," Nancy echoed her.

The women fell quiet and listened to the men talking about the haying soon to start. Esther suddenly said, "Maybe I can say something to..."

"No," Nancy stopped her. "You can't change how people feel."

The men joined the women in the parlor and for the next hour they talked about current events and things in the news happening in California. But their heart wasn't in it, and soon the Hunewills rose to leave. On the front porch Abe and N.B. shook hands for the last time with deep regret. Esther hugged Nancy and turned to walk away before anyone could see her tears. Nancy understood only too well that they were borne of frustration over a situation no one knew how to change.

The Carringtons wasted no time packing and getting started on their long journey. It was August and it would take them over a month to reach Lone Pine in the southern reaches of the Owens Valley. After making their way east to Aurora, they continued south to Warm Springs on the east side of Mono Lake, strained through the sands of Adobe Meadows, passed around Black Lake, and turned east to Benton Hot Springs. They were just outside the stage stop when Abe realized one of his wheels was cracked.

While the owner of the mercantile and the saloon's bartender helped Abe repair his wheel, they talked of the rumors that the Piutes to the east had killed one of their medicine men after his third patient in recent weeks had died. Although a traditional occurrence to the Indians, the settlers were frightened. When Abe said he planned to continue their journey anyway, the men of Hot Springs showed great concern for their safety. Abe persisted, and they were soon continuing south through a maze of roads separating a dozen small mines.

Eventually they passed through the rich grasslands of Fish Slough and headed southeast toward the Owens River. But to reach it, they had first to struggle through deep sand, ease the wagon along the muddy edges of creeks, and give several marshes a wide birth.

There were many joyful moments during this journey they would remember always. Several big horn sheep looked down at them from the top of a cliff; two eagles high in the air locked talons while falling as one until releasing from each other almost to the earth; more than once the setting sun cast orange fire into the sky over the peaks of the Sierra; and people all along the way offered kindness and hospitality.

Owensville was an example of that kindness. On the edge of the eastern shore of the Owens River northeast of Bishop Creek, the community was referred to as that of the "stone house people". The town consisted of stone cabins, a store to supply the homesteaders and local miners, and little else.

But the Horton family shared their dinner with Abe and Nancy, and their neighbor Mr. Jones helped a very tired Abe with his team the evening they arrived. Before they left the next morning, Mrs. Jones made sure they ate a big fortifying breakfast, and gave them a loaf of bread and a pint of milk to take with them. As the women bid one another good-bye, Nancy hoped that someday they would meet these kind and generous people again, but knowing they would be living 70 miles away gave her little hope of that.

When George Hightower came to see them off, he gave Abe advice about the best places to camp as they continued south. At the same time, young Tom Clark gave Nancy a small stone from his pocket and told her it was for luck. Years later, when he became the first white man to climb to the top of a 13,652 foot peak of the Sierra, it would be named Mt. Tom. Nancy would then remember the little black stone in her jewelry box and would set it on a shelf in the parlor.

When they reached Bishop Creek it was just in time to attend services of the Missionary Baptist Church, being held in a small adobe schoolhouse a mile east of Mr. Bishop's San Francis Ranch. There were only a dozen people present, but it was a restful hour listening to Reverend Andrew Clark. It was the first church in California east of the Sierra and the Reverend joked about those who were calling the area "gospel swamp". As they left, they passed through the lovely but marshy area and smiled.

Sixteen miles further at Big Pine Creek, they watched trees being felled that were destined for the mill above the town near a powerful creek. Houses and businesses for the approximately 50 people living near the creek were spread out along the trail coming down from the mill. Nancy looked longingly at this road that cut between large trees, and only hoped that there would be a home waiting for them in Lone Pine. That she knew nothing of the town made her uneasy.

Near the Owens River, they passed a family of Piutes spearing fish at the river's edge. The short thin man had tufts of rabbit fur stuck to his bare chest with pitch, and the two little boys with him were naked. Nancy was surprised to see that the woman was dressed in a calico dress that had been cut off to reach just below her knees. The Indians barely glanced at the couple in the wagon, simply continuing to fish, but Abe kept the wagon moving past. Having heard so many tales of the Owens Valley Indian wars, they held their breath until well along the river. Nancy turned to Abe. "Why do I have the feeling they're back there laughing at us?"

A few miles south of Big Pine Creek they were amazed at the acres of red and black rock that surrounded the narrow road. "It's an ancient lava bed!" Nancy exclaimed in wonder.

No less in wonder at her knowledge, Abe asked, "How in hell do you know that?"

"I remember Harold reading to me about this type of thing from one of his books." Nancy smiled to herself as she remembered that exchange, and at the same time she realized how easy it had been to refer to Harold with fond remembrance and only a slight stab of pain.

"Well, I'll be damned," Abe exclaimed. "Imagine volcanoes erupting right here."

Indeed, the ancient valley was very different from any place they had seen before. Although now much of their view was filled with waist-high brush and scraggly trees, the local tribes of Piute and Shoshone had traditions of a much different land. They told of extensive groves of cedar and willow, lush meadows where fish and game were plentiful in lakes lined with tulles and rushes, rocky nooks where artesian wells bubbled to the surface, and a river miles wide and filling much of what was now dry land. But then the mountains erupted and burned, and of course most of the lakes and streams dried up because of this violent tantrum by Mother Nature. Thousands of years since, it still looked much as it had then.

Because their wagon only covered ten to twenty miles a day, depending on the terrain, Abe and Nancy had a lot of time to fill. After exhausting discussion of those events that had brought them to that moment, they turned their conversation to what was ahead of them.

Abe told Nancy, "N.B. said some of the men we knew in Bridgeport had traveled through this valley from southern California to old Monoville north of Mono Lake back in the late 1850's."

"But mining is established where we're going?"

"Oh, yes. In early 1860 a Dr. Darwin French out of Visalia came over Walker's Pass south of the valley and discovered rich ledges in the Coso area southeast of Lone Pine. Four months later there were about 500 men in the area."

After awhile Nancy asked Abe, "The Lone Pine area has a number of ranches, doesn't it?"

"About ten years ago stockmen from the other side of the Sierra brought cattle into the area. They'd heard about the good grazing from miners passing through."

"How do you know all this?"

He looked at her and grinned. "Men talk. Other than drinking, burping and scratching, that's what we do in saloons."

"That may be what *you* do," she smiled, "but I know about other things that go on there when the fair flowers of easy virtue are present."

"Oh, Lord! Is that what women call them?"

"Oh, we have a few stronger names for them too."

Abe chuckled and nudged her with his shoulder. "Anyway, the first cattlemen settled in Lone Pine early in the last decade. They told people later that they had seen no whites from Long Valley north of Bishop Creek to Lone Pine Creek. But then Charles Putnam settled at what's now called Independence and called his trading post Putnam's."

"What else would he call it?"

Abe looked sidewise at her to see if she was being facetious, and noting her poorly hidden smile, continued his history lesson. "During the Owens Valley Indian wars people used his house as a fortress and even a hospital."

"What about the Bishop Creek area?"

"That's where Sam Bishop and his family settled. They came from the Fort Tejon area over the mountains in the summer of '61." He smiled. "He brought his wife, who I guess was the first white woman to settle in the Valley. He called his place the San Francis Ranch after her name, Francis."

"How sweet."

"I thought you'd like that part. But they didn't stay long and moved on to Kern County."

"What started the Indian wars?"

"Amasa Bryant told me it was the harshness of the winter of '61. By that time there were a number of settlers scattered over the area we're traveling through. Men say it was the worst winter in the history of the west. For 54 days it either poured rain or snowed. Streams were impassible and the usually narrow channel of the Owens River was as much as a mile wide and icy. The men in Placerville told me the Sacramento and San Joaquin valleys were flooded like an inland sea."

"Then how did supplies get into the Owens Valley?"

"They didn't. Not for months. Eventually the settlers only had unsalted beef left. The Indians had nothing, what with the floods wrecking their supply of seeds and grains. A Piute tried stealing a cow and was shot by its owner who himself was scared of running out of food. Then a Piute killed a white man in retaliation. Settlers and Indians got together and agreed things were even, but then a Piute Chief from southern Mono County came into the area and stirred up trouble.

"Over the months that followed Indians came into the area from the west side of the Sierra and even from nearby states. Most of the time the settlers were out-numbered about ten to one, but many of them were ex-army and knew how to utilize their few numbers to good advantage. Over time, soldiers came into the area from Fort Churchill, Nevada, and others from Visalia."

"They fought for five years?" Nancy was incredulous.

"There were periods of peace, I guess. From what I've been told, there was fault on both sides when it didn't last. By the time it was over about 60 whites and 200 Indians of various tribal groups had been killed. N.B. told me what the other men didn't, that in the beginning, with smaller numbers and fewer guns, the Piutes held their own. In fact, in May of '62 most settlers and miners had left the valley and the Indians were pretty much in possession of it.

"Of course, the government couldn't allow that to continue with so many mines here, so the Cavalry arrived July 4, 1862. They set up east of Oak Creek where the soldiers lived in caves they dug in a ravine. That's when most of the Indians fled to the mountains. Good thing, because the Cavalry had orders to kill every Piute they saw."

"How did it end?"

"Another treaty was signed. Those Indians that weren't from the Valley returned to wherever they'd come from, and mining began again in the Coso Range. Then gold was discovered in the mountains east of Independence about the time most of the soldiers had left the area. Men came from San Francisco, and the San Carlos mining camp grew larger."

"I suppose the Indians got upset again?"

"Not immediately. There were skirmishes and killings of freighters, lone prospectors, wood choppers and even a couple of families entering from the south. But that was mostly by the Kern River and Tehachapi tribes. Then the Indian depredations started up around Independence and Big Pine again so the soldiers returned and built a bigger fort. After several months of hostilities, the Indians and tired soldiers had pretty much come to a resolution and things calmed down. But a few blowhard whites who hadn't been brave enough to fight before, got a sudden surge of energy. They decided to kill a number of Indians, including women and children who were carrying messages of peace from their tribe."

"How terrible!"

"It almost undid all the work of settling the conflict. The white perpetrators were rounded up and sent to Fort Tejon on the western side of the Sierra, but N.B. said they were released in a few months. Reprisals continued on both sides off and on. Then in July of '63 about 900 Piute men, women and children were gathered up and herded like animals over the mountains to Ft. Tejon. They arrived eleven days later, but many had died and others had escaped along the way so they could return to the Owens Valley.

"The men I talked to had so many stories to tell of wins and losses on both sides that I can't remember them all. But well into '64, while we were settling into Placerville, immigration into the Owens Valley from the south was pretty steady, so towns were established. Men prospected, established herds of cattle, and began growing some crops."

"That was before the change of the county boundaries?"

"Right. That's when the north part of Inyo County now was then the southern portion of Mono County. That only changed recently. Some of the towns in the valley are pretty well established. Bend City, northeast of Lone Pine, has a number of adobe businesses and homes. Someone told me the town is fancy enough to have a couple of hotels, a tailor shop, and a laundry owned by a Chinese couple."

"So we're not going to be too isolated."

"Not really. But it takes six days to get from San Francisco to Visalia by stage, and more than that to get the rest of the way into the valley."

Of course, regardless of the number of towns Abe listed, and way-stations that he did not, these places were many miles and several days ride apart. Telegraph lines and rail roads had not yet reached the Valley settlements, and the only means of travel was by horse or wagon. Laws were few and the County Sheriff was an elected official that was more a final authority than a practical presence.

Nancy commented, "I had no idea the valley was so narrow. It feels like we could walk from the Sierra to the Inyo Mountains in a day."

"Don't forget how deceptive distances can be in places like this. We learned that lesson when crossing the plains and along the Humboldt. I estimate it varies from eight to sixteen miles across. With mountains so high on either side, it means it's a very deep valley." He would learn in time that it was the *deepest* valley in the United States.

The next few days were spent traveling south through small communities that sat like islands of rescue in the midst of acres of scrub. They were delighted to reach Oak Creek cascading down from the Sierra Nevada as it was near the protection of Camp Independence. Oak Creek was a place of great beauty and while picking wild elderberries, the air was fragrant with the scent of balsam and live oak.

Most of a day was spent at the fort where they met Major Clarence Egbert, the Commandant of the Camp. They also met Jacob Vagt and his wife Henriette, a German couple who lived just beyond the fort. They were at the mercantile store selling dried peaches and grapes grown on their property along with corn and alfalfa. Abe found pleasure in the long rows of white-washed adobe buildings gleaming in the sun and the smartly uniformed men.

Late in the afternoon they rolled into the town of Independence where they camped next to Tom Edwards's white wooden house, although he no longer lived there. Abe offered to get them a room at the Blaney Hotel, but Nancy said she would rather save the money so they could buy their own place as soon as possible.

Independence had been the county seat of Inyo since 1866, and a courthouse just completed the previous February was at its heart. It had cost $9,800 to build and the town was very proud of it. Little did they know that it would be the first of three, with the next to be built in 1876 and the last one in 1921.

On their way to George's Creek, their camp site on the Owens River was overhung with large willow and cottonwood trees shading a wide swath of tulles and rushes. Suddenly aware of her great fatigue, Nancy would have been happy to stay another day. However, she knew they were close to their destination, so as she had done so many times when crossing the country, she rose above her personal discomfort and climbed into the wagon.

Following the rutted road southwest, they saw in the distance the log fortification of the John Kispert ranch surrounded by fields of barley. The Kisperts sold this in Aurora at 36 cents for a two pound bag, and the miners used it as horse feed or parched it in lieu of coffee.

They spent the night at the Half Way House Stage Station where they could fill their water barrel at the rock well. As evening approached, they enjoyed the magnificence of a purple and pink sunset that created a black silhouette of the Sierra.

Abe sighed. "It's at times like this I wish I was an artist."

Nancy said nothing, too overwhelmed with the beauty before her. When the following morning greeted them with a red and orange glow over the Inyo Mountains to the east, Nancy realized this valley was a place for those who appreciated drama in their landscape.

Traveling further south they passed the ranches of Lacy, McGovern, Alpers, and Moffit. Fields of green alfalfa, and others of ripe wheat and barley, replaced the sagebrush. Young fruit trees surrounded most of the ranch houses, and large patches of potatoes showed promise near two of them.

The last night before reaching Lone Pine they camped near the energetic flow of a creek. Nancy stood beside the wagon and let her eyes travel slowly across the valley floor with its miles of blue sagebrush and yellow blooms of rabbit brush.

She remembered how she had embraced Placerville's green forested hills and established society, and then the wide fresh meadows of Bridgeport where everyone was starting new lives. If both those places had matched her needs at the right time, then what did it mean that they were now in such rough country seemingly in the middle of nowhere? She decided to proceed on faith alone, and as Bob Cook had once told her, know that it would somehow all come right.

The next morning they rose early, and while the day before Nancy had been intimidated by the starkness of the landscape, she now marveled at the sun lifting above the Inyos to add warm life to all around her. As they moved along the narrow dirt track, the sun warmed Nancy's back even as the crisp air chilled her throat and stiffened her lips. Her attachment to this arid landscape was born that morning with her first cool intake of breathless surprise as the Valley's beauty took hold of her soul and anchored it to the sage-covered Sierra foothills.

They finally approached a cluster of old wooden shacks and adobe buildings the same color as the earth. It had taken them a month, but the team and Flame were in good condition, and so were Abe and Nancy. Nevertheless, they were all relieved to be at their last stop. Flame, tied to the back of the wagon, sniffed the air and let loose a whinny that sounded to Abe as though he was declaring that he was ready to stop.

To the west, between the town and the Sierra was a barrier of low chocolate brown hills and beyond those a strange world of large granite boulders mounded in piles the size of buildings. They were spread over acres of what is commonly thought of as just dry brush, but is in fact plants of sagebrush, beaver-tail cactus, rabbitbrush, indigo bush, ephedra, spiny hopsage, shadscale and four wing salt bush, to name a few.

Nancy's interest was more focused on the little town ahead of them. She wondered what kind of home they might expect in such a small ramshackle place. A narrow muddy street separated five short blocks of buildings, with wooden sidewalks edging only a portion of it. The blacksmith shop had walls that leaned in beneath its wood shingle roof, and the corrals around the livery stable looked as though they had been there a hundred years instead of less than a decade.

"Oh, well," Nancy thought, "as long as I don't have to move again, I can be happy here as much as I can be anywhere else." The vision of a roaring wood stove near her rocking chair flashed into her mind and the longing for that reality choked her throat. As she looked up at the Sierra, a memory came to her from the past. "Abe? Remember Todd saying we'd find our own kind of gold at the end of our journey?"

"Yeah," he groused. "I'm still waiting for it."

"I think it's been with us ever since we got to California. It's the mountains. The Sierra has sheltered us, shared its beauty and fed our spirit for years."

Abe turned to his wife and found her smiling with a serenity he had last seen the day before he told her about selling the farm. Rather than break the spell of the moment, he said nothing and simply urged the team down Main Street into Lone Pine.

Their eyes passed over the small town and they were less than impressed. Most of the two dozen buildings were made of adobe mixed with chunks of granite, and were fronted by porch roofs that slumped in dejected repose. A few of the stores had a wood frame house or storage room next to the adobe structure that had then been roofed across. It gave the buildings a slightly lopsided appearance.

Several of the most prosperous businesses had glass in their windows, but most simply had heavy wooden shutters that could be opened to the fresh air. Of course, this also let in flies and mosquitoes, and tiny biting midges in spring that burrowed down to itching scalps. To avoid this, Abe would learn to keep his hat on and run his hands over the sagebrush and then his face, while Nancy would simply wear her closest fitting bonnet. Since both men and women's attire consisted of collars tight to the throat and long sleeves, that pretty much took care of the exposed skin.

At the entrance to the town, they passed an open plaza to their right where a stage pulled out past them and headed north. Just west of the plaza was a small Chinese district where the *celestials* lived. Abe and Nancy could see the Orientals, mostly men who did the labor that the local Piutes refused, sitting on the porches of their small shacks while smoking pipes.

The blocks of ramshackle buildings running south down Main were anchored by *Hunt's Livery and Feed Stable*, with its sign stating "Horses and buggies and the best of saddle horses to let at reasonable terms. Horses boarded by the day or week, at the lowest possible rates. Hay by the Feed or Bale. Rarely by the Sack or Ton." Next to it was a wagon shop, a blacksmith, a small house for the blacksmith's family, a saloon, a butcher shop and the *Loomis & Bros. Store* that also acted as a Post Office.

Continuing south were unidentifiable small houses between an hotel, Meysan's Merchandise, and several saloons, all of which were made of the ubiquitous adobe brick. While the businesses fronted the main road, the homes were set further back and the lots surrounded by picket fences. Nancy noticed that while only some of the pickets were broken, almost all the fences were in need of new paint. Abe drove their wagon slowly through Lone Pine Creek where it crossed the main road between an empty lot and a house facing the side road. The creek flowed out of town to the east, past the new town hall and the jail, and eventually poured into the Owens River that flowed south into the highly saline Owens Lake.

That impressive body of water was 17 miles wide and about 35 miles long, but only thirty to fifty feet deep. Although no fish lived in its briny depths, there were many ducks and shore birds that flocked to it for the brine shrimp that thrived in its waters and the tiny lake flies that swarmed the shore. But the birds were in competition with the Indians for this last. Just like those Indians at Mono Lake, the tribe here also gathered the larvae to pound into a mush, creating a staple that helped them survive the winter.

The Carringtons drove past the ranches south of Lone Pine with their fields of hay, wheat and barley. The small home-steads hosted fruit trees and vegetable gardens, and although all had a number of sheds and storage buildings, some also had a large red barn.

As dry as the soil appeared, it only needed water to bring forth an abundance of life, and the creeks cascading down the canyons of the Sierra provided that. Some ranch houses were partially covered in the large green leaves of hops, and many were surrounded by fences that trailed grape vines, while others had bee hives clustered on the edges of the fields.

After turning around, the Carringtons returned to the town and stopped in front of the Orleans Hotel. It was a pleasant whitewashed building with a covered porch next to a new mer-chandise store. The waitress in the dining room told them that the hotel used to house its merchandise down the street at Anna Heppner's warehouse, but a French family had moved into town the previous year and turned it into the Meysan Merchandise Store.

Nancy fervently hoped there would be a room available for them at the hotel, but it was full to overflowing with miners and travelers, and those who lived in the hotel on a permanent basis. As they negotiated the muddy rutted streets they passed a large number of freight wagons, the lifeline needed by the miners in the Inyo Mountains. After delivering their goods, the freighters either returned to Lone Pine for what few supplies they could obtain there, or continued on to Aurora or Carson City.

One of the first things Abe and Nancy realized was that Lone Pine was a town of many diverse cultures. At least half of those present were from Mexico, but there were also those from England, Ireland, France and Germany. A group of these men stood on a sidewalk loudly and vigorously talking about their plans for a schoolhouse, their various accents mixing together like musical notes.

The roads in the town were slick with mud after a recent thunderstorm, even though the winds had blown for several days. The Carringtons would quickly learn that rain was a rare occurrence, and dry air and powdery dust much more usual. The area averaged only six to eight inches of rain a year, with a foot or two of snow reaching the valley floor every year.

Surprisingly, trees of a size larger than one might expect in such a young town grew along Main Street and around all the homes. Besides those in town, there were willows along the road through Lone Pine Canyon that led up into the Alabama Hills. At the mouth of this canyon grew the only Jeffery pine in the area, shading the edge of Lone Pine Creek. It was the inspiration for the town's name.

Abe stopped the wagon at the side of the plaza near a water trough so the horses could drink their fill. He then introduced himself to Mr. Hunt at the stable where he inquired about a place they could camp.

Mr. Hunt pointed to the grove of trees on the north side of the plaza. "Under those trees will do. Staying long?"

Abe glanced at Nancy. "Permanently, I think."

Mr. Hunt smiled broadly beneath his long mustache. "Well, that's just fine. Welcome to Lone Pine. If you need water, the creek's close by and you just ask if there's anything I can do for you."

"That's most kind of you. I'll need to stable my team and my riding horse."

"No problem. What kind of work do you do?"

"I drive teams, and I can do carpentry work too. I've raised cattle, sheep and chickens, and I can help with the haying or other harvests."

"Well, you shouldn't have difficulty finding work then."

Nancy spoke up. "When we lived in..., I mean I've been known to sell pies to hotels. People seem to like them."

"We can always use a good cook 'round here. Let's get the horses unhitched first. You can settle their keep later."

They set up camp among the trees where they were partially hidden from view but could see the busy happenings of the town. After the horses were stabled and contentedly munching hay, they found their way to one of the town's two restaurants. The people they met on their way smiled without hesitation and the men tipped their hats. They immediately felt at home.

That night they stood by their wagon and watched the sun fall behind the ridge of the Sierra, casting shadows across the valley onto the Inyo Mountains and its subtle pastel hues. With his arm around his wife's waste, Abe looked at her and thought how pretty she was even after their exhausting weeks on the trail.

Abe told her, "I don't know why, but I feel that we'll not move from this place."

"I think you're right." Yes, Nancy felt at home. With this sense of finality, however, came also the memory of their life at the beginning of their long journey from the east. It was not their land, or house, or possessions that she remembered. It was the memory of how full their lives had been when filled with two rambunctious boys and a sweet baby girl, and the promise of an old age filled with grandchildren. Now it was all gone. Yes, she had a grandson, but she knew she would probably never see him. It was a fact that she had almost, but not quite, accepted.

They found that the night hours in the town were far from peaceful. The nearby saloons were busy places full of shouting men who became louder after hours of drinking, and angry enough to use their guns. Two bursts of gunfire from down the street woke them at two in the morning. The streets were packed with wagons until well after dark, and if the whistles and curses of the freighters during the day had seemed loud, they seemed doubly so at two in the morning. Eventually the noise did stop, and they dropped off to sleep around three in the morning, only to awaken early when the first freight wagon left town.

After a leisurely breakfast, they walked down Lone Pine's short streets. Being that there were so few, their walk should not have taken long, but they were stopped often by shopkeepers and citizens. How it had so quickly spread through town that they were new arrivals who were staying, they couldn't imagine.

These hardy settlers were practical, but they were not willing to be without at least the semblance of refinement and comfort. As they walked, Abe and Nancy noted that even though a building may have been a long narrow rectangle, the front often had a short decorative flat wall protruding above the entrance to give the image of grander proportions within. Crisp curtains at windows and benches outside the doors of shops added a sense of comfort.

One family had built a house that far surpassed the usual modest cottage. At the south end of town, on the east side of Main, they admired a yellow two story wooden house with five small sycamore trees newly planted across the front yard. Nancy waved to the little girl who stood on the front porch steps and whose long curls were held off her face by a blue ribbon. She wore a crisp blue dress with a white apron over it, and Nancy wondered at a mother who took such care to keep her child clean while playing outside.

While Abe enjoyed a lager in the Pioneer Saloon, Nancy wandered through the three small merchandise stores. When they met up again on the wooden sidewalk outside the hotel, they compared notes. Nancy listened to his litany of local gossip for five minutes, then cut him off. "I can't keep silent any longer." She gripped his hand. "Mrs. Heppner told me there's a small house that a Mr. Begole had rented to a young couple. But they left yesterday."

"I wonder if he'd be willing to sell it to us? I don't want to rent again and be at the mercy of some damn landlord."

"I figured you'd feel that way. She thought he might sell. He's lived here since the early '60's and he and a Mr. Moore seem to own most of the town."

They immediately went to look at the house. It was small and made of wood instead of adobe, with a roofed front porch shaded by a young cottonwood tree. The small yard was enclosed by a freshly painted white picket fence, and Nancy felt it had been prepared just for their arrival.

Other than a good sized kitchen, the house had a small front parlor, a bedroom larger than any they had so far enjoyed, and a solid outhouse a reasonable distance from the back door. Abe assured Nancy that he could easily build on a storage room at the back, and the fact that it was partially furnished was a definite plus, given their circumstance.

Without too much effort they found Charles Begole, a nice man in his mid thirties with a warm smile, curly hair sticking out from under his hat, a long beard and friendly eyes. He accepted their offer for the house and welcomed them to Lone Pine with a grin and a strong handshake.

CHAPTER TWENTY
LONE PINE, CALIFORNIA
1871

"The mountains and Valley floor are covered in snow. This is the season for those who rise early. Only then can one view nature's best morning tapestries. While the Alabama Hills are still dark shadows in the Sierra foothills, the sky lightens to a muted blue and reveals the jagged white Sierra peaks. But as soon as the sun rises above the Inyos, the Sierra's white peaks catch fire beneath a band of golden light. After a few minutes of that glorious sparkle and glow, the full majestic valley is revealed and only a full turn of the body can take it all in. I have fallen in love again, only this time it is with a valley."

Nancy

"Lone Pine isn't as refined as old Placerville, or as quaint and green as Bridgeport, but it is one of the most determined towns I've ever seen."

Abe

Nancy awoke to the sound of fists banging on the front door of the house. "Abe, wake up." Nancy shook him several times. "It sounds like Bill Moore shouting."

Indeed, Abe's bleary eyes focused on his friend's large frame filling the doorway, his face flushed with urgency.

"Get your pants on. There's a fire at the Miller ranch."

While Bill Moore urged his horse south, Abe quickly dressed, saddled Flame and raced out of town. Expecting to see the ranch house engulfed in flames, instead he saw only a small shed smoldering in its ruins. As it burned to the ground, the men who had gathered to help, made sure the fire didn't spread.

When the opportunity arose, Abe asked William K. Miller, better known as Gold Tooth, "What started this?"

The rancher sighed. "I fired one of the Piutes who was working for me. I was angry and yelled a lot."

"So he burned down your shed?" Abe was aghast.

"Yup. It happens pretty regular. It's their way of showing their displeasure."

"Really? What'll happen to the Indian?"

Gold Tooth shrugged. "Probably nothing. I can't prove he did it. I just know he did."

So Abe returned home, and along the way enjoyed the ride while anticipating a good breakfast.

Nancy found great joy in setting up housekeeping again, and each day looked forward to some new event or friend that might enter her life. Whenever possible, she and Abe enjoyed the times they could explore the trails through the Alabama Hills, she on a rented horse and Abe of course on Flame.

Not long after arriving in Lone Pine they had finally met John Kispert, he of the fortified house on George's Creek. Nancy found his Prussian accent charming, although she was less charmed by his long scraggly beard. In 1859, when he was twenty-two, the young trapper had come into the valley in search of a place to settle down and build a ranch. In '61, John had homesteaded 400 acres on George's Creek and had built his stone and adobe house, sharing the broad sweeping plain with several other families with smaller holdings. He named the creek after Indian George who lived nearby on a small ranch. In 1866 John had been named County Constable, and then in '69 he had married the lovely Augusta. Recently he had been appointed as District Judge.

The Kisperts invited Abe and Nancy to stay with them for a couple of days when Abe volunteered to help John with repairs to a stone storage building. Nancy found that John was a gentleman with a handsome face behind his jagged square cut beard, and Augusta a gracious young woman who eagerly welcomed the company of another female.

On their way back the next morning, Abe and Nancy passed the Owens River where it divided, flowed around a mile of lush green grass, and created what the locals called "the island". Abe and Nancy climbed down off their horses and rested in the shade of a cottonwood where they watched a flock of white geese feeding on the lush grasses along the edge of the island.

Soon the large birds took off in a surge of white with their honking calls echoing down the valley. They would continue on to the Owens Lake where they would merge with teal and coots by the thousands. Abe thought of his friends and wondered when they could set out together to do some hunting at the tree-shaded ponds north of the lake. If he shot enough ducks, he could sell them at Meysan's Merchandise store.

Not long before the Carringtons had first come to Lone Pine in 1870, a large family had put down roots and created quite a stir. They were French, outgoing and industrious, and had immediately seen the potential of Lone Pine. Charles and Madeleine Meysan had wasted no time in turning the Heppner warehouse into the Charles Meysan Merchandise Store as the large sign over the door proclaimed.

They had made a home for their family of six young children in the back of the store while building another room on the north side of it. At the same time, Madeleine had planted several rose bushes behind their house that quickly became the source of starts for the other women in town. Although Madeleine had a lovely soft voice and a most attractive smile, when serious or irritated she could appear severe in her expression, accentuated by the way she wore her hair tightly pulled back from her round face. None of this made her unapproachable, however, and children flocked to the Meysan home not only because there were so many playmates there, but also because they felt welcomed and nurtured.

Charles was 45, several years senior to his wife and a little on the short and portly side. Sporting a trim beard and side whiskers but little hair on his head, Charles always dressed smartly in a suit with fresh collar and cuffs on his white shirts.

Finally the roads opened in early spring and freighters began arriving with goods for the Meysan Store, while the locals brought to Charles their extra produce, honey, poultry and hogs. He gave their items prominence in the middle of the store between the long side counters so all customers would have to see their neighbors' goods.

The Meysan's competition was from Rockwell Loomis at his Loomis Brothers Store and the C. & M. Cohn Opposition Store. Not considered real competition was Mr. Zahn's store, as it was smaller and carried more clothing, and Dr. Gelsich's store that specialized in drugs and sundries. Meysan's store was prosperous enough that Charles was planning another at the big mining town of Cerro Gordo atop the mountains beyond Owens Lake.

More than just a store, Meysan's had become a popular morning meeting place for the town's male population. Charles had installed in the front corner of the store a small stove and surrounded it with five chairs, and this allowed men to gather for a morning break from chores that may have started before dawn. Here they could exchange the latest news (it was called gossip when the women exchanged it); compare hunting successes (the missed shots never made the agenda); mining productivity (which impacted sales of everything in town); and current articles in the Inyo Independent (the local newspaper published first in July of 1870). It didn't seem to matter whether or not the stove was lit, so summer mornings saw as much convivial chatter as on cold winter days. If news was sought, this was the place to be.

Madeleine Meysan at that time was the mother of five daughters ranging from 21 down to one and a half, and one five year old son Felix. Nevertheless, she always found time to show the ladies new arrivals in fashion such as hats, shawls and gloves. While she struggled to improve her English, they struggled to understand her thick French accent. She was kind and helpful, and she gave them excellent advice regarding the doctoring of their children, who were often at the store where the nice lady gave them candy buttons.

Nancy also liked shopping at the Loomis and Brothers store because of their broad range of products. Not only did they have items as large as spring and curled hair mattresses and agricultural implements, but also kitchenware and fancy stationery. It was the only place in town that Abe could find boots that fit him properly.

Abe found great pleasure in sitting near the stove at the Meysan Store and visiting with the other regulars. Charles Meysan, who had no problem with English and enjoyed serving up more than his store's goods, had immediately become involved in the affairs of the town. He made the effort to attend any meeting where people gathered to discuss development, regulations, elections, cattle or farming.

Charles Begole, Albert Johnson and John Lucas, three friends who enjoyed fishing together along the creeks and the river, often came together in the store to visit.

If Charles Meysan was at every meeting held in the town, it was usually Charley Begole who called for the meeting. He had come west from Michigan and in '61 had tried his hand at mining at the Monoville diggings before coming to the Lone Pine area in '63. There had been no town then, but Charley clearly saw the potential for one and was therefore jokingly referred to as the curly headed dad of Lone Pine. He was 36 and single. Nancy told Abe he might change his marital status if he stopped hiding behind a long beard and shaggy mustache that made his mouth practically disappear. But he always had something nice to say to everyone, and few there were in town who had not been befriended by him in times of need.

Charley had claimed squatter's title to hundreds of acres of land that now composed the town and even some of the outlying ranches. He and his friend Bill Moore had constructed the first buildings, laid out the arrangement of streets and received the town's first patent in June of 1868. A number of those arriving had purchased their lots from Charley, or simply been given the land so as to help establish the town. Abe soon realized this was why they had been able to purchase their house and ten acres so cheaply.

Along with his abundance of ranch land, Charley also owned the Lone Pine Pioneer Saloon where it was reported in the paper that he "keeps on hand all kinds of the finest quality liquid refreshments. The most gentlemanly bar-keeps are regular scientific mixers in constant attendance." In July of 1871 the men were discussing how well Charley had refitted and embellished his saloon.

Charley's friend Al Johnson had a ranch southeast of town where he hired a lot of Piutes as ranch hands. Back in January of '65 he had donated a small corner of his land for the town's cemetery upon the death of Mrs. McGuire and her seven year old son Johnny. However, when the water table in early summer was too high to allow interment in the cemetery, the townspeople buried their loved ones northeast of town and later in the fall transferred them to the Pioneer Cemetery. Some bodies, however, would not be moved, creating a cluster of graves near the curve in the road down to the river. Their families either moved on or preferred their loved ones remaining further from town in the beauty of the desert.

The McGuire family had lived at Haiwee Meadows Station twenty-five miles south of town throughout most of the Indian wars. They had never been bothered by Indians, possibly because they were so far south of the main fighting. But on the last day of December 1865, while Mr. McGuire was in Big Pine, his wife and son had been attacked. Mr. McGuire had returned home to find fourteen arrows in his wife and six in his son, which Mrs. McGuire had pulled out before succumbing to her wounds. These had included marks of strangulation on her neck.

Their deaths precipitated retaliation on the Piutes living at the south end of Owens Lake where a large group of men from Lone Pine descended on the village there and herded the Indians into the caustic alkali waters. Faced with the agonizing pain of the water eating their flesh or a quick death by a bullet, many chose to emerge from the water. Only three children, a boy and two girls, were spared. The girls escaped east, and the boy was adopted by one of the men who had argued for his life.

Some people doubted that the McGuire deaths had actually been at the hands of local Piutes. Two white men had been staying at the station when Mr. McGuire left for Big Pine and they had somehow escaped to Little Lake with only slight wounds. They gave conflicting stories of what had happened, but at the time they were believed. Although as the years passed some people said they didn't think the attackers were from the local tribes, the townspeople continued to claim it *was* the locals who had killed the McGuires. Whether this was in order to quell further fighting, or so those involved in the massacre could better live with their conscience, no one now knows. Whatever the truth of the situation, it was the last time the townspeople sought such violent retribution on the local tribes.

Bill Moore had been the County Sheriff since November of '68. He was also a frequent visitor to Meysan's store, where he repeated often that he was looking forward to turning "the sheriffing" over to someone else. He had in mind who he thought that someone should be.

Tom Passmore, who would indeed be the Sheriff in a few years, stopped by the store occasionally, as he did one day in the late summer of '71. Like Bill Moore and Charley Begole, he had seen his share of fighting in the recent Owens Valley Indian Wars. He had also built a free bridge over the river to Bend City to bypass the raft ferry that charged a toll. Tom had blond hair, a full mustache not quite long enough to be called a handlebar, deep-set eyes, and brows that arched each eye and gave him a look of perpetual surprise. But he had seen too much of the world for that. Tom had served as the County Clerk, Auditor and Recorder a few years back, and had recently purchased land in Olancha where he had been asked to serve as the Postal Clerk.

John Shepherd was in town from George's Creek, a long slow trip in a buckboard, and he didn't do it often. Unlike many of his friends, he always kept his hair short. It accented a long face that was partially hidden by a mustache and short goatee. John had been a County Supervisor since '69, but his term was about to expire. After stocking up on supplies, he stopped by the stove to say hello to his friends.

Shepherd told the assembled men, "I was talking to Smith and Engle at the Black Rock Sawmill and they told me two bars of bullion were shipped out from Kearsarge on a Wells Fargo Express wagon. I guess they're doing better than I thought, considering what little is left of the town after the '67 avalanche."

John Kispert had come into town the day before, and as a stage raced past heading north, he commented, "That'll be the Citizens' Stage Line from Cerro Gordo to San Francisco." The others nodded without comment, although none of them took such important transportation for granted.

Kispert commented, "If there's a quick draw expert from Cerro Gordo on board, I hope he keeps on going. There's been several shootings, a knifing and an untold number of fights up there at the mine recently."

"Recently?" Mr. Meysan laughed. The others nodded, knowing that such violence was a common occurrence at Cerro Gordo. Any ruffian looking for a place to hide seemed to gravitate up the mountain to the mining town.

Maybe it was the thought of such violence coming to "his town", but Abe noted that Charley Begole's mouth tightened as he looked out the window at the retreating stage.

Al Johnson asked, "Did any of you hear about the increased number of bears people are seeing in the mountains?"

"Must have something to do with the availability of food," John Lucas mumbled. He was reading last week's Inyo Independent, but was determined not to miss any of the conversation around him. He smirked and said, "If the bear can get through my new wire, he's welcome to my crop."

None of the others commented, and for a few minutes there was an unusual silence around the stove. Early the previous year the use of barbed wire had come to the area and it had caused as much argument in Lone Pine as in the rest of the country, although without the bloodshed. The wire cost twenty-five cents a pound and rough lumber sold at $55 per thousand feet, so it was a cheap way for ranchers to surround their crops and keep out of their fields the 200,000 cattle, horses and sheep that were herded through the valley.

When driven between the valley and their summer ranges in the mountains, it was not uncommon for these herds to destroy acres of unfenced crops. When a law had been passed that decreed the stockmen were responsible for any destruction of crops, they were forced to adapt even if moving their herds around fenced lands made for longer travel and took off some of the cattle's weight.

Worse than this to the cattle men was the fact that the cattle were not accustomed to the wire and sometimes were badly cut up when they charged into it. Even if the collision didn't kill them, the damage to their hides would mean a lower price offered for them. Resentment of the wire policy had created grudges between families and old friends, so the men usually chose not to bring up this subject. It was, however, often on their minds.

A miner came in from his claim in the Inyos and after purchasing supplies, decided to sit for a few minutes with the others. Although Abe hadn't met him before, he could tell that Luke Howith was well-liked by the men by the way they made room for him near the fire.

"How's things going, Luke?" Charley Begole asked him.

"Fine."

No one pressed him further. That had been enough to let them know he was still getting enough out of his claim to keep him supplied with food. And that meant he was still hanging on to the hope that his claim might yet pay off big.

These were some of the leading men of Lone Pine's approximately 100 citizens in those early years. They had homesteaded the land, organized a government for protection and growth, and remained positive about the town's future. To prove it, they put down roots that would go deep, and like other towns of the Eastern Sierra, the descendents of many of these pioneers would be living there into the next century and beyond.

The subjects discussed by the men of Lone Pine may not have been of momentous import, but they were important to them because the town's prosperity was important. Isolated as they were from the commerce of large cities, their days were instead filled with mining, cattle, crop yields, weather, and the availability of supplies. Only occasionally did they feel that the rest of the world had anything to do with them, and then only when it impacted them directly by the building of roads, the establishment of laws, or the results of elections. The Inyo Independent, published each Saturday, dedicated only one page in each of its issues to the news beyond the Valley.

There were far fewer women in the town than men, but they had been very kind to Nancy. The first one to formally introduce herself after they had moved into their small house had been a petite dark-haired lady with gentle eyes and a rosy complexion. Nancy had opened the door one afternoon to find the smiling woman standing on the porch and her arms laden with baked goods.

"Hello," the woman greeted Nancy. "I'm Anne Kennedy. My husband Ben and I live on Main Street just south of town with our daughter Pauline."

"It's nice to meet you. Won't you come in?"

After they had talked about the town for awhile, Anne learned that the Carringtons had traveled across the country on a wagon train. Anne commented, "I notice you have no children." Her unspoken curiosity was evident.

"No. We had a baby girl but she fell out of the wagon on the way west."

Anne looked stricken. "I can sympathize with you. My girl is 12 and I don't know what I'd do if I lost her."

Nancy nodded and thought to herself that she knew what Anne would do if she lost her child--she would find a way to cope. Anne looked up and said, "We had thought we would never be blessed, but when I was 34, there I was expecting."

"My girl was born when we'd been married twelve years."

Anne Kennedy sighed. "A surprise to have her, and then a shock to lose her. How sad."

Nancy wanted desperately to change the subject. "Where in town do you live?"

"At the south end where the ranches begin. They're all around us. Right now my Ben is home building a dumbwaiter to carry items from the first floor to the second floor. Last week he made Pauline a desk for her room, and he's talking of a bath house. Next he'll be building something else."

"He's still working on the house after two years?" Realizing her tone might have sounded abrupt, Nancy quickly added, "He must be a busy man elsewhere."

Anne chuckled. "You'd think. We have plenty of money from his mining and freighting days, and he's spending it on building this big two-story house for 'his girls'." She laughed at that.

"Men do like to keep busy. It sounds like he's made this his job."

"I hadn't thought of it that way, but maybe that's it. I wish he'd find something else to do, but I suppose it's better than him getting drunk every day."

Nancy smiled at her new friend. "And eventually you'll have a really nice house."

"Oh, we moved in a year ago. The kitchen is done, as is the downstairs. Now, he works on finishing the rooms upstairs when the weather is too poor to be outside. He's got a shed out back where he makes furniture." Anne laughed. "You'll have to come see the huge kitchen table he's just made me. It takes up a good portion of the kitchen, but it sure is nice to have when I'm making pies."

"My husband Abe makes furniture. As you can see from the mess my kitchen is in, he's putting in hanging cabinets."

"Where is he now?"

"Probably at the Meysan Store if he hasn't signed on for an odd job somewhere."

"Oh, yes, the Meysan Store. Ben hangs out there too occasionally."

"Abe hangs out there a lot."

For some unaccountable reason, the two women laughed. They then began exchanging stories of married life, although Anne later realized that she had done most of the talking.

Thus began the closest friendship both women would ever know, filling their lives with the acceptance and trust for which both had yearned. Nevertheless, unwilling to test such a precious bond, Nancy would never tell Anne about Todd.

Nancy made other friends too. Susan Swan was a woman her age. She and her husband John often spent the evening with the Carringtons playing cards after dinner. They hailed from Tennessee and so the two couples felt they had something in common. Abe and John sometimes went fishing at the river with Reuben Van Dyke, who had a ranch south of town. The men would spend two days camping, which gave Reuben's wife Mary the opportunity to invite Nancy, Susan, Mary McCall and Anne Kennedy to the ranch for tea. Mrs. Van Dyke had a son, Dave Holland, from a previous marriage. Reuben's sister Lilly and brother James also lived nearby in Lone Pine.

Mary McCall was a widow with a daughter, Cordelia, and being the same age as Nancy they enjoyed one another's company. Mary always seemed to know what was going on in the town, sometimes even before the men at the store. This privately tickled Nancy, and gave Abe access to events that he could be the first to announce.

Abe and Nancy often rode out into the rocks of the Alabama Hills. They would pack a picnic lunch and eat it while perched on one of the giant boulder piles. As they ate, they enjoyed their closer view of the Sierra, and although the previous winter's snow on the valley floor had melted by the summer of 1871, the northern shoulder of Lone Pine Peak was still dressed in a light drape of white. The snowy jagged peak of an even taller mountain showed beyond that peak's northern and more steeply sloping side, meaning it was much taller. Although men often talked of trying to climb it, no one as yet had made the attempt.

Only when Abe and Nancy were alone out in the Alabama Hills, in the open theater of nature and absolutely assured that they were out of range of prying ears, would they talk about the past. Although they still missed the children, the last few months had been happy ones.

"One of the men said that Seth Sneden has a store on Bishop Creek where he's also the Post Master."

"The same man that was Sheriff in Bridgeport back in '65?"

"I think so." Each felt a slight tension in knowing someone from Bridgeport had moved closer. "Actually, he's several days ride away and probably won't come this far. Besides, he's a tactful sort and knows how to keep a secret."

Some of the high canyons of the Sierra were lined with huge pine trees, but from the valley floor they looked like mere bushes. There were no longer forests in the valley, or on most of the slopes of the Inyos. Trees had always been sparse between scattered thick clusters, but now they fell rapidly before the onslaught of miners desperate for fuel. Dozens of mining camps had been established throughout the valley, but the greatest ore production was up at Cerro Gordo and the need for fuel to run the mills was pressing. Even some of the sagebrush had been scrubbed out for fuel.

Trees in Lone Pine had importance other than fuel. Fast growing black locust trees had been planted in town as well as in a forest of their own west of the town. They thrived in the alkaline soil to grow fast and straight, so they could be cut for fence posts.

Men hired out as wood cutters and harvested the single-leaf pinyon and juniper, and after reducing it to charcoal would haul it up to Cerro Gordo. Considering the limited production of this charcoal, it was costly, time consuming and exhausting work. But one man thought he had a solution.

Colonel Sherman Stevens came into the store and joined the men gathered there. Sitting down in a chair vacated for him by Al Johnson, the Colonel stretched out his legs and scratched his neck where his long johns itched his neck. He removed his hat to reveal a bald head with just enough hair on the sides to run into his long side whiskers, creating the appearance of furry parenthesis enclosing his face. The Colonel had a claim high in the Inyos on Buena Vista Peak, but it wasn't yielding what he had hoped. However, he wasn't one to lack ideas.

"I hear you're thinking of setting yourself up in the charcoal business," Ben Kennedy commented. The Colonel looked at Ben and frowned. Ben was tall, thick through the chest, and clean shaven. He was also curious about everyone's business when he wasn't working on what most people thought a ridiculously large house.

"I've been thinking on it," Colonel Stevens admitted cautiously. "I've been talking with Jim Brady over in Swansea about a way to get the charcoal from the west side of the lake to the east side so it can be hauled up the mountain. He has an idea for building a steamboat to take it across."

James Brady was the superintendent of a smelting mill at Swansea, a tiny village between the edge of the lake and the base of the "yellow grade". This was the road through a yellow rock canyon that led up to Cerro Gordo and gained almost 6,000 feet in elevation in eight miles. It was a nightmare of a haul for freighters. Brady had just the year before recruited several men from Southern California to come to the area, all 75 of whom were Masons and now in the process of formally founding a lodge.

Al Johnson, only a year from turning thirty and his goatee the shortest in the room, nudged Charley Begole's shoulder as he said to the Colonel, "Bet you and Jim get together in the old Boomeray Meeting Hall." The Colonel smiled, but did not deny it. The Boomeray was known to be a popular saloon on the far side of the lake.

The men often scoffed at the Colonel's wild ideas, one of which was to bring golden trout from the South Kern River to Cottonwood Creek. And in 1876 he would do just that, the beginning of great joy for fishing enthusiasts for centuries.

Colonel Stevens told his friends, "Until Jim, Dan Ferguson and I get our plans laid out, I'll have to continue using flat bottomed scows to cross the lake. I'm building some more charcoal kilns and extending the flume thirteen miles down the Sierra."

"You'll need to enlarge your sawmill up in Cottonwood Canyon," Ben told him. "That flume will only work with manageable sizes shootin' down it."

"I thought of that." Turning to Abe, he said, "You can drive mule teams, can't you?"

"Sure can."

"I'll have mule teams hauling from the bullion trail three miles from the lake shore to the wharf at the landing Ferguson is building near Cottonwood Creek. It's going to be costly, but my sons are going to help me. We'll figure it out. In the meantime, Abe, let me know if you want a job."

Before Abe could answer him, young Archie Livingston came into the store. He was a twenty year old teamster from Olancha, and even though there was no room for him to sit down, he stood by the door and shifted his weight.

"Okay, Archie," John Lucas laughed, "unhinge your jaw and tell us what's on your mind."

Archie leaned against the wall and said, "Did you all hear that Mrs. Barry is buying the Lone Pine Hotel?"

He was gratified at their reaction of surprise and was proud that he was the first with the news. Not to be outdone, it prompted the others to volunteer their own bits of *first to know* news. It was another hour before several of them realized they were supposed to be somewhere else.

July 4 of 1871 was warm, cloudy and inclined to be showery, but nothing could put a damper on the celebrating. The day was filled with explosions (dynamite in the hills and gun fire in the town), contests between the miners (to determine the fastest to shovel a pile of rock or first to drive a stake in the ground), box lunches for sale (made by the women of the town and placed in decorated boxes), games (three-legged race, sack race, and egg toss), speeches (by any politician wanting their presence noted), and music (fiddles, box banjos, guitars and harmonicas).

The day following the celebration, the ground beneath the town began a mild shaking. Every day at different times, the earth shook from Swansea to Lone Pine, and north to Independence. One man described it as about two horse power in strength, but by the time the shaking reached Bishop Creek, it was barely felt at all. Needless to say, the shaking became a popular topic of conversation at the general store, with much speculation as to what caused it.

The area was prospering thanks to the many mines in the area. The development of agriculture continued, along with the growth of the Shorthorn and Durham cattle herds and a few flocks of sheep. There were also men in Lone Pine and Independence becoming known for their talents as horse breeders, but the greatest pride was reserved for the Cerro Gordo Mine and its continued increase in production.

In 1869, local freighter Remi Nadeau had begun hauling Cerro Gordo's bullion to Los Angeles. He had relay stations at strategic points across the desert and a large staff of drivers. By the end of 1870, 340 tons of Cerro Gordo bullion had arrived in Los Angeles and bars of the bullion were on display at banks, hotels and major businesses throughout the city. The farmers and businessmen there then shipped their crops and other supplies needed at the mines back to Cerro Gordo with the returning freighters. It was this exchange of goods that caused Los Angeles to grow rapidly at this point in its history.

Cerro Gordo's notoriety brought hundreds of miners to the Valley looking for their fortune, but few stayed after they realized how harsh life was in the lawless mining community, and how difficult it was to find their own strike. Those criminals looking for a place to hide, however, loved the mining town's difficult accessibility. Even so, in 1871 there were over a thousand location filings on record in the district.

All of this gold and silver prosperity, and the many miners working the claims, had created a need for alfalfa, wheat, hay, barley, potatoes, and corn. The ranchers in the area grew it, harvested it, and hauled it where needed, while market gardens brought forth enough produce for the town's citizens as well as extra that could be shipped out to the mines.

It took three weeks to get a wagon to Los Angeles, but only freighters hauling silver from the mines wanted to go there, so the distance across the desert was of little interest to anyone else in the Valley. The freighters brought back news of Southern California events of any importance to the Owens Valley, and the men in Meysan's store disbursed it eagerly.

"The plans for the San Pedro breakwater have been completed," Charley Begole reported. "It's expected that three to four thousand feet of it will be completed this season."

"My wife is more impressed with the fact that the restaurants here in town are going to have ice cream on Sundays," Abe commented.

The other men laughed and had to admit they too were looking forward to it.

"Daneri and Stewart's store is closing," Rockwell Loomis told them. "They're offering to the public their assortment of goods at cost. I hope to get there before the public."

Tom Passmore said, "I was talking to Elder and he told me that he's running for re-election as County Sheriff."

A man entered, and having overheard Tom, said, "There's four others running against him." They shook hands with John Turner, a miner in his mid thirties who worked up at the Cerro Gordo mines. "I also heard that a new merchandise store is opening in Fish Springs. It's owned by Mr. Murry, the old quartz man. It'll be in what used to be the Westerville and Ryan Store."

Fish Springs, southeast of Big Pine, was where dozens of ponds converged and watered a forest of big trees. It was a favorite fishing and picnic spot for those living in Big Pine and Bishop Creek, as well as a perfect respite for travelers. The more Abe heard about it, the more he lamented that he had detoured around the area on their way to Lone Pine. But another store anywhere in the Valley was good news, as it meant more freight wagons heading through town, and the possibility of more business for everyone.

Mr. Meysan asked the men gathered in his store, "Did you read in the paper about the Atlantic and Pacific Railroad? It's to follow the 35th parallel from St. Louis to San Francisco."

Abe nodded and said, "Considering that it won't have to tunnel through the Sierra, it's a pretty good route."

Ben Kennedy shook his head slowly. "Maybe, but there are still all those miles of hills and sandy deserts across the country, and lots of unhappy Indians to scare the hell out of people."

The men continued to debate the route chosen, and whether or not the railroad would even be completed. Railroad routes had been planned and abandoned before, and citizens on the east side of the Sierra had learned not to believe all that they were told about such progress.

"Hey Abe, I saw you helping Curt Harvey building his blacksmith and wagon shop. Guess he got tired of Cerro Gordo."

"Yeah, we're almost finished. Nice guy. I should be working there for awhile, since he's also building a house for himself and his family."

At the end of September, 1871, Curt Harvey joined Abe where he was framing Curt's house. "Good morning, Abe."

"Morning, Curt."

"Did you hear about the big prison break?"

"Prison break? Where?"

"Carson City. About 30 prisoners broke out on the 17th and high-tailed it out in several directions after killing a guard. One of 'em is a nineteen year old kid. God, you've got to wonder what he did to get into prison so young." Both men shook their heads. "The group the kid is with ran into a young mail rider and killed him. His father is now part of the posse out of Benton. Dangerous bunch, and some are heading toward Bishop. They're asking everyone who's willing to join up with a vigilance committee to get to Bishop." When Abe said nothing, Curt asked, "Think you'll go?"

After a moment Abe said, "No. If they get around Bishop, they might head to Lone Pine and I'll not leave Nancy alone."

"They could do that," Curt agreed. "If they do, they'll probably be heading for Cerro Gordo."

That was the end of that conversation, but needless to say not the end of the speculation. It would last until a few weeks later when the convicts were either recaptured, hanged by the posse out of Bishop, or given up as escaped.

CHAPTER TWENTY-ONE
LONE PINE, CALIFORNIA
JULY, 1871 - MARCH, 1872

"I sure wish these damn earthquakes would stop. They interrupt meals, work, and sleep."

Abe

March 25, 1872: It is still and cool tonight. Today I helped Anne hang curtains in her many upstairs bedrooms. I wonder how they will ever use so many rooms. Our life here is very satisfying, if somewhat routine. Within that routine there is contentment, and I am happy to have no more surprises in my life. We have felt no shaking today so hopefully it has ended for good. But like everything in life, it is just something to be dealt with. And after all that we experienced on the trail, we can certainly handle a little shaking."

Nancy

The year of 1871 was a good one for the Owens Valley. It had 5,000 cultivated acres and was producing 250 tons of grain in the form of corn and barley that was selling at 4 cents per pound on the field, with Harris and Rhine in Independence the principle grain dealer. People felt prices were a little high for those necessities purchased at the markets, as they paid twenty-three cents a sack for green coffee and $1.25 for a five pound can of lard, but they were just happy to have it so readily available.

Seven steam and two water-powered quartz mills serviced the 100 stamps crushing the ore from the mines, with four furnaces to melt it down; twenty primitive arastras were still active crushing the ore at the small mines; and freight from Los Angeles cost ten to twelve cents a pound to haul into the area. Locals bragged that bullion weighing as much as 1,500,000 pounds had been produced at the Cerro Gordo furnaces.

Just north of Independence, a flour mill had been built on Oak Creek by Andrew Bell, and when most of the mill burned in April of 1870, what had survived had been rebuilt. There was also the Bishop Creek Flour Mill owned by Joel Smith and A. A. Cashbaugh, although it meant six days of round trip travel for those of Lone Pine. However, flour was almost as valuable as ore, and no one could eat for a day without it.

Lone Pine had a brewery that made lager beer, owned by Louis Munzinger and Joe Fernbach, who called themselves the Pioneer and Germanics Breweries. A horse drawn malt mill in back of the brewery west of town served as mild entertainment. People often stopped to watch the big old horse walking in circles pulling the stone that crushed the barley. When the hopper was full it began walking without prompting, and as soon as the hopper emptied the horse came to a halt. It was often the source of a wager won from someone new to the area.

There were only a few regularly traveled roads threading through the landscape. Besides the rough trail from Lone Pine to Bend City, there was one from Bend City west through Independence to Kearsarge. Another road led from Independence to the north line of the County that was then marked by Big Pine Creek. A narrow wagon road ran from Cerro Gordo to the summit of the Sierra, created to haul wood down to the edge of Owens Lake for fueling the mines. For many years people had talked about a wagon road between Independence and Visalia on the other side of the mountain, but it remained just talk.

The southern Piute population still lived in small groups throughout the foothills of the Sierra in brush huts and wooden shacks that nevertheless withstood the elements well. No major battle had marred the peace for several years, and the men of the tribes had slowly merged into the labor force on the ranches, making 50 cents a day and their food. Some of the tribal women did laundry in the town's homes or worked in the gardens.

Mail came into the area twice a week on a stage that started in Reno, Nevada before passing through Carson City, Aurora, Bishop Creek, Independence and finally into Lone Pine. Since the government was willing to pay for only one delivery, the stage company carrying the mail generously paid for the other out of appreciation for the communities that kept it in business. A petition had been circulated to secure a tri-weekly mail service, but it would take several years for that to happen.

Abe came into the Meysan store in the summer of '71 and walked to where Charles was standing behind the long side counter. Nodding in the direction of a man hunched before the cold stove, Abe asked, "Who's that?"

"Not sure. He's a soldier from the fort though."

"What's he muttering about?"

"It's something to do with the Wheeler Expedition."

"Oh, yeah. I've heard talk about them."

The Wheeler Expedition had come to the valley in July of that year to map and record all aspects of the Valley; botanical, geological and topographical. They were supported by the government and had hired local guides out of Independence to assist them while in the area.

Abe approached the soldier cautiously. When the man looked up, Abe realized that he knew him. "Hal? You look like you've been on a six day bender."

"Only three days." A thin man in his early twenties with a pale clean-shaven face, the frown over his light eyes was a combination of anger and puzzlement.

Abe had met Hal when he had been hired to take some paperwork to the fort for the Sheriff. Hal had been the clerk and they had enjoyed a convivial evening the night before Abe returned home. Now, Abe realized Hal was more boy than man and placed a hand on his shoulder reassuringly. "What's wrong?"

"My brother-in-law was hired by Lieutenant Lyle with the Wheeler group. He was to be a guide through the area north of Bishop Creek. He's an educated man as well as a mountaineer. He even did some mining in that area back awhile."

"Is this leading up to something?"

"He's gone missing. He was sent out to find water while the expedition was in the desert northeast of Big Pine Creek. He was told that if he returned without having found it, he'd be shot."

"Do you think he died out there?"

Hal hesitated a moment, then looked at Abe and lowered his voice. "No. I think he just kept on going. Probably into Arizona, since we've got friends there."

"I hope for your sake, you're right."

That week was an extremely warm one. Just after dark one evening, while their hot kitchens cooled, Anne and Nancy decided to take a stroll through town. Around eight o'clock, Anne grabbed Nancy by the arm and pointed up into the sky north of town. "Look!"

Streaking across the sky was a long cluster of smoky light. Nancy gasped softly, "Why it's a meteor!"

"How do you know that?"

"Harold...I mean, I read about such a thing in a book once." Anne started to ask who Harold was, but when Nancy turned and walked so quickly back toward home, she thought better of it. Maybe some time in the future, she mused, I'll ask why Nancy avoided saying anything about this Harold person. But the longer Anne knew Nancy, she realized there were some things one just didn't ask about, and the name never came up again.

Charley Begole walked into the Meysan Store and told his friends assembled around the stove. "I heard there's another rumor going around about the Wheeler group."

"Oh, yeah? What now?" Al Johnson asked.

Charley shrugged. "Don't know for sure. Something about another guide."

So Abe told what he knew. "I've talked to Hal again and he says they still haven't heard from his brother-in-law. And now another of Lyle's guides has gone missing south of here. Lyle reported that the guide had broken off from his group to try and connect with Wheeler's group. But then he disappeared. No one has heard from him and no one was sent out to look for him."

"Damn!" Ben exclaimed. "That sounds mighty suspicious to me."

Since many stories had been picked up by those in Lone Pine of the expedition leaders' brutality with men and animals, the local citizenry felt there had to be more to the disappearance of the guides. Lyle was heard to say that as far as he was concerned the men were deserters, and if he ever saw them again they would be shot as such. The resentment this caused, especially since the men knew they couldn't do anything about the situation, was great. The problem was discussed at length in every saloon, and certainly in the corner of the Meysan store.

Mr. Mulkey changed the subject one day by announcing, "Did you know I'm the agent for the new Independence Express and Passenger Line?" They took their cue and offered fulsome congratulations. "It'll run through the area on the first and 15th on its way to Los Angeles. I'll connect with the Opposition Line of Steamers for San Francisco. First class passage is $27.50

and second class $24.50." Everyone was excited to hear this, as it meant easier and faster passage for people into the area. And that meant more money exchanging hands in town.

January of 1872 was windy and cold, but this was not unusual for the valley. While adjusting to the cold, they were also trying to accept the daily earth tremors. The Piutes, whose ancestral stories included such things, said they would stop as suddenly as they had begun.

February of '72 was cold and wet, and after a heavy snow kept wagons from passing through town, a sense of isolation set in. This increased the men's need to gather every bit of news available.

Tom Passmore arrived at the Meysan store carrying several pieces of wood. Throwing a small log into the stove, he asked Abe and Ben, "Did you hear that a Mr. Grannis purchased Hunt's old stand at the plaza?"

"I hope his prices are as good," Mr. Meysan commented.

"And that he maintains the stables as well," Abe put in, his consternation showing. "He's always been good with my horse Flame."

Tom caught Ben's eye before asking Abe, "Are you as fond of your wife as you are that horse?"

"Just about." Abe enjoyed the men's laughter.

John Lucas arrived and after warming his hands at the fire, asked, "What's this I hear about some Mexican kid trying to kill Sheriff Elder?"

"Yeah, the kid put powder in a stick to go off in his stage," Tom Passmore said. "It blew up before the kid could do it right. No one was hurt, thank God."

"Wonder what Elder did to anger him so bad?" Abe asked. This led to speculation that took up the better part of an hour. When facts were scarce, nothing filled the gap like speculating about what they might be.

At the end of a week that saw the snow beginning to melt, Abe and Ben Kennedy arrived at Charley Begole's saloon late in the afternoon. No matter the weather or how busy the man, there was always time for a drink shared with friends, although at this time of day, there were less than a dozen men present.

"I hear Canty is fixing up The Orleans Hotel," Abe commented as he and Ben stepped up to the bar.

Charlie poured them a glass of lager. "More important is that he's built on an attached bar and has wine, liquors and cigars now. Pretty fancy."

"Speaking of fancy," Ben said, "has anyone seen the new American Hotel up at Cerro Gordo ole Simpson just finished?"

Abe shook his head. "I hear it's got two stories with an upstairs balcony across the front overlooking Main. But then, our Lone Pine Hotel has a new front."

Charley told them, "Burkhart the jeweler is building a new place of business with a house attached. And Loomis and Brothers are making an extensive addition to their storeroom."

John Lucas and Al Johnson walked over from a table where they had been playing cards. John smirked and said, "You'd think Lone Pine was prosperous or something." The laughter that followed had an edge to it, since many towns along the Eastern Sierra had over the past decade disappeared almost over night.

Not to be outdone, Al told them, "Joe Fernbach was in here earlier. Did you know that he's raising hemp from seed. He says some of his plants are eight feet tall now."

Ben smirked and said, "I wouldn't think there's enough hangings in the valley to make it profitable." When the others laughed, he added, "I know, I know, he's making rope."

The summer before, Clarence King who worked for State Geologist Josiah Whitney, had declared that he had reached the top of the tallest peak in the Sierra directly west of Lone Pine. Some of the locals had disputed this, claiming he had climbed another mountain less high, and they were still debating this in the new year. When John Lucas and Al Johnson again brought up the subject, Abe decided to leave.

That they were correct would not be confirmed until August 18, 1873, when Lucas, Johnson and Begole climbed the actual highest mountain before Mr. King could return to correct what he realized was indeed his error. The Lone Pine men wanted to name it Fisherman's Peak, but it eventually ended up being called Mt. Whitney, just as Mr. King had always wanted.

Dan Ferguson and James Brady finally built their flat bottomed steamer and called it the Bessie Brady after Mr. Brady's daughter. As soon as Colonel Stevens completed his charcoal plant on the west side of the lake, the Bessie Brady began ferrying his charcoal from Ferguson's Landing across the lake to Swansea, and Abe found as much employment as he wanted. However, when he told Nancy that he had been asked to haul the charcoal up the dangerous yellow grade to the Cerro Gordo mills, she put her foot down and he gave in to her wishes.

The main thing that never changed for Abe and Nancy was their enjoyment of the natural beauty that filled their days: mountain peaks blue in summer that disappeared beneath blankets of white in winter; almost every mountain canyon having a willow lined creek that rushed across the valley toward the river; lush swampy meadows filled with long grass and wildflowers; cottonwoods, tamarisk and locust trees around every home; hundreds of acres of strange brown boulders between the town and the Sierra; fields of wheat, barley and alfalfa surrounding ranch houses enclosed by white picket fences; and the reflection of the Inyos on the 600 square mile surface of Owens Lake.

As spring hinted its near presence, everyone was excited about the new Lone Pine Race Track. There were usually only two races, a single dash of one mile for a purse of $150 and one of half a mile for a $100 purse. They were called "free for all races" and Mr. Mulkey's *Lucy Dale* was usually a favorite.

In early March, Mr. Meysan turned the store over to Madeleine while he set off on a trip to Los Angeles. Eleven year old Alice had problems with her eyes that a specialist in the big city thought he could help. Alice almost immediately was overwhelmed with missing her mother and sisters, and cried so much that Mr. Meysan relented and returned with her to town. He told the men that he would try again in early summer when one of Alice's sisters could go with them.

On March 26, 1872, at 2:00 in the morning, the highest peaks in the United States looked down on the small town of Lone Pine as it had for millions of years. The night was cool, and most of the 200 people of the town and its surrounding ranches were sleeping soundly. Sixteen miles to the north in Independence, people were also settled down for the night, as were the soldiers at Fort Independence. The few people still in the saloons, livery stables, and riding the ranges while tending cattle were looking forward to soon getting some rest too.

Nancy awoke at 2:15 to the sound of dogs howling, chickens cackling and roosters crowing, all at a frantic pace she had never heard before. The stray cat they had recently adopted crawled to the head of the bed and dove under the covers, which awakened Abe.

At 2:30, as they sat up in bed listening to their cow bawling as though needing to be milked, the earth let out a great groan followed by the sound of cracking and popping. After Nancy and Abe were thrown onto the floor, they immediately rolled under the bed only to find that somehow the cat had gotten there before them. The noise of rumbling deep in the earth was in itself a shock, but the length of time that the hard convulsing and jarring of the ground continued was even more frightening.

When the shaking stopped after almost five minutes, Abe and Nancy ran outside just in time to be thrown to the ground by a rolling upheaval of their front yard. As they lay on the ground, they watched the Sierra shedding boulders that crashed into each other as they fell and set off cascades of sparks. Some people down the street shouted that a volcano was erupting and was covering the town with smoke. Then they choked on it and knew from the familiar taste that it was just their dusty dry soil filling the air.

Then the earth shook again and no one was left on their feet. When the movement stopped, the Carringtons made a tentative effort to stand up. They hurried into the house to dress before setting off for town.

Looking down Main, everything had changed. Every brick building that lined the road had crumbled beneath its wooden roof, and even some of the wooden buildings were now slumped sideways. Men and women were swarming the area, diving into the debris in an attempt to reach their friends and families that were screaming for help, as well as those who were silent.

As the rumbling and shaking continued, Abe and Nancy both joined Bill Moore who was tossing aside timbers and bricks so the family buried beneath could be reached. They then moved between rubble piles that had been a home to a large pile of bricks that had been a store, and stopped only when the earth shook again and they were challenged to stay on their feet. Realizing that this work required more physical strength than she could provide, Nancy grabbed a bucket and dipper from the debris of a store and filled it at the creek.

Abe continued on to the Loomis store and came upon Bill Covington just as he found Rockwell Loomis buried in the debris, which included supplies of black powder. A lantern left burning had caught a wooden box on fire, and Rockwell was in imminent danger until Bill stomped out the fire not far from the explosive powder.

Abe helped Bill carry their limp and bleeding friend to the open area being manned by Dr. Geleich. Rockwell had an ear and part of his scalp torn away, but the doctor sewed it all back together, minus part of the ear. Messrs. Columber, Lesesne, Grannice, and even Charley Begole, were among those who had enough knowledge of wounds that they could help the doctor.

Mrs. Joslyn called out for help from beneath the ruins of her house near where the doctor was working. On his way to help her, Dr. Geleich motioned to Abe to join him, but both men were prostrated by another shock. The doctor fell against a post and was hurt so badly that he began spitting up blood.

"Doc, you stay here," Abe told him. "I'll see to the Joslyn family."

"No, I'll be okay. They need me." He climbed to his feet and soon they reached the family, relieved to find that Mr. and Mrs. Joslyn and their two girls only had a few scratches. But their little boy was dead. While the doctor turned to others who needed his care, Abe helped Mr. Joslyn carry the boy to the Harvey Livery Stable that was being used as a morgue. As they left, Mr. Joslyn collapsed and Abe sat him down on the edge of a surviving portion of sidewalk.

"My poor wife clung to George's body until I forced her to let him go." Abe patted him on the back until he stopped crying, all the while fighting a desire to shed his own tears. But there was no time to give in to such self-pity, and both men moved on to help others escape from the rubble of their homes.

Abe passed the remains of the building that had housed the doctor upstairs and a dry goods store downstairs. He found Fred Austin sitting in front of it in great pain. Abe took him to the doctor where his arm and three broken ribs were wrapped in strips of sheeting being made by women who had volunteered for the task. Fortunately, Mr. Austin's wife and baby had escaped just as the side walls and roof had fallen in.

Someone hollered that the brewery of Munzinger and Lubken (who had recently bought out Fernbaugh) was partially destroyed.

Mr. Munzinger's greater tragedy was finding the crushed body of his son inside their house.

Nancy found Abe leaning against a tree wiping his face with a soiled handkerchief and made him drink a dipper of water from a bucket she was carrying. She couldn't help but note her husband's pale face beneath the sweaty grime and asked, "It's hard to see all this suffering, isn't it?"

Abe nodded as he coughed out the dust choking his throat. "Al and I found a Mexican woman buried beneath the rubble of her house. She was in bed with her daughter and son. They were all dead. Her ten year old boy survived with his nose broken and a foot crushed so we carried him to the doctor. But poor Geleich is himself injured and he's quickly becoming overwhelmed."

After Nancy gave him a hug and a few words of encouragement, she continued on her mission to give relief to the thirsty. Abe then went to the house of Juan Ybesta, a well-liked and prominent gentleman of the town from Chili. He found Juan dead with his skull split open, and Abe suddenly found out that he *did* have time to weep. But he quickly blew his nose and moved on to the next house.

No one was spared the loss of a loved one, whether relative or friend. Nancy soon learned that two women she knew well, Lucy and Antonia, had been crushed to death by the walls of their homes. Someone told her that Abe's friend Henry Tregellas, Superintendent of the Eclipse Mill, was dead. She dreaded having to tell Abe, but as she had done when on the trail, Nancy pushed her grief away and allocated a time in the future for reacting when she wasn't so urgently needed.

Abe knew that his friends Tom Gardner and John Heckel had been out sharing a night of heavy drinking and feared the shack in which they usually slept it off might have collapsed on them. As Abe approached the sagging wooden cabin and saw the men on the street, he joined others who were laughing at Mr. Heckel standing there in his longjohns. When Mr. Gardner collapsed, however, they rushed to his side, grateful to find that he was only in a state of mild shock.

When they got to the C. & M. Cohn's Opposition Store, they found most of it fallen in and the goods inside ruined. The elder Mr. Cohn was slightly hurt, but at least his son had gotten out okay and had set about helping others.

Mr. Deneri of Deneri and Stewart had a close call when the large store collapsed, as did Mr. Zaun when his store was destroyed. However, both men were too busy looking after the dead and injured to bother with their stores, and later their selflessness was commented on by many.

Abe and Ben Kennedy decided to check on those in the town's outlying shanties and small frame houses, where they found people wandering around dazed and covered with bloody dust-covered cuts and scrapes. After making everyone sit down before they were knocked off their feet by the next shock, Abe and Ben cleaned and bound their wounds. When finished, they hurried back into town to help those more seriously hurt or still buried.

Few who survived did so without a cut, torn scalp, or broken bone. The Carringtons soon had at their house Mr. Cervantes, a mill worker friend of Abe's with a broken leg; Mr. & Mrs. McCall who had many deep cuts and their daughter who was more shocked than physically hurt; Mrs. Burt with a broken leg; Fred Austin who would be laid up for some time with his broken ribs; and for the first two days after the quake Mr. George Burkhardt and his wife. Nancy and Abe nursed them, fed them, helped them with personal needs, and changed the dressings on their wounds. This same scene was repeated at the Kennedy's house, where all the rooms suddenly had a purpose.

The dead were taken to Curt Harvey's blacksmith shop and what was left of Charley Begole's Pioneer Saloon, while others were laid out on the bar-room floor of the Orleans Hotel and the lobby of the Lone Pine Hotel. In some cases, whole families died in an instant and lay together awaiting burial. Among the twenty-seven who died in Lone Pine was eleven year old Alice Meysan, crushed by a side wall of the house.

The Inyo Independent called the tragedy *the great visitation* and reported that the financial loss to Lone Pine was estimated at $132,100. Deneri and Stewart lost $18,000 in stock and buildings, Munzinger and Lubken lost $16,000, while Loomis and Charley Begole sustained losses of $10,000 each.

While grieving and still in shock, the men dug a large common grave at the north end of town on a rise of land at Curt Harvey's ranch, thereafter known as Harvey Hill. The citizens gathered to pay respects and bury 15 coffins in a row, one of which contained a mother with her child still clutched in her arms. Most buried that day were Mexican, but there were also three from France, one from Germany, one from Ireland, and one from Chili. The rest of the dead were buried nearby, at the small Pioneer Cemetery southeast of town, or on private ranch lands.

Those adobe buildings that did not crumble were bent and twisted and warped, and many people lived for months in tents or lean-tos made from what scrap wood they could find. The Meysan store was nothing but partial brick walls and wooden shelving mixed with the remnants of its inventory. But the corner stove was unscathed, resting on its stone platform in the nook of two partial walls as though waiting for someone to pull up a chair.

Not only were the lives of the people instantly changed, but so was the landscape. The valley floor dropped twenty feet; the top of hills moved back from their bottom halves by over a dozen feet; the Owens River shifted its course by a quarter mile; and while ponds that had been used as a water source for decades went dry, others opened up and became lakes. The western floor of Owens Lake dropped so quickly that a wall of water rose up and a new eastern shore line was created when the water settled 200 feet from the old docks.

Underground springs burst through the floors of several buildings and dozens of broken lanterns started small fires. Dust hung over the valley for two days and obscured the mountains on both sides. The earth split in dozens of places to create deep crevasses into which animals fell to their death, and small out buildings disappeared. Fence lines that were straight before the quake were now curved or sunken into the ground. Post Street had a new jog in it, and the road south out of town had a new sharp bend in it. For years to come the locals would reference everything as before or after "the quake".

Although Lone Pine was at the center of the quake, much of Independence had been hit hard and the courthouse lay in a heap. Mining camps throughout the area sustained heavy damage to buildings and mine shafts, or found themselves no longer sitting on the edge of the suddenly diverted river and therefore with no water to run their steam equipment. With the Fort Independence barracks now piles of adobe brick, the soldiers still managed to help the people in the valley with money, time, and medical aid. Oddly enough, the miners at Cerro Gordo barely felt the shaking.

Eventually it was learned that the earthquake had been felt as far north as Oregon, as far east as Salt Lake City, south to the border with Mexico, and west to the coast. It would later be classified as 8.3 on the Richter Scale. The survivors only remembered that the aftershocks continued for three months. They would also learn that on the same day a volcano erupted in Colima, Mexico.

As the citizens set about reestablishing their community, they constructed their buildings using wood. Much of this was brought down the hill from Cerro Gordo by the miners who also donated $700 to the town. Adobe bricks that could be used again for outbuildings were stacked around the town, and small boys were given the task of pulling square nails from boards so both could be used again. As soon as the debris was removed, teams of men began the construction of the businesses on Main Street.

While still healing and building, everyone waited for promised financial aid from Los Angeles, since Visalia had already sent $300. Eventually, in order to get it, the town sent a representative to Los Angles who met with the mayor, and eventually the town received the promised money. San Francisco meanwhile put up the money for lumber that Los Angeles merchants offered Lone Pine at half price.

That summer saw an outbreak of measles, and although the adults afflicted eventually regained their health, one child died. It was Pauline Kennedy, and only seeing to the needs of so many friends kept Anne from succumbing to her grief. Ben ceased visiting the Meysan store and the saloons with his friends, and buried himself in construction projects for the house. Consequently, when Anne needed a shoulder to cry on, it was to Nancy that she turned.

Before the following winter arrived, the town had risen from the ashes of its devastation. Although some people had immediately fled the area, those who stayed built larger and sturdier buildings, nicer homes, a new church, a wider main street edged in longer runs of wooden sidewalk, a larger plaza, a town hall, and a school.

This dedication to Lone Pine became the signature attitude of the town's citizens. Because of the early pioneers' willingness to focus their energy on one small town in the country's deepest valley, Lone Pine would remain on the map. And forty-seven years later it would be discovered by a new industry in a small town called Hollywood when it would bring to the Alabama Hills the charge of the Light Brigade, the elephants of Gunga Din, the good deeds of the Lone Ranger, and the melodies of the singing cowboys.

Emily Eastman, 1946

AFTERWORD
1895
BY EMILY EASTMAN

My close friendship with Nancy and Abe developed quickly from the time I arrived in Lone Pine in 1878 at the age of 21. Early in our relationship Nancy confided in me the story of Harold, although her other friends knew only of the loss of little Alice who she always said had fallen out of the wagon. It was the last time we spoke of her children for many years.

As the wildflowers lingered into the summer of 1895, Nancy looked out her kitchen window at Lone Pine Peak and Mt. Whitney. As she did every day, she thought of Todd and tried to picture in her mind what he might be doing. Then she found images of the 1872 earthquake filling her mind. "We fared so well," she thought, "and we were able to help so many others. Was that why we were meant to end up here?"

For years she had felt there must be some profound reason back of all that had happened to her family. She and Abe had started their journey west with the hope of a better life for their children, and instead their decision had meant death for two of them and shame associated with the third.

Her mind returned again to visions of the earthquake and all they had done to help the wounded and later assist in the rebuilding of the town, something that never seemed to end. She smiled and concluded that maybe in some small way their life *had* after all had a purpose to it. One thing she knew for sure. Time had given her an acceptance of all they had lost, while Lone Pine had given her the contentment of permanency.

In late June many in Lone Pine noted a stranger riding through town. He was dark of skin but fine of feature, with long hair protruding from beneath his hat, and several men standing outside the Meysan store assumed he was a half-breed dressed in the typical dusty trail attire of a ranch hand. He created some considerable interest when he stopped to inquire at the livery stable where Abe Carrington lived.

After receiving directions and before riding away, the stranger asked if Mr. Carrington still had the stallion that had been sired by the son of his old riding horse Flame. He was told he did, but that Abe would never sell him. The stranger smiled and tipped his hat. Everyone at the stable settled back into their routine, satisfied that the stranger would soon be leaving town without the horse. Only one man thought to question how the stranger knew about old Flame, now dead for eight years.

Nancy was shaking a rug on the front porch when she saw the man approaching. He stopped near the gate to the Carrington's small front yard and for a long moment they looked at each other. Not a breath of wind moved the leaves on the trees, nor ruffled the mane of the man's horse that remained as still as its rider. Several people walked past and wondered at this strange tableau.

"Is Abe Carrington home?" the man finally asked.

"Not right now," Nancy told him, her eyes not leaving his face. After a moment's hesitation, she asked, "Would you like to come in and wait for him?"

"Thank you. I could use some water." He tied his horse to the fence post and walked toward the front porch that was now completely shaded by the large cottonwood tree. Nancy turned and led him into the house.

Although Abe had not yet returned, an hour later the man walked from the house with Nancy close behind. He mounted his horse and with a quick smile and a tip of his hat to Nancy, he urged his horse forward and rode north through town.

A young girl in her teens with long auburn hair approached, her green eyes focused on Nancy who stood by the road looking at the retreating man. "Who was that, Mrs. Carrington?"

Finding her voice, Nancy said, "Someone we knew a long time ago."

"Where's Mr. Carrington?"

Turning slowly toward the girl, Nancy said, "He's taken the wagon to the blacksmith for repair."

The girl shifted her weight impatiently. "Are we going to bake a cake today?"

"No cake baking today, Whitney. I'm afraid I'm not feeling up to it." Then she smiled fondly and added, "Can you tell Emily I need to see her as soon as possible?"

"Yes, ma'am." Whitney frowned, aware that something was amiss, but not sure how serious it was. "I'll go home right now and tell Mother."

"Thank you." As soon as Whitney had started for home, Nancy retreated into her kitchen and sat down at the table in its center.

Half an hour later when I arrived as bidden, Nancy was still at her table. Her hair was pulled out of its pins by hands that she kept running over it and the lines around her eyes were deep. The face that looked up into mine seemed years older than her normally robust 64 years.

Lying in front of her on the table was a small package wrapped loosely in brown paper, and I could tell that it had already been opened. I pulled out a chair across from her and sat down. "Nancy, what's the matter?"

It was then that I noticed the rosy glow of excitement brushed across her cheeks. "Emily, when you first arrived in Lone Pine, I told you the story about how I lost my little girl. As you know, I told only you how Harold was lost from us. But I omitted part of the story and I want to tell you the rest now. Do you have the time?"

My husband Frank was moving cattle from one pasture to another, so in answer I got up and poured us both a cup of coffee from the pot on the stove. I returned to my chair and braced myself for whatever she would tell me.

"Abe will be gone for several hours," she said, "so we shouldn't be interrupted."

"What is it you want to tell me, Nancy?"

"I had a third child." She said it simply and without emotion. Instead of telling her that I already knew that much, I simply kept my eyes on her and waited. "We were parted from him while on the trail, but he's still alive."

At that revelation I gasped, as I had assumed all three of her children were deceased. From the seat of the chair next to her she lifted two leather covered books. "One of these is the diary I kept during the journey West. You know a lot about our time on the trail, and even something of Abe's adventures in Virginia

City, Aurora and Bodie. I've told you most of what happened after we arrived in California before coming to Lone Pine.

"But I didn't tell you why Abe traveled to Virginia City and those other towns, or why we left Placerville and Bridgeport. I guess I got into the habit of writing in a journal, because through the years here in Lone Pine I've written in a second one on a regular basis and in considerable detail. It helped me handle all that we endured during the aftermath of the earthquake, and all that happened in the years that followed. But I'm done with that now."

"You want me to read these diaries?"

"I want you to keep them." She ran her hand over the worn leather covers and smiled gently before looking me in the eyes and saying, "And someday, if you think it's appropriate, maybe let Whitney have them."

"When did you last see...?"

"Todd. His name is, or was, Todd. I saw him today."

"But Whitney said there was an old Indian just leaving here when she arrived."

Nancy looked down at the small package on the table. "He's not so old. He's only 47, and his name is now White Elk."

Realizing what this meant, I merely murmured, "Oh."

"I hadn't seen him for 32 years. Still, I knew immediately that it was him. I pretended that I didn't until we were inside." She smiled gently. "It was so good to hold him in my arms again. He's lived with his adopted Piute tribe in Nevada since he was nineteen. All this time, I've been terrified of what people here would say if they knew.

"You see, he was aware that we'd suffered from public opinion years ago when people found out about him in Placerville and Bridgeport. He told me that when he saw Lone Pine, he realized he was out of his element here and still doesn't feel free to bring his family to live with us. But we had a lovely talk, and at last I feel at peace."

I didn't know what to say. Part of me couldn't believe that she would let her son just ride away like that, but I was also aware that I didn't know the whole story. So I said nothing and looked down at the package she held in her hands.

"He left me this before leaving." She removed the brown paper and revealed a photograph in a small velvet hinged case with a tiny metal clasp. On the back was stamped the name of the photographer in Carson City. A tear ran down Nancy's cheek as she handed the small case across to me.

I studied the four adults and two children in the photograph for a long moment before opening a small fold of paper enclosed with it. In a neat hand was written: "Me, my wife Sandra, our son Andrew age 27, his wife Dorothy, their two children Mary and Nancy aged five and eight. Carson City, Nevada 1894"

I looked up at her and smiled. "He's very handsome, and his wife is lovely. His first granddaughter was named after you, so he must have told his family about his parents." She looked pleased and nodded. "And you're a great grandmother to two adorable children."

"They have Piute names, of course, but he said I don't need to know them. He doesn't know that I'm aware that he can't tell me what they are."

"Why not?"

Her smile was a bit rueful as she shrugged and said, "Because I'm white."

"But you're his mother. Surely he could trust you."

"No. He must adhere to his traditions."

"*His* traditions?"

"Yes." There was a tone of defiance and pride when she said, "My son is a Piute."

Somehow I knew that was the first time she had ever said those words aloud. I was very eager to return home and read her diary, but instead I told her, "At least you know where they live."

"Yes, and I was able to hold my boy in my arms again. I'll never forget the feeling of his lips brushing my cheek before he left." She sighed deeply and said, "I understand now why Todd had to leave us all those years ago, and I'm surprisingly okay with the way things are. Of course, if Abe feels I did wrong to let him go, we can travel to Carson City and find him."

But Abe didn't think she had done the wrong thing. Ever a practical man, he told Nancy, "He's obviously happy where he is, surrounded by his family and his tribe. He'd soon feel restricted by a small town such as Lone Pine, and his wife and children would grieve for the rest of their kin."

Beaming a smile at Abe, she walked to him and wrapped her arms around his neck. "I feel very much at peace now, my love.

And after all, there's regular mail stages running between here and Carson City now. So we can write often."

"Ah, Nan," Abe grinned, "you're such a great old gal."

"Well, not too old I hope." When she pressed against him in a way that had been familiar to him for the last 47 years, he laughed and moved to lock the front door.

November 1, 1895:

"Lone Pine is a place for putting down roots, and ours won't be pulled up again. Nancy has made many good friends among the ladies, and she enjoys their company on a regular basis, whether gathered around a quilting frame at one of their homes, gossiping over a cup of tea in Anne Kennedy's parlor, or cooking with Emily Eastman and her daughter in our kitchen. People here are not interested in our past, only in what we contribute to the community.

"Nevertheless, Nan need not know that I saw Todd before he reached town. Or that I told him I wasn't willing to risk Nan's hard-won serenity by his wanting to now move here with his family. I will let nothing threaten her happiness again, not even if it means misleading her into thinking that Todd is still happy to be so far away. So I told Todd to ask at the stable about Flame's grandson before going on to the house to see his mother, but that I then wanted to see him moving on.

Abe

"...to strive, to seek and find,

and not to yield."

Tennyson